W ̶ ̶ ̶ ̶O̶F̶F̶E̶R̶

FOR A REASON

WRITTEN BY

LARRY Z. WILLIAMS

WE SUFFER FOR A REASON

CHAPTER 1

Typical wet, wet weather here in Georgia during the rainy season.

James peers through the windshield watching buckets of water coming down from the heavens while awaiting his wife and daughter to make it from the house out to their car.

"Did you say something dad?" his son Eli asks from the backseat.

"No son, I was only thinking out loud."

"'Mama, I'm sorry for leaving the umbrella at school. It was such a beautiful day Friday that I didn't think I would need it," Elisha was telling her mother as they stood together on their porch watching the rain pound the distance between them and the car.

"It's okay sweetheart, it's not the first time an umbrella has been forgotten due to a day of sunshine," responded her mother Elizabeth. Always the one to drop a nugget of knowledge wrapped in a parable.

"Okay now sweetie hold on to my hand really tight as we run together out to the car," Elizabeth was saying before they bound toward their car, having their heads partially covered with plastic. Once inside, James didn't hesitate to begin his protest.

"Honey, are you sure we need to attend this morning's church service? Wouldn't it be better to wait and see if this weather will let up any?" he asked.

"No, I don't think we should, because this rain may never let up," she said having a stern look upon her face. Elizabeth knew she must be persistent due to her husband's stubbornness. Once he has his jaw set, he's absolutely relentless. So, her face remained austere as she pointed toward the street, indicating the route he should begin taking.

After turning onto the street, James asked, "Are you calling your mother to let her know we'll be running a little late due to this downpour?," James asked.

"There's no need to pick her up this morning. She's already at the church, prepping for this morning's service," Elizabeth informed.

"What, when did Ella make it onto the Usher board?" he asked with a look of astonishment slash fear across his face.

"She hasn't, she's just filling in for someone who couldn't make it," Elizabeth said.

"Someone who couldn't make it, probably due to the tsunami we're experiencing huh," James stated and went on to say, "We should be some more someone's who couldn't make it. This may be the Lord's way of telling us to stay on in this morning," James said. Overhearing the conversation from the rear seat, Eli offered, "Maybe the Lord and his angels are also sleeping in this morning." Always the one to stand on his dad's side. But he was given a look by his mother that spoke a language he could understand well.

Elizabeth then turned back to her husband and calmly said, "This weather may be one of the devil's deterrents trying to prohibit the children of God from hearing His word." Leaning into the steering wheel peering through a windshield that windshield wipers were unable to keep clear, James was silenced.

"Elisha, Eli, put on your seatbelts and James I'd appreciate it if you would put yours on also," Elizabeth exclaimed, bringing to everyone's mind, the click it, or ticket rule.

Only James replied. "That's not going to work for me bae, I can barely see as it is. I have to lean forward in order to see the road. How did your mother get to the church this morning? What did she do, buy a boat?" he asked in humor.

"No James, she did not. Let's just get there sweetheart. I don't want to be late for the worship service."

"We'll get there, but in the meantime you kids look on your left, and on your right. Perhaps we'll see it at the same time," their dad proclaimed. "See what?" asked the kids in unison.

"Noah in an ark full of animals," exclaimed their dad with amusement.

Then it happened. All of a sudden, out of nowhere, without warning an SUV t-boned their car with such impetus force that everything went to black. The only thing Elizabeth was able to remember to this day is her pulling her husband's lifeless body the rest of the way out of the driver's side window and onto the pavement. Her only thoughts at the time was to conceal the bloody disfigured body from the eyes of their children, whose screams caused her to move and react in an unexplainable fashion,. It was as if it was not her mind guiding her, but some unseen force.

Eli who'd only received minor scratches and a few bruises was able to assist in getting his sister, who had suffered a broken arm, to safety.

Elisha's screams of pain were compounded with cries of agony, because she knew. They all knew, that he who loved them unselfishly was no more. Two whole years after the accident, Elizabeth sat transfixed in thought. Her mother Ella's voice nudges her back into the now.

"Liz, sweetie I love you so much, but please tell me why you believe things would be any better a few, or even many miles away? And to have to take my grandbabies away from me. Baby, running away has never been the right answer. Only the Lord has the answers to our most difficult problems," Ella says as she attempts for the umpteenth time in hopes of persuading her daughter to remain in Georgia.

"I know you're right mama, but this is just something that I have to do for their sakes, just as well as for my own. So mama please let me do this my own way. I promise to call you everyday to let you know how me and the kids are doing. Mama I promise you. Come on kids, finish up your goodbyes and let's be on our way."

Before pulling out of Ella's driveway, the first words out of Elisha's mouth was, "Mama do we have to leave Nana here all by herself?"

"Elisha, she's not by herself. Pam will be staying with her now, and she also has her entire church family also."

"Yeah, but we're her family and she's ours. And mama who do we know in Louisville, Kentucky?" asked Elisha.

"It's pronounced, Louisville, and your granny lives there, your father's mother."

"Our dad's mom lives in Louisville, Kentucky?" asked Eli.

"Yes," replied his mother. And then went on to say, "She wants and needs to see you both really bad. So we'll stay with her for a little while until we find a place of our own."

The trip north to the state of Kentucky, city of Louisville took approximately eight hours and forty minutes for Elizabeth to achieve. Forever driving slightly under the speed limit, adhering to every traffic law and constantly checking to make sure the kids remain buckled up. It has been her motto ever since recovering from her head injury she suffered in the accident. A concussion she hadn't even realized while she sought out the well-being of her children.

Elisha's broken right arm, and Eli's minor cuts and bruises could have been far worse considering, but her discovering James' lifeless body hanging halfway out of the driver's side window had done something to Elizabeth that day and forever more.

To this day she still doesn't know where the strength, nor the will to conceal that view from Elisha, and Eli came from. Only thankful for it, she mentally summates as she makes her exit at Muhammad Ali Boulevard, downtown Louisville.

CHAPTER 2

Finding her mother-in-law's house was simple enough. Straight down Muhammad Ali Boulevard to 22nd Street, turn left, continue straight for about 8 blocks and then make a right onto Garland Avenue. Just two blocks til the 2400 block, the sixth house on the left, 2400 W. Garland Avenue.

But there was no welcoming committee, nor a single soul standing outside awaiting their arrival, which wasn't surprising. Her mother-in-law's last words over the phone were, "We're family, so just come on with my grandchillin. Someone will be here whenever you get here, and the front door is always open."

And just as she had said, the front door was wide open and the television blaring. A game show where a contestant had just won a trip to somewhere.

Elizabeth peeped inside and recognizes her in-law over on the couch, knocked out, sound asleep with what appears to be a half pint of liquor in one hand and a lit cigarette burning away in the other.

Pushing the children into the house right in front of the couch where their granny was leaning, Elizabeth didn't get a chance to wake her, because she sprung to reality, took a swig of the beverage, then a long pull off of the cigarette as she brought into focus the three figures that now stood before her.

"Ms. Bee, it's us. We're here. We've made it. I just hope you're really okay with us. . ."

"Hey babies, oh come on around here to your granny Bee, so I can get a real good look at you. And don't you even say what you were about to say out of your mouth. I wouldn't have invited you if it wasn't what I really wanted. And even though Debra, Reggie, and all the rest of 'em are here, don't mean nothing. It's more than enough room in this big ole house. Now y'all come on over here and give me some sugar.

"Umm Elisha you're a big girl, tall and pretty, just like your mother. Just look at this long pretty hair. Okay lil boy, get your butt on over here and give your Granny Bee some of your sweet sugar. We don't do shy in this house. Come on here, looking all like your daddy. Like he spat you out. Now that's a good boy.

"You know your Granny Bee is so glad to have you all staying here with us. We're family and don't you ever forget it.

"Come sit yourselves down. Where's y'alls stuff at Liz? Still in the car? Well, just leave 'em there for now and let's get to know each other. It's so amazing how much this boy looks like his daddy, my James! Even though me and my son didn't see eye to eye on a lot of things, like him moving down south to Georgia, where one hundred years ago black folks would have given their own lives to get out of Georgia, just so they'd be able to die and be buried somewhere free. It's all the same, I love him with my whole heart and there's not a day that goes by that some of my thoughts aren't of him, my son. "Oh baby, what's the matter? You come and sit right here next to me Liz, and tell me why you're looking so sad," instructed Mama Bee.

"It's nothing Ms. Bee. I just . . ."

"Call me Mama Bee, cause I ain't been a Ms. or a Mrs. in quite some time now, but go ahead and tell me what's bothering you."

"Well, it's just that no one has called me Liz but my mother and James at times. And hearing you say it just caused a flood of memories."

"That's what this is about ain't it? Listen you two, y'all go out back to the yard. Darrick and Larry and all the rest of them are out there, but they've been too quiet, so I know they're probably up to something they ain't got any business doing. And if they ain't out back y'all come right back and let me know, because I told them this morning, not to go no further than that fence at the end of the yard. Y'all go ahead.

"Now Liz, first of all, is it okay with me calling you Liz?
Yeah, I guess so . . ."

"Well to me it just seems so natural seeing that your name is Elizabeth, but I want to make sure you're comfortable with it, and judging by your face, I ain't too sure."

"Ms. Bee, I'm okay with you calling me Liz, really. It's just that when James used the name Liz on occasions, usually whenever he wanted to get back on my good side, or else he wanted something special from me. Other than him, Mama has been calling me Liz ever since I can remember. But when I heard you say it, it caused me visual memories," explained Elizabeth. "Well, I hear you, but I feel that there's a little more to it than just that, because I saw a little pain in your face and I can hear the sadness in your voice. So honey, if you ain't going to be able to talk to your Mama Bee, then who are you going to tell it to?"

"It's just so many different things and several mixed emotions. I just wouldn't know where to begin."

"Start at A baby, cause it's the only way to get to Z. As a matter of fact, I'll help you with A, because that's where I keep ending up at every time I try to go forward. I lost a son, and you lost a husband, the father of your two children. And even though the accident happened two years ago, the pain is no less."

"Ms. Bee you're absolutely right. Every day I awake it's a challenge for me to make it through. At times on frequent occasions I blame myself, because he asked me to agree to stay home that morning. But me being me I wasn't having any of that, and I knew I would get my way with James. I always have, even when I demanded that he move to Georgia from here, from home with his mother. Could you ever find it in your heart to forgive me Mama Bee?" she asked with a steady flow of tears.

"Stop that crying child. Come here and let me tell you the truth. I've never held anything against you for my son's leaving home. As a matter of fact, I was delighted to see him go. Otherwise, he would've ended up marrying my friend Bunch's daughter. I show didn't want any grandbabies of mines having any part of Bunch in 'em. And when you see Bunch, you'll understand why. I believe the children's joke goes something like, 'Put Bunch back in the game coach it'll score.' Anyway, little girls should not look like football

14

players, so I thank God that I don't have to worry about my granddaughter being a Bunch.

"Sweetheart, if it seemed like I was displeased or upset, it had nothing to do with you. Sometimes a mother has to put up a front in order to keep her kids in check."

"I understand, but why was there no stronger relationship between you and James? I've always felt that I caused it by causing the separation. So, I believed you didn't like me."

"You didn't cause anything. Me and my son's relationship started off on the wrong foot when he had me in labor for seventeen hours. Anyway, we're supposed to be dealing with your pain. So why don't you tell Mama Bee all about that."

"Well Mama Bee it's not just trying to cope daily with his passing, it's also my feeling that I betrayed my mother as well. Even after two years I'm still having to explain to her that I just couldn't take it anymore. But I'm sure she feels as though I just up and left, and took her grandchildren away from her, after all the love and support she has provided me and the children. I don't know, I just feel bad about doing my mother that way. But you don't understand I just couldn't remain in Georgia another second. Do you hear me?" she asked.

"I hear you and I understand. If anybody understands, I do child. But all I can say about it is that you need to make certain that Ella understands and even if she chooses not to, your decision has been made. So, she will eventually come around to dealing with it, at least."

"I've tried so hard to get my mother to understand that if I didn't get away I would not be any good for my children."

"Listen, you listen to me Liz. You've done what you felt in your heart you had to do. I, for one am so glad that moving here and staying with me is the choice that you've made. Now, you should be feeling good about making such a decision for yourself, and for the sakes of them chillin of yours," Mama Bee concluded.

Walking out onto the back porch, Eli and Elisha stood there and looked at several kids around their own ages and a couple of older ones in the backyard of their Granny's house, kicking a ball, running around and some were even wrestling with one another.

But all of a sudden a little boy around the age of 10 or 11 walks up on the back porch where they were standing and asks, "Who in the hell are y'all and who told you that you could come in my damn yard anyways? After a brief pause he continued, "I know the cat ain't got your tongue, because we ain't got no damn cat' A Reggie y'all look at them."

"Who are they Darrick?" asked Reggie as he made his way forward.

"I don't know. They won't say nothing. They're just standing here looking all stupid," Darrick told them.

All of the children who were in the yard gathered on and around the steps leading to the back porch. That's when Elisha says, "My name is Elisha and this is my brother Eli, and we are not stupid. Our Granny told us to come out here with you all."

"Your Granny," Debra questioned, as she walks up the steps.

"Yeah, she's in there talking to our mother right now. And we all just came to live here with you all from Georgia," Elisha said.

"Where in the hell are y'all going to sleep at?" asked Darrick.

This time he received a slap upside his head from his brother, Reggie, along with a threat. "If you say one more cuss word I'm a tell Mama you out here cussing again. And you already know what she said she's going to do to you the next time."

17

"Man, I didn't even say nothing, so don't be going to Mama lying on me."

"So, you're calling me a liar and you a pretty boy, cause I heard you with my own two ears."

"Cursing, and telling lies are sins," says Eli in a barely audible whisper.

"Man, you can shut up!" was all he received for pointing out a fact.

"Come on y'all let's go ask Mama," Reggie says. "Because if he's lying we're going to gang him." Running into the living room, everybody screaming at the same time, "Mama, Mama are they staying here in our house with us? Huh Mama?"

"What? What are y'all yelling about now?" Asked Mama Bee as she tried to shush them all.

"Are they going to be living here with us, Eli 'em? Huh Mama, are they?" asked two or three at the same time. "First of all, quit all of that screaming and hollering inside of my house. And yes, they are going to be staying here in my house, with me! Listen to it, my house! They're our family," Mama Bee adds. "Elisha, Eli, and this here is y'all's Aunt Elizabeth. They just got up here from Georgia. Elizabeth, this one here is the

18

oldest boy Reggie. He's around nineteen, or twenty. Boy how old are you exactly?"

"Mama you know I'm only fourteen. I just turned fourteen in January."

"Well if he's fourteen then that one right over there, Darrick, he's thirteen. Cussin Darrick is what they call him. But if I ever catch him again he won't have no more lips to cuss with, cause I'm gonna knock the ones he got right off of his face. Ain't I Darrick?" Mama Bee asked as she glared at him.

"Yes ma'am," was his reply in a very low decibel. "Granny, he was just—" Eli wasn't able to get the entire tattle tale out before his sister had put her hand over his mouth.

"What baby? What was you about to say he was just doing what?" asked Granny Bee with a small touch of violence in her voice.

"Nothing, I wasn't going to say anything but—nothing," Eli stammered.

"well, I bet not catch him just saying nothing. And that's y'alls cousin Larry over there. He's twelve." "I won't be twelve until the 18th mama. I want a bike and some weights, and some money for my birthday cause

19

you said if I pass to the sixth grade you would get them for my birthday. And mama they wanted to pass me to the seventh grade and put me in Darrick's classroom," Larry said with great excitement.

"Alright, alright Larry! Girl he's so damn smart, and my baby is going to grow up and write books some day. Ain't you baby?"

"Yes Ma'am, that's what I'm gonna do with the money you give me for my birthday. I'ma buy some pens and paper and stuff."

"Okay boy. And that little chubby yellow girl over there, messing around in your child's hair is Debra and she's the oldest, and grownest of them all," Mama Bee said having a look on her face.

"I might be a little chubby, but I'm cute though," Debra responds because she doesn't like being called chubby. And you just might get cut if you use the word fat around her. "Like I said, she's older than the rest of my children. Yeah, the first one in the world, and no doubt the first one I'll end up taking out with her smart ass. And get out of that gir's damn hair!"

"Who is this little cute one all up under you?" Elizabeth asked.

20

"Oh, this little big man right here all up under my ass is called Bootie. Well, his name is Tremaine, but we call him Bootie," Mama Bee explained.

"Bootie, what kind of a name is Bootie?" asked Elisha, which caused Tremaine, a great deal of embarrassment.

"Mama, I told you I don't like being called Bootie."

"Boy, that's your name, because you're my little Boo Boo. Elizabeth, don't you know my grandmother gave him that name when he was only six months old. That was almost nine years ago. The last time I saw her and my Mother together, your grandmother's niece," Mama Bee says with heartache that could be heard and felt in her words.

"Oh Lord help me. Anyway, I'll share that story with you some other time. Just in case you did't know, your grandmother and my grandmother were sisters, born about thirty-seven years apart. In short, we're all related in one way or another," she says as she pats Elizabeth on her knee.

"I sure do look forward to hearing it, because I never knew and my mother has never spoken to me of family. So, who are these other children?"

"Oh, they are from all around the neighborhood, and those two girls right there, they live right next door. How is your mother doing?" Mama Bee asks.

"She's doing fine," says Nikki, and LaDonna, both answering at the same time.

"Okay now, y'all can all go back outside and play. Let us grownups get finished talking. Then I can think about what to fix y'all to eat."

"Mama, can we have some hotdogs and pork-n-beans?" Bootie asked having a smile from ear to ear.

"I'll cook you porky the pig if he's back there in that icebox. Now gone outside and play like I said and don't go past that fence back there, or else! Cause if I catch anyone of y'all out there in that alley, that's where the ambulance will be picking you up from," Mama Bee threatened as she pointed. "Girl, them children of mines are a hot hot mess. Every last one of them, but they better stay under control before I lose control."

"You know Ms. Bee—"

"I said Mama Bee, call me Mama Bee baby."

"I'm sorry, Mama Bee, but you mentioned grandma and I've always wondered why my grandmother and my mother have never seen eye to eye. I thought maybe you could tell me something."

"Well, it's kind of hard seeing eye to eye when you're looking through the same pair of eyes. But, let us try and deal with your issues first before beckoning your mother's issues also, okay?"

"Alright that's fine by me, because I sure do have enough of them," Elizabeth confessed with a sigh.

"So, you were saying before the children came barging in here," Mama Bee encouraged.

"I was saying that I believe that Mama, well actually, I know that my Mother feels betrayed by me, you know, for uprooting myself and her grandchildren. As strong as she is, I saw pain and hurt in her eyes this morning as we were leaving. And . . . And I feel so selfish now that I'm really thinking about it all from her perspective. Mama Bee, I completely overlooked the pain it would cause her because, I was so busy worrying about all the heartache and the pain I'm having to deal with',She doesn't understand that it was right there in my own home where the pain became too hard for me to bear. You know, the constant memories and even at her house the memories would bombard my heart. So after these last two years had past I just knew it was time to just pack me and the kids up. Even though I'd been contemplating it for over a year now, I made my mind up completely a few months ago. I knew I was going to get me and my children out of Georgia no matter what. Even if we had to stay in a shelter in Omaha!" "Well, you don't have to stay in anybody's shelter anywhere. You and the children are staying here with their Granny Bee, and that's final. But I do understand exactly what you've been telling me. And child there's been so much pain delved out onto our poor little ole family that time and alcohol won't even heal it. But that's neither here, nor there.

"The fact is Liz, I want you to take however much time you need. You use this change of scenery to get yourself together. Somewhere along the way you'll discover what you want the rest of your life to be. Even more importantly, what you intend to mold the lives of Elisha and Eli to become.

"See, the Lord knows I love all of mines, even though I can't stand the sight of them half the time. My soul knows what this clan has been through, survived, and is still going through. But it's these kids who must go it this next leg of the race. And it just might be your job to guide the way," Mama Bee said having a distant look upon her face.

24

"I know what you're saying Mama Bee. I heard your every word and I think the same things all of the time. Which was one of the reasons why I was so determined to pack up and leave my home. I'm only afraid that my mother will never be okay with my decision."

"Sure she will. In time she'll at least deal with it better. Eventually she'll see you did what you felt to be best for you, and your children."

"Yeah, maybe, but in the meantime do you mind if I use your phone to call her to let her know we've made it here safely?"

"I don't mind at all, and while you're doing that, I'm going into the kitchen to see what I can whip up for supper."

"Would you like for me to help you?"

"Of course not sugar, you go ahead and make your phone call to your mother and send her my hellos. Afterwards you should try getting yourselves a little rest before supper. I imagine y'all are plenty tired from your trip. Or did y'all rest any along the way, because it sure did take you an awful long time to get here from Atlanta?"

"No, no we didn't rest any. I'm just a really cautious driver," Elizabeth replied.

CHAPTER 3

"One of y'all go upstairs and wake up your Aunt Liz and tell her I said to get her and her children ready for supper. It'll be on the table in fifteen minutes," Mama Bee said to no one in particular.

"I'll go do it," Darrick said as he breaks away from his brothers and heads for the stairs.

Approximately fifteen minutes later everybody was gathered around the table in Granny Bee's diningroom. Mama Bee, Elizabeth, her two children, and Mama Bee's five.

A few had begun eating, while others were about to, when Elisha asked, "Aren't you going to say grace?"

That's when Larry said, "Where is she and who told her she could eat at our house?"

Receiving a chuckle from only Darrick, while everyone else's eyes were fixed on Elisha as she begins with her head down and eyes closed. "Lord we thank you for this meal and ask that you bless it as well as the cook. We are so fortunate to have such a God as you who is always caring and providing for us. In Jesus' name, thank you.

Amen."

"That was really nice sweetheart," Granny Bee told her. "Come on y'all, lets eat this meal that God has just blessed."

"Mama, why come we never been asking God to bless our food before, especially your brown beans?" Debra asked.

Her brothers laughed and they all received mean stares from Mama Bee. But that doesn't stop Darrick from saying, "Or them damn, I mean, dag-on greens."

"Boy, get over here right now!" Mama Bee shouts.

"Mama, I didn't say nothing."

"Darrick, I ain't going to tell you again. Get up and bring your butt over here!"

"Mama, it just slipped out. I didn't mean to say it," he said in protest.

"I know it, just like I'm not going to mean to knock you into next week. I'm aiming for the weekend, Saturday at the latest."

POP! Mama Bee's left hand connects with cussing Darrick's lips and both of them instantly swelled. When he sat back at the table next to Larry with his sniffling,

Larry looks him right in the face and says, "When we go swimming Darrick, at least you won't need no inner tube. You can just use your lips." And everyone at the table busted out in laughter. All besides Liz, and maybe Mama Bee. With Mama Bee you really couldn't tell, because she had her head down looking into her plate. But I believe the edges of her mouth was turned.

Anyway, after all the laughter and other joking had ceased, Reggie asked Liz, "Aunt Elizabeth, what's the matter with your son?"

"What do you mean, what did he do? Tell me," she asked with a touch of curiosity.

"Nothing really, he just woke up from his nap screaming something."

"That's called a nightmare, boy," Mama Bee answered. "I didn't have any nightmare. I just couldn't sleep, besides it wasn't even nighttime," Eli managed to mumble.

"Well, you woke up screaming and hollering something but I couldn't understand what you was saying," added Reggie.

"Eli baby, are you okay sweetie?" his mother asked. "There's nothing wrong with me. I'm just fine," Eli yells as he gets up from the table and storms to the room, slamming the door behind him.

Mama Bee says to Elizabeth, "You better go get him before I do. Gone in there and see about him." Then she turns to Reggie and says, "There's a time to say something and there's also a time to be quiet."

"Mama, I was just—"

"This is what you was just doing, shutting up and listening. You didn't have to put his business out there for everyone to know. You could have called his mother to the side and just told it to her, couldn't you have?"

"Yes ma'am, but . . ."

"But nothing, now y'all finish up eating. Clear the table, and Debra you do these dishes."

"Mama, I always gotta do the dishes, everyday!"

"So you should be used to it and it shouldn't be no surprise to you."

"I'll help you," Elisha told Debra, before Debra could release that one back talk that causes Mama Bee to snap.

Nighttime came suddenly, and almost everyone was reluctant to go to bed, but Granny Bee wasn't having none of that. She issued out the sleeping arrangements and as always, insisted on Bootie sleeping with her, even though he wanted to sleep in the bed with Darrick like he used to before Granny Bee kidnapped him.

Regardless, after Mama Bee turned off the living room television and lights, she tucked Bootie and herself into bed and the both of them watched some show on cable until they both fell asleep.

In the boy's room, sleep would'nt be so soon, because they had Mama Bee's schedule down pat. And they never went right to sleep, not even on school nights. This was summer, and tonight's topic of discussion was whether or not to break down the alley and knock on J.J., and Arney's bedroom window.

The Eubanks had been Reggie, Darrick, and Larry's friends ever since they could remember. That fact alone now made them all partners in crime. And other times there cousin Rita was down for whatever.

Why crime? Because Mama Bee's money came slow and hard, so she didn't give it away unnecessarily. "Reggie, Reggie, man I know you ain't asleep," Darrick said as he shook Reggie by his shoulder. This causes Eli to stir.

Eyes wide open, Reggie asked, "What's up? Man I was pretending to be asleep so this guy would fall all the way asleep.

That way we wouldn't have to worry about him snitching on us."

"Are you a snitch Eli?" Larry asked.

"A snitch?" Eli says.

"Yeah, a tattletale, a pigeon, a ratfink, a snitch," Larry asked him.

"If you ever snitch on us you are going to get your ass kicked," cussing Darrick slides his two cents in. "I'm not going to snitch on anybody about anything," Eli informs the brothers. "But what do you plan on doing anyway?" he asked.

"None of your damn business," Darrick scolds.

"Darrick, your lips haven't even went all the way down yet, and you already cussing again," Reggie informed him.

"Man, forget you!" replied Darrick. "Eli, put you some pants on, but leave your shoes off until we're out of the house, because Mama can hear the floor squeak so good she'll tell you exactly where you're standing from behind her bedroom door. So just follow us, and do what we do," Larry tells Eli.

Approximately twelve minutes later Reggie's lifting Eli up to J.J.'s window so he could knock on it softly. But before he even gets the chance to, Arney sticks her face in the window, which in turn scares the I don't know what out of Eli, who almost falls off of Reggie's shoulders.

Arney lifts up the window and J.J. sticks his head out and says, "You all go down to the end of the alley by Mr. Jones' house, before Brownie starts barking." "Man, that dog ain't going to do nothing with Darrick back there, probably feeding her now, or laters. Y'all just come on before we do it without y'all," Reggie tells them.

"You go ahead out the window J.J., and stay with them. I'll meet y'all down at Mr. Jones," Arney said.

"Okay, listen," Larry says after they all was gathered behind Mr. Jones' house. "This is our cousin Eli. Y'all met him earlier today at our house. He's going to go through the window and open the back door for us."

"What! What are you talking about?" Eli asks no one in particular. Because as he asks, he's looking back down the alley towards Granny Bee's house, wanting to make a break for it.

"What we're talking about is, if you don't open up the back door we're going to let Brownie eat you! I told her your punk ass taste just like now, or laters. The green ones," Darrick threatened.

"Why don't you chill out Darrick," Arney said as she walks over and places her long, slender brown complected arm around Eli's neck. She then walks Eli away from everyone else a few feet, for a few seconds. Afterwards, everybody crosses over to the other alley and entered the backyard belonging to some people who had recently moved on the block. That's when she said, "Y'all wait here by the garage while me and Eli go up on the back porch."

Moments later Eli was through the window and seconds after that he was exiting the back door.

"Larry, what did she say to your cousin in order to get him to do that?" J.J. asked.

"I don't know exactly, but I imagine it was something like she told me when I stole her a big red and a bag of Grippos out of Mr. Joe's candy store.

After just under a hour spent inside not leaving a drawer unsearched, nor a mattress, or rug unturned, the loot was

34

taken back down the alley and placed inside of the empty house two doors down from Mama Bee's. "The Club House".

After the money was divided, everyone parted ways. J.J. and Arney to their house, about six houses down and on the other side of the alley.

Reggie, Darrick, Larry, Eli, and Brownie began the walk, two houses over until J.J. whistled out and called Brownie's name.

In their backyard, Eli said, "We weren't supposed to do what we just did. We stole those people's stuff. Their TV, toys, microwave, and . . ."

"And you said it out of your own mouth. We stole, all of us! So that means you too!" Reggie expressed. At that very moment Mama Bee's bedroom light went on. Everybody stood frozen in their tracks. Eli petrified, everyone else watching for Mama Bee's shadow to go by the window in order to determine which way to re-enter the house.

It looks like the basement way is out, so that leaves the side window, the roof, or the front door. Larry advised the others, "Being that no one went upstairs to unlock the window, that leaves the side window with Nikki, and LaDonna's dogs right there. If they hear us, then

Mama will definitely hear us. Come on, we don't have any choice but to use the front door." After everyone made it completely inside to the living room, BOOM! The lights went on and everybody's heart jumped out of their chest.

"Mama is going to kill y'all if she catches y'all outside," Debra said as she stands there with some leftovers in a bowl in one hand and the other hand extended, awaiting hush hush money.

Everybody digs in their pockets and comes out with various amounts, but everybody is also waiting to see what the agreed upon cost is going to be.

"Looks like two dollar a man . . . Good going Darrick," the brothers thought. He was up front and closest to Debra, and first to put only two dollars in her hand. "Where's your two dollars at?" Debra asks Eli with her hand still extended, who first hesitated, but then dug into his pocket and came out with some ones. After giving Debra two, he turns and goes into the boy's bedroom barefooted.

"Who is that?" came Mama Bee's voice from her back bedroom.

"Mama, it's just me using the bathroom," Debra answered, while the boys all went into their room.

"Well, you bet not be using no damn bathroom in my damn living room!" "Mama, go back to sleep."

"What, what did you just say? You yellow heifer."

"Nothing Mama, I didn't say nothing."

"I know damn well you didn't, cause I'll get up out of this bed and knock your head around like that little girl on the scary movie. And Bootie scoot your butt over, give me my damn pillow. What you need with two pillows?"

CHAPTER 4

The sun was bright, but not scorching like Georgia's summers in June.

It was absolutely a beautiful morning in Louisville. The sky a very pretty light shade of blue. And the light wind now blew over Elizabeth's gorgeous light skin oval shaped face.

Out on the front porch raking her hair with her fingers, she inhaled deeply, exhaling out some stored tension, as well as some frustrations. Now feeling slightly invigorated by last night's sleep and this morning's new outlook on life, she was ready for this new start.

Her talk with her mother-in-law has given her additional strength and more than a touch of curiosity about her family's history.

My mother's mother and my mother-in-law's grandmother are sisters. Lord I don't even know my grandmother's sister's name, but they're related by blood. That makes Mama, and Mama Bee cousins, I think.

This is all so very interesting, but I have to learn—."
"Mama, mama," Elisha called out, bringing Elizabeth back from her thoughts.

"Huh, oh, what is it sweetheart?"

"Mama, why aren't you dressed?"

"Dressed, dressed for what honey?"

"It's Sunday. Aren't we going to church?"

"No baby, I don't think we'll make it in today sweetie."

"Why not Mama?" Elisha asked having a look of disappointment.

"Because it's going to take us awhile to find us a good church to attend, sweetheart."

"I thought we would be going with Granny this morning."

"Um (throat clears)! Baby, I don't attend any church," Mama Bee says from behind the screened door. "Mama Bee, you don't go to church, ever?" asked Elizabeth.

"Well, I used to a long time ago, but it's been years and I don't think I'd feel right if I just up and went today, or any other day for that matter."

"Mama Bee, I have to find a decent church for me and my children. We've always had that spiritual foundation to stand on."

WE SUFFER FOR A REASON

"I hear you," Mama Bee said. "And you sound just as I did for many years. To the point where I imagined the cares of this world has just took its toll on Mama Bee."

"I'm sorry to hear that Mama Bee, but that's why we attend, in order to see the difference in the two. Always being encouraged to lean on the Lord and not on our own understanding."

"Proverbs, chapter three, verse five—Trust in the Lord with all of your heart, do not depend on your own understanding. I can quote scripture with the best of them, but that ain't the problem. My problem is the flesh seems to keep winning the wars over my spirit. Like right now, the flesh is screaming to be fed some of these pancakes, and sausages, I'm about to pull out of the skillet as soon as I get finished whipping over the stove' So, we can talk about it all some more after breakfast. Come on in here and give your Granny Bee some help with the table setting zbaby," she beckoned Elisha.

CHAPTER 5

Elizabeth and her kids transitioning into their new environment was easy enough. Liz noticed that Elisha remained outgoing as she has always been. But it was Eli who concerned her most. He being so standoffish, and having very little to say, she knew this behavior was due to the absence of a little boy's Dad. So, she tried unceasingly to bring her son out of the shell he was attempting to place around himself.

And these last few months she noticed a slight change, due mostly to his cousin's constant activeness, which is why she had decided to allow their interaction to evolve opposed to her treating him like a baby and causing him embarrassment. Oh, but he was still her baby. "James our baby misses you so—"

"Liz, sweetheart, do you mind giving your Mama Bee a ride to the grocery store?" she tapped on the door, then entered to ask. "I need to get to the Big 'G' grocery over on Dixie Highway."

"Mama Bee, I don't mind at all. Besides, I need to pick up a few more things, because I don't want me and the kids eating up all of your food."

"Baby, I don't worry myself about things like that, but it does make me feel good knowing that you continuously help."

"Just let me get myself together and then I'll get the kids rounded up, so we can take them with us."

"Round the kids up, for what?"

"You don't want to take the children to the grocery to give them the chance to get out for a little while, plus let them pick out a few of the things they like?"

"Child, let Mama Bee share a couple of things with you. First of all, those kids ain't got no money so there wen't their need to go to any store. Secondly, I already know everything they like to eat. And that's whatever I buy, cook and put on the table."

"I was only suggesting—," Elizabeth began. "What you was suggesting was to give us both early morning headaches. Now go ahead and get yourself together baby, and I'll get my purse and my other wig. I'll be waiting for you in the kitchen."

"Okay Mama Bee, I'll need about ten minutes, fifteen at the most."

In the car and on their way to the Big 'G' grocery, Mama Bee said to Liz, "Next week will be five months that you've been here in Louisville and I must say, I am proud of all you've done so far. You got your children into good schools, you've been working that job for what, three months now, going on four? And you done traded your old car in for this nice one you got here. All I got to say is 'You go girl!'

"Mama Bee, I haven't done nearly enough because I had planned on having a place for me and the kids by now. But when that old car of mines began to really act up, I knew I had to get rid of it. That set me back a little."

"Are you in that much of a hurry to get away from me, and my crew?" Mama Bee asked.

"No, it's not that Mama Bee. Although I have wondered whether or not you was tired of us." "I'll never be tired of my son's children, my grandchildren, ever. You either for that matter. And ain't you learned anything about your Mama Bee by now. How I speak my mind and if you get on my nerves, I know how to get you off of 'em.

"Anyway, about you moving. Just know, and understand that you're welcome to stay with me forever. But I know you're a woman who really wants and has to have her own. As if you got something to prove to the entire world."

"Not to the world Mama Bee, only to myself." "And that's just fine, and I believe if you stay with that attitude, some help from other sources will soon come your way."

"I sure do need it, because it seems like every time I take a step in the right direction, something from out of nowhere knocks me two steps back."

"Things will get better for you baby. Just wait, you'll see. Listen, pull right over there beside the green van over there," Mama Bee directs Liz into an available parking space in the Big 'G' parking lot. "It sure is crowded inside of here," she says to no particular person as she removes a shopping cart from its rack and wheels it toward the rear. Liz does likewise, following close behind Mama Bee.

"Honey, I'm going over there to the meat department. You go ahead and find the things you need, and I'll meet you at the car when you're done."

"Mama Bee, I was going to pick up some meat myself, and I thought we could do it together so we wouldn't be purchasing the same things."

"Sounds good to me, but Liz I want you to know something. Thanksgiving is a week away and I got a whole lot of mouths to feed, so I have no intentions on paying these high ass prices for this meat. So it might be a good idea if you go your way and let me go mines."

"Mama Bee, you're talking about stealing? Now you know that isn't right. Besides, you have the money to pay for it. And if you don't have enough, I'd be more than happy to give you however much you need"

"You just keep your money and do whatever you want to with it, like I plan to keep my money and do what I want to do with it. But this meat, I ain't paying one red cent for it. Not one dime," she said to Liz as she places a high priced ham with the bone in it into her shopping cart and then guides it off and away from Liz.

Liz goes in the opposite direction of Mama Bee and she shops around for about fifteen minutes, doing way more thinking than shopping. Mostly about Mama Bee's actions.

The nerve of her mother-in-law to be in the grocery store stealing. Her children's grandmother stealing meat.

As she continues on down a grocery aisle, she can see Mama Bee further down the same aisle, placing items from a shelf into her grocery cart. But what really catches Elizabeth's attention is the tall, dark complected man who appeared to be watching Mama Bee's every move.

As the realization hits home, Liz becomes instantly fearful for Mama Bee, because she realizes that this guy is following Mama Bee because he's store security. So, she speeds up in front of him and makes her way right beside Mama Bee and her cart, then whispers, "Don't look behind you, but store security is following you!" Afterwards, Liz places an item from the shelf into her cart and pushes off, Questioning her actions, but at the same time she knows she would hate to see anything bad happen to her mother-in-law, especially an arrest. After paying for her groceries, Liz exits the Big 'G' and places her groceries into her car. She then watches the front doors of the grocery store through the rearview mirror and occasionally she peers over her right shoulder in hopes of seeing Mama Bee walk out safely. Low and behold after sitting there for over twenty minutes hoping, and praying for Mama Bee to exit, she finally does. So Liz starts her car and drives to the front of the store and helps Mama Bee put her grocery bags into the car.

On the drive home, Liz is reluctant to say anything, believing any word spoken by her would come out wrong. She was so mad about the situation Mama Bee had placed her in.

Instead of speaking, she used the moment to review her own life and she saw that she had never stolen anything in her whole life, nor has she tolerated or condoned stealing of any kind.

"Liz, if you have something you would like to say to me, then I wish you would just go ahead and say it," Mama Bee spoke first.

"There's nothing that needs to be said," Liz replied.

"The expression on your face says otherwise."

"Well, then yes, Mama Bee. There's a whole lot that I have to say!" "Say on, I'm listening."

"Mama Bee, how could you involve me in your theft and in your taking a chance on going to jail? What if that security officer would have caught you, or even worse, caught me with you and arrested us both? We both would be locked up in the jailhouse right now, and then what would've happened to our children? My children, your children, who would be there to take care of them?

"I didn't want to leave them home by themselves in the first place. Mama Bee, how could you?" Liz asked with tears now streaming down her face.

"Elizabeth, stop crying and listen to me. I admit I was wrong," Mama Bee began. "I was absolutely and totally wrong, in my asking you to bring me out to the grocery store. Involving you was a huge mistake. I apologize and I promise you that it'll never happen again."

"You're not going to steal anymore, and you did pay for all of the things from Big 'G' that you put into your shopping cart, is all that I'd like to hear."

"I've been shoplifting for over two years now, and I do not plan on quitting anytime soon. So, no I didn't put back any of those items," said Mama Bee as she began to pull a ham and coffee, candies, and various other items from various places of her body. Items that were easy enough for Mama Bee to conceal, being that she was a big woman. Not insanely huge, but Mama Bee has plenty of meat on her bones. If you know what I mean . . .

"Listen sweetie, I am sincerely sorry for placing you in the middle of my mess. And believe me, it will never happen again, but the truth is there are a few families depending on me for Thanksgiving. Children who will

48

not be eating any turkey or ham, or any of America's traditions, unless I do what I do. And I'm not talking about just my own children either'

See, whatever doesn't go on my table this Thanksgiving or on the tables of the families who I try to help out, will be sold and the money will be used to purchase the things that are needed. I don't expect anyone to understand or agree, but it is what it is," Mama Bee said as they pulled up in front of the house. That's when she reaches over and started blowing the cars' horn.

Immediately the children came rushing out through the front door and to the car, knowing that Mama Bee always brought back goodies from the grocery store.

After putting the groceries away, giving the children candy bars, and sodas, then sending them all to other rooms, Mama Bee sits Liz down at the kitchen table. She places a hand over Elizabeth's hand and begins saying, "I really want you to know that I am truly sorry. I make no money for myself for doing what I do. Like my card parties, the profit is not mines either. Speaking of which, do you remember me telling you there'll be one this weekend? So, you'll get to see for yourself.

"I guess what I'm really trying to say in order to have you to understand, is we are a real close knit community when you really look at it all. But some of us are less fortunate than others, like my friend Bunch across the street. That's why I never mind it when her grandchildren have supper here with us nor do I mind it when they take Bunch a plate of food when they leave..

"Honey, I done had neighbors who had resorted to eating their dog's food."

Well, eventually I said enough is enough, because the Lord knows Mama Bee will knock off Bank of America before she sees any of hers go hungry.

"I tell you the truth Liz, one winter about two years back, we were almost there. Right on the doorstep to the poor house. That's when I made my mind all the way up to do something about my situation and my family's future. And maybe I didn't choose the wisest course of action, but I be damn if I be broke, or hungry ever again, not Bee!

"You can leave me, or judge me, hate me, or love me, just don't make the mistake of calling me selfish." With that being said, Mama Bee rose up, went to her bedroom and closed the door behind her, leaving Elizabeth sitting there at the table with her own thoughts.

After Liz prepared chicken and rice smothered in gravy, green beans, candy yams, and hot watered cornbread, she sat it all out on the dining room table, then she knocked on Mama Bee's bedroom door.

"It's open, come on in and leave the light out." "Mama Bee, it's me. I just wanted to say, obviously you have your reasons for doing what you do, like you've said, and you've promised to never involve me, so the only thing I'll add is, please think about your own safety, and your children's welfare. And other than that, I wanted to let you now that dinner is ready."

"You mean supper?"

"Supper, dinner, what's the difference between the two?" Elizabeth asked.

"None really, but when I was a little girl I used to think that a person had to go to a diner in order to have dinner. And back then we wasn't allowed in any diners, so we always had supper."

"Mama Bee, about when you were a little girl, I really would like to hear more about it, and I would like for my kids to know about our past."

"Well, I'll tell you what. After we all have eaten, I'll sit you all down and recite some real history. How about that?" Mama Bee then said to Liz as she gets up out of bed, moves over to her back window and yells for the neighbor's dogs to shut up their yapping. "Go ahead and call the kids to supper and send their company home."

"I thought you said you feed the neighborhood children."

"That's exactly what I said and it's exactly what I do, but there's a way in which you go about giving away food that you don't really have."

Elizabeth, having stepped out onto the back porch calling the children to supper and excusing their company, returned to the kitchen where she found Mama Bee looking through pots and opening the oven to have a look see.

"Mama Bee, this is not my first time preparing din—. I mean supper all by myself, so why are you looking like that?" asked Liz.

"It's certainly not your first time doing supper, but I do believe it's your first time going all out like this," she said as she continued her examination.

When Mama Bee had finished yelling at the children to wash up before they dared touch anything, she grabbed Darrick by an arm and instructed him to place two chairs from the kitchen and put them at the dining room table to accommodate their friends.

Once all were seated and before anyone touched a thing, Bootie asked, "Mama can I talk to God over our food?"

"You sure can baby. Everybody close your eyes and bow your heads. My Boo Boo is going to say grace." "God I thank you for my cousin Elisha and Eli and Aunt Liz, and I thank you for my brothers and my sister Debra, and especially thank you for my Granny." "And we thank you for this wonderful meal. Amen," Mama Bee interjected.

Then everyone said in unison, "Amen."

"Mama I wanted to do it," Bootie whined. "Boy, you did do it. I just helped you with the end," Mama Bee explained.

"And you definitely needed help cause you was about to thank God for the neighbors, the people across the street, and the old man who be yelling out, 'Watermelon, I'm selling fresh watermelon," Darrick said to achieve laughter from all.

In an attempt to end his embarrassment, Bootie took a swing at, but missed Darrick by a quarter of an inch.

"I'm just playing with you lil bruh. You ain't got to get so mad," Darrick said.

By this time the attention turned to Eli, cause Reggie had asked, "Eli, why are you so quiet everywhere but your nightmares?"

"I'm not having no nightmares, for your information Reggie, so why don't you just leave me alone about it."

"He don't seem to have any trouble talking when he be on the phone with my sister," squealed J.J.

And without a hint, nor a warning, Arney punched J.J. so hard in the mouth that it placed Mama Bee in a state of shock for approximately seven seconds before she scolded Arney for putting hands on anybody in her house, at her table.

J.J. didn't do nothing but sit there with his mouth wide open. Nor was he going to do anything. He never did, none of the times his sister had taken flight on him. Later it would be learned, after years of J.J. witnessing his Dad punch on his mother, he had vowed never to hit a woman or a girl.

"You are a cold punk, and a hot sissy," Darrick told J.J. "I think you're only tough when you got Brownie with yo punk ass." "When we get outside we will see who the punk is," J.J. warns Darrick. Which causes him to

54

laugh and say, "You know if you put your hands on me, Reggie will kick your ass.

"Ms. Bee," J.J. began, but Darrick cut him off by saying, "Eli, why are you so quiet forreal though. It seems like the only times you talk a lot is in your sleep." "Granny Bee, will you please tell them to stop bothering me. I don't say anything because I don't want to say anything," Eli states matter-of-factly.

"Well, Eli I did tell you when you first got here that we don't do shy in this house. If there's something bothering you, just let your family know what it is so we can work together to fix it," Mama Bee calmly expressed.

"How many times do I have to tell y'all that there's nothing wrong with me. Why don't you all just leave me along about it," Eli tells them all in a certain tone.

"What?" questions Debra looking directly at Mama Bee and allows the question to linger.

And since there was no immediate reply from Mama Bee, Debra went on to say, "Now Mama you know if that was one of us to mouth off like that you would have been done snatched up a weapon."

"Well, obviously he's going through something and we all need to just give him time to sort it out," said she with a look of concern upon her face.

"So you're just going to let Eli get away with talking back to you like that?" Debra asked.

"Debra, would you just let it go before you and one of them weapons become intimate," threatened Mama Bee.

"See Mama there you go, you don't never let me get away with nothing. You always want to embarrass me, or hurt my feelings every chance you get," exclaimed Debra with eyes filling up with liquid.

"That's because your healthy ass don't know how to let things go. You just keep on and on until you push my beat your ass button."

"And that's exactly the reason why I never wanted to come and live here in the first place," Debra voiced, allowing the first tear to roll down her cheek.

"Well, I'm quite certain my front door is unlocked, so all you have to do is open it up and roll your smart round ass on through it," said she, never being the one to back down from a fight. Not even if her opponent is a sixteen year old.

"I can't wait until my mother comes back and takes me away from the meanest old lady I've ever known in my life," Debra exploded as she stomped her way up the steps to her room.

"I've been waiting on that day for three years and she hasn't pulled up yet, but if you want to, you can pack you a bag and wait out on the porch for another three winters," Mama Bee was saying to the air because Debra had slammed her door shut a good twenty seconds ago.

After a calm had covered the inside of the dwelling, Elisha was the one who approached her grandmother with her inquisitiveness.

"Why do you want their mother to come and get her? Isn't she your daughter now?"

"No sweetheart. If she was mines I would have been done caught me a body, especially on that little round heifer upstairs," said Mama Bee illustrating that her calm was of an outward appearance only. "They're my daughter Lee, Lee's children, but I've raised all of them so it's like they're mine and if she ever comes back for them who am I to try and stop her," she said having a look of perplexity.

But then added, "That's a conversation for another time. I'm supposed to be sharing some of our other family history with you all. So who knows what slavery was all about?" Mama Bee asked, changing the subject from the one she was not ready to continue in.

"I do Mama," said one of the boys.

"I learned about it in school," said another. "Let's all move into the living room and we'll see if them school books tell a whole truth, or a half truth," Mama Bee said as she made her way into the next room.

Elizabeth sent Elisha to retrieve Eli as she herself traversed the stairs to persuade Debra to join them in the living room.

When all was gathered together, amongst the excitement you could hear Larry telling Eli to pay close attention cause Mama tells amazing stories. Debra was silent, but in great anticipation cause she too knew Mama Bee to be an awesome storyteller. But Darrick was the loudest as he began his narrative of learning from his school books about how the negro was brought to America in chains to pick cotton for food and shelter and if they refused to pick cotton they were whipped, or hung by their necks by their white masters.

"Shh, shh," Mama Bee ceased all the rumblings in the livingroom, and then said, "That's only part of it, but there was a whole lot more to slavery than the beatings and the hangings. But even still, the most horrible unforgiveable part is what continues to go on to this very day. Black people seem to have forgotten that with the beatings of our backs, our self pride, and communal strive has been beaten out of us. And we're not seeking to regain it, or anything else together as a whole."

"A whole race! It's so sad for us to forever lose ourselves and our self-worth."

"Y'all stay quiet and listen now," Mama Bee told them, instead of answering the barrage of questions aimed at her.

"Did they beat your back Mama? Why do they hate us so much? Why didn't you just leave the plantation?"

"Listen," I said. "Since the story demands to be told beginning at slavery, then I guess I might as well start right there.

"I remember my great grandmother saying to us, 'You chillin, hear your Granny with your hearts. These here white folks ain't gonna have us bound up like this forever, and it's the very message I received from my parents. A time is coming when you'll truly be free! But as God is livin, I tell you that the only way to get the devil's foot off our necks is if we women give 'em our very own souls. Seems like it's the way the good Lord intens on it. Hee, hee, hee!!'

"Granny is three years shy of reaching a hundred years old. And all of my life I ain't never seen a day go away that color folks ain't have to live in constant fear of dying, or in fear of something worse.

"It was right here on this Bodiford plantation that I was born, ninety seven years ago in the year eighteen and fifty. When I was old enough to question my mother about our surroundings, that's exactly what I set out to do. Well, Mama didn't tell much, but I had myself a Auntie Tee who told it all, and some.

"Even when she went to work in the Big House, she still managed to sneak away from master James and come and visit with me. And never without a hanky full of some of her sweetbread.

It was my dear sweet Auntie Tee who explained to me why my uncles and even my brother was no more. Either hung til dead or sold off by the overseer, who was employed by the Bodifords—Tom Woodward, the son of Satan.

"My Auntie didn't need to tell me much about the overseer, because I seen him with my own eyes doing his father's deeds. But it wasn't until I saw him snatch Glenda, my little precious baby sister out of my mother's arms and hurled her into the open flap of the coal stove, that I knew for certain him and the devil shared the same blood.

"My Great Grandmother wouldn't tell 'em of her brother's whereabouts, because not even she knew if he had really escaped and fled to the north, never to be heard from again.

"Her last and only remaining brother . . . Granny realized they were trapped in a hellish nightmare and that there was no awaking from it.

"They past it down to us that, 'We were a proud people, Africans living in our own land, a numerous amount of family, too many to count. All living and enjoying life.' But one night like a swarm of locusts, the white man assisted by other black clans came and bound our people in chains of steel. Her and her entire tribe, which consisted of her whole family, they were captured and shipped to this strange land, where her sisters were sent away in one direction and her brothers in another. Her uncles and mother's sisters treated likewise. But her and her children were sold to a plantation owner in Alabama.

"Later she was traded for cattle to a man named Bodiford who was a ruthless and evil man. One who didn't fear man, nor God. But it was there on that Bodiford plantation in Georgia where she was reunited with other members of her family. It was also there that birth was given to my Grandmother who later gave birth to baby Glenda.

"My great grandmother Bernice stayed there on that plantation and watched many of her family members travel to the north, after being freed by the Civil War," Mama Bee explained.

"When Bernice grew older, she believed things would be no different for a race of people hated in a land not their own, no matter where they were in that land.

"Of course she was often asked why she never left that awful place of so much misery, and she would say,
'After her mother's passing away, she went and married herself unto her Eli. They settled right there and raised their children up and into proud God fearing souls.'
"Now, Eli, he wouldn't have had it any other way. Being the stern and stubborn Reverend Eli Lewis, pastor of the flock that gathered every Sunday evening in the

field behind the barn on the Bodiford's land," Mama Bee said. With a knowing smile she then paused at the wonderment she saw emanating from her grandson's Eli's face.

"So," she said with great joy, "You see Eli your father named you after his great great Grandfather, Eli."

"My dad's great great grandfather was a slave in Georgia, where we used to live?" Eli asked.

"Yes, he was a slave, but he died a free man, who delivered the souls of many from bondage," Mama Bee announced, having a look of joy.

"You tell a story very well," Elizabeth tells Mama Bee as she moved close enough to her to place an arm through hers.

"It's easy enough to do when it's the truth being told," she replies.

"So, tell me something Mama Bee."

"And what might that be?"

"Was my grandmother Glenda named after the baby sister your great grandmother witnessed being murdered?"

"Absolutely. And let me share this with you because it seems like your mother has neglected to share with you important family history. First of all, we would still be family even if you wouldn't have married my son James.

See, you're absolutely correct. My great great grandmother's daughter named her second female child Glenda, who is your grandmother, your mother Ella's mother.

"My mother Rose, who passed several years ago and Glenda were cousins. You see after my great great grandfather Eli was accused of forming a rebellious revolution in and through the gospel, for which he was eventually murdered, Bernice later passed away, but not before embedding in her family the importance of the only way to get the devil's foot off of our necks.

"She worded it just like that on many many occasions in order to instill its importance into our minds and our hearts. She explained that it could only be the devil himself who could enslave a race of people for over four hundred years, and spread demonic hatred through so many generations.

"She often compared the hundreds of years of slavery of the black race with the hundreds of years of slavery done unto the Jewish race. Two races hated by an unseen entity of satanic origin dwelling in the hearts and minds of their captors.

"She would say that black folks was doing the first part of what the Jewish race had done to ensure their deliverance, trusting in God. But they would neglect to do the second part that would forever guarantee that they would never be enslaved or oppressed ever again. "See, my great great grandmother not only learned from the word of God, but it was like she had something or someone else working with her, in her and through her, giving her insight into distant things.

"I don't know what it was or what she had, all I know is she tried until she died to guide us as a whole into a future filled with promise. Never promising that the road to be traveled would be an easy one, but the opposite. 'You women will be called upon to give your very souls, but be mindful and certain of, unto whom your soul is being given,' " she would say to us when she had us all gathered together like that. "Like I've said, I was young and I didn't fully understand all that she was instilling in me, but I was aware of its importance. When that time came that I fully and completely understood my Grannie's words will be told to y'all at some other time," Mama Bee told her family.

And for doing so, she received some huffs and a few puffs.

Then Darrick said, "Dang Mama just when I was trying to understand—"

Mama Bee cut him off and said, "Boy you're telling a damn lie. You was over there knocked out asleep slobbering all over your brother's arm."

Darrick looked around, wipes off his mouth and says, "No, I wasn't Mama."

This brought on laughs from the ones who weren't asleep. And it also brought on an assault of questions mixed with ramblings that Mama Bee dismantled by saying, "I said we'll get back to the history lesson about our family tomorrow night, after the hamburgers and French fries, but during the triple layer double chocolate cake."

That brought on excitement that rattled the entire room.

Mama Bee told Bootie since he was now wide awake that they all could stay up for a little while longer.

Most of them began yelling and wrestling with one another, but it was Eli who remained sitting there stone-faced, as if he was in a trance.

WE SUFFER FOR A REASON

"Eli, are you feeling okay?" Elizabeth asked him. "Eli, if you're not feeling well you should go lie down," his mother added.

"Mama, I'm okay. I was just thinking about something." "Do you mind sharing your thoughts with your mother, or have you gotten too big to talk to me about everything?"

"It was nothing really Mama. There's just a lot of stuff Granny Bee said tonight that I don't understand, but I would like to know everything. Especially the things about my father's great great grandfather Eli, and his wife. All of their family! Our family Mama, our family who were slaves, but survived. And some even moved North, but where to in the North? Wouldn't you like to know too Mama?"

"Yes, I would like to know Eli, and maybe one day we both will. But until then we'll both learn what we can from Mama Bee. So, why don't you go ahead and play with the rest of the kids in there and we'll talk a little more tomorrow. Goodnight Eli, Mama's going to bed. I love you, please know that." "Goodnight Mama, I love you too."

"Eli, come on, Mama said we can go out on the front porch as long as we don't leave off of it. Come on,"

67

said Larry as he and the rest of the boys headed for the front door.

Outside it was dark, but starry. A sky filled with bright shining stars. So bright in fact it almost seemed as though you could reach up and touch you one. It was also noisy out front due to the break in school and the unusually warm weather for a November night. Kids out on the sidewalk and a very noisy bunch right next door on Nikki and LaDonna's porch.

But Reggie and Larry wasn't worrying nor concerning themselves with all of the ruckus. They was focusing their attention on two houses down, to the front yard of their clubhouse where they just saw Brownie, J.J., and Arney's dog run back to the back of the house.

"Man, did you just see what I just saw?" Larry asked.

"Yeah, and if Brownie is down there that means J.J. or Arney or both of them are down there too," Reggie said.

"Whose going to go down there and check it out? We all can't go, because if Mama looks out here and don't see none of us out here, you know she will bring the pain," Larry warned them all.

"Darrick, why don't you run down there and see who has Brownie out while I go around back and see what I can see from our backyard?" Larry asked.

"Man, you're crazy! I ain't going nowhere. You go down there and see. Send Reggie around back and I'll sit right here and holler at Nikki's cousin."

"Look at her over there sitting on the porch swing in her pink sweats, and fluffy pink house shoes."

"A Nikki, Nikki, what's your cousin's name? Stacey, Tracey? What is it?"

"She can talk, ask her, She probably won't tell you anyway, because she don't like you, she likes your cousin Eli, she said he's cute," Nikki yells loud enough that anyone with ears could hear.

Eli stood up and was on his way to the door, but Reggie grabbed him and asked, "Where do you think you're going?"

"You know he's scared, he was scared to kiss Arney the other day," Darrick said.

"I'm not scared. I'm going to make sure that Mama and Granny Bee are asleep, so I can go down there and see who's down there with Brownie," Eli said.

Reggie, Darrick, and Larry asked at the same time. "What!?"

"I'm going to go down there and see who has Brownie out," Eli says again, before walking into the house to make sure the coast was clear.

Upon his return, Reggie told him, "Larry's checking around the back, so you go ahead and run down and check the front."

"Why run, when I can just walk without letting anyone know that I'm coming, or what I'm doing?" questioned Eli.

"Man, do it whichever way you want to, just hurry up before they get away."

"Okay, but Reggie back home in Georgia your name would be 'Capped up Shawty.' " "What?" asked Reggie.

"Nothing," said Eli as he left off of the porch casually and headed toward the clubhouse. When he arrived around to the side of the house there was no Brownie. Only Larry standing on a milk crate peering through a side window.

"Eli, come here and help me hold myself steady so I can see in here better. Stand right here and let me hold myself up by your shoulder."

"How are you going to be able to see in the dark?" asked Eli.

"That's what I'm saying. There's a light on inside."

"What, when we were in there the last time there wasn't any electric. Lets just go around back, go inside and have a look around," Eli suggested.

"I tried the back door before I came around here, and it was locked," Larry told Eli. "What do you think is going on?"

"I don't know. Hold still, I'm trying to see if there are any movements. It looks like someone has been painting, and fixing the place up. There are tools everywhere!"

"Come on, let's go back on the front porch before one of our mothers wakes up," said Eli. "Or even worse, before Elisha, or Debra comes outside, because when I went in the house they were in the kitchen playing cards."

"Hold up for a second. Let me ask you something, Eli. I know you don't talk much and we be giving you a hard time about it, mostly Reggie, but my question is, why don't you want to hustle with us and make some money and at the same time fit in with everybody else?"

"Larry, when y'all be hustling, y'all actually be stealing and stealing is wrong. Cousin Larry, I don't know if you will understand this or not but I didn't get the chance to spend a whole lot of time with my father, but during the time we did have together he taught me a few things. One of those things was, God is always watching. He sees everything, recording the rights and the wrongs."

"I don't know anything about God Eli, but it sounds like Him and Santa Claus are working together. No but seriously, I've never had anyone to teach me about God. I just believed He was up in heaven and we was down here and whenever a person died, they went to heaven."

"But you do know and believe there is a God?" Eli asked Larry.

"Yeah, I just said He lives in heaven, didn't I? My Dad would say to me when I asked how can God see everything, that heaven was too small, cause God is so big. He fills the whole world."

"But what's important is that we know and believe," said Eli. Then added, "Thank you cuzzin."

"For what, what are you thanking me for?"

"I guess because I needed to hear someone my age say when you die you go to heaven."

"They do, now come on. Lets get back to the porch."

"What took y'all so long?" Reggie asked, when Eli and Larry had made it up the steps and onto the porch. "Y'all know Debra and Elisha been out here meddling, asking where you two were."

"What did you tell them?" Larry asked.

"I told them y'all had to take Brownie home, because she was out loose."

"A, Eli this girl wants to talk to you. It's Nikki, and LaDonna's cousin, Stacey," Darrick stressed.

"Tell her to wait a minute Darrick and come here for a minute," Larry told him.

"Yeah, what's up? Did y'all see J.J. or Arney?"

"Naw, we didn't see anybody, but what we found out is we don't have a clubhouse anymore."

"What are you talking about?" Reggie asked.

"It looks like somebody is fixing up the place down there," Larry explained.

"Painting and everything," added Eli.

"Well, it's a good thang we got most of that stuff out of there," Darrick said.

"Yeah, all besides that big ugly microwave."

"What about all of our other stuff we've put in there?"

"What we need to do is go down to our clubhouse one last time and pick up all of those power tools somebody left laying around," Larry suggested.

"Power tools?" Darrick and Reggie said at the same time. Then Reggie asked, "Is the back door still open?"

"You know Mr. Keith will buy all of the power tools we bring him."

"Come on, lets go. I'm trying to get enough money together so I can buy some red chucks and a red skull cap," Reggie said as he headed towards the steps. "Hold up a second," Larry said. "We have to make sure everything is straight before we just go and do it. We not only have to be sure that Mama is still asleep, we have to make sure that Debra don't see us either."

74

"You have to make sure Elisha is sleeping too because she'll worry about where everybody is," Eli said.

"What?" asked Reggie. "Your sister better keep her worrying to herself if she knows what's good for her. Besides, what are you worried about it for, you know you're not going to do no hustling."

"You don't know what I'm going to do," Eli responded in anger.

"I know you're not trying to make your own money, but whenever we go around to Joe's corner store you be asking your Mama for two dollars," Reggie told Eli, getting all up in his face.

Eli pushed Reggie back up off of him and told him to get out of his face. Reggie grabbed Eli and put him in a head lock so quick and unexpectedly that Eli didn't have a chance of avoiding his vice-like grip.

The neighbors, Nikki, LaDonna, their friends and their cousin Stacey were standing at the edge of their porch screaming over at Reggie to let Eli go.

He eventually did, not due to their screaming, but due to the fact that Eli no longer put up any resistance. Now free of Reggie's headlock, Eli looks around briefly, and then looks Darrick in the face and tells him to make sure everyone's asleep in the house. Then he turned to Larry and says, "Come on lets go through the back." "You don't have to do anything if you don't want to," Larry tells Eli as they take the steps and head around the side of the house toward the back.

"I know I don't," said Eli, and that's all he said before picking up his pace as they made their way through the backyard.

By the time they reached the back door of their former clubhouse, Reggie had caught up with them, and Darrick was just reaching the back fence of the yard.

When Darrick made it all the way up to them he said, "Man, don't y'all know Bootie had his ass up talking about he wanted to come back outside with us."

"What did you do?" Larry asked.

"I gave his ass some cookies and told him to take his butt back to bed before I take him in there and put him in bed with Mama."

"So, he's back in the bed?" Reggie asked.

"Naw, he's in my right shirt pocket. Yeah, he's back in the bed."

"Shh, listen," Larry said. "I told y'all that this door isn't open no more, so how do we get in?"

"Lets check the windows over here," Darrick said.

"Try them and see if they open."

"What about the ones up there over the door, right here?" he added.

"How are we going to get all the way up there?"

"I'm going to go around to the side, and to the front and check those doors," Reggie said.

"What if somebody sees you, like Mrs. Neil or her husband?" asked Darrick.

"What if anybody that's out front see you, then they will know that we were over here."

"Chingle lingle ling." The back door window went crashing to pieces and making an amplified noise in the still of the night, because Eli, without warning, had thrown a brick through the windowpane of the door.

And in shocked terror, mixed with a higher percentage of fear, the three brothers broke for their house. Several seconds after making it there to safety, Eli came trotting up through their backyard laughing and saying, "I turned around and y'all were gone. One second y'all were there and then in the next you was gone. I turned around and y'all wasn't even in the yard at all."

While Eli was still laughing, Reggie was up off of the back steps and saying, "Man, are you crazy or something? You could have told us you was going to do that, you big dummy."

"Leave him alone Reggie. He did what we should have done in the first place. Now all we have to do is wait for a little while and make sure the police, or nobody else comes. Then we can go back and get what belongs to us," Larry said before walking around to the front porch of their house.

Darrick followed behind him, then Reggie and Eli brought up the rear from where he said loud enough for all the brothers to hear, "Scary Dudes!"

Larry took the steps two at a time to the front porch.

Once all were on the porch, questions were asked as to what kind of tools was inside and how many. What was the potential worth and where would they be stored until sold.

These questions as well as their answers were interrupted when Nikki's cousin, Stacey hollered over and asked, "Are you alright Eli?"

Eli looked over at her and responded, "Yeah I'm okay. Thanks for asking." Then he turned and went into the house.

"A Stacy, you know my cousin Eli already has a girlfriend, don't you!" Darrick stated. "He goes with Arney. They have been going together for awhile now. They might even get married. Now, if you need a boyfriend, I'm not going with anybody right now, so what's up?"

"You still ain't going with anybody," Stacey said as she turned to enter LaDonna's front door.

Reggie and Larry were laughing when Darrick turned to face them. All Darrick said was, "She wants me." Around twenty minutes later the decision was made to go back to the clubhouse and get every piece of valuable in sight.

"I'ma go in the house and get Eli," Larry said as he opened the door and walked inside.

"Eli, are you going to go with us down to the clubhouse?"

"Larry I can't go, and I never should have did what I did in the first place. But Reggie and y'all are really going to think that I'm the scary dude now."

Larry chuckled, then said, "Naw, Reggie and Darrick are going to think that's more money for them. Later they may say you chickened out, but so what. If you don't want to do something, then don't do it. Don't care about what anybody says or thinks. You have your reasons, right?"

"Yeah, I have my reasons, but before you go let me let you know something. I think you are a pretty smart dude, too smart to be doing what you are about to do," Eli informed his cousin Larry.

"Thanks for saying that, but as for my doing what I'm doing, the reasons are being seen through a different pair of eyes. Mama gives us money, but not all of the time. She buys us stuff, but not the stuff we like to wear. So, we all decided to get the things we want and like on our own. Speaking of which, I'm out," Larry said, then left the room, closing the door behind him.

"Man, what took you so long?" Reggie asked Larry without giving him the chance to get all the way out of the door.

"Making sure the coast was clear," was all he said before asking, "Are y'all ready?"

"Yeah, we're ready. We stay ready, that way we never have to get ready," Darrick voiced.

Going inside of their former clubhouse and gathering all of the things of value was easy enough. The power drills, and power saws with their rechargeable batteries.

80

The brand new table saw was extremely heavy, but manageable by two of the three. Plus it was known by the three to be of the most value. And last, but definitely not least was a brand spanking new paint sprayer.

But most of their time was consumed by the viewing of their former clubhouse. Yeah, they knew it would no longer be their clubhouse, despite their stealing the tools being used to complete the remodeling of the house.

As they walked from room to room—living room to bathroom, upstairs and throughout the downstairs, they were all wondering how so much work could be done in the two days that they were last inside.

"How could anybody come in here and do all of this without us knowing it, or even seeing anybody?" Darrick asked.

"I don't know, but they did," Reggie answered.

"Listen, we've gotten everything, so lets get gone," Larry told them as he re-entered the kitchen. "We show could have used another set of hands," Darrick said in the middle of his second trip to the clubhouse.

WE SUFFER FOR A REASON

"We should have brought Eli and had him helping us, because I know damn well that you are going to give him some of your money anyway," Darrick informed Larry.

"Yeah, you show are right. We definitely could've used him to help us carry the table saw," Reggie commented. Then said, "Larry, we still haven't figured out where we're going to put all of this stuff at."

"We'll put it all down in the garage across from Arney and J.J.'s house until in the morning, but first lets get everything into our backyard."

"Do ya'll think we should have went and got them, because we could've—"

"Hell naw," Darrick and Larry said in unison before Reggie could complete his suggestion.

Darrick, because he had already visualized the outfit he was going to purchase. And right in time for Thanksgiving.

Larry didn't desire any additional help because he had already decided to give Eli some of his share. He figured it was Eli who made access possible and easy enough, and only at the expense of a little fright!

Having every piece of merchandise tucked away in the vacant garage, the brothers made their way back around to the front porch where they discovered that there was not a single soul outside. No one out on the sidewalk, nor anybody out on Nikki and LaDonna's porch. No one was out anywhere, it was assumed until they heard, "So everything went okay?" Eli asked from the darkest corner of the porch.

Trying not to look shocked, or scary, Reggie said, "What does it matter to you. You're supposed to be asleep, or playing asleep so you wouldn't have to go and do any of the dirty work."

"Sleeping or not I'm definitely going to try to avoid doing dirty work," Eli said in response to Reggie's words, but looking at Larry as he responded.

Larry briefly cast his eyes away from Eli's and toward the ground. Then lifting his head he said, "I'm going in and going to bed. I'll holla at y'all tomorrow."

"Man, hold on, I'm going in too," said Darrick. And everyone else followed suit.

In the boys bedroom there was very few words spoken, only a couple of comments about the kinds of shoes and outfits that would be purchased for Thanksgiving and how clean they was going to be looking in them at the Skating Rink, Thursday night.

Afterward, sleep came suddenly to all besides Eli. He remained awake a little while longer wondering why he was so different. Believing his difference had little to do with his sense of right and wrong and his desire to do right.

He fell asleep thinking thoughts of, *"No matter what, he would remain good in order to please his father, who was always looking down on him from heaven."*

CHAPTER 6

"Where in the hell have y'all been all morning?" Mama Bee asked Reggie, Darrick and Larry as they came creeping through the back door.

"Mama, we been out asking people if they needed their leaves raked, so we can make some money. We raked three yards and had two people tell us to come back in a few hours," Larry said. Then he added, "Is it okay if we go back and do them other yards mama?"

"I don't care," said Mama Bee, "but you're taking Eli with y'all the next time."

"Okay Mama, we will. What's to eat?"

"It's over there on the stove, probably cold by now," Mama Bee said before heading into the livingroom to watch her game show, then a soap opera on the big television.

"I don't know Eli," Elizabeth was saying to him as she looked into her son's big pretty eyes.

Eyes that were identical to James' and reminded her so much of her late husband. The more she looked into them, the more she knew she couldn't say no to him. So she said, "Eli, first I'll have to check my bank account and see if there's enough in there for you and Elisha to buy some new outfits."

"Okay, mama, thank you. I love you," and then he kissed her on her jaw!

"I didn't say that I would. I said I'm going to see if I could," Elizabeth reminded him.

"I know, I'm just thanking you ahead of time because I'm trusting in you."

With that being said, he left out of the room in a hurry, accidentally bumping into his sister Elisha as she was coming into the room.

"What are you so excited for?" Elisha asked. "You almost knocked me down."

85

"I'm sorry sis. I didn't see you. Have you seen Larry 'em yet?"

"I haven't seen no one besides Debra, but I think I heard the rest of them downstairs awhile ago."

Heading down the stairs, Eli was wondering about how much fun the Skating Rink would be, if only he knew how to skate. Which is why he didn't go with them the last time and was full of regret. As he sat and heard all of the stories of fun and laughter, they all told when they returned.

"Granny Bee, where's Larry 'em at?" Eli asked his Granny when he reached the bottom step.

"They're back there in the kitchen. When you go back there tell one of them I said to bring me a glass of ice water. And tell somebody to turn that thermostat down back there. It's hot in here!"

"I'll do it Granny Bee," Eli informed her.

"Thank you. I sho wish the rest of them was as willing as you."

"Good morning Mama Bee," Elizabeth said as she took a seat next to her on the couch.

"Good morning baby. I sent for you when I was done fixing breakfast. Why didn't you come on down and eat you something?"

"I couldn't move a muscle Mama Bee. And after Elisha and Debra finished their yelling in my ear, I rolled right on over and went right back to sleep."
"Well, if you're hungry, you fix you some breakfast. But first tell me something, does it feel hot in here to you?"

"No, not really, but do you want me to turn the heat down a little?"

"No, I already told Eli to do it, but you can check it and make sure it's set on seventy."

"I will, but first I want to ask you something. Do you intend to buy Debra and the boys outfits for Thanksgiving? The reason why I'm asking is because Eli asked me for an outfit, but I don't want to buy him and Elisha new clothes and your children didn't have new outfits."

"Baby, you go ahead and get your children what they need. I have a lady around the corner on Date Street who will bring me some outfits for the children for half

87

the price. I'll call her after while, cause we only have a few more days, don't we?"

"Yes ma'am. I'll go tomorrow myself and pick them out a little something," Liz said as she raised up from the couch and made her way to the back of the house.

"Eli, where are you and your cousins off to?" asked Liz as she entered the kitchen and saw the boys leaving out through the back door.

"Mama, Granny told them that I could go with them and rake some yards in order to make some money."

"Where are these yards, and didn't you think it would be a good idea to let me know where you're going before just taking off, Eli?"

"Yes ma'am, and I'm sorry, but can I go?"

"Yeah, as soon as you tell me exactly where it is that you are going."

"Aunt Liz, it's a couple of blocks over, right there on Howard. We have two yards to rake. Mr. Thomas' front and backyard and then we are going to rake Ms. Annabell's whole yard too," Larry explained to his aunt.
"Listen, y'all don't be gone all day," she told them.
"And don't make me have to come out looking for y'all either."

"Yes ma'am," said Eli and Larry. Then they left and caught up with Reggie, and Darrick toward the end of their yard.

But before reaching the alley, Larry turned back, jogged to the house and grabbed the rake from the back of the house, where he witnessed Liz still peering out the kitchen window. So, he gave her a little smile, then caught up with the rest of them down the alley a little ways.

"Man, hide that rake over there," Darrick said to Larry as he came jogging up to the side of them.

"I'm a hold on to it just in case Aunt Liz decides to ride around. I told her we would be raking a yard over on Howard."

"Why did you tell her that?" Reggie asked.

"Because she asked me and Eli where we was going ."

"Man, your mother sho be meddling too much, like some old lady," Reggie said to Eli.

"Why don't you just keep my mother out of your mouth!"

"What? You must want to go back inside of one of my headlocks, talking all crazy like that!"

"Man, y'all chill out and lets turn back and get the stuff," said Larry as he took the initiative and leads off towards the side of the garage.

"What stuff?" asked Eli, confused.

"The stuff we got out of the clubhouse, dummy," Reggie said. "Do you really think we're going out to rake some leaves, stupid?"

"I'll rake a yard if somebody needs theirs raked," Larry said. "Because all money is good money." "All I want to do is sell this merch, and get my cut," Darrick said as he began putting power tools and the power tool chargers into a gym bag.

"Hold on with that stuff, Darrick. Mr. Morgan told us this morning that he would give us a hundred and eighty dollars for this table saw, if we would bring it over there to him," Larry reminds them as he lifts one end of the mountable table saw, testing its weight again.

"I ain't carrying this damn thing all the way over to no Mr. Morgan's house!" Darrick yelled out in protest. "Man, be quiet. I ain't talking about carrying nothing all the way over there. I'm talking about getting it over to the junk yard, because that's where he said he'd be." "That's still far to be hauling this big ole thang," Darrick said as he walked back over to the table saw.

90

"Why don't somebody run back to Nikki's backyard and get their little red wagon, then we could pull this stuff around in it," Reggie suggested.

"Why don't you go and get it, since you said it," Darrick told him.

"You're right. I did think of it, so why don't he go get it," Reggie said as he pointed his finger in Eli's face. "I'll go get it. It ain't nothing but a stupid wagon." "Eli, what are you going to say if your mother sees you, or if Donna's mother Ms. Coralette sees you, and needless to say, if Mama catches you?" Larry asked.

"I don't know, what should I say?"

"Don't even worry about it," Larry informed him. "I'll go get it and if someone sees me, I'll just say, 'we're using it to haul the bags of leaves away.' "

When he returned with the wagon, they all loaded it with the stolen merch and took off down the alley to its end. They then headed to the junkyard where Mr. Morgan gave them one hundred and eighty dollars so quick that they began to think they were being taken advantage of.

Suspicions increased when Mr. Morgan gave them another twenty dollars, when he learned their reason for having a rake. Having told him that they were willing to rake leaves, he told them to go on over to his house and rake his front and backyard.

That's when he gave them the twenty dollars, and that's when they walked away, discussing the possibility that the brand new table saw could have been worth way more than Mr. Morgan had given them for it. Which, in turn, sparked the discussion of whether or not to actually go over and rake his yard.

But the yeahs outnumbered the nahs so they all decided to go ahead and rake his yard, but slum job it. Larry mostly wanted to go over to Mr. Morgan's neighborhood due to the juke joint that sat on the corner. It was there at the five and halfs that he planned on selling a lot of the merch that they had.

"Go ahead and give me my seventy dollars," Darrick told Larry, since he had the whole two hundred in his pocket.

"You don't get no seventy dollars, because two hundred divided by three will never be seventy."

"Well, give me my sixty six dollars and sixty six cents, cause I can add, multiply and divide. I just try not to subtract too often," Responded Darrick. "You'll get it as soon as I get some change." "Why do you get to hold the money anyway?" Reggie asked. "I'm the oldest, I should be holding all the money."

"I'm holding the money, because he put the money into my hand," Larry said as he dug into his pocket and brought out a hundred dollar bill, a fifty, two twenties and a ten.

"Here Reggie, here's sixty dollars and when we get some change I'll give you your six dollars and sixty six cents." "Why does he get it? I'm the one who asked first," Darrick whined.

"Who's acting like a hot sissy now? Here, you hold this hundred until we get to the store," said Larry as he placed the hundred dollar bill into Darrick's eager hand. Once over on Kentucky Street Larry told Reggie, "since you are the oldest, go inside and tell somebody to come out and take a look at what we got to sell, but first look around for any of our regular customers."

"Man, I know what to do, just like I know exactly who to look for, plus I see his truck parked right over there." "Sho is Mr. Proctor's truck right there," Darrick said.

"Okay, we'll be over there by his truck while you go in there and get him."

"Let him know everything we got," Larry told Reggie as he departed.

Sure enough. Mr. Proctor, the construction worker, bought almost everything that they had to sell. He even gave them a hundred and twenty dollars for the brand new paint sprayer.

Now that they all had over a hundred dollars, everyone besides Eli that is, they then made their way to Mr. Morgan's house right down the street. They really didn't want to rake Mr. Morgan's yard even though it was only a few houses down from where they were, but because it was now freezing outside. But despite the fact that the temperature had fallen considerably, they reluctantly raked the front and put the leaves into piles. As they headed for the back, Mrs. Morgan invited them all inside to warm themselves. She offered and then gave out tea and sandwiches and then cookies. She then gave them trash bags and warned them not to stay out in the weather for too long.

It had appeared as though she had taken a special liking to Eli, and on their way out of the Morgan's yard, Mrs. Morgan called Eli back to her front doorway. Moments later he caught back up with the rest and said, "Look she gave me this twenty and told me to share it with y'all."

"Come on with my five dollars then," Darrick told him.

"I got change for the twenty," Reggie said.

"Man, why don't y'all just let him keep the money, so he can have something for Thursday," Larry told his brothers.

They both hesitated, but then said, "Go ahead and keep it."

"We got enough money for clothes, and shoes. All we need to do now is sell the rest of this stuff so we'll have some extra money in our pockets," Larry said as he caused them all to pause right there at the corner, across the street from the five and halfs.

"Y'all hold up right here and I'll go in there and see if I can find somebody else who wants to buy these last few items."

"I already asked everybody," Reggie said, a little agitated by the cold.

"Yeah, but there are way more cars out here that wasn't here before," Larry pointed out.

After about five minutes, Larry came back out of the juke joint only to grab the bag of power tools. Ten minutes later he came back out counting money.

"We made another fifty dollars a piece, plus here go you, twenty five dollars Eli," Larry said when he reached them on the other side of the street.

95

Unlike he thought, his brother made no mention of his giving the twenty five dollars to Eli. Maybe because they were that anxious and eager to get out of the cold.

As they headed home, the brothers explained to Eli the importance of keeping the amount of money they had away from the rest of the family. So they came up with some numbers, two thirty dollar yards and one twenty. "We split eighty dollars four ways. So that means you'll have to hide your other twenty five dollars away from your mother, our mother, and especially from Debra, because she will definitely blackmail you."

"When we get in the house we'll show you a good hiding place for your money," Darrick said.

Larry looked at Darrick, then at Eli and said, "And if you fall for that, I'll show you how you can put your twenty five in my pocket and turn it into fifty as soon as it connects with my hawala."

They all were laughing as they made their way up through their backyard. The laughter was more welcomed due to their joy of knowing they would soon be in a house of warmth.

Once inside, their laughter immediately came to a halt, because it was total chaos inside of the house. Mama Bee was hollering and cursing. There was three or four men there who appeared to be the object of Mama Bee's verbal assault. There were two cops there attempting to calm things down, but both visibly showing some fear of Mama Bee's rage!

One of the men standing in her living room shouted, "She has to be crazy if she thinks I'm going to complete a job that I haven't been fully paid for doing, without having my tools to do the job with."

That's when Mama Bee said, "You'll get paid when you finish the work that you've been hired to do." This is when Elizabeth, Elisha, Bootie, and Debra came through the front door.

"Mama Bee what's going on? Is everybody alright?" Liz asked while putting shopping bags to the side. "Yeah, everybody is alright, but everything isn't. Why don't you take the kids upstairs . . ."

"Everything ain't alright," one of the men said. "I'm out of about a thousand dollars worth of power tools, and she expects us to finish the work."

"What work, what's going on?" Liz asked looking directly at Mama Bee.

"Ma'am, there was a break-in a couple of doors down at twenty four, zero four, where these men here were hired to do some work for Ms. Bernice Lewis. Upon returning to the before mentioned residence, these men discovered the burglary and theft, then called us," the female officer reported.

Then the male officer announced, "We compiled a list of the stolen items. They'll be put in the system just in case they turn up in a pawn shop. And in the meantime we'll patrol the area and see if we can get some info from one of our CI's. That's all we are able to do at this point," he added before looking the entire room over and intently into the faces belonging to Eli and the others.

Before leaving they left their number on a card behind with instructions to contact them if they should hear or remember anything further.

"Y'all come in here talking like what happened was my fault. Like I'm the one who made you leave your tools inside of the house over night. Who does that anyway?" mama Bee asked the workers.

"Ms. Bee, we're not saying that it's your fault. It's just that you're yelling, and cussing at us about having the job done by weeks end. And all we're trying to get you to understand is that that's impossible, unless you give us the rest of the money, so we can purchase the tools we need to finish."

"What I'm trying to get you to understand is that I'm not going to have the rest of the money no time soon," Mama Bee replied.

"Mama Bee, you hired these men to remodel the house down the street. Why? I didn't even know you owned any house besides this one," Liz expressed.

"Well, it was supposed to be a surprise, or even a early Christmas present for you and your children. But I guess the cat is out of the bag now. Liz, I got you a place of your own, so you can have your independence and some privacy, you and my grandchildren. I just wanted . . ."

Before she could get another word out, Liz burst into tears and went over and hugged Mama Bee around her neck, sobbing and squeezing until Mama Bee was nearly suffocated by love to the point that she had to pry Elizabeth's fingers loose.

She then hugged Liz and began to shed tears herself. Mama Bee gathered herself soon enough, and said,
"Look at us carrying on like two big babies and in front of folks no less."

"Y'all give me a few minutes to brush my good wig out, and I'll walk you down there, where we all can have a look around."

"Ms. Bee, can we all agree on some extra time and me and my workers will work on getting some more tools. First we'll check around and ask around and see if anyone sold any of our tools around the neighborhood," the older looking renovator said.

"We have to tell them where their tools are," Eli caught himself whispering to Larry.

"Man, be quiet for a minute, before you get us busted," Reggie responded to Eli's audible whisper.

"What was that you just said?" the tall guy standing right next to Eli asked.

"I was talking to my cousin. I said . . ."

"He said let's ask them if they need any help looking for their tools," Larry spoke up for Eli.

"Do y'all want us to ask around the neighborhood and see if we can find out anything?" Larry added.

"Naw, we'll take care of it," the guy said looking back and forth between Eli and Larry. Then he gave Reggie and Darrick a suspicious glance.

After him and the older renovator made eye contact, the older one asked Mama Bee upon her return to the living room, "Ms. Bee let me ask, did these boys know that there was work going on down there at the house? They look like they . . ."

"What?! Exactly what are you asking, did my own children have something to do with your tools being stolen? You stand here in my damn living room and accuse my own family of being thieves?! The nerve of you, you petty, overcharging, dishonest bastard. You get the hell out of my house, and take your flunkies with you. Y'all are all fired. And give me my damn door keys," Mama Bee screamed with fury in every word. Then added, as the workers were on their way out the door, "I guess you called and told them you would be leaving your damn tools in the house last night."

After those words were said, Mama Bee then slammed the door behind them. She then walked to the couch, flopped down and sat there and wore a very sad expression.

No one uttered a word for several moments. It was Elizabeth who reached over and took Mama Bee's hand as she sat next to her on the couch.

"You are a wonderful woman Mama Bee. I still can't believe you bought a place for me and the children to live. I can't believe that through your struggles you still manage to do so much for others. I love you Mama Bee and I do thank God that we are family."

With that being said, everyone gathered all around Mama Bee and Liz.

It was a very huge group hug. The flow of electrifying love broken only when somebody said, "Mama I'm hungry! When are you going to cook us something to eat?"

"You're always hungry Debra, with your chubby ass," Mama Bee said.

They all laughed a little, then began saying, "I'm hungry too mama." "So am I Granny Bee." "Mama what are you going to cook?"

"Mama Bee, you just rest yourself for a little while and I'll find something in the kitchen to cook," Liz said.

"No baby, that's okay. I'm just fine and besides, I already have some chicken wings thawing out in the kitchen sink back there. But I did want to take you down the street and show you your house. The grass needs cutting, and we'll get you some storm dorms and a alarm system so y'all feel safe down there.

"I don't know how much the workers got done on the inside, but we will go down there later and see. Then we'll find somebody who will make sure you're able to move in as soon as possible.

"Elisha sweetie, get the police officer's card off of the table right there and give it to me so I can put it in my purse. Liz, you remind me to give them a call in a couple of days. We have to make sure they catch the ones who broke into your house. Do you hear me?" Mama Bee asked while looking at the policeman's card she now held in her hand.

CHAPTER 7

Standing in the freshly painted living room of the house Mama Bee provided for her and her children, Liz became emotional again. Tears streamed down her face and she tried to speak words to Mama Bee that just wouldn't come out.

Mama Bee took Liz into her arms and said tenderly, "I know sweetheart, I know."

Finally, Liz regained her speech and thanked Mama Bee. "Thank you for everything. And even though I can't pay you back anytime soon, I can ask my work for more hours so I can take on some of the responsibility of the final expenses on this house."

"That won't be necessary Liz, sweetheart. This house is paid for, and by the looks of things there's very little work left to do. We'll just find someone to finish painting the kitchen, and the upstairs bathroom, repair the back door that the burglar smashed, and then it will be ready for you and the kids to move into." "How about we do the needed work ourselves?' Liz asked, holding Mama Bee's arm while looking into her face.

"We? Honey, I'd rather pay folks that know how to do some painting, rather than get in here and mess things up."

"Mama Bee that's pure scared talk, and you know it," accused Liz.

"Scared? Scared of who, scared of what? Girl, Mama Bee ain't scared of nothing but snakes. And that's why I keep my grass cut."

"Well, you shouldn't be afraid of a little paint."

"I ain't!"

"Then it's settled. We'll go buy paint and brushes, rollers and pans. And while we're out we'll find a place that repairs doors," Liz said. "Doing these things ourselves will definitely save money," she added. "I'm all about saving my money," Mama Bee told her, then looked over to the kids that just entered the room and said to them, "Y'all got some work to do and if you do a real good job you just might get paid for doing it." "Mama, I'll work for twenty dollars an hour," Darrick said.

"Just give me ten," Reggie expressed.

"How about I just give both of y'all a threatening statement?" Mama Bee asked with a serious look.

"Elizabeth, I'm freezing in here. All of that cold air coming in through that back door window that's broke up back there, I'm going home and get on the phone and call around until I find somebody to come out now to fix that door. Are you coming?" she asked as she headed toward the front door with Bootie in tow.

"Bee, sweet child of God, where you been in a housecoat, and your good wig?" asked Ms. Bunch as Mama Bee entered into her house. "I've been here for almost a half an hour, watching these two showing off their Thanksgiving outfits."

"Outfits! Where'd y'all get them clothes from?" she asked after recognizing Debra and Elisha in brand new attire.

"Mama bought these for us," Elisha answered. "She bought Eli and Bootie, I mean Cookie some clothes for Thanksgiving too. She said she's taking us all to church."

'There's been so much going on around here I done forgotten all about some damn outfits," Mama Bee said more to herself than to anyone else.

"Bee, you always wait until the last minute before you do anything," Ms. Bunch told her. "And what you got to sip on?" she asked.

"You know what I got to sip on, because you've already been in it. I can smell it on your tongue, you cow," Mama Bee called Bunch in a semi-playful manner.

"Let me get on this phone and see what I can come up on, at the last minute."

"Just like I said, it's always the last minute with you. Do you even got my stuff you promised me two weeks ago?"

"Hold on a minute Bunch. I know you can look out of your good eye and see that I'm on the telephone. Hello, Rhonda. This is Bee, Is your mother home?" "She is."

"Do you mind putting her on the phone?"

"Mama, let me talk to Rhonda when you get finished talking," Debra said.

"How are you going to talk with no lips. Now interrupt me one more time while I'm on this phone . . . Hello, hey Jackie, this is Bee.

"Hi, how are you doing girl?"

"Me, I'm doing fine. Listen, I was wondering if you had anything around there that would fit these little bad ass kids of mines. Thanksgiving outfits, you know?

WE SUFFER FOR A REASON

"Oh, you do. Well, girl I don't care if it is plaid and they bet not say nothing, even if it was polka dots. So, when . . . huh? Naw, I ain't silly. They silly if they think I'm a keep spending my money on their bad asses.

"Anyway, how long will it be before you can bring those that you have around here?

"Oh, forreal. Well girl come on because I supposed to be stepping out for a few minutes. So I'll be waiting on you to bring them so they can try 'em on. Okay, bye."

"Elisha, why do y'all have them new clothes on?" Elizabeth asked as she came through the front door.

"Mama we was trying them on again and showing them to Granny Bee's friend, Ms. Bunch."

"Okay, now y'all can go get out of them, before y'all dirty them all up."

"Ooh, mama. Are you going to take us to get some new clothes?" Darrick asked.

"I want to put my new clothes on mama," Bootie said.

"Sit your ass down. You're not putting on nothing until you take a bath."

"Uh-uh mama. I don't want no bath."

"Mama, can we go to the store and get some clothes and some shoes so we can wear them to the Skating Rink Thursday? Can we mama? Can we?"

"I know one thang, y'all are starting to get on my nerves with all of these questions. Now, one of y'all ask me one more, so I can make an example out of you."

"Mama, can I get the door, somebody is getting ready to knock on it."

"Come here Darrick, get your little narrow ass over here, cause I done told you about playing with me."

"Mama, I'm not playing, there's . . ."
Knock. Knock. Knock.
"Come in, come on in," Mama Bee yelled. Then said, "I'm still going up top on you for playing with me so damn much."

"Jackie come on in here. I want you to meet my daughter-in-law. This is Elizabeth and of course you already know Bunch over here."

"Hi Elizabeth and hello Ms. Bunch."

"Bunch, Bunch, Girl Bunch done fell asleep! So anyway, let me take a look at what you got."

"Like I said over the phone Ms. Bee, most of these things I have left are plaid, but they are all name brands."

"Let's just see if they fit, because they know better than to complain. They better be glad that they're getting anything at all.

"Here, y'all go in there and try this stuff on." "I ain't wearing no plaid," Darrick said. Followed by Reggie, then Larry.

"You'll wear it, or you'll be wearing last years zoot suits."

"We didn't wear them suits last year. We burned them!!"

"Yeah, and I burned y'all asses too!"

"Mama, do we have to wear this stuff? Don't nobody wear plaid no more."

"Get your butts in there and try them things on. I ain't going to tell y'all no more," Mama Bee warned. Larry returned to the living room wearing high waters, but a decent fitting polo shirt saying, "The shirt is all right, but these pants wouldn't fit a midget." Reggie was right behind him wearing a too tight mixmatched plaid outfit that had Debra and Elisha laughing their heads off.

"Darrick, Darrick, come on out here so I can see what they look like on you," voiced Mama Bee.

From behind the wall he answered, "I ain't coming out there!"

Reluctantly, Darrick finally came out in some plaid capri pants and a skin tight red shirt that showed his navel.

"Mama, I don't feel right. These pants keep on going up in my butt!"

"Boy, go take that stuff off," Mama Bee said, chuckling as she said it.

Everybody was hysterical in laugher. So much so that even Ms. Bunch awoke and joined in on the clamor.

"Jackie girl, what was you thinking when you boosted that stuff?" "I was thinking about the people who had ordered it. But I thought they got all of the capris that they had ordered. I'm a have to take them back over there to them, and get me my twenty five dollars."

"Well, I ain't gonna be able to use none of this stuff I'm sorry for wasting your time".Mama Bee said.

"That's okay Ms. Bee. I don't mind coming around here. You've always been good to me and mines," expressed Jackie. "I just wanted . . ."

"Mama, mama, I want this polo shirt," Larry said. "It fits me and everything. Now all I need are pants and some shoes."

"Shoes? Who's going to buy all of y'all some new shoes?" Mama Bee asked. She then mumbled, "Christmas, right around the corner."

"Mama we got the money to buy our own shoes. We just need a ride out to the mall," Darrick made it known. "Where did y'all get enough money for some new shoes?" Mama Bee asked all of them at the same time.

"We made it raking yards, and anyways Chuck Taylor's don't cost that much out at the mall," Reggie answered.

"Let me catch y'all running around here doing something y'all don't got no business doing. We went through this last summer, when I had to beat the brakes off of y'all, all the way from the juvenile detention center."

"Mama, we haven't done nothing but rake leaves. You can call over there and ask Mrs. Morgan," Larry said in a shaky voice.

"Mrs. Morgan! What in the hell was y'all doing all the way over there?"

"Ms. Bee, I was asking for twenty four dollars for the polo shirt, but you can just give me less than half price— say twenty dollars," Jackie bargained.

"Bootie, go in there and get Mama's billfold out of my room and bring it to me."

Jackie got paid and then left after promising to come by this weekend to show Mama Bee a variety of merch, and some handbags large enough to handle her business with. She kissed Mama Bee on the cheek and said her goodbyes to everyone else.

Elizabeth closed the door behind her, then turned to face Mama Bee. "Mama Bee, I want to show you the outfit that I bought for Bootie."

Elisha interrupted her mother by saying, "Mama, we agreed not to call him Bootie anymore but Cookie instead".

"Yea, I forgot Elisha."

"Mama Bee, while we were out I couldn't just buy them things and not buy him something as well." "I haven't said anything," Mama Bee told her.

"I see that the boys don't have there's yet, and I want to help you out with theirs too."

"You just heard what they said, they have their own money for shoes. All they need is a ride to the mall. So, if you want to help out, you can do it by giving them a ride."

"I can do that!" Liz said as she sat down beside Mama Bee and kissed her on her jaw.

"What was that for?" Mama Bee asked.

"That was for being you, and for having a heart so huge that it can't help but to give."

"I know what this is all about. You're still excited about your house."

"Yes ma'am I am excited, and happy, but I'm just as impressed by your constant, unceasing care for others," Liz told her.

"What house are y'all talking about?" Ms. Bunch asked as she helped herself to a nice swig of Mama Bee's half pint of Old Fosters.

"My Granny Bee bought us a house. That's where me and Debra had just come from when we met up with you out on the porch," Elisha answered. "I'm going to have my own room again. Thank you so much," Elisha

114

told her Grandmother as she hurried around the coffee table to hug and kiss on Mama Bee's face.

"You act like you are in an awfully big hurry to get out of my room," Debra said to Elisha.

"Who wouldn't be in a big hurry with all of them bread and cracker crumbs you keep in the bed, drawing them damn roaches," Mama Bee said.

"Mama, you ain't gonna keep talking about my size. That's why I'm going to live with my mother," Debra stated.

"Here, here goes the telephone. Call her and tell her I said she can come and get all of y'all today."

"Mama Bee, you don't mean that. These are your children now," Elizabeth intervened.

"No, they are not either. They are my daughter Lee Lee's children, and she can come and get them. Especially Debra, with her grown smart ass!" "Mama Bee, you told me yourself they've lived here with you so long now that they have all become as your very own children, instead of your grandchildren."
"They are all my children. I just hope she would come and see about her kids sometimes",

WE SUFFER FOR A REASON

"Well, where's your daughter Lee Lee at? How can we locate her?" Liz asked.

"That's my point exactly, where is she? I say, when my daughter gets tired, she'll come home to her mother and give me back my chance to share with her all of the things she so desperately needs to know. The Lord knows she can't identify none of her essence out there. Out there don't have nothing to offer a black woman but trial and tribulation. I know, but she don't want to learn it from her mother. And it hurts me to my heart that my child would choose the hard way. That's why I do what I do, cause that's the only way you're gonna get anybody to listen. If I can get just one of them to listen this place wouldn't be such a mess. But they ain't listening. They believe them streets has all the answers.

"Mama Bee's heart aches just thinking about it. Lee Lee baby, come on home so we can point these children in the right direction together. The way it's supposed to be, before it's my turn to leave away from here for good." Mama Bee sums up her sadness. Then she abruptly gets up and hastily heads toward her bedroom.

More than a little upset that Bunch had hurt her Old Foster the way that she had. "Bee, where you going?" Bunch asked. She then looked over to Elizabeth and the rest of them and says, "She always gets emotional like that when she gets to talking of her daughter, Lee Lee. Don't she Debra?"

"Yeah, but she be all mad at me too, and she's the one who be starting things most of the time," Debra says as she looks at Ms. Bunch with a sad face.

"Well, you know exactly how your grandmother is. She doesn't mean no harm Debra, and you know it."

"You always take her side, blaming me."

"No I don't either. Debra, you know I don't be taking no sides."

"Ms. Bunch, you sitting there saying that when you know y'all gang up on me if I start to get the best of one of y'all!" Debra said looking at Ms. Bunch sideways, before walking away.

"Come back here Debra and straighten out that lie you just told. You know I don't be taking nobody's side," Ms. Bunch is saying as Debra is walking up the steps to her room with Elisha right on her heels, asking her questions.

CHAPTER 8

"I know y'all don't, but I do. As a matter of fact I have to tell my mother that we were the ones who stole and then sold the workers' tools out of Granny Bee's house. A house that she has given to us to live in. You see why I have to tell the truth?" Eli asked the brothers.

"Man, you bet not open your mouth about it! I'm telling you and I ain't playing with you," Reggie said threateningly into Eli's face.

"Your threats don't mean anything, nor does your headlocks or your punches. I know what I have to do," Eli said.

"Eli, you want to get beat up, don't you?" Darrick asked. Then added, "Reggie go ahead and kick his ass, while I watch out for Mama!"

"Ain't nobody going to jump on nobody. If Eli feels like he has to rat everybody out then we can't stop him. But at least we will know who we got living with us," said Larry, never breaking eye contact with Eli.

"I ain't no rat! I just don't like it that we did this to Granny Bee, our own grandmother," Eli exclaimed. "Listen Eli, what's done is done and can't nothing change that. It ain't like we knew we was taking stuff that belonged to Mama. We didn't even know she owned that house. But the worse thing that can happen now if you tell, is we all will be in some terrible trouble. We won't be able to go skating and what Mama will do to us might land her in prison.

"If you go in there and tell, we all will go to jail, because Mama said she wasn't going to get us out ever again," Darrick told Eli and at the same time reminded his brothers.

"Again?" asked Eli. "Y'all have been to jail before? Why did y'all have to go to jail?"

"It happened about three weeks before y'all got here," Larry began. "Why do you think we were confined to the backyard almost all of the summer?"

"I didn't know, but what did y'all do?" Eli asked.

"Larry, don't tell him nothing! We didn't confess to it then, and we ain't gonna say we did it now," said Darrick.

"I'm not confessing. I'm just telling our cousin that we were accused of snatching a purse and charged with robbery."

"Yeah, charged with a robbery that we didn't do. All we did was find an empty purse," Reggie said.

119

"I asked that judge if we did it, then where is the three hundred and sixty dollars at, since the suspects were captured immediately after the crime," Darrick said with water beginning to fill his eyes.

"Listen Eli, all we're saying is, if we go back in front of that judge, he will take us away from Mama and lock us up somewhere," Larry told him.

"But if I don't say nothing, what can we do to maybe get the tools back so the work can get finished?" Eli asked.

"We might not be able to do that without letting it be known that we took the tools," Larry told Eli. "But if all of us agree to it, this is what we can do. We can clean up the mess down there and tell Mama that we'll do whatever she needs us to do for free."

"For free?!" Darrick asked. "I don't know about free, but we can do it for less."

"Less than what?" Larry asked. "We do it for free, we have a happy Thanksgivings and we get to go skating!"

"Yeah, we go skating," Reggie said with glee in his eyes, and a softer tone towards Eli as he continued. "Eli, we're family and family can't be telling on one another." "Y'all tell Granny Bee on each other all of the time," Eli responded.

"Yeah, but that be for petty stuff, not anything serious," Darrick told him.

"There isn't going to be anymore telling . . ." Larry began saying before he was cut off by Reggie who asked, "Isn't?"

"Where'd you get that word from?"

"Isn't," Larry answered. "I got it from our cousin Eli. He told me that ain't isn't a word."

"I can't tell that it ain't," said Darrick and then they all began to laugh, including Eli!!

* * * * *

Knock. Knock. "Mama Bee it's me. Is it okay for me to come in?" asked Liz.

"It's open," responds Mama Bee.

"Mama Bee, I just wanted to make sure you're okay back here."

"No, I'm not okay back here. That heifer Bunch just sit out there and sucked up all of my drink."

"Mama Bee, you shouldn't be drinking no way, that alcohol isn't any good for you, and you know it."

121

"It ain't good for who, people who don't drink? Cause I beg to differ," Mama Bee told Liz having a look on her face that said 'Let us leave the topic alone.' "Well, anyway Mama Bee, I wanted to know if you would like to go with me to take the kids to get their outfits, and then we could go to the paint store together."

"Naw baby, you go right ahead. I'm going to stay right here and figure out a way to get back at Bunch. I know she's waiting on me to bring out another bottle, and she'll be waiting cause I ain't got no more. She done drunk it all. And I'm so mad at that sea cow right now.

"Here, you take this with you. It'll help you with their things, plus the paint, and painting supplies," she says as she hands Liz a roll of bills from her purse. Then she said, "I would ask you to bring me back two half pints of my drink, but I already know you'll have something negative to say about it."

"All I have to say is, I don't need this much money. I had intended to write them a check."

"How are you going to know how much you're going to need until you get there?"

"I guess I won't!"

"Y'all be careful while you are out. I'm a have them girls help me get some things together for supper tonight."

"Okay, and I'll help y'all when I return," Liz said as she left Mama Bee's bedroom, closing the door behind her.

CHAPTER 9

It was Wednesday, one day before Thanksgiving. Mama Bee had insisted on Elizabeth taking the boys back to exchange the street wear Elizabeth had allowed them to pick out on their own.

Since her money had been spent, they would be dressing up in what she wanted them dressed up in. She had the good mind to go with them and pick their clothes out for them, but she decided to spare them the experience. Besides, she had more pressing business to tend to, like teaching her granddaughters how to prep for Thanksgiving supper.

Upon returning to the house, Elizabeth and the boys were immediately "sense assaulted," by the aromas emanating from the kitchen. For there was a symphony of oh's and ah's as they fast paced their way to the origin of the delicious smells.

"Mama, it smells too good in here. What are we eating?" asked Darrick as he entered the kitchen. "Boy, these things are for tomorrow," Mama Bee said without taking her focus off of her task, giving Debra and Elisha instructions all the while.

"Mama, we hungry now," Reggie whined.

"Get your ass in there and sit it down somewhere before I break it," Mama Bee said with a look of seriousness that wasn't just a look, because Reggie knew she had skillets that could actually break an ass.

"Mama Bee, I want to help," Liz said as she sat her bags down.

"Well, we're almost finished in here. The only thing that's left to do is straighten up a little bit."

"Okay then, let me put these things away. Where's Cookie?" she then asked.

"Bootie cried himself to sleep when I told him he couldn't go with you this time."

"Granny, he wants to be called Cookie," Elisha reminded her.

"Baby I know, I just been calling him Bootie for so long now."

124

"He was almost in tears in the car when we went shopping, wasn't he Debra?"

"She knows he don't like to be called Bootie, who would?"

"Well, he ain't never said anything to me about it, anyway I said I'll do my best to call him Cookie, but what the hell is a Cookie?"

"Granny, you know the way he's always eating cookies, so I just wanted to call him Cookie instead of Bootie," Elisha explained.

"So, you're telling me that you don't like the name my Grandmother, your great great Grandmother gave him?" mama Bee asked Elisha.

"Granny Bee, you know it's not that," Elisha replied. Then added, "Speaking of my great great gram, I'm just as interested as my mother is to learn where we came from. Cause for me it just may help with learning where I'm supposed to be going. My Mom has only been able to tell me so much. That's why I'm glad we moved here to be with you. So, I really do want to learn about your Mom, and your Grandmother too. So when are you going to tell us more about her, and about your great great Grandmother Bernice ?

"And about Glenda, cause I would like to know why her and my mother be at each other," Liz asked from the doorway of the kitchen.

"I'll tell y'all what," Mama Bee began. "Tomorrow after we've had our Thanksgiving meal, and things are all cleaned up we'll talk about it all."

"Mama, why we got to wait to talk about it tomorrow, when we can listen to you tell us now?" Debra asked.

"I know you're trying to get my blood pressure up, but before I let you kill me that way, I'll give you a ride out to the lake, and then lie way better than that white woman did," Mama Bee told Debra, who didn't know if she was playing or serious.

"So, what do you have for me to do?" Liz asked.

"Nothing child, nothing at all, just rest your nerves because that's sho what I'm about to do. Go in here and put Boo—, I mean Cookie. I'ma put Cookie out of my bed, so he won't be up worrying me all night."

Liz followed Mama Bee into her bedroom and once inside said, "As much as I didn't like the ideal, how could I ever say no to my Mama Bee?"

Then she pulled out two half pints of Old Fosters and sat them on Mama Bee's dresser.

126

"Oh, I see now! You want me good and drunk over the holidays! What are you after Elizabeth, my money or my man?" Mama Bee asked jokingly.

"I want both, because I have neither," Liz replied sounding more serious than she intended to.

"Liz, I know it's not my place to be saying anything, especially since you're my son's widow, but haven't you even considered another companion?"

"Mama Bee, I'm not having this conversation with you," she said with a perplexed look upon her face.

"Well, if not with me, then with who? Liz, you are going to have to eventually do more than just talk about it. You're gonna have to do something that's better done without talking, sometimes," Mama Bee told her. Liz turned and headed out of Mama Bee's bedroom, insisting on not talking about her sex life, or in her case, the lack thereof, with her mother-in-law.

"And sweetheart, thank you for the drinks," Mama Bee spoke at Liz's back.

"Yeah, you're welcome," Liz mumbled to herself as she made her way upstairs and to her room. There she began to search for things in preparation for her a long hot bath. Believing that a bath would somehow relieve her of some stress and tension. The soothing water was so relaxing and her mind had basically went to another place, and it was there that vivid pictures of lovemaking began to invade her privacy.

It's been so long since she has been allowed to succumb to her emotional needs.

"Lord, haven't I been the faithful widow long enough? It's not that I would practice any form of fornication, Liz told her body! But don't even I deserve to feel wanted, needed, sexy, alive? Oh Lord, help me," she said as she added more hot water.

Thoughts of her late husband James were portrayed on her memory screen and she began conversing as if he sat right there between her legs.

James, James, oh James, what would you have me to do with myself? I'm slowly dying from within, but my love for you remains strong, unbreakable. I block out my needs, believing I'm honoring you by doing so, but these many months have taken their toll.

I've used your former touch and gentle caress to provide me with comfort, but the more I neglect myself, the more my mind, body, and soul team up on me. How I miss the way you held me in your arms and you'd carry me to our bed, gently laying my body down, then you would stimulate nerve endings all over my body. You would take me places and then bring me back without us ever leaving the bedroom. You'd cause my back to arch and my toes to curl and leave my leg shaking, then you'd wait patiently for me to welcome you back into an embrace, where you would hold me so affectionately in a manner that made it seem that we was joined one to the other.

And there we'd lay until morning woke us to all the reasons why again. Life, oh my sweet dear James, why you? Why us James? I still can't seem to understand why this had to happen to us, and I probably never will. "I'm through questioning God. He has helped me see clearer. And all I know is I'll never ever betray our love by giving myself to another," Liz says aloud with warm tears flowing down her beautiful face.

Not even aware that she was crying, so she was jarred back to this realm when she distinctly heard Elisha on the other side of the bathroom door.

"Mama, is it okay for me to come in?" Elisha asked as she entered the bathroom. When she saw the tears that streaked down her mother's cheeks, she crossed the floor and kneeled beside the tub.

"What's the matter Mama? Why are you in here crying?" Elisha asked.

"I'm okay sweetheart, I just . . . well I think these tears was long overdue. But I'm fine now. You don't have to worry about your mother, okay?"

"But I do worry about you, you hardly ever smile anymore, and you have a beautiful smile. Talk to me Mama, tell me what's really bothering you, please." "I'll tell you what, my daughter, who's growing much too fast, you sleep in there with your mother tonight and we shall have ourselves a mother and daughter, okay?"

"I'm fifteen now, don't you think I'm just a little too old to be sleeping in the bed with my mother?"

"Never, ever, ever," Elizabeth told Elisha and then said, "Let me dry off and meet you downstairs."

"Okay Mama. I'll do that on one condition."

"And what might that be?"

"If you'll give your daughter a kiss to hold her over until I see you again."

"Don't you think you're a little too old to be giving your mother some sugar?"

"Never, ever—"

"Ever," Liz finished Elisha's answer, then kissed her daughter's mouth.

After drying off, Elizabeth spoke into the mirror, "James you sure have given me a lot. A wonderful, beautiful, intelligent daughter, and a handsome, bright, caring son who is your mirror image. I just ask that you speak to our son from time to time, because at times it seems as though he's lost without you.

"God, I thank you in Jesus' name for allowing me to realize that I still have my husband and your blessings rest upon me, and my family," said she, concluding her conversation in the bathroom mirror.

After dressing and joining Elisha, Debra, and Mama Bee downstairs in the kitchen, Liz asked Mama Bee would she like for her to start on dinner, "I mean, supper?" "That won't be necessary," Mama Bee replied. "Because we thought it would be a good idea if we ordered pizza."

"You did," Liz said as she took a seat next to Elisha at the table. She then asked, "Where are the boys? I don't hear them in the house anywhere," she added.

"They're probably playing out front—." Mama Bee didn't get the chance to finish before all five of them came barging in through the backdoor. One saying one thing and another saying something else.

By the time the girls heard what they was saying, it sounded like, "Mama we cleaned up the glass that was broken out and the other trash too!"

"Then we nailed up a board on the door and made sure it was locked," Darrick yelled over the rest.

"Mama, we did it all for nothing. We did it for free," Reggie said.

"All you have to do is give us something to eat," Larry said. "Cause we are starving!"

"Eli, what part did you have to play in all of this?" Mama Bee asked.

"I guess I helped," Eli responded.

"You guess you helped. Mama it was his idea, wasn't it y'all?" Larry exclaimed.

"It sho was," Darrick and Reggie admitted.

"In that case I guess all of y'all are entitled to some pizza," Mama Bee informed them. She then sat back and witnessed all of them go nuts!

"How many can we have Mama? Have you already called Papa Johns?"

"Mama, I want some Papa John's pizza too. Can I ride with you to go get it Aunt Liz?"

And on and on they went until Mama Bee said, "Liz, call and order what they want. Just let me know what the total cost comes to be.

"Speaking of total, you had plenty of change left over from what you gave me earlier. I only needed a little to put with what they had, and what I had, in order to get them all some shoes to go with their outfits." "But that was only because they agreed to go to church with us tomorrow. All we need now is for you to join your family, and the whole house will be worshipping the Lord together tomorrow, Mama Bee."

"Well, all I have to say to all of that is: one of y'all run around to Joes' and get your Mama a pair of eggshell white stockings and I'll be praising the Lord, and giving Him thanks with my family."

This caused the whole room to applaud and cheer with happiness and excitement!

Of course, Mama Bee was overjoyed as well. Although it had been awhile since she last attended a service, she was anxious, but well pleased that her family would be walking into that church tomorrow, lifting up God as her and her mother used to do.

"Mama, don't cry. Why you cry Mama?" Cookie asked.

"Boy, ain't nobody crying. Them onions in the food . . .
I mean when we used them onions," Mama Bee tried to
lie.

"Granny, I don't know why you're trying to tell a tale,
knowing you're going to church tomorrow," Elisha said.

"Y'all just leave ma alone. This is my family and I can
cry over y'all if I want to," she said as she went for her
purse for stocking money.

"Debra, and Elisha, do y'all want to go to the store too,
so y'all can get you something? I'm so impressed with
the way you handled yourselves in my kitchen." "Yes
Ma'am," Elisha said. Then told Debra, "Come on, let's
go get some sodas, and some chips for when we eat our
pizza."

"Y'all take Bootie with you," Mama Bee informed.

"Come on Cookie," Debra said. Then she added, "It's
Cookie Mama!"

"well, take Cookie's ass with you," Mama Bee told her.

After the children had left the house, Liz made her way
over to Mama Bee, and strong armed her out of a hug.
This caught Mama Bee by surprise!

"So," she asked, "what is this for? Tell me what I did to deserve this much love?"

"I do love you, and even though you be acting complicated, that's all you be doing is acting, because underneath it all, you're just a little sweet ole lady," Elizabeth told Mama Bee as she released her hold.

"Little old lady huh? Well, try me and find out why they call me big boned!!"

"Well, maybe you're not all that little," Liz corrected.

"Old either," Mama Bee told her.

"You know, each day that goes by is causing me to wonder about that as well."

"You don't have to wonder no more. I'll show you my birth certificate where, instead of giving my birth date, it has young, ready and about that life printed on it. I'll tell you something else too, while we're on the subject. Them half pints are my fountain of youth, in a bottle.

"Now the question is, would you like to take one of them down with me?"

"No, I do not. What would we look like showing up at church with hangovers?"

"That's the problem right there, too many folks worrying about what they look like at church. That's why they are more focused on showing out, than showing Christ!"

"You're right, a lot of people do go for the wrong reasons, but what can we do to guide ours in the right direction?"

"I don't know if you realize it or not, but you are doing a whole lot of leading by example. And would you just look at the way Eli has rubbed off on Larry," Mama Bee pointed out to Liz.

"Yeah, I've noticed a slight change as well, but it has worked both ways, because Eli has sho become more vocal since we moved here. So, I agree we are definitely good for each other. It's evident," Liz says as she begins to ponder.

"Mama, is the pizza here yet? I want a whole one by myself," was expressed by more than one individual.

"Naw, they haven't gotten here yet, but don't y'all eat any of that junk until after you have eaten your pizza," Mama Bee told them.

"Too late Mama. Bootie done ate a whole roll of them cookies right there," Reggie said.

136

"Cookie, Cookie??"

"Huh, yes ma'am."

"Do you want us to call you Cookie, instead of Bootie?"

"Yes Ma'am. I don't like being called Bootie no more Mama." "Okay baby, we will all call you Cookie from now on. Y'all hear that. this baby's name is Cookie and it ain't Bootie no more," Mama Bee told it to them all. "Alright Mama, we'll call him Cookie instead of Butt," Darrick said.

"But what if we slip and call him by his old name?" someone asked.

"We all may at times, but eventually we will all get used to it."

"Cookie," Mama Bee called.

"Yes Ma'am."

"Go ahead and put the rest of your cookies up somewhere, because if I see you trying to sneak one more into your mouth before you have your pizza, I'm a knock the whole roll down your throat!"

"Yes Ma'am. Can I put them in your room so nobody can get them?"

"Go ahead, then shut Mama's bedroom door back. Who else is that back in my kitchen?" Mama Bee called out.

"Hi Ms. Bee," Arney spoke up.

"Hi Mama Bee," J.J. followed.

"Oh, hello. How are y'alls mother and father doing?"
"They're doing fine," Arney answered.
"Are they ready for Thanksgiving around there?"

"Yes Ma'am. My mother is at home cooking now. that's why she put us out of her house. She said we was in her way," J.J. told.

"Liz, you ordered enough pizza didn't you?"

"Yes Ma'am, I ordered six different kinds."

"That should be plenty," mama Bee told her. Then she said, "Arney, y'all stay and have some pizza with us, you and J.J."

"I told you we was having pizza J.J.," Darrick said as they made their way into the boys room with Arney following close behind.

"Arney why don't you come upstairs with me and Debra?" Elisha asked.

"What for?" Arney replied, preferring rather to hang out with the boys, as she has always done.

138

"So you, me and Debra can get to know one another," Elisha said.

"Okay," Arney agreed, gave Reggie and the others a disappointed look, then headed for the stairs with Debra and Elisha.

After the boys had been yelled at by Mama Bee for the umpteenth time for wrestling and making all of that noise, they finally relented and came out of their room, just as the pizzas arrived.

And wouldn't you know it, Bootie—I mean Cookie jumped onto J.J.'s back and locked his arms around his neck, because J.J. had gotten the best of him inside of the room. It took two of his brothers to pry his little hands from around J.J.'s neck.

J.J. was a little embarrassed and a whole lot upset, but knew not to retaliate because the brothers didn't play the radio, about their little brother. And the looks on their faces reminded him of the fact.

So, after grabbing pizza boxes and going to the dining room table, they dove in, but not before dumping plenty of hot sauce on their pizzas. At the dining room table in the course of consuming pizza, the question was asked by Darrick, "Arney, what did y'all talk about when you went upstairs with them?"

"Debra and Elisha was telling me——."

"What we were telling you is none of their business," Elisha stepped in and said.

"Why not? What was y'all talking about boys?" Darrick asked.

"No, we weren't talking about any boys," Elisha responded.

"Well, our friend J.J. likes you Elisha. Are you going to talk to him?" Darrick asked.

"I don't like her," J.J. said.

"Yes you do, liar," Darrick told him, then added, "You're sitting there telling a damn lie, because you're scared of her."

This was overheard by Elizabeth, who responded, "Elisha is too young to be talking to little boys and besides that Darrick, you should be watching your mouth."

"Watching my mouth for what? I ain't said nothing."

"Yes you did say something, and haven't Mama Bee told you about using those curse words. If I hear you use another one I'll be telling her."

"I see where Eli gets it from now," he said.

140

WE SUFFER FOR A REASON

"What? What did you just say?" Liz questioned.

"Nothing!"

"You bet not have said nothing."

"I didn't say nothing, nothing but, tell whatever you want to. She ain't going to believe you no way," Darrick smarted off.

"Guess what. I don't have to tell her anything, because the next time I hear you use a curse word I'll smack your mouth myself."

"You'll do what? You ain't gonna do nothing to me! I got a gold nameplate that says, 'I wish you would.'" This caused his brothers to giggle, because he had quoted an old L.L. Cool J rap lyric.

Apparently Elizabeth was also familiar with the lyrics, but didn't appreciate them at the time, because she reached over and grabbed Darrick by the shirt collar and plucked him up and out of his seat. Then she guided him to Mama Bee's bedroom door, despite the fact of his and his brothers resistance, as they attempted to pry her hands from their brother.

But at the opening up of Mama Bee's door and seeing her standing there, the brothers fell back as did the soldier who had came to arrest Jesus in the garden of Gethsemane.

"What in the hell is going on out here?" Mama Bee asked thunderously.

"Tell her, tell your grandmother what you said out there at the table," Liz instructed Darrick.

"Nothing Mama, I didn't say nothing. She said she was going to smack me."

"What, who? What in the hell?" Mama Bee started saying.

"Yes, yes I did say I would smack—."

Liz was cut off when Mama Bee interrupted and said, "Listen to me, and listen to me closely. Ain't nobody God has breathed breath into is going to put a hand on these children of mines, nobody but me! Now take your hands off of him and let him loose Mama Bee told her viciously."I clothed them, I feed them, and it's only going to be me who beats them."

"But Mama Bee, he was in there—." Liz attempted to explain, but Mama Bee would not allow her a word in inch wide.

"I don't give a damn what they was doing. You come and tell me and I'll handle it. I'm their mother," she added.

Those harsh words spoken caused Elizabeth to shed a tear. When Elisha witnessed her mother's hurt, she eased up and took her hand, then led her away and they both went upstairs, followed by Eli.

"Arney and J.J. it's time for the two of you to be heading for home," Mama Bee said. "Larry, y'all get y'alls asses in your room and I bet not hear a single peep out of none of you. Not even a damn whisper!"

"But Mama, we didn't even do—"

Reggie tried to say something, but she wasn't trying to hear anything because she said, "Reggie, if I didn't make any sense to you the first time, come over here so I can knock some into you."

Darrick had already eased out of the striking zone, and once all of them were in their room, Darrick was feeling himself so, he said, "I knew Mama wasn't gonna let nobody put their hands on me. Elizabeth must be crazy coming in here thinking she can run something."

"Man, you're trippin. Plus, you was dead wrong," Larry said. "Now none of us might not get to go nowhere tomorrow."

"Is that all you think about is that Skating Rink?" Darrick asked.

"Naw, that isn't all that I think about, cause right now I'm thinking about Mama coming in here and beating the brakes off of you, then putting you on a punishment for the rest of your life!"

"For what, for saying one cuss word?"

"For that, and for not just letting it go. Add stupidity with that, then you'll have all you need in this room with you while you're serving your time. I'll be honest, right now skating is all I'm thinking about, and if you messed tomorrow up for us, I'm going to mess you up, but real bad," Reggie threatened. "Man, you ain't gonna do nothing," Darrick told him. Then he climbed up on the top bunk, just a little afraid of Reggie's body language.

CHAPTER 10

"Good morning Mama Bee. I've come down to see if I could give you a hand with breakfast," Elizabeth says being in a forgiving spirit.

"Yes, of course you can, but first have a seat right here."

"I'd rather stand Mama Bee, because I—."

"Please, it won't take but a minute to say what I believe need to be said."

"Mama Bee I—."

"Would you please let me say what I got on my mind child."

"Okay, alright, I'm seated."

"Good. Now listen. I have to tell you first of all that I don't know what came over me last night. I want to blame my acts on tiredness laced with a little bit of drink, but I know better. The honest to God's truth is there's been nobody here to help me with these kids. There wasn't anybody riding in that ambulance but me when Reggie broke his leg four years ago. It was just me by myself enrolling them into schools, and at the bus stop waiting on them after school.

"It has always been just me at doctors appointments, dentist visits, and back to school shots. And it was just me down there by myself when them girls down the street tried to jump on my Debra.

"So, I made my mind up a long time ago that it was only going to be me who would beat their asses. But now I do realize that I went off on you and I am so sorry, because you surely deserve better than that. You have been nothing but supportive, giving, and caring since you've been here. You have proven to love mine, just as much as I love yours.

"We are family and it makes no sense to use those words, but don't live them. Liz, to show you that I'm sincerely committed to family, I want you to take that extension cord, go in there and beat their asses. As a matter of fact, make sure you beat 'em for all of the things they think they've gotten away with! Here take it," Mama Bee tells Liz as she extends to her the extension cord.

"Mama Bee, I can't do that, and I most definitely couldn't use no extension cord."

"Nothing else works, and believe me I've tried everything."

"Well, Mama Bee, it's over with as far as I'm concerned. So we'll just move forward. I accept your apology and I understand your reasoning."

"But what you don't understand is, if you don't go in there and get him for whatever it was that he did, then I'm going in there with this cord and I'm going to kill all of 'em." "Mama Bee please, let's just let it go for now. Please, please?"

"Well since you're using words like please, I'll let it go, but I'll be damned if I let them go to a damn Skating Rink!" "Why can't they go skating?"

"Because, whatever they did, they caused this mess."

"Mama Bee it sounds like you don't really know what happened last night."

"Whatever they done it caused me to get angry with you, and it even made you mad enough to want to get at 'em," Mama Bee was saying in her confusion.

"Actually, it was only Darrick, and what he did was say a foul word out of his mouth last night. I told him that I really didn't have to go tell you anything, because I could smack his mouth myself if I wanted to. But, when I tried to do the right—"

"You don't need to say no more," Mama Bee interrupted.

147

"Oh yes I do. I have to say more. So Mama Bee please allow me to finish. When I tried to do the right thing by bringing your child to you, you became irate, and started yelling at me," Liz said as tears began to drop and roll down her face.

"Come here, put the eggs down and let me hold you as I tell you how sorry I truly am. You mean more to me than you know. You and those children have brought my son's spirit back into this house. So you listen to me. It'll never happen again, and the next time any of them get out of line you deal with them. That means whether I'm around or not.

"If you ask me," she continued, "I would go in that room in there and commence to tearing Darrick's ass to pieces, or you run the risk of him not respecting your authority. I'm telling you the truth. I know my children. They'll run over the top of you if you let them," Mama Bee summarized.

"No Mama Bee, I told you I don't believe physical punishment to be the only answer. Right now I'm feeling like, just as we have forgiven one another, we should also extend that forgiveness to Darrick. This time anyway," Liz added.

"Okay, Miss Elizabeth, but don't come in here running to me talking about they done tied you up and hung you upside down out of the upstairs window."

"They wouldn't do anything like that, would they?" she asked desiring a serious answer.

Instead of answering Mama Bee just gave Liz one of those looks as if to say, "Girl, I wouldn't ;put anything past them."

"You're not serous, you're playing aren't you?"

"Mama, Mama, I'm hungry," Cookie said as he came stumbling out of Mama Bee's bedroom.

"Happy Thanksgiving little boy," Mama Bee greeted him.

"Happy Thanksgiving Mama. I'm hungry." "Little boy you are always waking up hungry, like you went to work in your sleep. Breakfast is almost ready, and you can go wake everybody and tell them I said to get ready for breakfast. Now go on and do what I told you to. You in here talking about you're hungry."

"By the way Ms. Elizabeth, happy Thanksgiving sweetheart."

"Happy Thanksgiving to you too Mama Bee." Fifteen minutes later everyone was gathered at Mama Bee's dining room table, digging into some of everything. Bacon, eggs, biscuits, grits, some chopped up leftover pork chops and all covered with cheese and other condiments.

There wasn't that much conversation, mostly due to the unusually early time of their having breakfast. But the jump start was due to Mama Bee's commitment to attend church this morning. Which is why she said, "When you get finished eating, I want y'all to clean up and then get your clothes on so we can get to the 9:00 a.m. service on time."

The statement alone caused Liz's face to brighten, and for some reason she felt instantly rejuvenated and energized. Deep down inside she knew she was not just ready for today, but she was ready for life's challenges and she knew she would overcome them by the power of the Lord's might. So after everyone appeared to be finished, Elizabeth said, "Girls upstairs and boys use the bathroom down here. Let's go. Let's go!" she said a little bit louder than she intended.

But, it achieved the necessary result and at 8:25 a.m. everybody in the house—was almost ready to leave. That is, all besides Mama Bee. So, Liz went and tapped on her door a few taps, but received no answer. So she entered and announced herself.

To her surprise and shock she sees Mama Bee there, standing in front of the dresser mirror about to twist the cap off of her half pint.

"Mama, what are you doing? Why would you do something like—"

"I'm so nervous," she said, cutting Liz off. "It's been so long since I've been in a church. I've been walking wrong for so long it's as if I done forgot how to walk right, and it scares the hell out of me just thinking about it. So, I thought I would just knock the edge off with a small swig."

"Mama, you don't have to use the devil's brew to get you to step into the Lord's house," Liz said as her eyes watered.

Before Liz continued, Mama Bee jumped in. "I thought I was tripping the first time, but I know good 'n well I just heard you say it again." "Say what?" Liz asked.

"You called me Mama, and not once but two times."

"Did I?"

"Yes, you did," Mama Bee said as she sat the bottle down and reached out and brought Liz into her embrace.

"You'll cause my make-up to run," Mama Bee said. "I've already messed mines up," Liz said, slightly choking out her words.

"Oh baby, you're crying," Mama Bee says. "So are you," Liz said and hugged on Mama Bee some more.

When they were through with their embrace, Liz says, "Let us get ourselves together, then make sure our babies are together."

"First let me say this. There are some things that I must share with you and I intend on doing exactly that after we have our Thanksgiving supper this evening," Mama Bee tells Liz. "Maybe it'll help you to understand your mother and grandmother's bickering."

At the mention of her mother and grandmother, Liz came to full attention. Actually, she took Mama Bee by her hands and they both sat down on the bed. "Oh tell me all that you know, because I haven't a clue as to why they refuse to even speak to one another."

"Sweetheart, I'll share with you all that I know, but it'll have to wait until after church, due to the time."

152

Liz glances at her watch. "Oh my God, a quarter til nine. We have to get going! I'll meet you in the living room.

I have to go back upstairs to straighten up my face."

"I'll be ready in two minutes Mama Bee." Liz takes several steps through the kitchen, then she turns right around and goes back into Mama Bee's bedroom and gets the half pint of liquor before leaving again.

CHAPTER 11

"When we get inside of this church y'all bet not start acting a donkey, and whatever y'all do. Don't think that I won't put hands on you in the Lord's house. Cause I'll kill you, have your funeral and give your eulogy that expresses my sincere regrets this morning, and then get baptized. Amen." Mama Bee expressed her threat to all the backseat passengers.

"Mama, we gonna be good," Cookie said.

Then Larry said, "Mama, you look real, real nice this morning. I believe it's the best I've seen you look in a long time."

"Larry, thank you, but please stop your damn lying. We are on our way to the church."

"Mama, you can't be cussing and we're going to church," Darrick says. "Of all people!"

"I can and will do whatever I choose to do, like putting you out of someone else's car, right here! I'll tell you what you need to do, cussin Darrick. You need to pray for forgiveness. Because, if I don't catch the Holy Ghost, I'm a catch you by the neck and ring it," Mama Bee told him. Then said, "You better be finding yourself a nice believable way to apologize to your Aunt Elizabeth."

Liz squeezes Mama Bee's hand gently up there in the front seat of the car and whispered "I thought we agreed to forgive?"

"Oh, I forgive. I just can't seem to forget!"

"Wow, look at all of these cars at this church," Eli said from the backseat atop his sister's lap, as he peered out the window.

"My Lord, it sho is a lot of people already in there this morning, and I thought that this nine o'clock service wouldn't be so crowded," Mama Bee said as she looked out of her window.

"Well, I see a good place to park right over there. The Lord is good," Liz said as she wheeled her car into the available space.

Once out of the car, Elisha asked, "Granny Bee, what made you choose this church instead of the one Mama found for us to attend?"

"I don't know exactly why sweetheart. I guess it's because my mother and I attended this church when she was still alive, but oh how it has grown!"

"Mama, I have to use the bathroom," Cookie told her.

155

"Hold it."

"Mama, I can't hold it," Cookie whined and wiggled.

"You're going to have to hold it until we get inside." "Come on Mama, you're walking too slow," Cookie insisted.

Once inside, Mama Bee instructed all of them to go and relieve themselves, because there would be no getting up and down during service.

Before Debra took off, Mama Bee moved in close and told her, "You look really nice Debra. A lot like your mother, Lee-Lee."

Debra gave no response. She just turned and began to catch up to Elisha, but before she even accomplished three steps, tears began to freefall.

"Let's find some seats, if we're able to," Liz offered.

"Child, please, we're not moving from this spot without securing permanent seating arrangements for them little troublemakers."

"Bernice , is that you standing there?" a male voice asks from the immediate right of where Liz and Mama Bee stood.

As they turned to address the unknown voice, Mama Bee came face to face with—

156

"Bernice Lewis, I never thought my eyes would see the day that you would be caught dead in the same room as Holy Water."

"Poppa Charlie, that is you, ain't it? And I thought you had died in the early eighteen hundreds. How are you standing right here, right now, in front of me?"

"Bernice , Bernice you must have your dates and events mixed up, because as I remember it, February the fourteenth, Valentine's Day was the date, and 2400 West Garland was the place."

"And absolutely nothing happened on that date, or in that place, but you passed out drunk. Speaking of which, you must be high now speaking evil in the house of the Lord," she told Poppa Charlie just as the children approached with inquisitive looks pasted across their faces.

All besides Debra, who spoke, then gave Poppa Charlie a huge hug.

"Hey, my little Debbie, and you know to call me Granddaddy."

"And if she does, she already knows the eulogy is going to be short, but sweet," Mama Bee said as she pulled

Debra loose and guided them all toward an available pew, leaving Poppa Charlie standing there.

While getting situated in their seats the sermon was already underway.

The preacher said, "We as children of the living God have so much to be thankful for. We should always be mindful to thank God for giving His only begotten son for the remission of the sins of the whole world. This includes every sin we've ever committed, or ever shall. God did this because He so desired to have a family to love and to be loved by.

"As we spend this Thanksgiving with our families, lets be thankful for their existence and for the things that family adds to one another.

"Church, I can't speak of thanks without shedding a little light on the word, giving. So, I ask, what are we willing to give to pave the way for our family's growth, survival, happiness and peace?

"Most importantly we must continue to encourage their relationship with the most merciful, forgiving God of heaven. We must sacrifice our own selves in maintaining the relationship.

"When we are at our homes enjoying our meals, let us be mindful that it is these very same people who

158

surround us at the table who make us whole and complete in love. With the love of the Father's hedge of protection we are capable of fulfilling our predestined purposes.

"Now turn with me if you would to the Book of Psalms, chapter 28 and verse 7. Everybody there, say Amen? And it reads: The Lord is my strength and shield. I trust in Him with all my heart. He helps me, and my heart is filled with joy. I burst out in songs of 'thanksgiving'!"

"Again, I burst out in songs of Thanksgiving. I've come to tell you what God loves and that is the truth. Without a relationship with the Lord we have absolutely nothing to be thankful for. But I must preach to the Lord's church. You children called and chosen by God. A relationship with our heavenly Father grounded and rooted in Jesus Christ, His only begotten, we have as a promise, the Lord as our strength and our shield. "He asks of us to trust in that with all of our heart, and He promises to help us each and every time, so that our hearts may be filled with joy!

"He is saying to our spirit, with this knowledge and understanding, our hearts should burst out in songs of Thanksgiving."

Then the choir began to sing, "I just want to thank you Lord."

When the choir sang two more songs expressing thanks with the entire church's participation, the Pastor, Ronlee Murrell spoke from the book of God for over an hour, then concluded with, "Again, church turn with me in your bible to the Book of Isaiah, chapter 51 and verses 3 and onwards.

"And it reads: The Lord! Who?"

"The Lord," the congregation answered. "The Lord will comfort Israel. The Lord will!"

"So, stop trying to get it done on your own Grandmas and Mamas. Sisters and brothers. Grandfathers and Fathers. Quit trying to provide the family's comfort on your own without the Lord's help leading the way!

"For the word says, 'The Lord will comfort Israel again and have pity on her ruins. Her desert will blossom like Eden, her barren wilderness like the garden of the Lord. Joy, and gladness will be found there. Songs of thanksgiving will fill the air.'

"The Lord promises you that you will sing songs of thanksgiving, because you believed in His Word and you trust in Him to perform His Word in your life.

"Meditate on His unfailing love. Stand to your feet and let us close out in prayer.

"Dear Father God in heaven, we are most appreciative and thankful for your unfailing love. We are in awe and humbled by the love you've expressed by the shed blood of your Christ Jesus our Lord and Savior. "We pray and ask in his most Holy name that you enlighten the eyes of our understanding so that we may receive divine instructions by, and through your Word and your Holy Spirit. "Lead us into everlasting as we continue our faith in you. Let this day be glorious in your sight as we lift it up to you, allowing you to order our steps.

"Soften our hard hearts so that your Word may enter in to change us, molding us into Christ's likeness. We give you thanks, honor, and all of the glory, for you are worthy. In Jesus' name. Amen and Amen.

"Now, hold up before y'all start making a break for the exits. We always close out in our altar call. So, as the choir sings, all of those who know that the Lord has moved inside of you, pleading with you that you should give unto Him this day your entire life, forever! Come on to the front and invite Jesus into your heart to be your Lord and your Savior. For Jesus Himself said during His earthly ministry, 'No man, woman, or child come to the

Father except through Him.'

"What in the world is my grandchild doing?" Mama Bee asked no one in particular as she sat there and watched Eli make the trek down to the front of the church where members awaited to lead him in the sinners prayer.

Liz, and Mama Bee locked eyes long enough to notice tears filled them both. When mama looked up front to where Eli was now kneeling, it was then that she remembered herself just over fifty-five years ago kneeling at the very same altar while her mother watched from the pew.

A whole lot of things have changed since way back then, but the message is the exact same message that the Spirit of God used to draw her to Christ those many, many years ago.

"Mama, Mama why is Eli up there with all of them other people?" Darrick asked.

"Doing what you needed to be doing. Giving your life to Jesus, before I take it," Mama Bee told him.

"Can I go up there too?" Darrick asked.

"No, you cannot. You'll be going for the wrong reason, and that's not the way it's done. Now sit back and be quiet," Mama Bee concluded.

After Altar call had ended, her and her family mixed and mingled with members of the church because the atmosphere was filled with such warm and welcoming spirits of love. You could just sense and feel the sincerity of the hearts encountered.

As Elizabeth, Mama Bee, and a longtime church member named Sister Claire engaged in gossip or the gospel, it was hard to determine which, because these two were mixed and mingled by sister Claire often times.

A voice from their immediate left spoke. "Bernice as I tried to make it to my automobile the Lord guided my feet back here to you babe."

They all then turned and as Mama Bee seen that it was Poppa Charlie she asked, "Security, somebody get security and inform them that this man is breaking and violating an E.P.O. . . . ."

"Bernice , why are you treating me like this?" He asked.

"Fall back Charlie. Now is not the time, nor the place for your foolishness. And for the record, they call me

Bernice or Bee. But, I'd rather you didn't call me at all." "You can call me between the hours of six and nine," Sister Claire told Poppa Charlie.

"Ain't nobody trying to call you Claire, nothing but a greyhound. All them miles you got on you," Poppa Charlie exclaimed.

This caused Claire to excuse herself from the group, but not before she cocked her head toward Poppa Charlie and mentioned, "That's not what you were calling out a few summers ago," then she sashayed away.

"Anyway Bernice , I wanted to explain to you why I haven't been around your way in these last three years." "You don't owe me any explanation. I just assumed your family gave you a private send off," Mama Bee said.

"A private send off?" he questioned.

"That's what they do when they don't want anyone other than family members to attend the funeral services," she answered.

"Naw, I didn't do any dying. It's not my time for that, but I did have to travel up to Boston so I could tend to my mother who left us after losing her battle with cancer."

"I'm sorry to hear that, but as I've already expressed to you, you don't owe me any explanation. All I ask of you is to slide to the side and allow our passage," Mama Bee said in a base manner.

"Why do you treat me so cold Bernice ? I know I should have contacted you somehow in these last three years, or even in the few months that I've been back here, but—"

"Charlie, let me jump in right here just to remind you that we never have been, or shall we ever be in any relationship, so your words you're using must be coming from some fantasyland you've decided to move to. Are you taking any medications for mental health?" Mama Bee asked.

"Okay Bernice , I understand," Charlie said in sadness. Before turning away, he looked into Elizabeth's eyes and said, "Talk to her for me, please." And then Poppa Charlie walked away with his hat in his hands. "I don't want to hear it," Mama Bee said holding her hand up to Liz, not allowing her to get them words out that she thought about saying.

"Let's just go out here and round up our little gang before they hotwire your car and leave us stranded."

When they reached the foyer, there stood the pastor's wife with her arms all around Eli, and Cookie. having the rest of the gang in front of her when mama Bee approached them the first mother looked up and recognized Bernice Lewis instantly.

"Bee sweetie, how have you been my dear heart?" Mother Murrell asked.

"I've been doing okay Mother," Mama Bee answered, as they embraced one another.

Having chatted for awhile and all of the formal introductions completed, the pastor and his wife invited Mama Bee, Elizabeth and all of the children to their home for the Friday after next.

It was expressed in conversation how much the Murrell's had missed Mama Bee, but scheduling had prevented them from visiting. Their prayers had been continual, and one actually answered and manifested, because here their dear friend Rose's daughter stood in their church again.

"Praise God, praise Him who always answers prayers lifted up to Him in faith!"

Once back inside of Liz's car and everyone settled down, Liz couldn't help but to say, "Mama, you are well loved by everyone and you know that we have to

166

discuss you know who as soon as we get somewhere that little pitchers don't have big ears."

"There's nothing—"

"Did you just call my Mama, Mama?" Reggie asked.

"Yes, I did," Liz answered, then asked, "Why?"
"But Mama, you already have your own Mama," Eli voiced from the backseat.

"Now I have two. I've always had two, and I love them both.   Just like you have two Grandmothers," she explained as she peered at Eli through her rearview mirror.

"Y'all put them seatbelts on as best as you can back there!"

"We got it Aunt Liz," Debra says.

Then minutes later they pulled up in the front of Mama Bee's house, and after the kids exited the vehicle, Mama Bee and Liz remained inside.

Elizabeth just came right out and asked, "Are you going to tell me all about the conversation you just had with Mr. Poppa Charlie that had your face showing all sorts of mixed emotions?"

"I told you there was nothing to tell," she answered stern faced.

"Come on Mama, obviously theres lots to tell, because there's so much that I don't know."

"And what makes you believe you're entitled to know my business, Elizabeth?"

"You yourself obviously have questions, and concerns and I'm sure you have some fears too. And like you're always telling me, 'If you can't share it with me, then who can you share it with?' Besides, this will be our first mother and daughter talk," Liz added. "Well, you are right about the questions, and the concerns, but dead wrong about Mama Bee having some fears, because I done told you once before, I keep my grass cut. Now come on in this house, before we sit out here and run out all of your gas."

"We are not going to run out of gas if we sit here for a little while longer." Mama Bee's response didn't surprise Liz in the least bit. So she had no choice but to turn the car's ignition to off, then exit the car herself.

When she pulled up along side of Mama Bee, Mama Bee said to her, "One day soon we'll get the chance to discuss it all, but today I just don't want to think about it. I want to get inside of this house, warm up what all needs warming, and fix myself a plate."

"Okay Mama, fair enough, but whenever you feel like getting any of it off of your chest, I'll be a good listener," Liz told her as she took one of Mama Bee's hands and they traveled the rest of the steps together.

That's when Liz glanced down and noticed that Mama Bee didn't have her heels on. So she asked, "Where are your shoes, and aren't your feet cold?"

"My shoes are in my purse, and I can't begin to tell you how good my feet felt standing out on that cold concrete," she said as they entered the house.

"Mama, Mama, Mama, Debra went in your pot and she's eating up all the food," Darrick said as soon as Mama Bee stepped both feet inside of the door. "If I knock her down for going in my pot, then I'm gonna have to hit you with an overhand right for being a tattletale."

"Mama, all I did was put the greens on the back burner and put the fire on low so they would warm slow. Then I turned the oven on two hundred so the meats would warm too. So you should slap Darrick for lying so much," Debra said as she looked at Darrick with that look like, I'd slap you myself if Mama wasn't standing right here.

"Thank you Debra. Now y'all go get the table ready and tell somebody to bring me my house shoes and my other wig. Here, take this purse and this wig and put them in there on my dresser, Darrick."

"I ain't touching that thing," Darrick said taking Mama Bee's purse and looking at her wig all silly as she removed it from off of her head.

"Boy, you better do what I told you to do and take my stuff back there."

Elizabeth sits in the chair directly in front of Mama Bee and just looks at her for a spell. Long enough for Mama Bee to notice, but before she could say anything to Liz about her staring, Elisha came into the living room and asked her mother was she taking them to the Skating Rink.

"Yes, I guess I am. What times does it start?" "I don't know exactly," Elisha says, then she calls to the back of the house for Larry.

"Larry, where are my house shoes at?" Mama Bee asked him as soon as he came into the room.

"Do you want me to go in your room and get them?" he asked.

"Yes please. Darrick was suppose to be getting them, but obviously he's gotten lost."

"Granny Bee, I'll go get them," Eli said from behind Larry.

"Thank you baby," she told Eli.

"Larry, when does the skating party start up tonight?" Elisha asked.

"It's from eight til twelve."

"Twelve? Y'all won't be staying out until no twelve o'clock midnight," Mama Bee almost yelled.

"Ain't no school tomorrow, and it won't really get off the chain until around ten thirty, or eleven o'clock," Larry pleaded.

"I don't care if the world was coming to an end tomorrow. Y'all won't be staying out until no twelve o'clock like I said. And I know I don't have to say it no more, or y'all can just stay right here in this house," Said she, loud enough for the whole house to hear. "What you need to be doing is asking Liz what does she think would be a good time for her to pick y'all back up."

"Aunt Liz," two, or three said her name at the same time.

"I don't know. Let's eat and after we've eaten I'll have had enough time to think about it," Liz told them.

"Debra, go in there and check on the food. If the meat ain't ready, just turn the oven down to about one fifty."

"Mama, I already turned everything down some more. We need to be putting everything out and on the table," Debra told her.

"I'm on my way in there now," Mama Bee said with a sigh.

"You just sit here and rest for awhile and we will take care of fixing the table," Liz told her.

"I still need to go back there and take these clothes off and these stockings before they get a run in them."

"Okay, but before you go anywhere there's one thing we all want to know. Are you still going to share with us some more of our family's history?" Liz asked.

"Y'all don't want to hear no more old boring stories from me," Mama Bee said as she raised herself up and off of the couch.

"I don't know about them, but I definitely want to learn as much as I can about my family and where I came from," Elizabeth told her.

"Me too Granny," Eli was the first to say standing right in front of her taking her by the hand, after placing her house shoes on the floor.

Then everyone else chimed in with their, "I want to hear about our family, and I love it when you tell us stories Mama."

Then Cookie said, "Tell us Mama so I can fall asleep in your lap."

"Alright, alright y'all done twisted my arm. After supper we'll all meet back up right here," Mama Bee said as she left the living room and headed toward her bedroom, leaving everyone in glee!"

CHAPTER 12

"Everything looks absolutely wonderful," Liz says as she looks over the table set for a king's banquet.

"Mama, you've outdone yourself," Larry comments.

"Granny, everything does look just delicious, all besides the chitterlings," Elisha said. "Well baby, don't knock 'em until you've tried 'em. You see, not only does my chitterlings melt in your mouth, they are a family tradition. And I fix them only on Thanksgiving, Christmas and New Years," Mama Bee says.

"Mama, why are they tradition?" Darrick asked. "Well, it's sort of a long story, but I'll give you the extremely short version before these grow cold. You see they were thrown out to the colored slaves as the lowest of the lowest, pigs' intestines, but us color folk know how to turn their evil intent into our smorgasbord."

"Are you gonna tell us some more about slavery, before we go skating mama?" Reggie asked.

"I planned on it, but first lets give thanks for our meal."
"Mama, I want to," Cookie said.
"Naw baby, Mama got this one, okay?"

"Okay Mama," Cookie answered.

"Y'all bow your heads and close your eyes," Mama Bee told her family, then she began. "Dear father, I know I don't come into your presence as much as I should, but I come before you today to give you thanks, asking you to bless this meal that we are about to received. Bless those who are less fortunate. Please have mercy on our humble community that struggles through these hard times, and those few families that I try to help this day. I take no credit, but rather give you all the glory for putting the will to do, in my heart.

"Thank you for your Word today at the church and most of all, thank you for my little family and for your unfailing love. And Lord wherever my Lee-Lee is on this day bless her heart with your love so she'll feel her mother's love too. Amen."

As foods were being passed, jokes were being told as usual. But for the most part hearts were filled with the rare joy that's only obtained through a family's gathering, and that knowledge alone delighted Mama Bee.

Elizabeth's face was actually glowing, her heart was so filled by the spirit. She was watching the faces of her family and her thoughts immediately went to her and her mother's early morning conversation.

She couldn't bare to hear her mother cry, so she had to pass the phone to Elisha and Eli until she could regain her composure. After saying their goodbyes is when she knew she had to visit her mother, and soon.

As Elizabeth sat transfixed on her son now, she asked, "Eli sweetheart what made you decide to go down to the altar call?"

Everybody quieted down. I guess because everyone was curious as to why he walked forward.

"I don't really know exactly why Mama. I just know that when me and Elisha went forward back home with all the other kids it just didn't feel real, or I didn't even really know why I was going to the altar. But when we were at church today it was as if I was being pulled, cause I just got up and went down to the altar knowing why I was going."

"Why was you going?" Larry asked.

"To give my life to Jesus, and to obey His Word. But for some reason it was like my eyes were made to open and I really understood." "Not only did your eyes open, but your mouth too. That's the most I've heard you say at one time since you've been here," Darrick said and drew a few laughs.

"The next time we go to church I'm going to give my life to Jesus too," Larry told everybody. It was followed by a couple of me too's.

"We all need to live our lives for Christ Jesus, because it was Him who gave His precious life for us," Liz shared with the table.

"When did He do that?" Debra asked, having her interest peaked.

"It was over two thousand years ago when He died on the cross for the sins of the whole entire world," Elizabeth told them.

"If Jesus died more than two thousand years ago how can He save people now?" Reggie asked with interest and also having confusion written all over his face. "Because Reggie, Jesus is the son of God, and He was born into the world for that very reason alone. In order to save God's creation from the wrath of God," Liz answered.

She then said, "it all may sound complicated right now, but once you're able to hear and understand it from the beginning, it's easier to comprehend."

"Aunt Liz start from the beginning so we'll understand," Debra said.

177

"Well Debra, it's an extremely long truth, but I promise to tell it to you all on a day that there isn't so many other things going on. But what I would like to share with everybody today is this particular writing by an unknown author entitled, "Alpha." "And it goes:

'In the beginning was the word and the word was with God, and the word was God. He was in the beginning with God. And the word became flesh and dwelt amongst us, and we beheld His glory. The glory of the only begotten of the Father, full of grace and truth. Full of Grace and truth!"

'Actually He overflowed with the two, to the point that He willingly extended grace and truth to me and you. Let me first thank you with a sincere heart for allowing me the opportunity to share with you some truth I've discovered concerning this grace and the truth that the word that became flesh and dwelt among us delivered to us during His dwelling time. 'Bare with me as we begin at the beginning. The word was at the beginning. The word was with God. And the word was God. Then this exact

same word who is God took upon Himself flesh and blood and dwelt amongst us.

'Now we are understanding that this same word that was God became the only begotten of the Father and called His Christ. Better known as Jesus, the son of God. No wonder He has been recorded as saying He and the Father are one. And before Abraham was, I am! 'I thank God for showing us the beginning. This helps in our understanding of the other beginning, that we are more familiar with. The beginning of creation, when God created Adam and Eve. They, our original parents, sinned against God by disobeying God and how crafty the serpent at his deception.

'It separated them, and us from God, for sin had entered the world. This relinquished the authority God had given His creation unto the serpent, who is Satan. Sinning against God separates us from God, the wages of sin is death, an eternal death, eternal separation from God.

'The wrath of God poured out on all those too naive and/or rebellious to repent, turn to the word and trust in the God who loves you and who came in the flesh to suffer on a cross.

'He was raised on the third day, that all who believes in Him shall not die, but be saved from His wrath and receive eternal life. This is Grace!

'He is the Alpha, the beginning of all things even our salvation. So, He has given us His word in order that we may learn to trust in and believe in Him who He sent for the remission of sin.

'All who believe in the name of Jesus shall be save. For, if you believe with your heart and confess with your mouth, you shall be saved. This is truth.'

"There was no author's signature when I pulled that from the net. Although I'm able to take a real good guess as to who wrote it. But what's important is the contents of the writing. It speaks the truth about what Jesus did so we could all have a loving relationship with His father and our Father, God."

When she had spoken all of this, Liz simply paused, knowing that there would be an onslaught of questions. The table didn't let her down either.

"Aunt Liz, God is our Father too?"

"Yes, He created us for Himself."

"Jesus died for us?"

"Yes He did, because He loves the children God created."

The questions went on and on for a while but it was Eli who asked, "Mama why don't everybody accept Jesus as their Lord and Savior?"

"I don't know the answer to that one sweetheart, but I do know that the Lord uses long suffering, and His mercies endures forever. So, we'll continue to pray for the lost and let God soften their hearts, like He did ours." "Aunt Liz, I've been thinking about the way I acted toward you, especially last night, and I felt bad all day and I know I won't feel any better until I tell you that I'm sorry for treating you so bad after how good you be treating us.

"You even gave us the extra money we needed for our shoes and stuff. So, I'm sorry and it won't ever happen again," Darrick said. Then he put his head down and dug off into his macaroni and cheese.

"I accept your apology sweetheart, and the only thing I want everyone at this table to know is me, and Mama love all of y'all and at times when we seem to y'all to be mean we only want y'all to do right so we love you more."

"In other words, be good so we won't have to beat y'all asses," Mama Bee said. "Liz, sweet child of God would you be so kind as to go and get me what belongs to me, because turkey and Old Foster has always went well together."

"Yes ma'am, just this once I'll get you your drink. But this is suppose to be a time for family and tradition and to give thanks," Liz said as she got up from the table.

"Believe me the family knows, I thank you all for not messing with me, and Mr. Foster's tradition," Mama Bee said, smiling to herself.

When Liz returned to the dining room and handed Mama Bee hers, Mama Bee told her, "If you'll go into the kitchen and get me a glass of ice, I'll be ready to ask you what I got to ask you."

"What do you have to ask me?"

"The question will be right here waiting on you for when you get back, I promise."

"What do you need some ice for? You usually hit it straight from the bottle," Debra asked.

"Why are you all up in my business little girl.? Ain't you got none of your own? I guess you don't, judging by that naked turkey leg, you done handled your business. Liz, bring Debra the pot of chitterlings so she

182

don't have to keep on getting up and down." After she had said all of that and the laughs subsided, Debra responded by saying, "Mama you always want to throw some jokes at somebody, but you know you can't take it when somebody starts to get the best of you. Like that time when Darrick said, that's why you took that picture with your wig on crooked."

Right in the middle of the light laughter that the remembrance brought on, Mama Bee told 'em, "Y'all know I don't play no games about my wigs."

"Don't tell me y'all are in here at it again," Liz asked as she gave Mama Bee her glass of ice.

"Sit down baby, and y'all hush up a minute, because this is serious," Mama Bee told everybody as she poured herself a drink.

After taking a nice swig, she asked Liz, "Sweetheart, you've asked me on a few occasions to tell you what all I know about Ella and Glenda's bickering's. Well, before I say anything at all about your mother and Grandmother, I have to ask you, do you wish for your children to learn about it at the same time that you yourself learn about it? Or would you rather that they be told by you at a later time?"

"I imagine it'll be fine because they have been affected by it as I have, plus I don't like the idea of keeping any secrets from them," Elizabeth answered.

"Okay, let's scrape the plates and sit them in dish water to soak and then follow me into the living room," Mama Bee told everybody.

It was Cookie who first said, "Mama we don't get no desert? You said you baked cookies."

"After we clear the table, everyone grab a paper plate and get their desert," Mama Bee said as she took her plate and a couple of other dishes into the kitchen.

At approximately 6:15 p.m. everybody was gathered around the coffee table in the living room, all waiting in anticipation for Mama Bee to come from the back bedroom where she went to get herself another half pint. She said she needed it to go with her slice of caramel cake.

As she walked into the living room and took her seat on the sofa, it was almost total silence except for the few lips that were smacking due to the desert. Otherwise, you could've heard a mouse pee on cotton with a pair of brand new Nikes on.

"Come on Mama tell us," Reggie said and shattered the stillness.

"Hush up! Y'all just hush up, cause this here ain't for y'all. It's for Liz, so she'll see things more clearly," said Mama Bee.

"Liz honey, I don't know why Ella hasn't told you these things herself. I can only imagine she was afraid of how you might take it. Really, I don't believe it's my place," she added before she stopped to take a sip from her glass but then started to drink straight from the bottle.

"It's not my place to tell you, but just as you have grown close to my own heart as if you was my own child, I feel as if I have to let you know certain things."

Elizabeth didn't say not one word. She wanted to, but out of fear of taking Mama Bee off course she remained silent and very attentive.

"Your Grandmother Glenda, whether intentional or otherwise, it was never determined. She entertained a love affair that would eventually hurt all those involved and continue to affect with a ripple effect of lies, deception, and pain.

"The burial of the event only shows that if something that's still living gets buried, it has the ability to crawl out from its grave and continue its journey of pain that causes hurt," Mama Bee said as she felt the alcohol travel through her veins and coat her senses. But this

185

didn't affect her ability to share the truth. It actually enabled her to tell the details from a place of courage.

So she continued, "Your Grandmother Glenda fell in love with a man who was not her own. When the affair began, no one truly knows, but what's certain is the fact that it did happen. Although the man wasn't married, he was involved with a woman who was with child that no doubt belonged to him.

"It's safe to say that Glenda was aware that her lover had a child on the way and that he was very involved with this woman who was having his baby. But she made the decision to involve herself in relations that would lead to disaster, and devestation. knowing that the affair would even tear her very own home apart. She violated a sacred trust and crushed the heart that was so closely entwined with her own. "Glenda neglected to consider the fact that her acts would throw her family into peril. The unborn child did not go to full term. Her mother had her a couple of weeks earlier than expected, with the father nowhere to be found on the day of the child's birth, nor the couple of days that followed.

"Early on the morning of the fourth day of the childs birth the mother left the hospital in search of her daughter's father. She searched and she searched and

186

just about had given up. She decided to go to her mother Glenda's house because she was unable to return to the hospital due to her pain. As she entered the house she called out for her mother, for she was in tremendous pain. But she received no answer.

"As she struggled, she finally made it up the stairs to her mother's bedroom door, from where she immediately began to hear sounds coming forth from the other side. Reluctantly, she turned the knob of the door and to Ella's shock and horror she witnessed her fiancé William, the father of her newborn daughter Elizabeth who she had named after William's mother, in the bed and engaged in an act of unbridled lovemaking.

"She screamed loud and long before turning to flee.

"When all of the pieces were allowed to fall where they may, all of the horrific truths were exposed and they forever formed a wedge between Ella and Glenda. One that still causes separation til this very day. "Back then it took time and the mutual love for a precious Elizabeth to bring the two into anything that would resemble a relationship between a Mother and her daughter. But the damage had been done and the wounds were deep. Although after awhile, several years actually, the clashes were few and far between. But there were still

187

clashes. It wasn't until Elizabeth was beginning to take her first steps that Glenda and Ella had all but completely stopped speaking to one another.

"I myself only knew the explicit details because me and my Aunt Glenda had remained in close contact even after I moved here to Kentucky."

After Mama Bee had spoken these words she looked over at Elizabeth's face and it was totally soaked in tears. She reached out and squeezed her hand and asked if she should continue.

Liz motioned and whispered through her hurt her answer.

Mama Bee told them, "There's really not much more that needs to be said. Other than the fact that after Ella realized she could no longer stand to be near to either Glenda nor William, she moved a distance away from them both to an area of Atlanta somewhere on the west side, right off Bankhead, in one of them Zones.

"After severing those ties she learned that the two of them, William and Glenda continued their romances up until his departure when you was still young." "Mama Bee, are you sure you really know all of the facts and you've told me everything?" Elizabeth asked, still crying and clutching on to Elisha as Eli watched his mother from across the room.

"I told you everything that Glenda has phoned and shared with me over the years. She expressed how her heart ached that she lost a daughter and how she didn't know which way to turn because she loved William. At the time that those things were happening there were so many terrible words being said, and feelings were hurt and deeply damaged. I felt at the time as if I was caught in the middle, or at least on the end of a whirlwind.

"Many times I attempted to speak with Ella but she wasn't having any of that, because she had convinced herself that I had taken Glenda's side. I'm almost certain that it wasn't until you were in your second or third year at Spellman that your grandmother and mother had actually sat down together and talked without spitting venom at one another. And of course the truce was due to your scheduled wedding to my James."

While Mama Bee spoke Elizabeth reviewed her past in her mind's eye and she recalled so many events inwhich she was able to see much more clearer now.

She often assumed that her mother and Grandmother didn't socialize with one another because of the distance that they lived from each other. But now as she even recalls telephone calls, she never can remember seeing them on the phone with each other. On those few occasions it was only her and her grandmother, briefly. But never Ella and Glenda conversing.

Elizabeth raised herself up from where she sat right next to Mama Bee and then told everybody that she would be back in a few minutes.

Eli asked his mother if she was okay, and Elisha immediately followed her mother up the stairs.

"Mama, is she going to be okay?" Larry asked. "Is she going to be able to take us to the Skating Rink?" someone else asked.

"You might not be going skating," Mama Bee informed them.

"Why not Mama? Why did you have to tell that story anyway? You was supposed to be telling the slave stories," Darrick asked.

"That can wait for some other time. We have to make sure that your Aunt Liz is going to be okay."

"Oh, I'm okay. As a matter of fact I'm more than just okay," Elizabeth said as she made her way down the steps. Once she had reached the bottom stair, having

Elisha right on her heels, the door came flying open, almost knocking Elisha backwards and back up a step or two.

"Hey Mama!" Lee-Lee said barging in carrying several bags in both her hands and arms.

"Come on Reggie, Darrick, and y'all look what your Mama got for y'all! I got some more stuff out in the car too. I even got some gifts for you Mama," Lee-Lee said as she gave the packages to her children.

"Happy Thanksgiving," she said loud enough and then locked eyes with her mother.

"Lee-Lee, where have you been child, and why haven't you left no number with nobody in order to get a hold of you, just in case something happened to one of your kids?"

"Come on Mama, don't start on me with that."

"Don't start on you with that!" Mama Bee yelled. "And what if something happened to you out in them streets?" Mama Bee asked. Then added, "What am I supposed to do, read about it in the paper, or catch it on the evening news?"

"Mama, there you go. Why can't I just come over to visit without you going through all of that?"

"You sho sound like a visitor, but you know what, you spend some time with your children. Your children LeeLee!" Mama Bee said before leaning back into the couch with her bottle.

Lee-Lee turned to face Elizabeth and her children, and asked, "You're my brother James' wife, aren't you?"

"Yes of course, I'm Elizabeth and these are my children, Elisha and Eli."

"I remember you well enough. It's just been a few years since I seen you last."

"Hello," Elisha said extending her hand and asking, "You're Darrick and Larry 'ems mother. You look so much like Debra. I mean Debra looks like you."
"Yes sweetie, yes I am and I'm your Auntie."

"Mama where's Debra at? Call her and tell her to come and get her present that I brought her."

"She hears you well enough. I guess she plans to wait until you leave before she comes back in here."

"Debra, Debra! Come on in here girl and see your mother," Lee-Lee yelled. "Oh, by the way, there's somebody that I want everybody to meet," Lee-Lee said as she went to the door and yelled out to the car.

"Rufus, Rufus King, you hear me," she yelled out from Mama Bee's front door. "Bring the rest of the presents, the ones that I brought for my Mother.

"And I believe we'll be able to find something in one of those bags for you as well Elisha. And I know there's something here for you Eli, looking all like my big brother James," she said while gazing upon Eli's countenance, as her friend Rufus entered through the door. "Hey, how are you all doing?" He asked as he sat a couple of gift bags onto the coffee table. He then extended a gift to Lee-Lee and said, "I believe this is the one for your mother."

Lee-Lee took it and handed it to Mama Bee, saying, "Here mama this is for you."

"I don't need any gifts Lee-Lee. I need some answers and some hands on help raising these children of yours. I'm old and I won't be around much longer," Mama Bee expressed to her daughter in sadness.

"Oh Mama please, please don't spoil things for everybody else. Why can't you just accept and appreciate what me and Rufus are trying to do?" Mama Bee held her tongue, out of fear of what she just might say. She took the housecoat her daughter had given her and laid it on the back of the sofa.

193

"Debra, come and see what your mother has given me," Elisha called out as she tried to put the bracelet on her wrist.

"Come here and give your Mother a hug and some sugar," Lee-Lee said to Debra while attempting to wipe her lipstick off of Bootie's jaw.

They all told Lee-Lee several times a piece that his new name is Cookie, given to him by Elisha.

Debra was being a little standoffish, but accepted every last one of her Mother's gifts.

Elizabeth received earrings, and Eli a book and a ball cap. Needless to say, the boys were all very happy and excited. Despite the fact of their gifts being distributed out to include Elizabeth, and her children. As they were playing with their various gifts, unbeknownst to them, their overjoyed expressions was causing Mama Bee a little discomfort and just a touch of disappointment. Because, all she has ever tried to do was just put some happiness and joy into her grandchildren's lives, while keeping clothes on their backs and food in their stomachs.

Her daughter Lee-Lee's obvious neglect of her own children pained Mama Bee due to, and for the children's sakes. It was they who have had to suffer the loss.

"Lee-Lee have you and your friend had anything to eat?" Mama Bee asked her. She didn't' wait on an answer, because she already knew it. So, she told her daughter to fix her, and her friend Rufus some plates of food.

"Y'all just continue doing what you're doing, and I'll go fix the plates," Liz said.

"That won't be necessary," Lee-Lee told her. "I know exactly where everything is!"

"Well, I'll just go with you just in case you need an extra hand," Liz told her before they both walked off and into the kitchen.

Once Liz and Lee-Lee began putting food onto plates, Liz said, "You know your mother is a wonderful person and she misses her daughter dearly."

"Yeah, I know my mother has a real loving heart and for it I'm truly thankful."

"The only reason why I'm saying anything is because before I arrived she was here all alone taking care of the children. It's not that she minds doing it, it's just that she hopes to have you here with her, helping her every step of the way."

"Well, for your information Ms. Elizabeth as soon as me and Rufus get us a place that's big enough, I'm going to come back here and get my children."

"Get your children, you mean take these kids away from Mama?" Liz asked in a tone with attitude. Then she went on to say, "That would just break your mother's heart."

"What do you expect me to do. Live in this house under the same roof with my Mother? Why do you think I left in the first place? It was so I could get away from my Mother," Lee-Lee answered her own question. "But why, what could she have possibly done to you?" Liz asked.

"Elizabeth, I don't know exactly how long you've been here living with Mama, but I'm sure it hasn't been long enough to really know her."

"I've been here for almost six months now and I believe it has been more than enough time to know a great deal about who she is, so I certainly have grown to love your mother for who she is to me."

"That just may be, but it still only leaves me to believe that you've yet to learn that my mother is an extremely difficult person to get along with or maybe she's only that way with me, her only daughter," Lee-Lee told Liz as she locked eyes with her.

Breaking eye contact Liz said, "Maybe she's just harder on you because she wants so much more for you."

"What about what I want, what about that?" Lee-Lee asked a little louder than she intended.

Elizabeth looked at her for a moment and then told her, "Shouldn't your wants be secondary now that you've birth five children?"

"First of all sister-in-law, my priorities are my priorities, but since my business is such a huge concern of yours, then you should be informed that I am presently with child," Lee-Lee said as she took a hold of the two plates they had prepared and took them into the dining room and placed them onto the table.

Liz followed close behind and said, "I imagine your friend in there is your expected child's father?" "Yes, he most certainly is, and he loves me so very much."

"I can believe that he does, but you'll have to wait and see if he will extend that love to all of your children."

"Of course he will," Lee-Lee assured Liz before calling out for Rufus to join her in the dining room.

"Hey baby," Rufus exclaimed as he entered into the dining room. "Everything sure does look good," he said as he took a seat.

"Enjoy," Elizabeth told them as she made her way back into the living room, where all of the children were engaged in the enjoyment of their gifts.

"Aunt Liz are you still going to take us to the Skating Rink?" Larry asked as she sat down on the couch next to Mama Bee.

"What time is it getting to be?" Liz asked as she viewed the time on her wristwatch. "Oh, it's fifteen minutes after. We'll be leaving at about twenty minutes before eight, if it's okay with you Mama?"

"That'll be just fine by me, but don't y'all want to spend some time with y'alls mother and go skating some other night?"

The kids all looked at one another, expressing awkward looks. It was Larry who said, "Mama we've been waiting all month to go to the Skating Rink tonight. Please don't make us stay here. If she wants to spend time with us she can just stay here and spend the night." "Yeah Mama, will you ask her to spend the night?" Darrick asked.

198

"I'm not going to ask her anything. Y'all want Lee-Lee to stay over, so y'all should ask her yourselves and leave me out of it," Mama Bee told them.

"Ask me what?" Lee-Lee asked overhearing her name and their conversation from the dining room.

"Mama, we want to know if you plan to spend the night over here, because we're on our way to the Skating Rink." "Mama already said we can go," Reggie said.

"Oh, so you are going skating and leaving y'alls mother here by herself? " she asked jokingly.

"We've been working hard and saving our money all month to go skating," Reggie told her.

"Where are y'all going to, Robins Roost, or Broadway Roller Rink?" Lee-Lee asked.

"We're going to Broadway," Debra said.

"Well, at least let me and Rufus give y'all a ride over there."

"That's okay," Mama Bee said. "Liz is going to take them and she's going to tell them what time they better be outside waiting on her when she comes back to pick them up."

"No, it's fine, she can drop them off if she wants to and I'll just pick you all up at eleven o'clock," Liz said.

"How in the world am I going to fit all of them folks off in my car?" Rufus asked looking around at all of the kids scurrying about.

"We all fit in my car just fine this morning," Liz said. "We sho did, and we even had Mama in the car too," Darrick said.

"So what is that supposed to mean Darrick, with your narrow ass?" Mama Bee asked, knowing he made his comment because of her size.

"Don't be talking about my baby like at Mama, that's not nice at all," Lee-Lee said.

"You better take his ass on out of here before I beat it," Mama Bee told her daughter as she gave a vicious look toward her grandson.

"Mama, I really don't want to go. I don't even know how to skate," Eli told his mother.

"What, you don't know how to twerk eight wheels?" Lee-Lee asked Eli as she placed her arm around his shoulders.

"No Ma'am, no one has ever taught me how to." "Your Aunt Lee-Lee learned a long time ago and I don't believe I'll ever forget how to. So you should learn how so you can take it off of your to do list."

"Mama, you know how to skate?" Darrick asked.

"When was the last time you been?" Reggie asked. "It's been awhile, but like I said, once its on your to do list, its like riding a bike. You never forget".

"We're just about finished eating, but we'll get y'all there before it gets too crowded, so y'all won't have to stand outside in the cold," Lee-Lee said as she was re-entering the dining room.

After Lee-Lee, Rufus and all of the kids had left the house, Mama Bee and Elizabeth both sat back on the couch and exhaled.

It was Mama Bee who spoke first. "Do you see what I mean?" she asked. "That girl never wants to listen to me."

"Yes Ma'am, I see. Just like I see where Debra gets it from. But that's why at times you have to let the other person say all that they have to say until they've said it all. Then you tell them what they need to know," Liz said.

"You know what the problem with that is don't you?"

"No, what's that?"

"Well, with my Lee-Lee she never sticks around long enough to talk about anything with me. And I'm afraid

201

that now that she has left, I won't be seeing her again, not anytime soon anyway," Mama Bee said as she began to cry.

Liz took Mama Bee into her arms and began to console her, realizing herself how fragile a mother and daughter's relationship truly is. As they both sat on Mama Bee's couch weeping, all sorts of thoughts were traveling through Elizabeth's mind.

She immediately began imagining her and Elisha's relationship. The stage that it was in now, how to develop it into a bond that's unbreakable, established in trust, and honesty. But mostly, a relationship between her and her daughter cultivated and sealed in love.

She promised herself in determination that for the rest of her days on earth she would work toward a bond with Elisha formed in solidarity. Her thoughts also led her to what she had learned pertaining to her own Mother, and Grandmother's relationship.

How could they have allowed theirs to grow out of control, or even let sex, a man, or love for a man to come between their bond. But obviously they never took the time and necessary steps to formulate a secured bond. A true bond, sacred as the blood they both share.

Yes, I'm beginning to see things clearer than I ever have before in my life, Elizabeth told herself. Which is why I shall not allow my Mother and Grandmother's problems to take a hold of me and hinder my forward progress. Because life is supposed to be constantly progressive.

Examples experienced are to be delivered to the next generation so they'd know and recognize the building blocks of achievement.

Women, she continued in thought, the life givers are obviously central to it all. It's been given to us, entrusted to us to provide the necessary knowledge and guidance.

It's no wonder we've been trampled on, beaten, bruised, and all but destroyed, then labelled the weaker vessel, Because if we are ever allowed to carry out and fulfill our calling, our purpose, our God given right, the whole entire world would become Eden.

Dear God Almighty, I see it. You've opened the eyes of my understanding and I can now see vividly, and clearer than I ever have in my whole life.

Someone said, "We women must give our very own souls. We women will have to give our very own souls," Elizabeth said to herself once more, but only this time it was audible.

CHAPTER 13

"It show is crowded out here," Debra said as they turned onto Broadway and were traveling toward the Skating Rink.

"Rufus, pull over in front of those double doors," Lee-Lee said. "Right there behind that blue car." As Rufus slid in behind the blue car that was dropping off passengers, Lee-Lee let her window down and called out to the woman who was taking the admissions.

"Toni, Toni is that you girl?"

"Who is that?" Toni asked as she brought the rest of her body out of the doors for a better look, then asked again, "Who is at?"

"This is Lee-Lee. How have you been girl?"

"Lee-Lee, what's up big sis? I haven't seen you in forever. Girl where have you been?"

"Hold on, we're coming in!"

"We're what?" Rufus asked as he put his car into park.

"Baby, let's go in for just a little while. It'll give me the chance to talk to Toni. She's a real good friend of mines who I haven't seen in a long time."

205

"You asked me to bring these kids over here. You didn't say nothing about staying," Rufus told her with a little tone.

"Well sweetheart, I didn't know I would run into such an old friend."

"Look at all of these cars. There's no damn where to park. And would you just take a look at all of them damn children running around everywhere like they don't have no sense," Rufus complained. "Where is all of this coming from Rufus. You're starting to sound crazy," Lee-Lee let him know.

"Ain't nobody crazy, but I'll tell you who's crazy. You are, if you think we're going in a Skating Rink with a bunch of raggedy ass kids," Rufus spat as he got out of the car and lifted his seat so that Reggie and whoever else that was on that side could exit his car.

Lee-Lee screamed, "I know for certain that not only have you done gone crazy, but you done lost your entire mind, talking to me like that.

He stuck his head in the car and yelled, "This ain't no debate or discussion. Let them out over there on your side and bring your ass on so we can be leaving."

"Listen Rufus, you obviously have something on your mind other than treating me, or these children with
206

respect. So until you get the right things on your mind and tighten up I'll be hollering back at you later.

"Come on y'all, let's go," Lee-Lee said as she stepped out of the car and onto the sidewalk headed toward the double doors of the Rink.

She didn't get a chance to take a good four steps before a huge strong hand grabbed her by her right shoulder, spinning her and almost causing her to trip and fall. "What the f#@$ do you call yourself doing. You ain't going nowhere without me giving you the say so!"

"And I ain't said. so," Rufus yelled as he grabbed LeeLee by her wrist.

He made attempts at snatching her by her hair, but she avoided that with various squirms.

Lee-Lee yelled out in protest as people began gathering for a closer view.

Even Lee-Lee's friend Toni stuck her head out the door, and when she noticed it was her friend who was in trouble, she screamed, "I'm calling the police!" The threat didn't dissuade Rufus' behavior in the least bit. If anything, it seemed to have intensified.

He didn't let go of his grip until after the "Swop!" Caused by the two by four that was used by Reggie to smack Rufus upside of his head with.

And that was followed up by hits and throws being administered by Larry and Darrick's sticks and bottles. The damage they were doing was so severe that Lee-Lee began to scream at them to stop and get inside of the Skating Rink, where Toni awaited and did assist.

Lee-Lee looked down at Rufus' extended hand, asking her for help, but his actions caused her to respond, "I can't believe you put your hands on me. I never want to see you ever again."

She then joined her children, her niece, and her nephew inside of the Rink.

Lee-Lee made sure that everyone was okay, while answering Toni's questions. Even the one she asked about what she should tell the police, because they were definitely on thee way.

"Just tell them that we left and you didn't see what kind of car we got into."

"Alright," Toni said, "but I would have had his ass locked all the way up."

WE SUFFER FOR A REASON

Then she told Lee-Lee and her group to go on inside and refused to accept any admissions fee from them. Once inside of the Skating Rink the brothers began questioning Eli as to why he didn't help them beat down Rufus.

They then told him to remember that when one fight they all fight an outsider and especially a big person!

Then they strolled off into the complex looking around at all of the faces as they made their way toward the skate checkout window.

"I don't need any skates," Eli began to say, but was cut off when Larry reached down and started removing Eli's shoes from off of his feet.

"He needs a size eight Chuck," Larry told the checkout guy.

"I'm serious cousin Larry. I can't skate, because I've never tried to before."

"Out of your own mouth the truth has come. You have never tried," Larry jokingly teased Eli.

"What's going on?" Lee-Lee asked the boys as she came up to where they were.

"Mama, Eli is scared to skate," Darrick said. Then he spun around in his skates and told Eli, "Look it's too easy."

"Ain't no nephew of mines going to be without any skating in his blood," Lee-Lee told him as she reached over and got the size eight's from Chuck. She then loosened the strings and told Eli to wait on her to get her some skates.

"Mama, you're going to skate too?" Debra asked.

"I show am," Lee-Lee said. Then she added, "I'm going to show all of y'all a thang or two. Not a thing, or two, a thang, or two," she said.

They all laughed, even though a few had their doubts.

"Give me a size five," Elisha said.

"Elisha, when did you learn how to skate?" Eli asked his sister.

"When we were little, I skated all of the time. Up and down the sidewalk out in the front of our house."

Once everybody was fitted with their skates, Lee-Lee took Eli by the hand and they both made their way towards the floor. Eli reluctantly, but once they went around a few times he began to feel himself. So, he told his Auntie to let his hand go.

210

Eli picked up a little speed and went to make his turn. He didn't quite make it. He went down hard, taking a little fellow with him.

But what made the matter worse was someone ran over his pinkie finger.

Aunt Lee-Lee came from behind and scooped him up and onto his feet. He complained about his finger and asked his Aunt Lee-Lee to help him make it off of the skate floor.

"Boy, you can't go out like that. Do you see all of them little girls looking. You'll never get a second chance to live this moment over." "Good he mumbled."

"No, not good," she insisted, bent down and kissed his pinkie finger and led him around the rink a few more times and then she guided him to the center of the rink. "This is where the inexperienced get their skills up!" Aunt Lee-Lee left him there and was on her way to the concession stand, but was intercepted by Larry. "Mama, do you want to skate backwards with me?" he asked.

"Boy, I'm on my way to the counter to get me something to drink. Come on and let your Mother buy you a soda and then we'll skate together, okay?" "Okay, but let me buy you the soda."

"Okay then, my little big man!"

Eli began skating around in the circle at the center of the Rink, but he immediately noticed how small the children were who shared the center with him as well as how often they seemed to fall.

He was now overcome with embarrassment and to make matters worse he had to deal with: "Cuz, what are you doing in the Kiddie City?" Darrick would ask every time he skated by.

The embarrassment accompanied by those taunts caused Eli to dig down deeper for his determination. This made him take on skating with a brand new resolve. He viewed this through eyes belonging to his inner being. So in that middle he dug down deep and committed.

"Debra, get your tail over here. You and Elisha, neither one of y'all need to be talking to them little boys over there," Lee-Lee told her daughter and niece. "Mama, we wasn't doing nothing but talking to them," Debra said with attitude, because Lee-Lee had just embarrassed her in front of them little boys.

"Little girl, you better get yourself over here like I told you to. And don't make me have to get up from this chair."

"Dang mama, we wasn't doing nothing but just talking to them," Debra said again as she finally made it over to Lee-Lee's table.

"You better believe your Mother knows what talking leads to. It leads to some little ones running around everywhere."

"Well, if I do have some little ones, at least I won't leave them with somebody else," Debra said, rolling her eyes at the same time.

"Let me tell you something Ms. Debra, no matter how wrong I may be, or how grown you think you are, I'm still your Mother and you are gonna respect me for that much."

Debra got up from the table and she skated off mumbling something like, "I don't know why she had to come no way, messing it up for everybody else. She ain't gonna do nothing but leave anyway."

Even though Debra was on skates, she didn't go a great distance before getting her last word out. She made certain her mother heard every mumbled word to. "I can't stand the sight of her sometimes, and every time I come around we end up fighting," Lee-Lee said to Cookie, Reggie, and to Larry as he had just skated up to the table.

213

"Mama, don't you know that Debra is right and it makes all of us mad every time we see you go," Reggie told his mother.

"You're not leaving no more, are you Mama?" Cookie asked.

"Can we not talk about this right now?" Lee-Lee asked them, then made her way to the ladies room.

"I thought I just heard you whisper the exact same words that my great great Grandmother Bernice used to always say, 'We women would have to give our very own souls".

"That was you wasn't it, who shared those most valuable words of knowledge with me that has been passed down to you," Liz remembered.

"Child, tell me what you're talking about so I'll understand you," Mama Bee said as she looked at the radiance that shined upon Elizabeth's face in her dimly lit living room.

"It's so many things," Liz began. "I can't completely grasp it all, nor sum them all up into an explanation. All I truly know is I believe I understand how everything I have learned, and the things I've been told most recently, ties in together," she attempted to explain. "But what's this about what my Granny used to say?" Mama Bee asked.

"Mama, I came here to you and ever since my arrival you've been sharing your soul with me. Now I see that it's my responsibility, my duty as a Mother, to give unto my daughter my own soul. A soul that contains parts of your soul, my mother's soul, and pieces of the souls that have been given unto you all.

"But before I'm really ready I have to continue to allow you to fill me to the full with all you are willing to share. Mama, will you please tell me more about our family's history and the things given unto you by your great Grandmother?" Elizabeth asked.

"So you do understand that our family's past will guide you into your future purpose?" Mama Bee asked. "It's definitely part of it, but I just need to know. To be given your examples allows me to understand and grow toward that purpose. Do you see?" Liz asked.

"I believe I do, and I'm more than willing to help you in any way that I can. I just thought since it's only you, and me here you would much rather want to talk about Glenda and Ella."

"No Ma'am, it isn't, because I've decided to allow their troubles to remain their own responsibility to work out. If their desire is to solve them, of course I support that, but I refuse to let their issues hinder my progress.

"And I must progress, even if it's in the sense that I put everything that's possible into the characters of my children so that they would be capable of deeply

216

loving others enough to become guides. "Elizabeth sweetheart, it sounds like you've made your mind all the way up and your heart is set on getting the necessary work done."

"It is, but I know I'll need your help, because just like I've heard my own mother say, 'It takes an entire community to raise a child.' "

"I know that's the truth," Mama Bee replied. "You can just turn on the news at any time of the day, or night and it shows how today's youth are suffering from a lack of love."

"So, you do understand exactly what I'm talking about don't you? You see that if there are not any true unbendable loving guides, then the people will really perish.

"Mama, I'm not only concerned about our children's future, I'm also concerned about the futures of all of our children."

"Go on," Mama Bee said subtly coaxing Liz to share more of her inner thoughts.

"If there isn't anybody standing up, willing to sacrifice, willing to do whatever it takes to guide a generation to self love, then the future of an entire race of people becomes bleak."

217

"Liz, dear child of God, I've been living in this house raising them kids for all these years trying to deal with the same concerns, but with no one to talk to about so much importance frustrated me to the point that I became angered and then found refuge right here on this sofa with that bottle of alcohol in my hand."

"Mama, you have to see that the situation is too grave to allow yourself to become mentally handicapped by liquor or any other substance."

"Yeah, I know. Plus we've snatched the whip out of master's hand so why should we turn around and whip ourselves with an addiction?"

"We can't go on screaming about self respect if we daily disrespect ourselves either. It's time to do what we were created to do here on earth. It's time for us to express the form of love that changes everything it touches," declared Liz.

"It's deeply rooted in my heart that all of my grandchildren will grow to become fighters of their rights and for the rights of others. And I know I'm hard on them at times, especially Debra, but she's the oldest and the one who's suppose to be guiding her brothers. "So, hell I'm just rough on all of them."

"Well, don't you think it's time for us, me and you to begin a more hands on approach by forming a plan that educates them and instills in them self-respect, and love for others? A plan centered around Christ Jesus?" Liz asked.

"What are you suggesting, that we take them to church every Sunday, and make them all attend bible study every Wednesday?" Mama Bee asked.

"You know Mama, I've thought about that and as I look at the churches that have been in the communities and in the lives of the parishioners for all of these many years and yet the people still seem to be headed toward self destruction.

"We both know that other institutions have to be established to assist in the guiding of love. You and I both know that sometimes love must be retaught to those who haven't heard it, seen it, or felt it in so very long.

"So really, it all comes full circle and starts right back at point A. Us women will have to give our very own souls in order to break the vicious cycle formulated or otherwise assumed for 'our children,' " Liz said before exhaling a sigh.

"You know I always knew you were smart. I just didn't realize how much so until just now," Mama Bee expressed.

"Thank you Mama, but let me say this. You put on that hood chic attitude, but I can detect the intelligence when you choose to express."

"Well, you know I read a lot back there in my room when I'm by myself, so I got me . No, better said, I've obtained myself a vocabulary."

They both laughed at that one, both of them knowing how Mama Bee had a habit of mixing her speech, but kept it mostly hood.

"You know you've placed a lot on my mind tonight," Mama Bee told Liz as the laugher died down.

"Like what?" Elizabeth asked.

"Well, for starters, where do we go from here? I mean, how do we do our part in establishing a foundation that the kids are able to build on?"

"That's a good question. Unfortunately, I don't have an answer for it. The only thing that I've come up with thus far is for us to form ourselves a coalesce."

"You mean a group of us women coming together to form a whole, or one voice?"

220

"A vociferous voice if necessary. But for the most part we will all learn, grow, educate, and guide the young women of the group into womanhood."

"I'm in," said Mama Bee as she looked into Liz's intense eyes that appeared to sparkle in the shadowed living room.

"That only leaves the boys to be tended to, because it sho seems as though they are the ones who are under attack, captured, and incarcerated."

"Mama, you are absolutely right. Hopefully it won't take us long to come up with a service that will inspire self love, because the Lord knows society has targeted black men.

"And if black men are not careful, or properly guided, they'll fall head first into the traps that have been erected for them."

"We sho have our work cut out for us. And I'm sure it's not going to be an easy task, simply because it's not the first time that it's been attempted," Mama Bee told Liz.

"What do you mean?" Liz asked.

"In my lifetime I've witnessed my share of leaders arising and rallying the people in a common cause, and there has always sprung a white fist to dismantle, or a black hand sent in to grab a hold of the black neck.

Either or, the people eventually return to what they've accepted to be the norm." "Well, we won't allow our coalesce to be dismantled. Mama, I swear to you this day to build our foundation on solid ground, overlaid with my sweat and my blood if necessary," Liz told Mama Bee in all seriousness. "I hear you," she replied. "And I intend to be as committed to our survival and success. We have a plan and now there's nothing left to do but be doers and take the first steps."

"I couldn't have said it any better," Liz said. "Tomorrow we will work it out on paper and see what we come up with."

"Sounds like a plan," Mama Bee confirmed, then asked, "What time is it getting to be?"

Liz looked at her watch then answered, "It's twenty minutes after ten. We've been talking for over two hours."

"I guess we have," Mama Bee responded. She then asked, "Can I bring you anything from the kitchen? I'm going and fix me another plate full of everything, and I'll probably doo-whop on desert, because conversing always make me hungry."

222

"Mama, stop lying. You know you couldn't wait on me to pause my talking so you could make a break for the kitchen."

"So, what are you trying to say?" Mama Bee asked as she pulled Elizabeth by the hand and practically drugged her to her feet and into the kitchen.

There, they both fixed one plate full of every food and sat at the kitchen table with two forks, digging in and mumbling through mouths full of food.

"Your macaroni is even delicious cold," Liz said as she filled her mouth full with more!

After finishing off the entire plate and discussing weight and the need for exercise, Liz told Mama Bee that it was just about time for her to ride over to the skating rink and pick up the children.

Before leaving the kitchen she told Mama Bee, "You know you still owe me some information."

"Yeah, I know. Tomorrow, I promise to sit you and the kids down and share our history."

"No Mama, I'm talking about some you, and poppa Charlie history."

She made the cross sign over her heart using her finger.

WE SUFFER FOR A REASON

CHAPTER 15

"Eli, didn't you hear me calling your name?" his sister asked him as she skated up along the side of him. "No, I couldn't hear anything over the music," Eli told her as the DJ changed tracks. "It looks like you got the hang of it," Elisha told him. She then took his hand, telling him to come on, because she wanted to teach him how to backward skate. "I don't think I'm ready for that just yet," he informed her as he attempted to pull his hand free from her grip.

"Come on Eli, it's too easy. All you have to do is follow my lead and do what I tell you to do."

"Look at Eli," Darrick said to Larry as they leaned over the rail, looking out onto the floor.

"Yeah I see, our little cousin catches on quick," Larry responded.

"Where's Mama?" Darrick asked.

"She's in the front talking to her friend Toni. That's who I'm standing here waiting on."

"Suit yourself," Darrick told him as he darted out onto the floor.

"Where are you on your way to?" Larry asked Debra as he reached out and held her arm.

"I'm going to take these skates off, because I'm tired of skating," she told him. "You ain't tired of skating, you're just mad at Mama. Debra, we all get mad at her, but right now tonight we have her with us and we're having some fun."

"But don't it make you mad knowing she will probably be gone tomorrow, if not tonight?"

"She probably will be leaving soon, but I rather not allow myself to get upset until it happens. That way, tonight I can have all the fun I want to," Larry told his sister.

"I'll leave these skates on for a little while longer just in case y'all want to do our trio and ride the rails later on," Debra told him.

"Oh, we're definitely going to ride them rails. It's a family tradition. You just need to start coming here with us more, because we done stepped our game up."

"If that's the case, then y'all should be on my level by now then!"

"Girl stop it! I been on your level, because it was I who set the bar."

"Whatever little brother," Debra said putting emphasis on the words "little brother."

"Just wait, you'll see it with your own two eyes when I put on for my City," Larry said smiling, but serious at the same time.

"Is that your girlfriend?" this caramel-skinned chic with long hair asked Eli as him and Elisha were just coming off of the floor.

"No, I'm not his girlfriend," Elisha answered before Eli had the chance to. Then she added, "I'm his sister."

"I was just asking because I saw you both skating backwards together."

"It's my brother's first time, and I was just showing him how to."

"You backward skate really well for it to be your first time. By the way my name is Mary, Mary Jordan." "Hi Mary. My name is Eli," he eventually said after being nudged in the back by his sister.

They shook one another's hand and talked as they rolled over to the concession stand, apparently having become oblivious of Elisha's presence.

"Mama, come on, you owe me a skate," Larry told LeeLee as he rolled up on her and Toni's conversation. "Boy you act like you're my man or something," LeeLee said as she got up from her seat.

"If he's a good one, I'll take him," said Toni. "Well, he's just a little bit too young for you," she expressed with Motherly protectiveness.

"No, I'm not. I'm old enough and what I don't know I'm willing to learn," Larry said.

"Larry boy, you are too grown," Lee-Lee said. She then told Toni, "Girl, I swear he has been here before."

"Come on here boy. Let your Mama see if you really know how to skate."

"I just hope you'll be able to keep up!"

"Boy, please. I was standing right over there waiting on them to finish putting the floor down, but you better be glad I don't have a pair of grease packs." "Y'all about to go out on the floor?" Reggie asked when he skated up on their side.

"Yeah, I'm about to show Mama that it don't matter what kind of skates you have, but who you got in the skates."

"Okay, okay," Reggie said in excitement. "I'll be out there in a second. I have to find that one girl who I was just talking to."

Everything was everything out on the floor. The song wasn't too fast and everyone was coupled up. Larry was enjoying his mother's company and his brothers continued to skate past, carrying smiles on their faces stretching from ear to ear.

To Larry and Lee-Lee's surprise they were just passing by Eli and a real cute girl skating hand in hand, backwards. Lee-Lee and Larry looked at each other until their smiles turned into laughter. Both impressed that Eli was such a quick study.

After one or two more songs the DJ began to play real slow music and Larry had already spotted this one chic who had been playing hard to get at school. So, he told his mother half of what he was actually thinking.

"Mama, don't you think it would be a good idea for you to go and talk to your daughter?"

"Yeah, you know I was thinking the same thing, but I was debating on whether or not to wait until later."

"Why wait, when both of y'all are right here right now?" he asked his mother.

"Yeah, you're certainly right. Boy how did you get to be so smart anyway?"

"I don't know, maybe it's in my gene pool."

"I guess," Lee-Lee told him. "I still say you've been here before."

As they got off of the floor and Lee-Lee was on her way to find her daughter, Larry took a hold of her hand and said to his mother, "Mama, remember she's angry, and she's hurting."

"Okay I'll keep that in mind when she starts trippin." Larry spotted the object of his affections and although he has never been intimidated by a girl's beauty before, he was for some reason hesitant to just walk up on Karen Mckenzie and her friends.

But just so happens, his reluctance allowed some dude the opportunity to push up on his Karen.

Oh "H" naw he thought. He was not having that. So he disregarded whatever it was that hindered him momentarily, and swaged over to Karen looking her directly in her eyes, he said, "Come here and let me tell you how the rest of your night is going to go." She followed him to the games area where he spun around and told her how nice she looked. "But I didn't pull you away from your friends just to tell you that. I have to let you know that you and you alone put butterflies in my stomach. And I think about you whether we're at school, or not.

"And butterflies are okay, but not when they're in my stomach. So, I thought maybe together we could figure out how they get there whenever you are around, or maybe if we're together we could keep them from flying around."

"I love butterflies. I have some all over the walls of my room," Karen said.

"For real. I'd very much love to see your butterflies. You know, just see the butterflies!"

"Yeah, I know exactly what you mean Larry."

"Wow," Larry said and just stared into her face.

"What are you wowing about?" she asked.

"The fact that you say my name like it's being sung in a song."

"Boy, you're too silly, aren't you?"

"I can be silly if you like a guy with a sense of humor."

"I like a guy who is himself and not what I want him to be."

"That's nice to know, because I'm not a good actor."

"Tell me something, who was that older woman who you were skating with earlier?"

"So, you were watching me all along, probably even followed me here. Ms. Mckenzie, you do know that in the law they call it stalking, but I'm not going to report you this time, because I like being stalked by you." "Ain't nobody stalking you! I saw y'all when you passed by me in the concession stand. Then I came out to the rail and saw y'all skating together."

"So you followed us as we went out on the skate floor," Larry said playfully.

"Boy, shut up!" Karen told him as she hit him on the arm.

"Do you hear that, they're finally playing my song," Karen said making her body move to the beat.

"That's your song, huh. Come on out here with me and show me how you turn up to it."

Karen looked him up and down, then said, "I sure hope that you can keep up."

"Oh, we won't be racing. That song is to be grooved to," Larry said as he took her by the hand and guided the way onto the skate floor.

Once out there, feeling one another out he slid behind her, wrapped his arms around her waist and said ever so softly into her ear, "Karen Mckenzie, there can't be but one of you on the whole entire planet."

"I don't know if it'll be okay to give out my Grandmother's telephone number. What if my Granny Bee answers the phone when you call?" Eli asked.

"Naw Mary, I think it would be better if you gave me your telephone number and then I will definitely be calling you tomorrow."

"Okay, I can do that Eli," Mary said then asked, "Do you have a pen or a pencil?"

"No, I didn't bring either one," he told her.

"So, you didn't come here looking for girls and getting their numbers?"

"I didn't come here looking for anything. I wasn't even going to skate. I just came along with my family."

"You said you was from Georgia, right? How long are you going to be here in Louisville?"

"For a while I guess. My Grandmother just bought us a house here. So I guess that means we're not going anywhere anytime soon."

"Good, because I want the chance to get to know you better," Mary told Eli as she smiled, showing her pearly white teeth.

* * * * *

"Can we talk?" Lee-Lee asked Debra as she rolled up to the table where she sat.

"I don't guess I have any choice, do I?" Debra responded.

Lee-Lee overlooked her daughter's smart remark, because she didn't want to let anything interfere with the talk they both needed to have.

So she took up the empty seat next to her daughter and said, "I know you are very angry with me right now, just like I know that there's no one at fault but me. Debra, you do have every right to be upset with me and my actions."

"But Mama, why do you keep on doing it?" Debra asked as she looked at Lee-Lee with old and new tears in her eyes. "Don't you know that every time you leave you leave behind pain?" "Yes, yes I imagine I do."

"Well, why do you keep on doing it for? Don't you care about us? Don't you even care about what happens to us?"

"Yeah Debra of course I do, you know that I do."
"Mama, sometimes I don't know. Sometimes we really do wonder. We think it's the opposite. We believe you leave us with Mama because you don't want us. And because you wish that you never had us."

"Well, that's just not true," Lee-Lee told her. "I called myself leaving my babies in hands more capable than my own. At least until I get myself together."

"Mama, what's the matter with you that you would leave me for so long?" Debra asked.

"That's a story that I'm still dealing with, but I'm getting better and the truth is, this day has brought so much happiness and joy to my heart that I'm truly able to see the road that I must travel."

"See Mama, there you go talking about traveling somewhere!"

"Well Debra, this time I'm talking about a good trip. One that leads right to your heart," she told her daughter, then wrapped her arms around her neck.

"Mama, we need you to be home with us everyday and not just every once and a while," Debra said into her mother's neck, trying to hold back tears that insisted on falling despite how hard she tried to prevent their fall.

"Hold up, let me get in on this hugging thing," Reggie said as he wrapped his arm around his mother and big sister, having his baby brother Cookie in tow.

"What's going on here?" Darrick asked as he rolled up on the scene. "It looks like a group hug to me," he said as he got in on the action.

"That's what I'm talking about," Larry said as he too came and wrapped his arms around everyone and at the same time telling Elisha and Eli to come on and get them some.

And they were more than happy to join in on the affection.

"All able bodies report to the skate floor. It's time for the trios to ride the wheels off of your skates as DJ Dirty plays the non-stop cuts," was announced over the PA system.

"Come on y'all let's do this partna," Larry told his brothers as they discontinued their embrace.

"Come on Mama, you can watch us put on," Darrick told Lee-Lee.

They went out onto the floor so full of excitement and energy, but more than anything else the brothers hearts were filled to capacity with a joy that was provided by a Mother's love.

The brothers rocked the Rink and rolled the rails so well that they had the whole entire Skating Rink in an uproar!

The DJ, DJ Dirty kept on hyping the crowd every time he witnessed the brothers put down a move even he hadn't seen before. But what took the show was at the end when the brothers rolled up on this girl group all dressed in pink and white. They rolled with them doing the exact same moves that the girls had practiced so long and hard to be able to perform.

When it was all over they exited the floor one at a time, and every single one of them was applauded, hugged, and patted on their backs by everybody that they came in contact with.

Eli was proud to tell his new friend Mary that they are all his cousins.

Karen hugged and squeezed on Larry as if she didn't ever want to let him go.

"I told you he knows something about them skates," Karen's friend Tish said.

"Hey, what's up Tish ? I see you got Tonya Bethal and Lavida with you."

"We are always together, looking out for each other," Tonya said. "So you better treat our friend right!"

"Me, treat Karen Mckenzie right? I plan on treating her as good as she'll let me. Especially if she keeps putting on that gold and maroon like she's already a Seneca cheerleader," Larry said with a smile as he tugged at Karen's skirt.

"Larry, look over there," Darrick said pointing across the concession area at their brother Reggie hugging all over the lead girl of the pink and white trio team.

All Larry could say was, "Sleeping with the enemy." "Attention, attention, attention!!! All skaters, please turn in all rental skates. Broadway will be closing in ten minutes. You don't have to go home, but you do have to get the heck out of here," DJ Dirty informed the patrons. After all of the goodbyes was completed and telephone numbers were exchanged, they made their way across Broadway and into Elizabeth's awaiting car.

238

"Lee-Lee, you went skating too?" Liz asked once they all were inside of the car. I've been out here for about fourty minutes waiting on y'all. I didn't know it would be so much traffic to make it through," Liz exclaimed as she sought an opportunity for her to make it back into traffic.

"Yeah, I went with them and I had the greatest time of my life with my daughter, my sons, my niece and my nephew."

"Mama, Eli has a girlfriend and he has her phone number," Elisha blurted out, dropping a dime on her brother.

"Oh, he does?" Elizabeth questioned looking through her rearview at her son in the backseat.

Eli broke eye contact with his mother and put his head down, but said, "Mama she's a really nice person and I didn't know it at first, but she goes to the same school as I do."

"Well, as long as she's a nice person," Liz told him. "Mama, you told me I couldn't date until I was thirty years old," Elisha said, which caused everyone in the car to bust out into laughter.

"That's how they do us girls," Debra said, when everybody had quieted down. "But the boys, the boys get to act like dogs in heat."

"Well, us girls have more responsibility and a higher standard is expected of us. I plan on discussing it all with you women of the Lewis family tomorrow. You to Lee-Lee if you're spending the night."

"Discuss what, with who?" Lee-Lee asked as she repositioned Cookie on her lap.

On the ride home Liz informed them all of her and Mama Bee's intentions to form a coalesce, a group to educate and motivate. But most importantly, to plant the seed of history so that it may grow into purposeful direction, clearly showing where they've come from and where they're presently at, which will aid us all into where we need to go.

The boys weren't put at ease until Liz told them that they too would have their own club of refuge. The word club was all they needed to hear. They were all for it, dishing out names that they thought it should be called.

The car was suddenly quiet when Liz said, "So obviously Mama is going to be thrilled that you are staying over."

"Yeah, she may be for awhile, but how long until the thrill is gone?"

"I guess it's up to the both of y'all, because you have both been given the opportunity to crumble the mountain that stands between you'," Elizabeth said to her as they parked in front of the house.

"Thank God we're here already. My feet are killing me," Debra said to everyones agreement.

"Mines are too," came a couple more responses. "Y'all are just playing with the truth. I'm going straight in there and soak my feet in some hot hot water," Lee-Lee shared as she got herself and Cookie out of the car.

Once inside of the house they checked on Mama Bee and found her to be passed out asleep at the dining room table.

"Mama, Mama," several voices exploded, which brought Mama Bee to consciousness.

"What, what? Why are all of y'all yelling at the other one for? What are you calling me for Debra?" Mama Bee asked, having a face of bewilderment.

"Because Mama, you're sitting here knocked out asleep, almost ready to fall out of your seat," Lee-Lee told her Mother.

"Wasn't nobody sleep," Mama Bee said wiping slobber from her mouth using her arm. "I was just resting my eyes for a minute, waiting on y'all."

"Mama, you still got a little bit of slobber left right there. Do you want me to get it for you?" Darrick asked as he pretended to reach for it.

"Naw, I don't need you to do nothing. And if you touch my face I'm a touch yours. And I ain't talking about no gentle touch either," she told Darrick as she wiped her mouth again.

"Lee-Lee, how did you end up taking them skating and bringing them back?" Mama Bee asked. " 'Cause we had to beat the brakes off of that sucker Rufus," Reggie volunteered the answer.

"What? What are you talking about?" Mama Bee asked as Elizabeth said, "Oh my God, what happened?" "It wasn't nothing, just Rufus acting crazy. Trying to tell me where I could or could not go," Lee-Lee said.

"He put his hands on you?" Mama Bee asked.

"Yes Ma'am, he put his hands on her Mama. And you remember how you told us that we better not ever let nobody put their hands on our sister, well we know not to let anybody put their hands on our Mother either or

242

any other female in our family," Larry said feeling angered again about the whole incident.

"Lee-Lee, did he put his hands on you?" I asked. "Now tell me what did he do?" Mama Bee wanted to know from Lee-Lee.

"Not really Mama. He was just trying to get me to –"

"Mama he was grabbing all on her, and pulling on her real rough like," Reggie interrupted.

"Well, he bet not ever come back around here no more, and I mean it," Mama Bee said in obvious frustration.

"Mama, it wasn't that serious. It was just as much my fault as it was his. I insisted on going skating when he had already told me of his plans."

"Listen to me, all of you. You can't make any excuses, because there are none. A man ain't got no reason to be putting his hands on no woman for anything," Mama Bee said. Then asked, "Lee-Lee has he ever put his hands on her ever before?"

"No, no not really. I mean, it wasn't nothing serious and it was my fault for not doing stuff that I already know I'm supposed to," Lee-Lee said in Rufus' defense.

"Do you know what, you sound like you could be a poster child for spousal abuse," Mama Bee told Lee-Lee before adding, "Elisha go into my room in there and get me that e-mail that I printed out laying on top of my desk."

When Elisha returned, Mama Bee told everybody to listen. She then asked Elisha to read it out loud.

So, she cleared her throat and read:

"This morning my body aches in places I didn't know existed. As I view my face in the mirror of the bathroom's medicine cabinet, I hate what I see. I hate myself, because no matter how hard I try I mess up and do something that displeases him. But it's nobody's fault but my own. I should have immediately cleared the table, then washed the dishes after serving him his meal last night. It was also my fault the night before last, because I'm the one who turned into bad traffic that caused me to be a few moments late arriving home from work. Speaking of work, I wonder if it's possible for me to conceal my bruises with a little make-up. The glasses will cover the bruise under my eye, but like Kathy said I will look

244

very foolish wearing sunglasses indoors all day.

Oh Kathy, sweet dear soul, she swears it isn't my fault, and that one day he just might kill me.

I'm so afraid and confused. I'm tempted to swallow this whole bottle of sleeping pills saving him the trouble.

I may never be able to satisfy him all of the time. I hate my life. I hate him. No. No. I didn't mean that. I love him.

He's all I have in this world and at times he tells me how much he loves and needs me. I well know that he wouldn't be able to make it on his own without me. So, I can't harm myself.

I'll just try much harder to do everything he expects me to do."

Mama Bee thanked Elisha for reading the poem and then paused, allowing the poems' message to seep into their minds.

"Lord, I sure would have loved to been able to share that message with one of my co-workers back home when she was trapped in an abusive relationship and always blaming herself," Liz said breaking the moment of silence.

"Mama, I'm not in an abusive relationship. Rufus has gotten out of line a couple of times and I put him back in his place," Lee-Lee said.

"Naw, you didn't put him in the right place, because if you had there wouldn't have been no couple of times. He would have been placed in the right cemetery after hitting you the first time," Mama Bee said after having her anger rekindled.

Just the thought of a man putting his hands on her child makes her blood boil!

"Listen, y'all go ahead and get them children ready for bed. It's almost 12:20 a.m."

"Dang Mama, it ain't no school tomorrow," Darrick whined.

"Somebody take Cookie in my room and lay him down. He's already asleep. Cookie, look at him," Mama Bee was saying. "He sho looks like a Bootie to me." "I like Cookie better than Bootie myself," Lee-Lee said. "Mama, do we have to go to bed already?" Reggie asked.

"Do what Mama told you to do boy," Lee-Lee said.

"You should be dead tired, and dizzy too after going around in a circle all damn night. Gone in that room, y'all ain't going to sleep no way. Probably try to wait on me to go to sleep, so you can sneak out."

After the children were off to their rooms, Mama Bee, Liz, and Lee-Lee sat at the dining room table talking, while Lee-Lee's feet soaked in some hot water.

Everyone tried to avoid the Rufus topic because Mama Bee had finally calmed herself down somewhat. Instead they discussed tomorrow's agenda.

Lee-Lee began retrieving blankets and pillows so she could sleep on the couch. When the first quilt touched her sofa Mama Bee snapped.

"I just know you don't think you're sleeping in there on my new sofa, do you?" she asked Lee-Lee.

"Now it's a sofa because it's new," Lee-Lee said as she continued preparing it so she could sleep on it.

"You're right. It's my new sofa that ain't nobody going to sleep on and wear it out," Mama Bee told Lee-Lee a little louder and with a little tone.

"Well, one day this sofa will be a couch and by then you'll be calling it a couch again. And Mama just in case you didn't know, ain't is not a word."

"It sho sounded like one when I used it. That's the problem with black folks today, they let other people tell them what is and what 'ain't' a word," Mama Bee said, being sure to put emphasis on the word "ain't."

"I'll tell you something else that's a word, 'beatdown.' It's a compound word that will leave a person with compound fractures for stretching their fat ass out on my sofa!"

"Mama, why don't you go on in there and go to sleep before I pay somebody for a witness signature and use the two to have you committed," Lee-Lee told Mama Bee and then reached over and turned the living room light off.

"So, you're gonna sleep on my sofa regardless of what I say, but if I came in there and hit you upside your head with the television, I'd be wrong."

"Goodnight Mama, goodnight Liz. I'll see y'all in the morning," Lee-Lee said while totally ignoring her mother's threats.

"Goodnight," Elizabeth said, turned and gave Mama Bee a kiss on her jaw and told her goodnight as well.

"I'll see both of y'all in the morning. I just hope y'all don't expect me to fix breakfast for the whole house,"

248

Mama Bee announced. Her way of requesting her daughters to help in the kitchen in the morning.

She then turned the dining room lights out and retired to her room.

Once there, she had to wrestle Cookie for covers and one of her pillows, which she wasn't successful in until after several threatening statements were made.

CHAPTER 16

The next morning Mama Bee awoke and came out of her room running right into all sorts of smells and aromas. Lee-Lee and Liz were in the kitchen whipping up all kinds of foods. They had the entire house engulfed in delicious fragrances.

When Mama Bee came in and took a seat at the table, Liz and Lee-Lee discontinued their laughter long enough for Lee-Lee to hand Mama Bee a steaming hot cup of coffee.

"Good Morning Mama. Did you sleep well?" Lee-Lee asked as she beat more eggs over the sink.

"Good morning," she told both of them," then said, "so, y'all just knew I was on my way out, already having my coffee ready?"

"We knew it wouldn't take you much longer to come out of there, judging by the way you was in there fussing with your grandson," Lee-Lee said.

"Yeah, it's just about time for him to go back into the room with the rest of the boys." Mama Bee let that fact be known as she looked over her shoulder at her bedroom door opening.

"Good morning little boy," was said by all three women.

Then Lee-Lee said, "There's not nearly enough room in there for all of them."

"There will be plenty of room soon enough," Mama Bee told her. "I'm having the finishing touches put on the house down the street so Liz and her two can move in.

"I'll tell both of y'all right now," she went on, "it was bought and intended for you Lee-Lee, but who knows when you're coming, or where you're going."

"Mama, Liz told me about it this morning and it's okay, because I have been missing in action."

"Why do you do me like this? Don't you know how much it hurts my heart?" Mama Bee expressed to her daughter before abruptly going back into her bedroom.

After looking at one another for a brief moment, Liz suggested to Lee-Lee that she should go in there and tell her Mother what she had just shared with her this morning.

"Go on, it's the perfect time to tell her everything," Liz said. "I'll finish up in here and then me and Cookie will wake the rest of the kids up for breakfast."

"Mama, can I talk to you for a minute?" Lee-Lee asked as she entered her mother's room.

"I ain't got no choice, you're already in here,"

"Mama, I'm serious," Lee-Lee said as she sat down on the bed beside her Mother. "Mama, I know that I have caused you and my children a great deal of pain. I realize I've done a lot of things wrong my whole life. And whenever things get tough I get gone. Neither one of us can take back any of the pain, nor none of the words we've said to one another. But we can take this day and use it as a starting point toward a better relationship and a better future. A better future for your grandchildren, especially. "I don't know if I'll still make mistakes and bad decisions, but I do know I'm going to do my best to support the development of my family. Liz explained to me, in great detail the plans to establish a woman's group, and I want to cast in my support of that as well." "You'll have to be here in order to be supportive," Mama Bee had to say.

"Mama, I'm here. I'm here and I don't plan on going anywhere anytime soon."

Those words brought a flood of tears to Mama Bee's eyes. A flood that overflowed and rolled down her cheeks.

Lee-Lee took one of her hands and wiped away her mother's tears, then she embraced her ever so tightly and affectionately and said into her ear, "This is the mood you're put it from sleeping on a sofa couch!"

Mama Bee laughed a chuckle and then told Lee-Lee, "I don't know what your mood will be like tomorrow then, but I do know your ass will be sleeping on the floor tonight."

They both laughed before making their way into the dining room, where Elizabeth had the table looking like a buffet.

"This looks absolutely wonderful," Lee-Lee told Liz as her and Mama Bee took seats.

"Thank you, thank you both, but I couldn't have done this without you," Liz told Lee-Lee.

"Where are the children, have you called for them yet?" Mama Bee asked.

"I sent Cookie upstairs about five minutes ago, but he hasn't returned yet," Liz said.

"I'll go get them," Mama Bee said in a somewhat threatening tone.

"No Mama, let me go get them all up. They need to get used to seeing their Mother's face," Lee-Lee said and then kissed her mother's forehead.

"Mama, Mama," Lee-Lee screamed and hollered as she came running back into the dinging room.

Mama Bee jumped up with Liz right beside her, both having looks of horror and fright covering their faces. "What is it, what's the matter?" Mama Bee yelled, more than a little alarmed as she looked at her daughter standing before her drenched in water. "Them bad ass grandkids of yours was hiding out waiting on me so they could soak me wet with them damn water guns," Lee-Lee shouted, but not being as mad as she would have been if her hair would have been fixed.

Mama Bee, and Elizabeth both busted out in laughter as they moved away from Lee-Lee's flood when she attempted to draw closer.

Reggie, Darrick, Larry, Cookie, and Eli all came easing their way into the room and at the same time laughing like crazy. This made Mama Bee and Liz laugh some more.

"Mama, you just stood there. You didn't run or move or nothing," Darrick said. "That's why you got so wet," he added.

"That's called shock," Lee-Lee told him. "I couldn't move, I wouldn't have believed in a million years that my own children would ever wet me up. And Eli,

254

you're suppose to protect your Auntie, not attack me boy."

"Aunt Lee-Lee it was too funny. You was just standing there stumping your feet and turning in circles."

"That's alright, you little knucklehead, I'm going to get all of y'all back. Mark my words. You too Cookie; come here. You set me up."

She began chasing him as he took off running and laughing around the dining room table, until he ran into Mama Bee's awaiting arms, who scooped him up and swung him away from his mother's grasp.

"She can't save you forever little boy," Lee-Lee informed Cookie.

"Yes I can and I will," Mama Bee said. "You need to go in there and put on one of my shirts and get yourself out of that wet one."

"Y'all think it's funny now," Lee-Lee said to all of her boys and her nephew Eli as she made her way towards Mama Bee's bedroom.

"Y'all behave yourselves," Elizabeth said with a giggle as she mushed her son's hair a little.

"Mama, why is it so much food this morning?" Eli asked.

"I don't know, I guess this is our way to express our love for you all through this cuisine."

"Well, I'm glad y'all did, because I'm starving," Eli said.

"Hopefully we'll be able to sit down and eat soon. We're now waiting on Debra, and your sister to make it down here. While we're waiting, tell me something, how much did you enjoy skating last night?"

"Mama, it was awesome. I had no idea it would be so much fun," Eli exclaimed.

"Did running into your new found friend have anything to do with the awesomeness of the whole thing?" "Mama, she's just a girl. I mean she's smart, she listens, and, and—"

"And what?" Liz asked. "And she's pretty. Is that what you was about to say?"

"No, I was going to say that she seems to understand me when I'm talking to her, you know, like she gets me."

"Somebody go tell Debra and Elisha to hurry up and come on," Lee-Lee said re-entering the room. "I'm too hungry from all of that running around." "I'm starving too Aunt Lee-Lee," Eli said. "I'm so hungry I don't think I'll be able to wait much longer."

256

"Come on then, help your Auntie with these plates and by the time they get down here we'll be ready to sit down and eat. Tell me something nephew," Lee-Lee continued. "How old are you and how did my little nephew get to be so smart?"

"Aunt Lee-Lee, I'll be thirteen in a few more months and I don't really know how smart I am."

"What took y'all so long?" Lee-Lee asked the girls as they entered the dining room.

"Mama, we had to brush our teeth and stuff before just coming down here breathing all in people's faces like some people be doing," Debra said as she sat down and looked at Reggie with an accusing look.

"Naw, she didn't," Darrick told Reggie as him and Larry sat down at the table.

"Yes she did," said Larry.

"Oh you got jokes this morning?" Reggie asked his sister.

"Who's joking. Give yourself the breath test. Breathe in your hand and catch your knuckles on fire." "Naw, what you need to do is breathe on your hair and see if it'll still take a perm," Reggie jonesed back and then busted out laughing.

257

It caused others to join in on the laughter. "I don't know what you find so funny Eli," Debra said.

This caught him totally by surprise, due to the fact that up and until that point he had evaded many joke attacks. But it didn't appear that he'd be so lucky today, because as soon as he stuttered for an answer, Debra fired on him.

"The way you was in the middle of the Skating Rink holding on to little kids, so you wouldn't fall." A floodgate of laughter erupted and right in the middle of it Larry said, "Cuz that one little guy couldn't have been no more than six, or seven that you took down with you."

And the laughter went right back up a few decibels. At Eli's remembrance of the incident he too began to laugh out loud.

Jokes, jokes, and more jokes were fired back and forth and they didn't cease until Mama Bee said, "Liz has something to say so y'all, be quiet for a minute and listen up."

"Oh yeah right, well just like I told you all last night in the car. We've decided to establish ourselves a coalesce. A group of us women who will nourish and foster the growth of one another as well our community.

"Lee-Lee, we will definitely need your help as well as Debra's and Elisha's.

"Us five women sitting here at this table will form the core, but we will have to branch out as far as we're able in order to express our love to others and extend the goals of the group."

After many many questions were asked, and the ones that could be answered answered, the women continued their conversation in the kitchen while they cleaned. Then they convened to the living room where Debra and Elisha equipped with pens and pads took detailed notes.

Lee-Lee instructed them both to head their top page with 'Goal!,' and then said, "We'll branch out from there." It was the boys fourth or fifth time asking their barrage of questions. Feeling left out, they asked, "What about a club for us?" But who could have guessed that it would be Eli leading the pack.

While the girls took the time to listen, he told them their club could reach out to others and they could also share ideas as well as take trips to places of learning.

Elizabeth was excited, because he was excited, and she assured the boys that they would be assisted in their developing a club. She also told them that if they were truly serious, they would eventually be partnered in with the women's group.

"Okay, that's enough work for one day. Now I have some other planning and preparing to do for my card party," Mama Bee said as she stood to her feet. At the sound of the words, card party, Reggie, Darrick and Larry's faces lit up like lightbulbs. And no doubt Debra's did too, because they all were aware of the endless opportunities for making themselves some money at Mama Bee's card parties.

And their thoughts were; it's been way too long since the last one. Almost eight months. "What is this card party all about again?" I remember Mama mentioning it once before," Liz asked.

All of the boys attempted to answer her question, and all at the same time, but it was Lee-Lee who explained it to her.

"Mama's card parties is where her and her friends come together and they gamble on bid whiz, spades, tonk, and a few other games that old people play."

"They be gambling for money?" Liz asked.

"What else could people gamble for?" Reggie asked.

"Boy, stay in your own lane and out of grown folks conversations," Lee-Lee told her son.

"Yeah, they play for a few dollars a hand, but since Mama is the house lady she doesn't do much playing. She cuts the hands."

"And what is, cuts the hands?" Liz questioned.

"You can't possibly be from Atlanta and be this slow," Lee-Lee said jokingly.

"Well, I wasn't raised in the City. I grew up outside of town. Then we later moved to Kings Grant Drive right there near Borne Holmes."

"Anyway," Lee-Lee continued, "cutting the hand is where the house lady is entitled to her cut off of every hand played. That's for her hosting the card party at her house. And my kids are thrilled to death, because Mama let's them serve her guests food and beverages."

"And it's my turn to serve the plates. Elisha you can help me," Debra said as she looked in her brother's direction, which immediately caused their response, "No it ain't Debra. You did it last time, because we did clean up and didn't make hardly any money, but what Mama gave us."

"You are telling a brand new lie," Debra told Darrick, and the rest of them.

"We did so clean up, but it's okay you can serve again if you want to," Larry said, because he had received a signal from Reggie, who obviously had some inside information.

"Aunt Liz, Mama told me to ask you if you would drive my mother to the grocery store to buy this list of stuff."
"We are not going to any store," Lee-Lee protested.
"She was just in here and she didn't even bother to ask us anything."

"I was hoping you'd say that so I would have to go myself. Then I would get my purchases at a tremendous discount." Mama Bee said as she re-entered the living room.

"Mama, why didn't you say something about going to the store while you were in here at first?" Lee-Lee asked her.

"What difference does it make? I was needing to go over my list again. And I'm glad I did. But like I said, I'll be more than happy to go myself."

"We'll go, if it'll prevent you from doing it the other way," Liz said trying to conceal from the kids Mama Bee's use of the five fingers discount.

"Can we go with you Mama?" Elisha asked.

"You all can go," Elizabeth said and told them to go get ready.

As they rushed off to ready themselves, Liz stepped close to Mama bee and said, "When we return you owe us some family history. So please be ready."

"In that case let me put some of my stay ready juice on the list."

"Mama, you do not need any juice, especially that kind of juice," Liz informed her mother-in-law.

"You sho don't need no juice, because you know that that certain amount will get you to trippin," Lee-Lee said.

"Aint' nothing wrong with trippin," Mama Bee said, "as long as you don't fall." And then she started laughing.

"We're not stopping at any liquor store," Lee-Lee said establishing the fact that she too was going with Liz.

"Now who's trippin? Not me," Mama Bee told them. Then said before leaving the room, "I keep me a plan 'B.' "

Elizabeth and Lee-Lee turned and looked one another in the face, giving quizzical expressions. It was Liz who asked, "What in the world is she talking about?"

"There's no telling girl. You know she thinks she's still in her thirties," Lee-Lee told her.

"I noticed that," Liz said. "And I pray that I be as vibrant, if the Lord wills that I live to be her age."

"I be hoping the exact same thing," Lee-Lee said, giving Liz high fives before heading to the bathroom to freshen up.

"We're ready," the boys said as they came back into the living room geared up.

"Y'all have to give us a few minutes to get ourselves together, but in the meantime y'all can take them coats off until we're all ready to go," Elizabeth told them.

Once they were all out the door, Mama Bee got on the telephone and began dialing numbers.

After reminding her select group of card players of the time and procedure, she told them all that they knew the place, the same place that they always left from; "BROKE!"

Her last phone call was placed to Timmy, her runner/driver. Right now she needed him to run to the liquor store and pick up her entire order, because experience has taught that an intoxicated card player was a discombobulated one.

"Who is it?" Mama Bee asked the person who now knocked on her front door.

"Uh, it's me Ms. Lewis. It's me Rufus, your daughter's old man."

"Oh, okay, hold on for just a second sweetheart. Let me go get me my key!"

Mama Bee scrambled to the rear of the house, retrieved her key from its place high up on the top shelf, then hurried back to the living room and sat back down on her sofa.

"Come on in baby, it's open," she announced.

Rufus stood in the center of the living room holding a beautiful bouquet of flowers in his hand. He made an attempt to express himself. But before a completed sentence could leave his mouth, Mama Bee drew her derringer and aimed it at Rufus' forehead as she quoted, "If you ever put your hands on my baby again I'll send you to your Momma in a pine box. Now get your punk ass out of my house."

Rufus stood there frozen in place, unable to make a logical decision due to his fright. Knees knocking, but legs unwilling to follow the command to go, he finally turned to leave.

"Rufus," Mama Bee yelled his name waving her pistol. "You can leave the damn flowers. I like flowers."

He complied, then broke out the door to his car and squealed tires tearing it down to get up through there!

Seconds later Timmy entered in and upon seeing Ms. Bee placing her little derringer pistol into her key shaped lock box, he now understood the guy in the red cars' urgent departure.

"Ms. Bee you keep on flexing with that little ole pistol knowing you ain't built like at," Timmy said, but believing the opposite to be the truth. "Little Timmy, you can say whatever you want to, because those are your lips, but I want you to know this for certain, I don't need no gun for you! Now here is this list and this money right here," Mama Bee instructed as she handed them both to him.

She looked him in his eyes and told him, "All you have to do is short change me and I'll make a believer out of you too!"

"Something tells me that you're a woman of your word," Timmy said as he took the list and the money. He then smiled at Ms. Bee and exited the house.

Mama Bee answered her telephone and spoke with her friend Ms. Bunch for a few minutes until she finally said,

"Just bring them on over here Bunch and I'll check them out myself."

Being that Bunch lived directly across the street from Bee, it didn't take her but several minutes to arrive in Mama Bee's front room.

"Bee?!" Ms. Bunch yelled as she came through the front door.

"I'm in here, come on back and quit all that unnecessary hollering, you ole crazy ho!"

"You got your nerves calling somebody crazy, with your mental health ass," Bunch retorted.

"Let me see what you got Bunch. I ain't got time for no BS. I'm trying to get things together for my Card Party." "I came to ask you in your face why come I wasn't invited to your Card Party?"

"What am I going to invite you for? You can't play a damn lick of cards."

"I don't have to play any cards Bee. I can become friendly with a couple of your guests."

"Girl please, don't nobody and I do mean nobody, want your ole wrinkled up ——. Girl let me stop."

"Bee, you know that right there hurt!"

"You trying to be friendly would hurt," Mama Bee told her and they both started laughing. "How many purses do you have?" Mama Bee asked.

"Here are the four that I got left. I already sold two yesterday."

"How much are you asking for these?"

"For all four, I want twelve hundred."

"Twelve, what they cost, a thousand a piece?"

"No Bee, they cost anywhere from seven hundred to eight fifty. And I need three hundred a piece, which is way less than half price. I figured I'd just give a deal on the whole slip." "Bunch, folks are struggling everywhere. Thanksgiving just past, and Christmas is right around the corner. Factor in bills and daily expenses. Now ask yourself, who in the hell has two hundred for a purse?"

"I wouldn't expect no one who's in hell to need one, but if you're on earth and you want one of these you'll be paying two, or you can go to the white folk and pay them seven."

"I won't be paying two or seven, cause I don't need them. Nor do I believe I'd be able to get rid of them at my Card Party."

"Why wouldn't you pay half price for one of these pieces of merch? You make me pay half for your merch," Bunch said.

"You know you're standing there telling a whole entire lie 'cause if that was the case you owe me for the ham and bucket of chitterlings I sent over there the day before yesterday," mama Bee scolded.

"What was you going to do, break tradition? You do at for us every year, now you want to go in my purse."

"I'm just kidding with you. I wouldn't go in your purse, but I am telling you to get these purses out of my house."

"Bee, you're a cold-hearted black winch when you want to be," Bunch said, then asked, "Can I at least come over tomorrow night and show my purses to your card players?"

"Hell naw, what you can do is leave them here and I'll make sure they are seen. But you, you're not invited or welcomed. Do you even recall what happened the last time?" Mama Bee asked Ms. Bunch.

"No, no I can't honestly say that I do," Bunch replied.

"My point exactly. You got drunk and lost all of your money, including your gas, and light money playing card games you never even played before in your entire life."

"I vaguely remember something like that possibly happening, or I could have been pick pocketed by one of your grandchildren," Ms. Bunch attempted to jones. "It might be a good idea if you kept my grandbabies out of your mouth before you find yourself knocked out and posted on the curb out there."

"Bee, you're still living in denial, aren't you? Bee, your grandbabies are bad as hell, running around here doing their little hustles and everything else under the sun." "Bunch, you honestly believe us to be too good of friends for me to slap fire from your face don't you? Now I done asked you once to keep my grandchildren out of your mouth, but you act like you ain't heard me, so I'm telling you for the last time.

"Now utter one more word about my babies and I'm going to see if I can have you touching everything in here, starting with the floor," Mama Bee said in that most threatening tone.

"I'm through with it Bee. I just hope you wake up before it's too late. What would it look like if they grew to be boosters like me, you and Jackie?"

"Ms. Bee, it's me Timmy," he announced as he came through the living room and into the dining room carrying two bags of items. "Where do you want these?" he asked.

"You can just sit them right there on the table," Mama Bee told him.

"Hello Ms. Bunch," Timmy greeted. "I have to go out and get the two cases of beer and that'll be it."

"Alright, then let me have my receipt for tax purposes," Mama Bee told Timmy before he left the room.

After her business was completed with Timmy and she insisted that Bunch leave her house, Mama Bee cleaned and straightened up a bit more.

She then made her way back to the living room clutching a half pint of her drink, having a feeling of accomplishment as she inhaled the deodorizing fragrance she had sprayed.

Propping her feet up she made a few more calls and by the time the last one ended she was finished and feeling herself. So much in fact she placed a call to Atlanta, Georgia.

"Hello?"

"Yeah, is this Ella I'm speaking with?"

"Yes, this is me. How may I help you?"

"You can't, my help doesn't come in the form of a person."

"I'm glad to hear that, so maybe you could help me by stating the purpose of your call, Bernice ." "My purpose comes in the form of a question/"

"Which is?"

"Why haven't you told your child the vital information about family that is a Mother's duty?"

"Listen to me Bee, Beetle, or whatever it is that they call you up there. You stay the hell out of me, and my daughter's affairs."

"Correction Ella, not your daughter's affairs, yours." "He was mines. He belonged to me first, damn it," Ella erupted.

"Key word being, belonged, as in past tense."

272

"You don't have the right to interfere in the life of my daughter, knowing damn well you've always taken Glenda's side!"

"This hasn't a damn thing to do with sides. This only concerns the right that Elizabeth has to know about your love triangle and how it affects her directly."

"I'm warning you, you old bat, if you don't let me tell my daughter what I feel she needs to know, I'll somehow, someway make you regret it!"

"That's my point exactly. You're only telling the parts you feel the need to tell. But I have these two things to say. Your time is limited being the first, and secondly save your idol threats. We both know you've been a coward ever since we were little, with your ole punk ass!

"Now make me come to the 'A' and go up top on you, on bankhead," Mama Bee told Ella before hanging up in her ear.

The boys burst through the front door laughing and playing so loud Mama Bee had to tell them to tell her what was so damn funny.

"Mama, while we were at the store we ran into Eli's girlfriend Mary," Reggie exclaimed.

"Eli's girlfriend," Cookie sung and then laughed his laugh!

"No, she isn't. She's just my friend Granny . They act like that because they've never tried to have a girl as just a friend," Eli defended himself.

"They probably haven't baby. Y'all put those things in there on the kitchen table," Mama Bee instructed then began to ask Lee-Lee, and Liz's whereabouts just as they came through the door laughing loud with Debra and Elisha in tow.

"what is it that y'all find to be so extremely funny? Are y'all laughing at my grandchild having a friend who just so happens to be a girl?"

"No Ma'am, we're the ones who told the boys to knock it off. And by the way the little girl's name is Mary and we took it upon ourselves to invite her and her mother Elaine Jordan to tomorrow's Card Party," Lee-Lee was excited to tell Mama Bee.

"You did what?" Mama Bee questioned, then she went on to say, "You must have forgotten this is Ms. Bee's Card Party. Not Lee-Lee's, Liz's, Eli's, or anybody else's.

"You don't invite nobody to Ms. Bee's Card Party. Only Ms. Bee has the authority to invite. So, I hope you

274

have her phone number so you can call and uninvited!"
"Mama, what's wrong with one more person attending tomorrow's Card Party? She appeared to be a good person, didn't she Liz?"

"Yeah, and that's exactly what I'm afraid of, bringing good to a cut throat environment," Mama Bee said.

"But you know what, let her come. Just know that she will be you and Liz's responsibility."

While putting away the groceries Lee-Lee said, "Mama, I really didn't think you would mind if I invited the woman. I imagined that she just wanted to meet the family of the little boy who her daughter had just recently met."

"When have I not, and further more you've attended enough Card Parties to know it ain't no kind of an environment to be trying to make a good first impression," Mama Bee told her daughter.

"But listen, what's done is done, so there's no need to discuss it any further. Like I said she will be you, and Elizabeth's responsibility. So don't be running to me talking about rescuing her from my friends." "I'll watch after her then Mama, because you are right, people definitely need protection from your friends, most of them anyway," Lee-Lee offered.

"Lord have mercy. I didn't realize we were gone for so long Mama, leaving you here all by yourself," Liz said as she came into the kitchen.

"All by myself?" Mama Bee asked, giving Liz a strange look.

Liz didn't catch the look so she went on to say, "We were gone for a little over two hours. One of us could have called and checked up on you."

"Called and got cussed all the way out," Mama Bee said, then asked, "Elizabeth, what makes you think I would need any checking up on, or a babysitter or anything of that nature?"

"I just don't like the idea of you being here all alone."

"Well, I guess I appreciate your concern, but rest assured that I am never really alone. I got a key for any stranger who may try my lock."

She then went into her bedroom closing the door behind her.

"Mama, can I talk to you?" Eli asked as he entered the kitchen.

"Sure you can sweetie, what's on your mind?" Liz asked. "Well, at first I wasn't even worried about Mary, and her mother coming over tomorrow, but now—"

276

"But now what? What has you so concerned and worried Eli?"

"I don't know, but what if she thinks like everyone else, that I like her as more than just a friend?"

"If she does, you just tell her how you really feel about her."

"Nephew, I agree with your mother." Lee-Lee entered the conversation. "You should tell her how you feel. The only thing I'll add is this, what if you begin to feel more for her after you tell her you only wish to be her friend?"

"I don't know, what do you think I should do?"

"Why don't you just let things take their own course and at the right time you'll know exactly what to tell her," Lee-Lee said.

"That's incredible," Eli said.

"Why is that so incredible?" Liz and Lee-Lee asked at the same time.

"Because that's exactly what I had planned on doing before I began to worry myself about it."

Lee-Lee moved around the table and kissed Eli on the top of his head and said, "You are entirely too smart, and I for one can not wait to see who you grow up to become."

"I can tell you that now Aunt Lee-Lee. I'm going to be a lawyer just like my Daddy wanted me to be." "Eli, you mean to tell me that you actually remember your Dad telling you that when you were only around four, or five years old?" Elizabeth asked.

"Yes Ma'am. Really I was four going on five because that's the same year I got that red fire truck with the sirens. He told me that he wanted me to be a great lawyer like Johnny Cochran when we were at Grandma Ella's and I was sitting in that little chair that Nana had bought for me," Eli explained.

"That's amazing, what else can you remember from when you were real little?" his mother asked.

"Like what?" Eli questioned.

"Like anything, what about the time we went to the lake and—"
"And I told Elisha that I could swim and she was about to throw me into the water, but you yelled at her to stop. Mama, I was so glad you stopped her, because I probably would have drowned."

"Elizabeth, it isn't that mind blowing that he's able to remember a few years back," Lee-Lee told her.

"I wouldn't think so either, but he remembers the exact words that were said."

"Mama, I can remember a whole lot of stuff. Like when we were in the car coming from that church we were invited to. You asked me on the way home what Pastor Stevens said about Eve when she disobeyed God."

"What was it that he said Eli?"

"I told you then that he said Eve had sex with Satan."
"What?" Lee-Lee asked when she heard that.
Elizabeth answered, "We went to a church belonging to friends of James and their Pastor's guest had a lot of abstract ideologies. And to make sure none of it had taken root in Eli's mind we asked him if he believed what the Pastor had said. I didn't even remember the man's name until Eli just said it."
"So, you didn't believe that pastor, did you Eli?" LeeLee asked.

"No Aunt Lee-Lee, of course not. Daddy told me he couldn't find that anywhere in the bible. See that's the only way to know if it comes from man or if it comes from God."

"Okay Liz, you're beginning to scare me now because you got a look on your face like your son is the Golden Child or something."

"No, it's not that, it's not that at all. But it is astonishing, because he couldn't have been no more than a few months past three when we attended that church." "Mama, did you hear that?" Lee-Lee asked Mama Bee as she shouted toward the door of her room, "You have a miracle child for a grandson."

"Oh, Lee-Lee I'm not saying that at all," Liz said. "I'm just playing girl, but it would be nice to have some good fortune to finally come to our family."

"We do have good fortune and plenty of it I might add," Liz said.

"I wish you'd point it out to me so I can recognize it," Lee-Lee told her.

"It's everywhere, all around us. For starters, we have each other. We have good health, peace of mind. We laugh and enjoy each other's company all of the time. These children are a true blessing because we are able and definitely responsible for shaping and molding their futures. And the list goes on and on. If we only look at the things we do have instead of the things that we don't."

280

"What are you out here yelling about now?" Mama Bee asked as she emerged from out of her bedroom. "We were just learning of how Eli is able to remember things and conversations that took place when he was just three years old," Liz shared with Mama Bee.

"I think that's just great that he has been given that gift, but Eli the older you become the more you'll realize that it may be a blessing and a curse.

The only way to numb the curse part is to wash it away with alcohol, she said to herself not allowing her grandson or anyone else to hear her remedy.

"Where have y'all been at?" Mama Bee asked Reggie, Darrick, Larry, and Cookie as they all came through the back door.

"Nowhere Mama, we just went around the block to see if Arney and J.J. could come outside."

"How in the hell could y'all go nowhere and somewhere at the same damn time?" Mama Bee asked them. " But don't go back out that door no more today," she warned them.

Then came the whining and the complaining, but she wasn't hearing it.

It was Liz who said, "You all might want to stay inside anyway, because Mama has promised to share more of our family history with us."

Then came the, forreal Mamas, are yous, and the whens as they ran up to Mama Bee pulling on her asking again and again.

"Yes, yes, and yes," she told them. "Go get Debra, and Elisha, then meet me in the living room."

They shot toward the front and she went into her room.

CHAPTER 17

When Mama Bee made it into the living room and sat down on her sofa, the children began repositioning themselves.

Lee-Lee threw her feet up under her on the loveseat and made a comment on the beautiful flowers her mother had received while they were out.

Elizabeth gave a compliment as well, before scooting her chair about two feet closer. "We don't want you to feel pressured by us to tell—" Liz began.

Mama Bee cut her off by saying, "Nonsense, I know how important it is for our people to never ever forget what was bestowed upon us. It's certainly obvious that as the years go by, the next generation cares less. It's like they feel that since they wasn't there and it didn't happen to them, or their mother or grandmothers, then why should they even bother themselves with the trips down memory lane.

"But I will tell you all why it's so very important that we never lose sight of the fact, nor allow the next generation to live a life uninformed. The exact same blood that runs through the veins of every black person in America was caused to spill in these streets of

America in some of the most excruciating, horrifying, dreadful ways that not even Satan himself could have conjured up. I say the same blood because the cost of our citizenship was paid for by the bloodshed of an ancestors.

"And if it was possible for that ancestor's cause of death to somehow be communicated to us today, we'd be face to face with the terror that pushes one over into insanity, or worse.

"I believe it to be important that I educate, before telling the history that was given me by my Granny. Because you could go to school for a hundred years and never discover none of these truths in any of them history books that they're teaching from.

"The Dread Scotts, the A. Philip Randolph's, Ella Bakers, Denmark Vesey's, and none of the Malcolm X's., They wouldn't be expressed and illustrated in the manner that explains that some deaths were welcomed so we'd be free to pursue pride, dignity, and a rightful place in a America that has been built on the black back; study Martin Luther's walk. A lot of deaths were untimely, because their lives were snuffed out in their prime.

"If I fail to give this generation what has been given to me, then I would be at fault as well," Mama Bee said and then sighed deeply.

She looked the room over, then continued. "It's a shame how we as a race of people have allowed ourselves to distance ourselves from our own roots. No wonder we've grown so far apart.

"Furthermore, how could we possibly expect to grow if we have willingly stunted our own growth. And without roots we wither and then we die. How horrible a death for a race of people who have endured so much hardship, and suffering.

"I was taught a very long time ago that if you won't stand for something, you will fall for anything. Look at today's society. We don't stand for one another in pursuit of forward progress. We, as a people, have been exchanged for I as an individual, who's out for self.

"I fear the future of my people, because the next generation is destined for complete separation and absolute consciou unawareness.

"I want y'all to listen to me very carefully and understand all that I'm saying to you. It's very important that you descendants of slavery never forget that lives were sacrificed in brutal deaths so that you would have the right to conquer your future.

"Drugs, prisons, and even the alcohol that I indulge in so often are all designed obstacles put in place to divide so that you may be conquered.

"Divide and conquer, is a known fact so the house slave was pitted against the field slave. Light skin against dark skin. And today, you witness the same form of selfdestructiveness when the one black gang member kills the other black gang member and then the murder cycle continues. How is that the young have the old as their opps? "My friend Bunch has never been accused of being the sharpest knife in the drawer, but she show expressed smarts when she said, 'The reason why the Klu Klux Klan took off their capes and hoods is because now they are able to say, 'the niggers are doing all of the work for us.'

"So, you have to believe that they're just sitting back, posted up in their higher up positions waiting on what remains after the fallout, so they can have their way with whatever survives, probably the black women. I look around, or whenever I turn on the news, I see it happening all over these United States of America; black men are slowly but surely on their way to becoming an endangered species.

"It hurts me to say, but the truths are evident. Our eyes have become so blinded that we're unable or unwilling to see that by allowing ourselves to become disassociated with our family, who were enslaved, brutally beaten, and killed, some eventually freed, but dehumanized. We are in reality ushering ourselves into a form of modern day slavery.

"Our minds handicapped and institutionalized into accepting our plight as being the norm. My great great Grandfather Eli, taught his wife Bernice to look closely at the history of our Jewish brothers and sisters. They too were enslaved, made to suffer for over four hundred years. They believed in and trusted God to deliver them out of bondage.

"Negroes got a hold of the same scriptures and cried out to God who's been known to set free and deliver. St. Peter was inspired by God to record: 'If God allowed His spirit to rest upon these people who I once called common, but then instructed by God not to call common, then who are we to deny them.'

"Black folks and Jewish people sincerely need a greater association, because it's so very obvious that both races have been chosen and called by God himself. He chastises those He love. We suffer for a reason, His reason! When will these two races of people allow God Almighty to enlighten the eyes of their understanding so that His will upon Earth may be done and our purpose achieved.

"If I can recognize that fact, me being an ole lady of Louisville, Kentucky, surely scholars and intellectuals around the globe are able to. And even if the divinely designed association ain't forthcoming, the black race at least should learn from the lesson Jewish unity has taught.

"Heaven, and Earth will pass away before the Jewish race will allow themselves to be enslaved ever again. As a matter of fact, you best to be careful about how you tread the holy land. But not so for our black race, we have allowed our minds to evolve into the stagnant subhuman state that has been embedded in us by those who enslaved us.

"Obviously, the effects of our enslavement has had sort of a post-traumatic affect. I say this because it is apparent, if any group of people are held back for hundreds of years and even put to death for even attempting to learn how to read as the Negro slave was; then after the elapse of that time is the immediate presence of the traumatic stress.

"Instead of developing adequate schooling institutions, they built prisons. Instead of adequate housing, they erected projects, places for blacks to wallow in their own misery.

"And instead of financial institutions being established for and ran by black folks, they instituted a welfare system that further handicapped the mentality of the negro.

"So many devices devised that prevented our race from realizing that just because the chains were removed, did not mean that slavery had ended.

"I also agree with others who argue that it is totally up to the individual to free his or her own mind from the slave mentality and then be provided with the government assistance.

"For I was able to see with my own eyes how they gave the Vietnamese housing out there at the Americana Apartments in 1985, with tax exemptions, and money to start up their own businesses. All that assistance for folks who had only twenty years prior killed hundreds of thousands of American children. But the black fingers that picked the cotton to enrich the country, receives nothing, even after fighting til death in those wars.

WE SUFFER FOR A REASON

"Don't get me wrong, I love America for one reason and one reason alone. I've been provided the freedom to worship Jesus, when, where, and how I want to. But it appears that too is in jeopardy. My point is: America has the strangest way of showing thanks.

"And lets not begin expounding on America's need to apologize to its black sisters, and brothers for the treatment of their parents and for the traumas we still suffer.

"Does it strike anyone as odd that slavery still remains intact in the 13th Amendment of the United States of America constitution?

"But that adamant attitude only signifies who's responsibility it is to demand retribution. And if the black race never discovers nor feels the absolute need to come together for this common cause, then it may be no hope for us as a race of people striving together for our rightful place in this new millennium.

"We, as a race of people, haven't got a clue. We are still being blinded by individual wants and desires. The need to become successful, and then, 'I can help others because, they'll listen to a rich man, you say.' Maybe so, maybe so. My point is, without retribution, our lives and our future remain in the hands of our oppressors, and if their plans for the world backfires on them, what becomes of us?

"We inadvertently become plunged deeper into the mire maybe until suffocation succumbs us. Our plea, our goal, our demand: Give us what we need to establish our own safeguards against future catastrophes that appear to be inevitable.

"Our suffering reminds us of many truths. We will prevail over the most demeaning and impossible obstacles. We were born with survival kits, built into our psyche. And most importantly, we are capable.

"So the question that smashes, breaks, and shatters the fetters from the mind is: How can I just sit back and allow my fate to rest solely in the hands of people who have shown me time and time again that they don't give a damn about what happens to me or my children? "This fact has been illustrated in an unrecorded history. So, ask yourselves: How on God's green earth can I simply sit back and leave my fate in the hands of folks who have shown me time after time that they don't give a real good damn about what happens to me or my babies. They don't even believe us to be responsible enough to lead and guide our own into the uncertainty of tomorrow.

"If it was otherwise, we would be provided with the necessary provisions that would guarantee the utilization of God given abilities. The same and exact abilities that have enabled us to sing and smile, even dance a little through and after four hundred and sixty five years of slavery.

"But I don't speak merely of the songs sung, nor the smiles, despite of. I point out the ability to overcome and go on to greatness.

"Now seeing with your own eyes that this greatness will never be allowed, due to their inner fears, we must achieve and introduce our greatness to the world by any means necessary. And afterwards, show the love that gives the ability to do the things that only God Himself could ordain.

"There's only one other race of people who has traveled through the valley of the shadow of death and prevailed to a position to become a light to others. I commend you my Jewish sisters and brothers. I'm not instructed to make you love my black sin, but I have been commanded to love you as well as your nation that is and always will be the apple of the Lord's eye.

"Whew, I know I promised y'all a story based on our family's history, but if you're not able to develop a thought pattern, or a need for action that prevents reoccurrence, then what's the purpose of discovering one's own history?

So, I thought I'd enlighten my own family with my thoughts that I've developed from learning, research, and knowledge passed on to me by my great Grandparents."

"Mama, it amazes me how you're able to speak as a scholar whenever you desire to, but most of the time you—," Liz began.

"She hasn't told you?" Lee-Lee intervened with the question.

"Told me what?" Liz asked.

"My mother taught psychology for two years and took courses in philosophy years ago."

"I did those things many years ago when people use to be interested enough to at least openly discuss black issues," she said.

"Granny Bee, I wanted to know more about my great great great Grandfather Eli, who I got my name from. And now I also want to learn why we have to suffer so much," voiced Eli with such a look of concern covering his face that Mama Bee wanted to comfort him with detailed answers. But instead she placed a hand to her grandchild's face and said, "And you will learn more, right after we figure out who's going to fix us some sandwiches, and what we're going to have to go with them."

"Lets have fried bologna and cheese with corn chips on the side," suggested Larry.

"Sounds good to me," Mama Bee announced.

"That's what's up," Reggie said as he slapped his brother Darrick upside his head, waking him up.

"Man, what's wrong with you. You got a death wish or something?" Darrick asked his assailant.

"Y'all cut that foolishness out," Mama Bee yelled and then added, "Get up and get ready to help your mother with them sandwiches."

Again Liz asked, "Mama, these are some really nice flowers. Where did they come from?"

"Oh, these things. They are some nice ones, aren't they," stated Mama Bee after easing over and gently stroking a petal.

When sandwiches and beverages were consumed and everyone had gathered back together in the living room, Mama Bee brought her grandson Eli close to her right side, looked at him and said, "I wasn't a bit surprised to learn that you too possess an extra ordinary ability to remember events and conversations of your past, because I too can remember with such vivid clarity that it sometimes frustrates me. Sometimes I even result to drowning some memories, but for you I'm certain that it's a gift from God to be used for the benefit of others. It just may be your mission to learn how to use it. "I was only nine years old at the time when I sat next to my great Grandmother as she shared with us these events; She said," she sat there atop a bale of hay as Eli preached to them the gospel. There were many folks gathered there, even quite a few from surrounding plantations. But mainly they was from that Bodiford plantation, on who's land they remained even after slavery was supposedly abolished. It was right there at the near edge of that plantation. A mere stone's throw from my Granny's shack that Eli would open up the scriptures like you wouldn't believe. My Granny would tease and say that an angel of God came down from heaven and explained them words to Eli.

"On this particular occasion he was telling the congregation that the words contained in the book of the bible are the absolute truth and have never wavered' He said, 'I spoke the words of this book many years ago while our hands and feet was still bound in chains. I told them of the Almighty's promise to all those who trust in Him, that He would send a Savior to His people who would lead them out of bondage.'

"And it was no sooner than them words had left Eli's mouth that James Bodiford, the wicked slave owner of the plantation, sprung from out of nowhere, smacking the bible from Eli's hand, grabbing him by the collar of his shirt and he then began spitting outlandish insults, and all sorts of blasphemous remarks about God and Jesus Christ.

"He uttered contemptuous profanities that he held for the negro race. His tongue was fixated on the use of the term, nigger. He shouted over and over again that a good nigger was a dead nigger. And he insisted that the North's law about slavery being over didn't mean a damn thing down here in their Confederate South. Nothing but hunting season year round, he viciously spat venom.

"And he spat into my great grandfather's face before knocking him to the ground, leaving them all there terrified and shaken as he walked back up the hill. "Granny, along with a few others went to Eli's aide, but he was such a proud man which was exactly the reason why he refused to leave the area that needed him the

296

most. He dusted himself off and retrieved the black leather bound bible, dusted it off as well, then picked up right where he had been interrupted.

'That Savior came in the form of a man as did the one sent to lead His nation of Israel out of Egypt. Our God, and Father seems to always work His great wonders through the means of those He has created. 'But in these last days He's sending His only begotten Son to lead us to Himself in heaven.

'So, why run away when God has provided us with an opportunity to stand. To stand and fight the good fight of faith. Trusting Him and His word that promised He will never leave, nor forsake us, but always provide us with a way of escape.

'We have to stay united and provide one another with the same strength that has been promised to us. There's no need for us to leave these lands that we have tilled and planted our crops on, or leave behind the schoolhouse my Bernice has toiled to keep active.

'We're destined to be led and fed by God to plant our faith, and reap a harvest of souls for the Kingdom. 'Let's bow our heads and lift up a fervent prayer for our persecutors, that they may come to the knowledge that together and soul to soul we all will fulfill our calling.'

"Yes, I'm able to recall so many things. It's like I spent time right there on that Bodiford planation," Mama Bee shared.

"Eli brought the people together and made everyone aware of the fact that no one was all alone. He was truly a leader and a guide, a light to and for many.

"Eventually some of the white folks began to listen, and they started to read for themselves exactly what the bible expressed about loving others. Unfortunately, it was that turn of events that was the beginning of the end, that would ultimately claim Eli's life.

"But I don't want to speak on that. Instead we'll reflect on better memories," Mama Bee announced, making an effort to keep herself from becoming tearful. "As I remember, something strange, but powerful came over my great great Grandfather that changed the way inwhich he administered the Word to others. These things my great Grandmother shared with me because the change began before I was even born.

"My Granny Bernice told my mother that she may be too young to understand, but she prays that she would always remember and never forget.

"So, my mother would tell me, 'Later, much later my own heart would be blessed by a light that shinned for Eli.'

"So, in my adulthood I searched the scriptures diligently, wanting the same awakening that my great great Grandparents had experienced. I never obtained it no matter the work and faith I applied.

"So, coupled with other events, I put the bible down which caused my relationship with God to falter and as I view through new eyes I see that I'm the cause of my own unassurance' Lord have mercy on me!"

"Lee-Lee, Liz, no matter where our little group takes us, we must let the Word of God be our compass. Do y'all hear me?" Mama Bee asked.

She received several yes Ma'am's, then she continued. "I'm supposed to be telling you all the good times. It just seems so hard to do when there wasn't that many back during those times. After those Sunday gatherings out by the barn our family would all go to eat at my great great Grandparent's place. Their little shack could barely contain them all, but somehow, some way, they managed every Sunday.

"They say way back in the day Eli seemed to always be upset with his daughter Jessie for giving birth to Stella at such a young age. She was only thirteen. And they were always at odds with one another.

"He would angrily tell her that the days of young girls birthing babies for the master's profit was over with, and the Lord's way was the only way now. He would tell Jessie about how much the Lord desired for her to live a holy life with a mind aimed toward Him and not influenced by a slave's way of thinking.

"She would fuss back at him, questioning her father with, 'How would you really know the Lord's way, or what do you know about schooling? Have you ever been? Do you really know what you're telling everybody and causing them to believe is really the truth? How do you know you're even telling us right when you never went to any school and learnt to read them there words of that there bible?'

"That day Jessie sprung up from where she sat and ran over to where the bible lay and after getting it she sat it down hard onto the table in front of where Eli sat. And despite the protests being made by her mother, Jessie, in tears, now shouted, 'Read it to me, read to me the part where it say thou shalt not have a child at thirteen or the Lord won't love you, or it.

300

" 'Go on, read it,' she screamed with more tears coming from her eyes, but looking sternly and intently at her Father.

"Eli gripped the bible with both hands and just peered down at it as if he could look right through it's leather binding.

"Everyone at the table looked on with perplexed and confused faces of anticipation. All but Granny, she having an encouraging look, she simply reached over and laid a reassuring hand atop of her husband's and then told her daughter that that would be enough.

" 'Naw Mama, I know that you too would probably like to know if you are being given the right words.'

"Bernice just looked at her daughter Jessie with a look that said, she meant that she had had enough.

"Even after Jessie had regained her seat, Granny's hand remained on top of Eli's as he slowly lifted his head and made eye contact with his wife. Squeezing her hand firmly, he used his other hand to open his bible. He looked onto the page he had opened up to and just peered at it for a time.

"Then he said, 'Spirit of God I do thank you for resting upon me. Thank you Lord for counting me worthy.'

"Eli took his finger and scrolled the page. He looked up at his family who surrounded his table. Then bowing his head back into the bible he began: 'What sh-all we say th-en? That Gen-tiles who did not pur-sue ri-ghteous-ness have at-tained to ri-ghteous-ness, e-ven the right-eous-ness of faith. But Is-ra-el, pur-su-ing the law of righteous-ness has not at-tained to the law of righteous-ness. Why?' "He then peered around his table at all of the faces that sat there, then continued dispute the fact of him barely being able to read well: 'Be-cause they did not se-ek it by faith, but -as it -were, by the-works of the law. For they stu-mbled at that stum-bling stone. As it -is writ-ten, be-hold I lay in Zi-on a stum-bling stone and rock of of-fense and whoever be-lieves on Him will -not be put to shame.'

"Before closing up his bible, Eli said, 'Ro-mans chap-ter nine ver-ses thir-ty thro-ugh thir-ty three.' Everyone's mouths were left hanging wide open. Everyone's except for my Granny's who sat there with a look of pride and one of knowing.

"You see, everyone at that table knew that Eli was just like all the other black folk in the south. At least ninety nine point nine percent of them. They were all illiterate, and the older you were the greater the certainty of your being so.

"So, no one understood how Eli was able to read from that bible. Just like his daughter had accused, he had never had any learning, but it certainly appeared that Granny knew something.

"When the subject was revisited, I was told that Eli had in previous times preached to the people messages that he had only heard told to him by white slave owners. Never having been taught to read, nor to write, so his messages were messages originating from their oppressors. This always puts into question the depth of the messages truth.

"But a time came that the teachings presented to the people by Eli changed. I was told by my great Grandmother, who's Mother had shared with her how Eli would spend hours upon hours alone speaking with God. Just him and his bible. He would emerge from the secret place sharing with Granny what book of the bible he would be speaking to the people from, as he rehearsed his message with her.

"She insinuated that Eli had a spiritual guide, a gift to our family that would bless us all through the generations. But unfortunately there seems to be more curses than blessings. But all in all we've endured and here we sit gathered together. The only part lacking is the most essential element of every household, the adult male figure."

As Mama Bee sat there contemplating on her own words, everyone else began in their own discussions, but it was Liz who spoke up to the whole.

"So it's clear that we can not and we shall not allow our group to falter, because not only is it essential to our family but to our community as well. So beginning Monday we'll revisit the notes Elisha and Debra took down and proceed from there."

"Sounds good to me," Lee-Lee said clearly indicting that she didn't plan on going anywhere anytime soon.

Eli still snuggled up under Mama Bee, had over a million questions running around in his head, but the only one he posed to his Granny was, "What can we do to make sure that all black people realize their Ancestors suffered for a reason?"

Apparently the question caught her off guard, judging from her facial expression.

Having thought about Eli's question for a moment Mama Bee answered, "I suppose it's our responsibility to do our part in making sure our people are aware of the fact that it's possible for this present generation to become oppressed mentally as well as physically if we all remain asleep. You see grandson, he who does not know his history is condemned to repeat it."

"Our generation's responsibility is to inform the next generation and so on and so forth," added Liz as she pulled up on the other side of her son. Then she went on to say, "Listen fellows, I want all of you to know that just because we women are starting up this group it does not mean that you all will be excluded. We will form classes that teach history lessons, our history. But what's most important is the care and attention that will be placed on everyones schooling. Making sure we produce a whole lot of college students. So, that being said, Debra, you and Elisha put tutors in the notes you both make. I'm so very excited about forming our group," she concluded.

"It's called Lynx Mama," Elisha said.

"I know what it's called, but it's ours, it's our group, but we'll share it with the whole world."

"That will be a good thing and like we've said, we will begin on the ground work for it on Monday. But for now lets get prepared for bed, 'cause I have to get up early to put the finishing touches on my Card Party," stressed Mama Bee.

Ms. Bee was in rare form on the night of her Card Party as she greeted her guest who entered her home. When she got a break from that she went into the kitchen to observe how her granddaughters were coming along.

"Debra on your next batch of chicken let them stay in the grease just a little while longer to allow them to come out browner," Mama Bee instructed her grandchild.

"Mama, I know what I'm doing. Everybody don't like their chicken dark brown and stuff."

"Little girl, I'm not going to let you get on my nerves today," replied Mama Bee, then mumbled, "Use that same skillet to beat you to sleep.," as she made her way to Elisha's side. "Sweetie, what them burgers doing?"

"They're coming out just fine Granny."

"Okay baby, 'cause you never want them to come up out of the pan with any pink in the middle. Well, I see you both got this, so I'll just go back out there and entertain my guest."

"Come on Bee and play a few hands with us until some more folks show up," suggested Bunch. "I was just about there, what's the game?"

In unison three people, including Bunch said, "Tonk."

"It is not your deal Elroy. Every time anybody sets the deck down, you grab it. That's how you know somebody is trying to cheat," voiced Waltlee.

"My man, let me explain something to you. Whenever you play against people as sweet as you all, there's no need to cheat," stressed Elroy.

"Let me explain a little something to you. If I catch you cheating tonight, I'ma cut your fingers off and leave you with just two thumbs. But at least you'll still be able to hitch hike from either side of the street."
"Ima deal right now so I can show you how easy it is to take the sugar out of sweetness."

"Bee, don't you hear somebody knocking at your door?" asked Pat.

"LeeLee, LeeLee get the front door," Mama Bee yelled from the dining room.

"Mama you call me from upstairs to get the door and all of y'all are already down here?" questioned LeeLee as she made her way down the steps and to the front door.

Knock! Knock!!!

"Hold your horses, I'm coming," she said as she opened the door.

"Oh my God!"

"Hey sweet brown sugar," Poppa Charlie tells her as he takes her into his arms.

After their embrace LeeLee took him by the arm and led him into the next room. When Mama Bee laid eyes on him she was surprised, and shocked to see him, but she continued on in the hand of tonk she was playing. "Bee, ain't you going to come over here and greet me?" asked Poppa Charlie.

"Yeah I'ma greet you alright, greet you with a well placed uppercut," Mama Bee told him.

"Who in the hell let the black alley cat drag him in here?" asked Bunch with an attitude.

"It must have been your black cat, you old wore out, worn down whistling warlock."

"You got your nerves you broke down, raggedy river roach," Bunch jonesed back.

"You two cut it out, 'cause I ain't going through this with you two. I ain't putting up with y'alls foolishness, and I mean it," yelled Mama Bee over top of both of them. "Bernie you heard her start it with me," complained Poppa Charlie.

"I ain't heard nothing and I ain't your damn Bernie."

"See what you done did. You done went and upset her you old old real old thirsty diseased Tasmanian devil donkey." "I done told you Charles, I ain't playing with you now." Mama Bee used his government expressing her seriousness.

"There she is, I remember you from church Thursday. How you doing sweetheart?" Poppa Charlie asked Elizabeth, changing the subject.

"I'm doing fine. How are you doing? Poppa Charlie, correct?"

"Yes, that is correct. Why don't you come over here and sit by me," he suggested.

As Liz sat down, Mama Bee got up and went to the front room 'cause she heard someone coming into her house without knocking. When she made it into the living room her young friend Jackie was being hugged on by her grandson Larry.

"Larry let that woman go. By the time you turn twenty one she'll be about forty."

"A cougar," said Larry as he released his hold on Jackie.

"Ms. Bee your grandson is a trip. This boy had your door wide open before I even made it up the steps." "Yeah, I know he's a trip, just like I know he's about to make me send him on a trip. Him and his hot nuts. And where are the rest of y'all at Larry?"

"They're outside trying to tell them other people where to park."

"What other people? Jackie you can gone in there baby, let me look out here and see what this boy is talking about."

When Mama Bee opened her front door, Tommy, and Kat was standing right there.

"How long have you been standing here? Come on in this house. Kat, girl how have you been? I haven't seen you since July girl?"

"Bee I've been down bad, but I'm doing fine now. So good in fact I decided to come around here and win me some of your money."

"You might win you some money, I'm not going to say that you won't. But it won't be my money, I can assure you of that," Mama Bee said before she broke out into laughter.

Kat and Tommy joined in on the laughter as they made their way into the dining room.

"Let me get some more chairs and set up another table over here," she shared with her new arrivals.

"Waltlee, you always running around Victory Park talking a bout what you'll do to somebody with your box cutter, but you haven't did nothing to nobody since seventy-one," Elroy stated having built his courage up.

"Elroy you just sitting over there begging for a buck fifty," threatened Waltlee.

"Ain't going to be nobody giving nobody no buck fifties up in here. You came here to play some cards and to purchase some of my granddaughter's fried chicken, and cheese burgers. So, what are you all waiting on?" asked Mama Bee.

"I'll take a plate and have them put extra macaroni on it and earn a tip," Waltlee expressed.

"My goodness Jackie, you sure have grown into a fine specimen. Why don't you slide on over here and join me," suggested Mark Wagner.

"I'm good Mr. Wagner, 'cause I ain't looking for no Sugar Daddy right now, and I don't need my eyebrows arched either." replied Jackie.

"Sweetheart, everybody needs a little sugar every once in a while. So, don't let a lil grey fool you, they come with experience." Mark the barber had to let her know.

"I done heard about you and them long rides in your long Cadillac," said Jackie in such a way.

"Don't knock it until you try it," He shot back. "Why don't you leave that girl alone Mark. You and that Cadillac are about the same age, antique!" Pat said and brought the room to laughter.

"Ain't you got your nerves. I seen that exact same wig on Tina Turner in one of her first videos and it looked good on her. Sitting on top of your head it looks like a lazy lonely leprous leeping lion's mane."

And the laughs escalated once more.

"Here you are in two thousand and four, sitting over there in a troop suit. Ain't nobody told you those went out of style at the same time your shag did? Ain't nobody trying to bring the eighties back but you."

Man you done gone crazy back in the eighties," chided Pat without letting up.

"Y'all let Mark alone before you cause him to lose his rent room money over here," Ms. Bunch chimed in. "Heifer you just taking Mark Wagners's side 'cause he probably pays your rent from time to time," Kat spoke out for the first time, and probably out of jealousy. "Mama, here's somebody I want to introduce you to," LeeLee said standing in the doorway.

Mama Bee sat in her chair for a moment because she hadn't a clue as to who this was standing in her archway. She finally stood and then approached.

"Mama this is Elaine Jordan, the woman we told you we invited, and this over here is her daughter, Mary, your grandson Eli's little friend."

"And that's all they are," voiced Elaine as she looked in her daughter's direction.

Mary didn't return the stare, but simply said, "Mama!"
"What are you insinuating, or are you bluntly saying your daughter is too good for my grandbaby?" Mama Bee questioned her with attitude.

"No Ma'am, I'm not saying that at all. I'm only reminding my child that her studies leave no room for courtship."

"Courtship? Girl where you from, out Prospect?" Jackie asked from the background.

"No, I'm not from Prospect. We reside in Anchorage."

"Same thang!" exclaimed Jackie

"It don't matter where you from. It's where you at," declared Darrick while selling Waltlee a soda.

"You stay out of grown folks business," Mama Bee advised him, then added, "But what he said." Then she went on to say, "I have no problem with you and your child coming into my home, but like I told my daughters when they told me you was invited, this is no ordinary gathering, but we're all family here, so at the end of the day everyone is welcomed." "How are you two, I'm glad you both made it, again I'm Eli's Mom Elizabeth and I assure you Ms. Jordan my son's mind is where it's supposed to be". Elizabeth made Elaine aware.

" Come on in here and take your coats off and make yourselves comfortable.
Mary, straight through there you'll find the kitchen and my two granddaughters. You can go and introduce yourself.

"Ms. Elaine you can come on in here and take Liz's seat,
'cause she's losing more money than we're making," Mama Bee instructed. Then she went on to ask, "Is everyone okay in here? Can I get anybody anything?"

"Yeah Bee, you can get me a new deck of cards. This deck here is being mean to me," exclaimed Proctor.

He being one of the more experienced card players at the table, he actually knew when to switch decks so that cards would flow in his favor. And the rules are: Any player at anytime can ask that the decks be exchanged as long as it isn't during the playing of a hand.

"Croc, you're always complaining about something, 'cause something ain't going your way," said Elroy. "And you're always minding everybody's business but your own. And the name is Proctor. So call me Proc, or Proctor or don't call me nothing at all."

"I'll call you nothing at all. You nothing as—"

"Hey, hey let's play nice now," Elizabeth interjected. "What am I supposed to do with these five cards?" asked Elaine while holding her cards up to her face.

"You're supposed to play tonk with them," LeeLee told her.

"Tonk?" questioned Elaine.

"Yeah, let me show you," Lee-Lee said as she stood behind Elaine viewing her card hand.

"Y'all don't mind do you? She don't know how to play," Lee-Lee asked the other card players.

"She don't know how to play, are you sure? She knows how to play don't she?" asked Pat with suspicion.

"I'll put up for her this first hand," Lee-Lee advised as she placed five dollars onto the ante pile.

Her and Elaine's first hand was a success and the five dollars had gained them an additional twenty-five dollars minus Mama Bee's five dollar cut for being the house lady.

"Mama, can we go upstairs and show Mary our notes for our club?" Debra asked.

Mama Bee answered, "Debra I don't care if y'all go up or downstairs, but if I have to get up and serve somebody a plate, you don't make anything."

"Mama we won't be long."

"You've been warned."

"Do anybody need anything before we go upstairs?" Debra asked the entire room.

"I can use another ice cold grape soda," informed Proctor.

"That's my brother's department," Debra told him. "Speaking of the boys, they've been extremely quiet, which means they're doing something they ain't got no business doing. Debra you go and find them and tell them I said get here right now."

"Dang mama, we was on our way to do something." "Girl, you better do what I told you to do before your company see you get embarrassed," Mama Bee threatened.

"Idle threats," said she as she made her way out of her Grandmother's presence.

Moments later the boys came running into the dinging room, everybody except for Larry and Eli. "Where are y'all at and what are y'all doing?" Mama Bee asked.

"We're right here in the dining room and we ain't doing nothing but standing here," answered Darrick.

"Boy, quit playing with me before I knock one of your tooth loose."

"Mama, we've been on the front porch throwing tennis balls across the street," squealed Cookie.

"You bet not throw no more balls across the street and if I catch you doing it I'ma start throwing balls across the street," she threatened. "Where is Larry and Eli at?" she asked.

"They sitting on the front steps, 'cause Eli's scared to talk to Mary," Cookie continued to tattle tale. "Boy be quiet!" Reggie said, giving Cookie a hard nudge. Not because of his concern for Eli, but more so, because he has been trying to break his little brother from telling Mama Bee everything they did.

Outside on the front steps Eli and Larry's conversation went something like this: "Man, what are you so afraid of? It's not like you don't know her," Larry explained.

"I'm not afraid at all. It's just that everyone is calling her my girlfriend, but it's not even like that."

"Well, she likes you, and you like her, so what's the problem?"

"I've never had a girlfriend before so I wouldn't know what to say to one."

"Man, it isn't any different. You say the same things you've been saying and maybe even more. But first you'll have to ask her if she wants to be your girlfriend."

"What? No, I couldn't do that."

"Yes you can and you'll never forget it either. I still remember my first time asking."

"You do? How many girlfriends have you had cousin Larry?"

"I don't know exactly how many, but you never forget your first time asking. Mines went like this: "Will you be my girlfriend. Yes or no square, check one. And she checked the yes square. And then it was on and popping.""

"What was on and popping?"

"What? Man, kisses, during recess. Well at least until school ended and then she started to go with Smooth because he had gotten a brand new green machine for his birthday. Thats not whats important. What's important is, Mary could be the one."

"The one?"

"Yeah she could be so perfect that you'll never need to look for another until next summer."

"I don't know, she might not want to be my girlfriend."

"Oh, yes she does."

"How do you know?"

"Cause if she didn't she wouldn't be here. So come on, lets go back inside so you can say something to her."

"Something like what?"

"Something like: Thank you for coming. Are you enjoying yourself?"

"And then what?"

"And then whatever's clever . . ."

When Eli and Larry made it into the house it appeared that the entire house was in party mode. The music was playing and there was dancing being done by many individuals in Mama Bee's living room. A old track by Escape, escaped through the speakers and flooded the house with sultry vocals that caused bodies to sway and made others groove.

It was festive and made Mama Bee remember why she loved her Card Parties. It was never about the money, but totally about the party part.

"Hey," Eli said when he made it over to where Mary stood.

"Hey," she replied.

"I was hoping we could talk for a little while, but it's so loud in here. Would you mind going into the kitchen with me?" Eli finally asked.

"Sure," she said.

When they were seated, Eli just took flight.

"It's embarrassing. I mean, I don't know if it's wrong or right, but to have everybody looking at me talking about me. It's just embarrassing."

"Slow down Eli and tell me exactly what you're trying to say."

"Well, having everyone think that you are my girlfriend and I don' know, I'm just embarrassed, because I don't want you to think that I gave them that idea."

"I don't think that."

"Good, 'cause I would never do that. Besides, we're only friends who enjoy talking to each other over the phone, and laughing and talking to each other. Oh, did I already say that once?"

"Yes, but it's okay because it's true. When we talk I can tell that you're not like other boys. You really put thought into your words, and—"

"And what?"

"And I really like that. I really like you," she said staring into his eyes.

"I don't think you like me half as much as I like you."

"What if I like you more than that?"

"Then I would have to show you my appreciation," expressed Eli.

"When are you going to being showing me?"

"Right now and then always."

"Pinky promise?"

"Pinky promise," he replied as he extended his pinky to connect with hers.

Even at the tender ages of thirteen, the world could not deny the sincerity contained in their promise.

Back in the dining room the music having subsided, Elizabeth was explaining to Elaine the family's commitment to start their group, Lynx.

Elaine told Elizabeth how the ramifications of such a group would be limitless.

Elizabeth liked the way Elaine Jordan thought. So much so that she informed Lee-Lee of their need to tell Mama Bee that Elaine would be a valued addition to their groups core.

"Lee-Lee if you was to carry her off to the side and pitch the idea, she would recognize your commitment as well," Liz suggested.

"Are you trying to con me girl?"

"No, I'm trying to get Elaine here voted in. She's really smart and I know she'd be able to bring so much to the table Lee-Lee."

"Okay, okay don't whine on me. Obviously you've discovered someone whining is my weakness."

Before Lee-Lee had the chance to address her Mother, Mama Bee had pulled up on them.

"What do you have going on? I see you all over here at the card table, but y'all ain't playing no cards."

"To be honest with you, I can't play the card games they're playing and the only card game I'm familiar with is solitaire," explained Elaine.

"Solitaire. Child what you know about solitaire?" Mama Bee asked.

"I win more times than I lose. Well, when I'm on a roll anyway," Elaine confessed.

"Yeah, but how many ways do you know how to play?"

"I know two ways. No, wait a minute. There's actually three ways that I'm able to play."

"Well, I'm at twenty-seven, and counting. I say and counting, because my grandchild has taught me how to find new ones on the internet."

"That's amazing you know so many ways to play solitaire. Let me ask you, would you mind showing me a few new ways to play if I was to show you the ones I already know?"

"I don't see why not. I think that's completely do-able."

"Mama there's something we'd like to run by you, Elizabeth and I," began Lee-Lee.

"What is it child?"

"We was wondering how you'd feel about Elaine here joining our group?"

"I feel like if she's able to carry her own weight then the more the merrier. Oh, and one other thing. The very first Lynx meeting will be Monday evening at seven thirty and nobody should want to miss our first meeting," Mama Bee advised.

Right then Lee-Lee showed an expression that you had to be standing exactly were she stood in order to truly appreciate. She placed her two hands over her mouth in pure surprise and with a tear coming from wide eyes she said, "Mama look behind you."

"Girl, what's wrong with you?" she asked as she turned in her seat.

"Oh my God!" Mama Bee shouted as she stood. "Sweet Jesus, is that you Rayvontez?"

324

"Yes, it's me Mama."

"Oh my goodness, when did you get home baby?"

"We made it into Louisville yesterday evening, Me and Joann."

"Joann, it's so good to see you too sweetheart. It's been so long."

"Hello Ms. Bee. I tried to get him here for Thanksgiving, but we had two flight cancellations due to the weather being so terrible over there," Joann explained.

"I'm just so glad you both made it. Now Ray come on in here and have a seat. Are you hungry? Let me fix you both a plate, please."

"Mama, that won't be necessary. We can't stay long. We basically dropped our bags off at the hotel, shopped a little, and then came here."

"Hotel, boy you got a big ole room upstairs. You don't have to be staying at no hotel."

"It's okay Mama. Now Joann picked out these things and we want you to open up your gifts. This one is for you," Ray said as he handed his mother a small box.

Mama Bee opened the box and brought out a gold broach encrusted with diamonds.

"Ray, you didn't have to do this. It must have cost a lot."

"Don't worry about that Mama. This is for you as well," he said as he handed his Mother a gift wrapped present.

Having opened her other gift, earrings that glowed from within the box, Mama Bee was now trying to hold back tears, but couldn't.

"I knew you'd like them when I first laid my eyes on them," Joann told her.

"Joann, I don't like them, I love them," declared Mama Bee.

"Mama, I have just one more gift to give you."

"Come on Rayvontez, you gave me everything I needed when you walked through that door." "Well, I hope you love this one more than all the others. I give you another daughter. Me and Joann were married three months ago in Florence."

"Y'all got married in Italy?" asked Larry.

"We sure did and I've been dying to share the news with my family."

"Why didn't you call Ray?"

"Because Mama, we decided to tell you in person."

"Well, I'm overjoyed."

"Come here lil sis, let me take a real good look at you," Ray said to Lee-Lee who'd been anxiously waiting to greet her brother.

"Ray, you look so good boy," Lee-Lee told him from inside of his embrace.

"You can thank Joann for it, 'cause she's my little health nut, strictly organics. Hey look here, don't think I'm not familiar with this one right here," Ray began as he reached out to take ahold of Elizabeth.

"It doesn't seem like you've aged one day Elizabeth. You look exactly the way you did on your wedding day."

"Thank you Ray, but I doubt that I look the same as I did fifteen years ago," Liz contested.

"Ray, I'm so sorry you missed your brother's— Mama Bee began, but got choked up. "Mama, it's not your fault. If anyone's to blame, it's me. I bare it alone. I was the one out of the country trying to discover me. The Lord only knows how Joann was able to track me down, marry me, and then bring me back home to my Mother."

"Ray, are you home for good?" Lee-Lee asked. "It looks that way sis. Here to show my sister and Mother how much I love and miss you both. Besides, how else I'm going to be able to get to know all these little ones running around here?"

The night went on in a most joyful fashion. No one had ever seen Mama Bee so happy.

The women explained to Joann the purpose of and hope for their woman's group. She became more than interested in attending the Monday evening meeting.

Unfortunately, everyone didn't remain in joy, because about the time of the card games conclusion Elroy in a semi-drunken state said, "Now which one of you little bastards pick pocketed me for my wallet?"

"What you got going Elroy?" questioned Mama Bee.

"One of your damn grandkids done went in my damn pocket and stole my damn wallet," Elroy shouted words in a decibel that reverberated throughout the room.

"Now listen here Elroy, I don't know if you done had too much to drink or what, but you standing here falsely accusing my children of stealing from you is something I'm not going to tolerate," shouted Mama Bee in a much higher decibel.

"Bee, I don't give a damn what you say, them little badass kids need their asses whooped, running around here stealing folks stuff."

"Now listen here Elroy, tone it down a little bit in this woman's house," Poppa Charlie voiced as he moved in between Elroy and Mama Bee.

"Watch out Charlie, I want him to explain his self and he aint' got long to do it," she said as her anger steadily grew.

"What I know is my damn wallet ain't grew no damn legs and walked off. Them kids running around here bumping into everybody. But hell you probably the one who taught them the hustle."

As soon as he let those words come out his mouth Pretty Ray had his hand around Elroy's throat. And the vice-like grip caused Elroy's eyes to become protuberant.

"I'll tell you what, you get yourself from my house before you make it worse on yourself," said Mama Bee as Ray shoved him to the front door.

"Bee you act like you blind and can't see what they be running around here doing. All over to five and halves selling power tools and paint sprayers. Stealing 'cause they're little thieves."

"What? Power tools, paint sprayers? You get the hell out of my house Elroy. If your wallet should turn up, I'll personally make sure you get it, along with its contents, if it's anywhere in this house."

Poppa Charlie and Ray escorted Elroy to his car as Mama Bee gathered the boys, and then she began her inquisition.

Once she had Reggie, Darrick, and Larry in their room with the door locked Mama Bee began, "I swear before God if I hear one part of a lie coming from any one of you, I'm going to kill all three of y'all." This was voiced with such anger, sadness, and disappointment mixed that the boys in unison responded,

"I'm sorry Mama."

"Not as sorry as you're going to be. Now get them clothes off."

Then the cries came. Then a knock on the door came. Then Eli's voice came.

"Granny, I need to tell you something."

"What is it Eli? I'm busy in here."

"It's important Granny."

Having unlocked the door, she opened it and asked, "What's important?"

"I have to come in and explain it."

She allowed Eli to come into the room, and once all the way inside he began, "Granny I'm supposed to be in here too, because I was with them the other night."

"You was what? I don't believe you. You couldn't have. Oh Eli, I'm so disappointed in you," she said as tears began to stream down her face.

Mama Bee sat on one of the twin beds and wept more, before finally asking through her tears, "Why? I mean I just can't understand why you all would do this to me. I do everything for you. Even when I say I won't, I end up doing it anyhow, because I love you all so much, but y'all break my heart like this, as if you don't even know how to love back. Is this who I've raised, some young men who don't care about nothing, or no one but themselves? Inconsiderate and uncaring? Are y'all

331

heartless? Are you all evil? If you are then I'm through with you. So you can just stay in here until you figure out what kind of men you want to be. Good or evil?"

Having expressed the depths of her heart, Mama Bee left them there to search within themselves.

CHAPTER 18

Monday evening came and in attendance for the first official Lynx meeting was Elizabeth, Lee-Lee, Joann, Elaine, Debra, Elisha, Mary, and of course, Mama Bee who had just entered the room bearing more refreshments.

The women mapped out their first major goal, which was to obtain a building which would provide office space as well as recreational areas, and classrooms. They devised four classes for the young women to take that would be mandatory. They appointed Saturdays to be for exercise and additional computer technology.

They all were excited about their roles as teachers and mentors. Aiding young women into adulthood was such a motivating force for them that they could barely contain their enthusiasm. They all were trying to visualize the endless possibilities, especially the one of being hands on in the shaping and molding of a future generation.

For Mama Bee it was like possessing an ability to birth doctors, and lawyers, scientists, and scholars into the world. Actually, the possibilities were limitless. They all agreed, Elisha, Debra, and Mary were assured to be the first fruits of this, their movement.

Ever so slowly an entire month had eventually gone by and the boys were still on the strictest punishment they had ever been on. Confined to their room immediately after school. Any and every attempt to do otherwise was always put to terminus by Mama Bee. She had become their warden.

Despite being extremely busy with obtaining a lease on an old building that formerly housed the boys and girls club in the Parkland neighborhood. Mama Bee had learned to multitask.

The old Boys & Girls club had been closed for years. Actually its closing was in tremendous relation to the increase of gang membership, although no one seemed to notice the correlation.

But Lynx would make a difference. It would turn the tide and provide its neighborhood and surrounding communities with an alternative.

Elizabeth, Elaine, and Joann had suggested to Mama Bee that for her securing the lease, a celebration was in order. With this Mama Bee had no problem. Only that it would be an extremely small gathering of family and close friends.

While they were preparing the necessary ingredients for said celebration, Mama Bee took the opportunity to address her grandsons. "Let me make myself clear. Due to your actions there will be no Christmas presents for you next week. I guess that's the bad news. The good news is you're off of punishment, with restrictions. Most of these restrictions you'll be advised of on a need to know basis."

The boys didn't immediately flee their place of confinement, but instead remained transfixed, but one managed to utter, "No Christmas."

"You heard her, and guess what, we hurt her so bad this time that there's no sense in asking later if she'd change her mind about it," voiced Larry.

"Best thing for us to do is be thankful we're off punishment, and pray that going outside ain't one of the restrictions," stated Reggie.

"Man, this is messed up. We'll be the only ones going back to school after Christmas break without any new clothes," Darrick stressed.

"The least we can do is try and find some way to make it up to her. Show her how much we do love her," Eli told them.

"Man you don't even have to worry about it like we do. You live down the street." Reggie declared.

"That doesn't change the fact, and besides only time I can come out of my room is when I'm placed here inside of you guys room Eli retorted.

On Christmas morning almost everyone was in the spirit except for the boys. Mama Bee couldn't have been more serious and adamant about her decision yesterday.

The girls were shrieking and exclaiming to one another about the gifts that they had received. But it appeared that even their excitement subsided due to the boys unhappiness.

After having a brief conversation with Mama Bee and Lee-Lee, Elizabeth informed everyone that she was going back home to place herself back into her bed until the evening. This her decision, was made because she couldn't bare to see her sons' unhappiness. And as Eli's heart ached so did hers.

Well, evening arrived as well did a somber cloud that engulfed 2400 West Garland Avenue.

Mama Bee refused to relent. As she put her finishing touches on the Christmas meal, she told herself, *Well it's too late now anyway, so even if I wanted to get them something I couldn't. All the stores are closed."*

Everybody had retired to their own rooms, so nobody heard the Ho-Ho-Ho coming from the living room. "Who is that?" Debra finally asked from the top of the stairs.

"Ho-Ho-Ho," was the answer she received. This caused her, and Elisha to come down and into the living room where they found Pretty Ray and Joann standing wearing Santa Claus hats and having their arms filled with presents.

Pretty Ray instructed Elisha to go in the back and get Mama Bee and he told Debra to get the boys. When Mama Bee came to the living room from the kitchen, her presence caused the boys to cease from unwrapping their presents.

"Ray, you're violating the rules of their punishment by giving them these presents."

"I know Mama, like I also know that if this day would have passed, you would regret it for many years to come. So I brought them one gift each and the video game system to share. Now come on Mama and open up your presents."

After all the presents were received and exchanged, the Christmas meal having been consumed, Mama Bee and her family sat in her living room almost completely in silence until Elizabeth asked, "Boys, why do we celebrate Christmas?"

"Mama I know the answer," said Eli.

"Why?"

"Because it's the day that God sent baby Jesus into the world," he answered.

"Is that right Aunt Liz?" asked Darrick.

"Yes, and no. I say that because no one knows the exact date of our Lord's birth, but I look at it like this. Just imagine if a baby was adopted by a man and a woman and there was nothing indicating the baby's birthday. But the new parents decided to celebrate the day that they received the child as the baby's birthday. Wouldn't it be better to celebrate that day rather than having no day that expresses their love for receiving this precious child into their lives?"

CHAPTER 19

January the twenty second two thousand and six, the construction contractor went over the blueprints that would transform the old boys and girls club into Lynx.

Exactly three years and three months later, Lynx had the first meeting in its new building. It wasn't the only achievement being honored tonight. They were also holding in high esteem the accomplishments made in the two and a half years they had officially become Lynx.

Now, having moved all of their assets from the rented warehouse to Lynx's formal home, they were compelled to present awards of achievement to members and staff. And just as important as all the other accomplishments was the high percentage of members who had graduated and those who were scheduled to make their transition into college next month. Among whom were Eli, Larry, and Mary.

Debra and Elisha graduated in 07, being among the first group that Lynx was hands on with. Elisha, now a sophomore at Spelman college, Debra remained full time at Lynx. And Reggie opted for the military the following year.

Now that all was full throttle, the vision was clearer and the possibilities were steadily increasing.

Tonight's theme was being brought to everyone's attention: "Ladies and gentlemen, we thank you for coming and celebrating with us the opening of your institution. An institution that promises to provide a alternative to the dead end that them streets offer our children. But with no further ado I present to you all. the one, the only, Bernice Lewis."

Mama Bee being introduced to the community by Elizabeth was good for Mama Bee somewhat. It helped to ease her fears a little, but nonetheless a reluctance remained intact. Add that to the fact that she was still disappointed that her daughter had stopped attending meetings months ago. Mama Bee was simply not feeling it tonight. But she persevered because this is what she instills in each and every person who walks into Lynx.

"I welcome you all tonight and I thank all of you parents who have taken the time to not only come out tonight, but also for supporting your child's efforts every step of the way. That's so very vital to their success. "Let me now make everyone aware of tonight's theme and its purpose. *We Suffer For A Reason.*

340

"Oftentimes we become caught up in our sufferings to the point that we're unable to see any further than the problem itself. Thus, we become habitual complainers. And there the cycle begins. But how often do we seek out the purpose for our having to suffer?

"Example: When I was just a child in 1939, there was a man by the name of Lint Shaw who was made to suffer a lynching. I may never learn the reason as to why this man was made to suffer, but I'm sure his great grandchildren and even his grandchildren could share with us all how their knowledge of his cruel suffering has caused them to learn some truths upon which they are able to build and grow. Isn't this why we all have a responsibility to learn and share?

"Gain knowledge of our Ancestors sufferings and share the knowledge with the next generation. I submit to you all that Lynx is committed and our purpose and aim is to utilize the knowledge of our past, link it to our present state, then when possessing the necessary tools we navigate successfully in building a greater future."

As Mama Bee handed the microphone back to Liz and made her way off of the stage, she received applause and adoration from her mentees and her peers.

The entire staff was elated and motivated to build, grow, and equip every single child that flowed through their hands with the necessary tools to achieve success.

Commitment was an understatement.

The following evening Mama Bee was exited, anxious and a little bit regretful that she was on her sofa instead of in Freedom Hall watching her grandson Darrick start for the University of Louisville College basketball team.

She, formerly a University of Kentucky basketball fan, but this season her heart had begun to lean toward the Cardinals.

During a commercial she sat and reminist over the past few years and the ups and downs that they were made to endure. Her grandchildren stereotyped and placed in a high percentage failure category, had beat the odds by dodging the strategistly placed pitfalls.

"Granny," Eli called to her. She didn't actually hear him, but the sound brought her back from that place in her head.

"Granny, do you want anything from the kitchen? Mary had been asking you."

"No, I'm fine. Thank you Mary, but I'm just fine."

More people arrived at Mama Bee's house during halftime, and they all stayed to witness Louisville upset Duke. Although Mama Bee had to wake Debra up again when the time had gotten down to the Chinese clock, but at least she was able to see the game winning shot, assisted by Darrick Lewis.

CHAPTER 20

Here of late it seems as though time had sped up. At least that's what Eli was thinking as he viewed his college choices.

His sister was in her second year at Spellman and he was seriously considering Georgia State. He missed his sister so much and hadn't seen her in like forever. "Yeah, my decision is pretty much settled, and if Mary is going to Spelman, my soul would definitely need to be in her close proximity."

They both had less than a month to make their decisions and then register. So Eli decided to make a dinner date and see just where Mary intended on going. As of late she too had been indecisive, not wanting to relinquish her responsibilities at Lynx.

Later that evening at one of Louisville's most prominent eating establishments, Eli sat across from the love of his life, holding onto one of her hands while gazing into her eyes.

"What is it boy, what's wrong with you?" she asked.

"What's wrong? There's nothing wrong. Right now right this instant everything is right in the world ."

"Then why are you looking at me like I'm a cold glass of Vichy?"

"Maybe it's because a brother needs to stay hydrated."

"Boy, I've told you, so we don't need to keep revisiting the subject."

"Baby, this has absolutely nothing to do with making sweet, slow passionate love to my future wife. I've invited you out for the evening to celebrate you, all that you do, and all that you've become."

"You're sweet and charming, but I can still sense something beneath the surface."

"Well, if you're sensing anything it's my desire to know your decision."

"My decision?"

"Yes Mary, I would like to know where you plan to attend school, so I can make a more intelligent decision."

"If your decision is based on where I attend, it's not based on intelligence Eli. It's based more on lust."

"Lust, Mary? I believe you're mistaking lust for love. I love you Mary and I want to be where you are and I don't want there to ever be any distance between us.

This is how I know I'm more than able to spend the rest of my life with you."

"Oh bae, I love you too, but I'm just unable to make my decision right now. I hope I'm able to see things clearer and soon, but I don't know Eli. I would love to go to Spelman due to all it stands for, and also I want to stay here and fulfill my obligations to Lynx and at the same time remain close to my Mother."

"Yeah, I'm well aware of you and your mother's bond. It's like my mother and sister's relationship, yet Elisha was still able to leave."

"You know that's mainly because she has wanted to attend Spelman every since her first day of middle school when you all still lived there in Georgia," Mary reminded him.

"Yeah, I know and I also know it's your decision to make. Just let me know the second you decide."

"Eli I don't want you making a choice based off of my decision. You have to do what's best for you Eli."

"You're what's best for me Mary."

After their meal Eli took Mary near the new Muhammad Ali Center where they star gazed and enjoyed each other's company outside.

They walked around and talked about many topics which somehow led to intimate discussions.

"I know that when we're both ready it's going to be easy enough. I mean I think of how uncomfortable it may be, but as long as it's with you, I know I'll be okay," she informed him.

"I don't want you to think there's any pressure from me. I'm willing to wait until our honeymoon if necessary. I just hurt sometimes, because that's the only part of you that you haven't given to me. So at times I feel as though I don't have all of you."

"Eli I don't ever want to be the cause of you having any pain. So please don't say it like that. It makes me a little sad to know you're hurting because of my decision to wait."

"Mary let me assure you that you made the right decision for—"

"But you wasn't made aware of that decision until after you was committed, right?"

"Yeah, but I'm okay with it now, I guess."

"But?"

"But I've never loved anyone as much as I love you, and I've never wanted anybody like I want you Mary."

"I love you so much Eli. You're my whole world, and I need you in order to solidify my existence."

"I feel the exact same way as you do baby," he said before taking her into his arms and kissing her so passionately that her knees tried to go weak.

Forty minutes later they were staring into one another's eyes searching for a glimpse of their future, because they both knew that tonight would be etched into their souls for all eternity.

Their gaze did not falter, nor waver as she removed her top in the middle of the Galthouse Hotel room where they now stood. Mary more nervous than she ever thought she would be. And her mind was telling her to put her blouse back on. And her body was telling her to hurry and experience making love with the man she loved.

"No, sweetheart there's no rush. Take your time and go slow," Eli told her as Mary began to remove her skirt. Eli sat on the edge of the bed and watched her intently. "Why aren't you undressing Eli?"

"Because I would like to savor this moment and commit it to memory forever."

She moved closer to where he sat and unhooked her bra. She then leaned forward and kissed his lips. He then kissed her stomach before standing to remove his shirt. He took her into his arms and used his tongue to taste hers. He slowly, then passionately, then hungrily kissed her mouth.

After removing his tongue from hers, he sat in the chair beside the bed and asked Mary to continue undressing. She obliged him as he reminded her to go slow.

When she was standing before him, completely nude, Eli placed his hands on her hips and drew her nearer. Again he gently kissed her stomach, then her thighs.

"Eli, lay me down on the bed," she moaned unable to contain, nor hold back her moisture.

He laid her onto the bed ever so gently and then removed his clothing.

Eli had to control his urge to rampage, so he went after Mary's neck, using the tip of his tongue to locate her hot spot.

Her moans were doing something incredible to Eli's manhood, but he maintained his control because this was all about pleasing his Mary. So he slid down and began using the tip of his tongue to trace her inner thighs. As he moved back up the length of her thighs with his tongue he began to caress her right breast ever so softly with the palm of his hand.

Again hearing her moan did something to Eli as if he'd been injected with an aphrodisiac.

He could no longer contain himself. He moved up her body needing to insert his phallus deep inside of her, but could not because she started using both her hands to push Eli's head back to where it was.

He, being a novice at it, did not dissuade him in the least bit. But following instructions given to him, he parted Mary's vulva and used his tongue to explore its contour. He used his mouth and the heat thereof to ignite her core. When he licked and pulled with his tongue on Mary's clitoris she involuntarily squeezed his head with her thighs while forcing his tongue deeper inside of her with hands still atop his head. Eli kept going despite the fact and eventually she eased up a little. He continued his exploration with his tongue, and mouth while using his hands to caress her body. He gently, tenderly caressed her nipples, her thighs, even her arms. Seeking nothing other than to pleasure this woman who he loved more than life itself.

"Eli, I need to feel you inside of me," she was barely able to moan the words.

He obliged her as he slowly entered into her matrix. Once there he willed himself to go slow, steady, and rhythmical to the tune that played in his head. He maintained his stroke, slowly, purposefully, in and out. Fifteen minutes later Mary was on her second or third orgasm. She no longer wanted to count, nor needed to as her next one was building, welling up inside of her as Eli began to go harder and faster as if he was aware of the climax her body had to obtain access to.

Mary wrapped her legs around Eli's waist making an effort to pull him even deeper inside of her. He continued his stroke as if destined to knock the bottom out of it. He took hold of the back of her knees and pressed her legs forward and into her chest as he stood up in it and beat it up like as if it threw a punch at him first.

She moaned, he grunted, she cried, he grunted as he released all of himself inside of her as she exploded at the same time. He collapsed on top of her and she welcomed his weight.

WE SUFFER FOR A REASON

They kissed passionately and sensually as Eli rolled to the side and shared with Mary the reasons why his love for her is eternal.

CHAPTER 21

"Surprise!" was the chorus that Larry, Mary, and Eli received as they came through Mama Bee's front door.

"What?" Mary was the first to ask. Then her smile lit up the room when she saw her mother standing over there by Elizabeth and Mama Bee.

"Yeah, what is this all about?" Larry asked. "This here is you all's going away to college party," Reggie told them as he entered into the living room.

The sight of such caused Eli, and Larry to step to him and snatch him into their double bear hug.

"Man, when did you get home bruh?" Larry asked.

"Yesterday at around eight o'clock, but I've known about the surprise party for about a week now." "Hey cuz, how's military life treating you?" Eli inquired.

"It's okay. I won't complain. It's what I decided, so I'll complete the task, but enough about me. I see you and Mary have remained inseparable."

"I don't know about all of that, 'cause you have to come together in order to separate, then come together, and separate, then repeat until your toes curl," Larry pointed out.

"I'm pretty sure her toes cured," Eli allowed some game to drip.

"What?" Larry and Reggie asked at the exact same time. "Fam you smashed?" Reggie asked requiring a more definite answer.

"Hold your voice down cuz. It wasn't a smash, it wasn't a hit, it was lovemaking on a cloud that orbited the earth."

"Man, what a rookie know about cloud nine?" Larry wanted to know. "I learned from the same person who you learned from. So, I basically knew what to do. I simply had to discover for myself how to."

"I learned from the big guy," said Larry, as he patted his big brother's shoulder.

"So did I, that's what I'm saying. I did too."

"Now you're not going to be blaming me for your screw ups," Reggie informed him.

"Screw ups. You trippin fam. I believe I did everything right last night. So, in short, you taught me well."

Those words caused Larry and Reggie to look over to where Mary now stood. And at that exact moment

Mary provided them eye contact, because she was already wondering what their conversation consisted of.

"Man, you two idiots, she caught y'all staring. Come on, lets go join them and find out what's on the menu," suggested Eli.

CHAPTER 22

At the beginning of Elisha's second year at Spelman she became a member of a sorority that she absolutely fell in love with, and they her. So much so that they allowed their new sister to establish a chapter of Lynx amongst them. Having the blessings and guidance of founding members, its potential was evident.

These women worked extra hard and developed ways of reaching out to their community that was fresh, exciting, and vibrant.

The attention that they received on and off campus was not only positive, but progressive as well. Their numbers grew as well did the community outreach programs. These women being more than willing to take time from their personal time and spend it with the elderly, hands on and extremely committed. And there was also a large number who volunteered their time to attend to the youth.

I mustn't neglect to inform on Elisha's brain child. A musical aspect that was taking shape due mostly to the talent that continued to reach higher expectations.

Once they achieved the vision she had strove to make manifest, they put on shows on campus and throughout the Atlanta area. Which in time brought huge awareness to their plight.

Lynx was now a household name throughout Atlanta, Georgia. From zone-one to zone-six.

Spring break had come upon Elisha so suddenly it caused to become indecisive when she took time to view her calendar. She knew not whether to accompany her girls on their scheduled performance dates, or go spend her break with her family, and especially her Mom whom she had promised that she'd spend spring break with.

So, her decision became clear as she recalled that promise. Besides, she was confident of the manager's ability to manage the girls through the completion of their last few scheduled apperances.

CHAPTER 23

In Louisville, Lynx continued to prosper and grow. It was actually branching out to other places such as Ohio, and Indiana, just to name a couple of places that had received approval for chapters in their areas.

There would eventually be many other places participating in the journey that is Lynx's mission.

All members had become extremely busy and tremendously involved in the day to day process that enabled the growth that they all welcomed, despite the hard and long hours.

Mama Bee had no other choice but to cave in and agree to hiring a personal assistant. Oftentimes becoming swamped in work she believed only she could sort out.

But cooler heads prevailed and she now had a secretary, two other volunteers under her, and Debra making sure her deadlines were met.

Lynx had to purchase a larger complex in order to accommodate its growth. And with new members signing up almost daily, a third building was being taken into consideration. But the achievements along with their statistics made it all worthwhile.

This is exactly what Mama Bee was thinking as she typed out a memo that she planned on distributing through their intranet.

Yes, they'd come a long way and as previously envisioned, there was absolutely no limit to their growth potential.

CHAPTER 24

Eli, despite his emotional mellifluous feelings for his Mary in her absence, is thankful that he's able to remain focused and make personal accomplishments, that he himself is proud of. He now believes that Mary's commitment to her Lynx obligations is not to be viewed by him as taking away from their personal time but rather that which continuously develops her into the woman she's so wonderfully becoming.

He had never seen her as happy as the day that Lynx granted her the necessary funds to open up their first shop and her passion. A wedding business that provides everything a woman could desire for her wedding day. Mary named the store, Bridal Workz and she made it a success.

Lynx had become huge on many different fronts. And it was apparent that Eli's family and friends were taking the appropriate steps to accomplish every goal that they set.

Eli was thrilled, happy, and comfortable with his decision to remain in Louisville, attend college, assist and help support his cousins and also volunteer his time to the Lynx chess club. He was sincere about helping to build this strong, vibrant woman's association in any capacity that they needed him in.

The following fall it was evident that everything had come full circle.

The women of Lynx' dedication, hard work, and late hours had solidified communities and with it had brought on broader recognition. And tonight their efforts were coming to fruition, as they were preparing to display their accomplishments and the mind blowing achievements of many, many intelligent youth.

Media outlets from both near and far were in attendance having cameras and microphones at the ready.

The behind the scenes activities was a little flustered. But as Eli thought to himself, he believed his mother to be more than capable.

"Yeah," he told himself, *"Mama is most capable of keeping their organization organized."*

"Hey little bruh, what's up?" Elisha asked him and jarred him back to the right now.

"Hey sis, how's it going?" he asked as he hugged and kissed her cheek.

"I see things between you and Mary have really gotten serious, huh?"

"Why do you say that?" Eli wanted to know. "Well, little bruh, you two have something thats to be envied. And just incase yoh haven't noticed, everyone else has, and everyone is happy for you guys."

"I appreciate it, but tonight isn't about me. It's the beautiful and lovely women of my family's night and I'm just thankful and proud to be of relations," Eli said and then kissed her cheek once more.

"We should be ready to begin in as little as fifteen minutes. My first priority is to get my chapter of Lynx onto the stage to open up."

"So let me go over it with them one more time," Elisha explained.

"Okay, you go handle your business," Eli told his sister as she was leaving.

"Hey you, come here!"

Eli turned to face the familiar voice that he knew all so well.

"Granny Bee, I had thought you walked around the corner with my Mother."

"Yeah, but she wouldn't budge. So I've returned so I could aim some inveiglement at you," Mama Bee said in all seriousness.

"What is it Granny? You know I'll do anything to help." "I know, and that's what I'm counting on. Here's a twenty. You go around there to the bar and get your Granny a bottle of her drink. No glass, no ice, and you can keep the change."

"Granny, you know I'm not going to do that, because we both know that you don't need it. All you need is the power of the Lord's might."

"Sometimes I believe that the Lord invented liquor for those of us who experience occasional stage fright."

"You know you don't mean that Granny Bee."

"Of course not, but I do wonder sometimes."

"The truth is you're a little nervous, maybe even slightly afraid, because of the huge crowd. But you are neglecting to take into consideration all of the supporting cast that you yourself have created. Granny, it's time for you to lean on them a little bit, because not even Jesus was able to carry His own cross."

"My, my you sure are a smart boy. Tell me how did you grow to be so intelligent? I know your destiny is to become a messenger for God, so that you may also do your part in leading your generation."

"Naw Granny, I'm going to school to become a computer science major and maybe help some people learn to use the programs that I create."

"Well, just remember, we can't always see the Lord's overall plan so easily. Besides, every time we make plans it causes God to laugh."

After Elisha, and her sorority sisters left the stage, Elaine, Mary, Joann, and Debra spoke about their efforts and continuing need of support in expanding the technology aspect of Lynx.

Afterwards, they introduced to the stage, "Shine." The instrumental composition consisting of three female singers Elisha had worked so hard to fashion into being bright lights unto others.

After the last guest speaker spoke about the job fair is company hopes to link up to Lynx an intermission was announced, during which Elisha and her sorority were being hounded by some guys who had their swags on autopilot.

And Shine were really getting their shine on. They were presently being interviewed, and photographed by a local magazine, which sparked the curiosity of the larger forms of media that were in that area.

Elizabeth and Eli had Mama Bee cornered off making every effort to prepare and calm her for her stage appearance that was scheduled to take place in as little as twelve more minutes.

"Granny, we've already been through this, and you'll be fine. If it was me who was going out there I would find me something in the back of the room to focus on, or I'd visualize the entire audience in the nude."

"Eli," Elizabeth said in protest. Then she turned Mama Bee toward her by her shoulders and said, "Mama you've spoken before a few crowds before, remember? Well, this is no different. Besides, it was you who said you needed no written speech, because you wanted to talk to your community straight from your heart." "Yes, I did say that. I said exactly that when I was still in the community without all these lightbulbs flashing, or them cameras being pointed all in my face. "Now, every time I hear a clap or hear the shouts, my heart jumps almost out of my chest," Mama Bee said holding her hand over her chest.

"Mama, once you've gotten over the first few seconds of being out on stage, you'll be just fine, I promise you," Elizabeth told her.

"Granny, if I could I would go up on stage with you and hold your hand all the way through," Eli told her.

She looked into the eyes belonging to her grandson and saw the sincerity that resided there. She drew strength from all of their encouragement just as well as from knowing that it is she who should be strengthening them. So, she took a deep breath, exhaled and exclaimed that she would be more than fine.

"I'll just go out there and tell my people how much I love and care for them all."

Her words put huge smiles across the faces of Elizabeth, Eli, and the woman who was attempting to put some more makeup on Mama Bee's face.

"Mama, are you ready? You're on in two minutes," Elaine informed.

"She's more than ready," Liz responded.

Crew members escorted Mama Bee to the stage while telling her to remember to stand on her mark.

Elisha, and Debra approached at the last second. Debra squeezed her grandmother's hand and told her to smile her beautiful smile, while Elisha gave her a few encouraging words.

She stood there on the stage and looked out into the crowd as if she was looking for someone particular. While the cameras flashed and hands clapped, Mama Bee stood glaring, searching and panning. "You have been announced as the host and one of the founders of Lynx, so may I ask you exactly what does Lynx stand for? I mean what does it represent?" a small voice belonging to a news reporter from Ohio asked. "Well, let me see," Mama Bee began after a moment of continued silence.

"Well, we all know that the Lynx is a wildcat and being a Kentuckian we're all wildcats with the exception of all of the Cardinals of course," she said causing a huge portion of the crowd to erupt into a cheer.

"Anyway, we decided to use the Lynx and the strength therein to symbolize our own strengths and resilience as we commit ourselves to fight and overcome misfortunes that are consuming our communities.

"We are on a course, a mission if you will, to link the past with the present in order to establish a future laced with knowledge of self-worth. Along with many other faculties that educate and motivate love for self and love toward others."

After answering over a dozen more questions and expounding on upcoming projects that are hoped to eradicate the project mentality out of the minds of many, Mama Bee announced that they all should be hearing the words of those who are in the world equipped with the messages of change.

"So I introduce to you all my dearly loved grandson, Eli, who will bless you all with his poem."

While the crowd exploded into applause, Eli was behind the curtain, shocked. Caught totally off guard and by surprise, having no idea that his Grandmother would put him on blast like this. Having no time to entertain these thoughts, because he was being ushered out onto the stage by family, and an usher.

Finally taking up a position beside his Grandmother, he could only look at her with a questioning look, like, why?

Granny Bee seeing her grandson's nervousness squeezed his hand and told him, "Would you just look at all of those naked people out there. They should be ashamed of themselves."

Then she left Eli with the audience as she walked from the stage, leaving the audience with Eli.

He cleared his throat and began, "I really don't know what to say, because I didn't prepare anything. So I'll just begin with a simple question. Where are the institutions that instill in black America black pride? That structures, that propel growth in our schools, churches, homes, and in our communities? That self pride and self-worth that enlightens us and opens our eyes as well as our understanding?

"I don't know exactly where all the rest of them are, but I'm so familiar with this particular one called Lynx. Created by all of the women in my life, including my Aunt Lee-Lee who unfortunately could not make it here tonight. But these women of Lynx have taught me and my cousins all about love for self and love for others, which is most important.

"I thank all of the women in my life, my mother Elizabeth, my Granny Bee who just introduced me to you, my sister Elisha, and cousin Debra. April, Mrs. Elaine Jordan, Joann, and the list goes on and on. But I give an especially sincere huge thank you to my girlfriend and founding member Mary Jordan. "And again, thank you Granny Bee for shaping, and molding me. I give you my heart in thanks as well as all of my love, for you have given me so much and you have asked for nothing in return.

"Thank you Ms. Bernice Lewis."

After the applause subsided Eli said, "Well, she hadn't asked for anything until she asked me to come up here unprepared and recite a poem in front of all of you, um unfamiliar faces. I hope I don't disappoint her as I speak as my heart compels me.

"I now embark upon a scar that America has across its face. A scar so ugly that it's almost too hideous to look upon. But we are forced to view it everyday. A constant reminder of the wound so deeply entrenched, we wonder if it will ever heal.

"A scar is suppose to signify healing, but America's scar reminds its victims of these two truths. It reminds us of the time the wound was first inflicted, and of its residual pain still being slashed across the backs of the burden bearers til this very day.

"Oh America, home of the free, it was you who inflicted the mark that remains. I've called it a mark as well as a scar but the definition of them both is "Slavery."

"A race of people kept in bondage by relentless oppressors who raped, mutilated, disgraced and destroyed black women in the presence of their children, while hanging the negro man from huge trees that remain as centerpieces to their modern day squares.

"How is it possible for us to forget, dare we should ever forget, or neglect to impress our history upon the minds of our children after us.

"There shall be no more deceiving black children with further deception.

"America treats you with contempt, because it knows no better. It has been raised by its parents to think and act as they.

"Oh but of course, that was then when the scar was made, so let us not blame this generation. I suppose we are to blame it on the past. What are we to do then, track down their children like the bloodhounds used to track down the slaves who risked their lives running for their freedom?

"We are now in this new millennium and some are asking for an apology. Well, if that's what's needed for them to make them oblivious of the scar that has swelled into a mark, I say lets all begin at the starting line, all at the same time.

"Hurry, hurry, line up at the line quick, before the guns go off!!!"

370

Eli stood there at the podium awaiting a reaction. These were not people sitting in the nude before him. These were people such as himself. Different ages, different races, but the same nonetheless. People seeking direction because they too were sick and tired of being sick and tired and needed a format from which to progress.

A few scattered claps ascended into the atmosphere as Eli started to turn toward the curtain.

Then a few more applauds and then suddenly Eli was enraptured by the elating sounds of approval. He viewed the audience after turning back toward them. He smiled a huge smile as he bowed his head in absolute appreciation and thanks.

Once behind the curtain Eli faced his Grandmother and instead of him complaining about her putting him on blast, he simply took her in his arms and hugged her affectionately.

"You done really well out there and they all seem to like what you said," Mama Bee told Eli while still inside of his arms.

His mother and sister came over and congratulated him as well.

WE SUFFER FOR A REASON

Eli placed a arm around Mary's neck and asked, "You don't think it was a little too much?" "Of course not," Mama Bee told him, then added, "It's time for the history lesson to begin."

CHAPTER 25

In the eyes of all those concerned, the Lynx introduction event was a huge success. And they received too many e-mails to read in a day. So Joann and Elaine took the liberty of separating them and then screening them according to their urgency.

One particular e-mail grabbed their attention immediately. It had been sent by the news media that employed one, Soledad O'Brien and the content was as follows: *In fairness we are contacting you to inform you of our upcoming broadcast pertaining to the panel that will be on hand here at our studio in New York, discussing "Lynx" and the platform it provides.*

The e-mail ended with: *If you wish to attend, discuss, and/or defend, feel free to contact our studio at the following number, or email address.*

When Joann showed the e-mail to Elaine they both were left perplexed by the one word, 'defend.' They instantly decided that they should gather everyone together and then decide in which way to proceed.

They scheduled a meeting for that evening to be held above the recreation center where one of the smaller offices was located.

Mama Bee was informed by Liz and they both pondered on what could possibly be meant by the need to defend, as they readied themselves for the travel to the meeting.

Elaine was seated at the round conference table as the members started to arrive, when Mama Bee and Liz entered, followed by Phyllis Galbreath and Henrietta Crawford they all took seats then shut and locked the door.

Elaine announced that she had e-mailed an inquiry, hoping to have received more information by the time everyone had arrived.

Liz read the previous email aloud and allowed the contents to linger in the room awhile. Afterwards she said, "It's very possible that this could become extremely important due mostly to the e-mail's mention of our potential need to defend. I'm concerned as I'm sure you all are about the panel that's scheduled to discuss us, our achievements, mistakes, or what have you," she added.

"Regardless of their criticisms we will continue to maintain a focus of commitment to the goals of Lynx," Joann exclaimed.

The computer alerted the room that there was an e-mail. Everyone paused and it seemed as if they all had stopped breathing for a split second.

Elaine said, "This is it everybody," as she stroked a key to open the email. She then proceeded to read it aloud: *Thank you for your efficient response. I've tried to reach your offices by phone to no avail. There has been a panel of concerned individuals who's desire it is to know exactly what the underlying purposes and agenda of your group may really be.*

The question posed is: Is it a platform for black anger, and rage? Judging by the poem recited at your recently held media event, entitled "America's Scar," Lynx! Please let us know if you would like to represent your group's standing in the defense of this matter by sending a representative to appear on the panel.
All travel expenses will be paid for by our studio. You only have to notify us promptly and arrangements will be made. Sincerely S. O'Brien.

After the reading of the e-mail the question was asked; who will we be sending to represent Lynx?

"Hold on one minute," Mama Bee interrupted the back and forth chatter. "We are not going to be sending anybody to represent something that speaks for itself.

You only need to look to the floor below to see the evidence of what we've been about since the very beginning."

"This we know," Joann began. "All of us are aware of the fact that we're all about the youth and especially the young women who will be called on to carry the torch after us. But obviously," she went on to say, "the rest of the people in the country are not aware of these facts, nor of the other issues that we take on."

"You're right but –" Linda started in.

But Joann continued, "Hold on, I'm not finished. Let me just add; I feel as though we should have someone on the panel to defend our interest and make the public aware of our goals and of our commitment to accomplishing them."

"You make a valuable point, but this isn't the first time we've been threatened, or scrutinized nor the first time we've been criticized. The point I make is, we didn't respond, because it almost always ends up like adding fuel to the fire," Elaine concluded.

"I support a non-response method despite the fact of it being my grandson who's the alleged cause of this attack.

They are obviously accusing us all of being a group from which black anger is allowed to be voiced," Debra spoke out. "Well, if that is their assessment of Lynx then what is there to defend? I am not ashamed to point out, if not Lynx, then who, or what vehicle will the race be willing to use?" She added.

"Let's remember our by-laws, which says: "All matters involving the entire organization must be put at a vote, where the majority rules. And veto power does not reside in the hands of one, but the five," Phyllis read from their laws.

That night, a couple of hours after the meeting at Lynx, Mary and Eli met up at Bristol's Bar and Grill for food, wine, and conversation.

Upon entering the place Mary spotted Eli at the bar talking with the tender, and after she had approached him they took seats at a back table where Mary instantly removed her heels, explaining to him that she had been up on her feet practically all day and couldn't take it another minute.

He jokingly asked if it would be sanitary for her to take her shoes off. She ignored his comment because she was in no mood.

"Eli, there has been a strange turn of events," she began.

"What do you mean?" he asked noticing her serious demeanor.

"There has been an e-mail sent to Lynx informing us that there has been a panel of critics erected and are scheduled to appear on national television on the last Friday of this month."

"I see, but you do realize that whether it's good publicity or bad publicity, it still equals free publicity."

"Eli, you don't understand. Like we discussed at our meeting today, we've dealt with criticism as well as naysayers before."

"Then what's the problem?" Eli asked trying to read her eyes. But she put her head down diverting them from his stare.

When she lifted her head again she stared him directly and intently in the eyes and began, "It's concerning the poem you recited at the convention center. It appears that some people believe Lynx is only used as a launching pad for anti-Americanism."

"You have to be kidding me. I say that although it's typical for the powers that be to oppose anything that shines light on their Satanism."

"Satanism? Eli is this how you view these individuals?" Mary asked.

"All I know is anybody who's dead set on dismantling Christian rites are the progeny of Satan. I said all of that just to say this: For any race of people to enslave and brutalize another should be labeled as such. And if the offenders never attempt to make amends then the ones violated should bring about an amendment."

"I know what you are saying is important and it's true Eli, but is it right for you to use what we're trying to do as your platform for your retribution address?"

"Before you make the mistake of labeling me Anti-America you should take this into consideration, two important facts actually. First of all, I could be doing what I'm doing for the betterment of my country by warning it to wise up and take heed to the new vibe that beats in the hearts of its black Americans and secondly, learn of the essence of Lynx and its motivating force, because if you are not willing to give your own soul if need be, to inform this generation of why a Country has been and is still hell bent on keeping them in bondage mentally and physically with their modern day mass incarceration then you should re-evaluate that which you are willing to give for and then go and be a part of

379

that," Eli voiced before abruptly storming out of the bar and grill, not even turning to respond to Mary as she asked him to wait.

CHAPTER 26

Five days later it was voted that Elaine and Joann would attend the panel in New York. Elizabeth and April would accompany them for moral support, and although some of the others wanted to attend as well, it had been voted that the ones chosen would portray Lynx in a most favorable light.

Mama Bee's opinion was known to all. She didn't feel any need to address the critics, because she knew that they would always be. She did consider, however, the shots that would be taken at her grandchild and she didn't like the idea one bit.

Not only was she the one who invited Eli to the stage to recite his writings, she has always encouraged him to use his work as a bridge between the past and the present. So if some idiots were accusing them of being Un-American for pointing out obvious atrocities past, and present, then it should be just as obvious to see that these are the very ones who attempt to redefine America's Christian core beliefs. That is Anti-America!

Mama Bee was brought back from her thoughts as someone had entered the house and spoke.

"Granny Bee, didn't you hear me?" Eli asked.

"I'm sorry baby, your Granny was somewhere else."

"I didn't mean to bother you Granny, but I just left from fighting with Mary again, and I'll be honest and tell you that our arguments stem from that email that you guys received."

"Why would that cause you two to argue with one another?"

"Because I stand firmly by what I recited at the Lynx convention and I disputed their claim of my being anything but for America."

"I hear all of that, but you still haven't answered my question Eli. I asked why would the email cause you two to fight."

"Granny Bee I felt as though Mary was in support of their accusations and that she neglected to see your initial reasons of a coalesce."

"My reasons and our goals have never changed. She was present when we set here and mapped out those exact same goals. She even voiced ideals that we as a group not only supported but developed into working elements. So, are you sure she's siding with anyone other than our initial cause?"

"All I know is it seems to me that just because the opposition are posing criticism and questions that she thinks the answers should be ones of appeasement."

"Meaning?" Mama Bee wanted to know.

"Meaning if they question the truth in what I recited, it doesn't cause it to be untrue."

"Of course not," Mama Bee agreed.

"Then why should we submit to inquiries instead of continuing to do what Lynx set out to do in the first place?"

"Which is?" she asked.

"To educate and inform. To provide with history unrecorded, and examples of those who died so that we may be made free. Free to strive toward our togetherness, while exercising our abilities to there full potential and if possible, beyond."

"It appears to me that you haven't lost sight of what your responsibilities or ours are," Mama Bee told Eli. Then she instructed him to have a seat on the sofa right beside her.

After patting him on the knee, she began, "Let me share with you what others having the same skin as yours were forced to go through, suffer, and overcome in hopes that some day someone would tell their stories to the world so that their deaths wouldn't be in vain.

"So listen. It was during a night that the south was in an upheaval. Slavery had long been abolished, but yet there were no laws protecting blacks.

"So the south still lived by the notion that black lives didn't matter and didn't possess the credibility, nor the right to accuse a white person. But on the other hand they would falsely accuse, try, convict, and persecute to death a black man, woman, or child. To them this method was perfectly legal and it was widely practiced.

"On the night in question, little David, a small negro boy only a year younger than myself at the time, who I had known for quite awhile, because he and his family attended my great Grandfather's vegetable crop, along with his Grandmother who was well acquainted with my great Grandmother, they never mind when they gleaned the corners.

"Being that little David and his family took up land on property belonging to former slave owners, he had grown accustomed to playing with the Wilbank children. Particularly, one Susie Q who was a couple of years older than he.

"My own eyes had seen the two of them out and about on occasions when I was allowed to accompany an adult into town. There, they'd be running around laughing and giggling along with other children, mostly black. "I'll admit the Wilbank's weren't fortunate. I mean, they didn't have much more than the average black family. They say that after their Grandfather died, the others allowed their farm to go to waste and eventually sold off all of their farming equipment.

"Anyway, on this particular night my Granny woke me from my sleep and told me to come and climb into bed with her. When I had gathered my senses, I began hearing all kinds of ruckus coming from the outside. Everything from dogs barking to voices yelling and screaming.

"By the time Granny had me all tucked into bed with her, Granddaddy came in the room sweating and acting really nervous and scared. She asked him what was they going to do and before he could answer, the door came crashing down and there stood three white men with their heads covered with white hooded masks.

"When two of them had a tight hold of my great Grandfather , the other one came over and he snatched the quilt off of me and my Granny. She started to holler, and scream as she took a firm hold of me and then covered me with herself.

"She cried, "You'll never take another child away from me." She screamed those words over and over again until one of them came over, shoving the first one out of his way and then he commenced to beat my great Grandmother about the back parts of her body and then all over.

"During that moment I didn't feel an actual lash of his whip, but each and every time she received a blow, a piece of my soul was torn away from me. He had beaten her unconscious before she had released her hold of me.

"The first one came back over and put his hands all over me reaching under my nightclothes, grabbing in places no man had any right to, but my mind was far from that, because lying next to me was my dear ole Granny beaten, and bloody, unable to move an inch. I couldn't tell if she was even breathing or not. I turned my stare from her only to discover the rope that they had tied around my great Granddaddy's neck, forcing him to watch all the while.

"They repeatedly hit Granddaddy about his head, demanding that he tell the whereabouts of the boy. But, all he would utter was, Lord please don't let this wickedness be done in thy sight.

"They cursed him and God and continued to smash his head as they ripped the night dress from my body. Eli, begged and pleaded, not once taking account of his own miserable state.

"Suddenly, one of the men silenced the others. "Granddaddy began to scream even louder until the assailant that held him by the rope around his neck wrapped that same rope around even tighter and then placed it in Eli's mouth causing him to choke and gag.

"Then there was nothingness, nothing but the faint whimpering that seemed to be coming from a deep well. The one who held me, let me be so that he could run into the next room where the whimpering appeared to be coming from.

"Then the tearing apart of that room could be heard. I went to my Granny's side and was a little relieved to feel her chest go up and down. I whispered Granny several times but she wasn't able to answer me. That's when I looked over to where my great grandfather lay. He still had the rope wrapped around his neck and all I could see in his eyes were their whites.

"I started to cry tears of sorrow and despair, wishing that all the others hadn't left to take the produce into the next town. I was left all alone and I hadn't a clue as to what

I should or could do. So, I did all that I knew to do. I placed my head to my Granny's chest and I prayed. "The hooded men dragged a small black boy and a woman to the entryway of the room. They took the rope from Granddaddy's neck and looped it around the child's neck.

"The boy's Mother cried and screamed as she tried to free her child from the rope, only to be snatched by the hair, by one of the white men. Then he began to beat her face with his fist as the boy cried out in agony. "This only caused them to tighten the noose around his neck tighter.

"My God there would be many deaths that night, I just knew it. And my fears were incomparable when one of the men ripped the dress completely from the body of the woman. His intentions were to rape the child's mother right in front of the child.

"He only stopped his savagery at the ordering of one of the others who commanded the two to take the woman and the boy out of the shack and tie them both to horses. 'What about these old niggers here pa?' 'What about them,' pa answered.

'Surely they'll speak to the law. Leave 'em for dead, and if they should live, then so be it. We are the law around here.' Then he laughed a devilish cackle that caused my skin to crawl.

" 'Go,' he commanded again. 'You have the little bastard that laid down with your Susie and as a bonus you get the whore to do with as you please.' "When I heard their horses ride off I had to control my trembling, and sobbing. Then I went for cold wet rags, and cold water for my great Grandparents.

"Several hours later the rest of my family returned home from their trip.

"The doctor was summoned and after many, many nights my grandparents health returned to them, but our mental health was caused to harden and become calloused. Well, at least mine became numb and I was unable to feel any emotions other than hatred. "It took my Grandparents prayers and of course time. Time showed me that not all white people hate me for the color of my skin. I learned to feel again after a long while, but I have never been able to forget. And I'll never forget that third day after the attack when I was being taken to the docs' house and there on the side of the road hung little David's mother, naked with her chest and stomach cut open exposing her insides. What was left intact anyway, the rest had spilled out onto the ground.

"The body belonging to little David was never recovered, but an interesting fact was revealed. Susie Q later told several people that her and David were fully clothed when her older cousin had come into the barn. And the only reason why they both were laying there is due to a joke they had been laughing so hard to.

"But later when she wouldn't give the cousin what she had down in her pants, he threatened to tell her Daddy that her and little David was laying together in the barn. It went from being a threat to becoming an actuality, because he lied the lie. And she made her Daddy believe that little David had forced himself on her.

"All of those lies caused the near deaths of my great Grandparents and the absolute deaths of Carla and her son little David Jenkins.

"See, I've told you the details of this story so that you'll never forget that just because these exact same atrocities are not happening to your race today does not mean that they and many other monstrous and unspeakable acts didn't happen to our brothers, and sisters."

"Granny, what happened to you all was awful," Eli said having watered eyes. "I can't even begin to imagine how you were able to survive it all. Most people would be mental patients on some mental ward." "No, my grandson, you're wrong, because many thousands of our people endured the hardest abuses imaginable, but yet there were survivors who instilled their examples into others. Told their stories to ones who cared and loved enough to go forth and make a difference."

"I understand Granny, I really do. I just don't know if I could possibly evoke unto paper and into my writings the pain and the agony, the suffering and the death that this early America caused my family to be recipients of. I do know that. I will no longer refer to us as just a race of people, black, or colored, but we are all family. Every one of us living in this world. I feel that we are all kin to one another. But Granny Bee, my feeling this way doesn't give me the ability to illustrate the facts that enlighten us by examples that bestow upon our minds needed knowledge and wisdom for our perseverance. I don't, I just don't believe myself to be capable."

"If you're not, then who is Eli?" Mama Bee asked.

"Granny, I don't know. All I know is it's a huge responsibility and I know that many people my age shun the responsibility because they set their minds on the fact that they wasn't there during that awful time of slavery, or even the twenty or thirty years after its supposed abolishment. So, we don't even feel that we are qualified to tell others anything.

"Fears, time, and the lack of willing example givers leads us all into a future of mental oblivion. And at the exact same time we embrace the truth in the fact that where there's no knowledge of where you've come from, then it's impossible to get to where you were destined to take it to."

"So Eli, you can not allow what others think to hinder your call. Nor can you afford to settle for the norm. "Grandson, let your entire generation fear their responsibility, but you give of your very soul and show your love for others as you express your knowledge of what's been instilled in you," Mama Bee told Eli.

"You've taught me so much, maybe even more than all of those books in school put together. What I research off of the web is good and helpful, but these examples that you share, hit right at the center of my heart and this lets me know that I'll continuen to write , and speak out to all those willing to listen."

"If that's your promise to your Granny then I can promise you I'll leave this world a happy woman." Eli kissed his Granny Bee and once he had, they sat and discussed Joann, April, Elaine and his mother's trip to the Big Apple.

Then came a knock at the door. "Who is it?" Eli asked as he was getting up and at the exact same time the front door came open and in walked Mary!

"Hell Ms. Bee, how are you?" "Hello Mary, I'm doing about as good as can be expected," Mama Bee replied.

"Eli, I can't believe you won't return any of my calls."

"I'm sorry, I just—"

"Yeah, you are sorry," she cut him off mid sentence.

"No, I'm serious," he said as he moved toward her. "I made a mistake and a rush to judgment."

"You've done more than that. You've hurt me deeply when all I've ever done was support you and your ideas, believe in you and encourage you to do that which your heart compels you to do. But obviously none of that matters to you because you don't hesitate to walk out on me whenever we argue."

Then Mary turned and walked out on Eli.

Eli stood staring at the now closed door, just looking at it.

"Well, just don't stand there, go after her," Mama Bee sternly instructed.

Eli snatched at the front door and then rushed through it. He caught Mary before she pulled off. She hadn't even started her car up yet. She was just sitting there crying with her head on the steering wheel.

Eli tapped on the window after trying the door handle.

Mary shook her head no a few times which caused Eli to say: "Please, I thought we were finally past the episode at the Bristols. Please Mary just open the door. We have to talk before we allow something to happen that we'll both regret."

She yelled, "Why didn't you think about that before you left me sitting there feeling hurt and looking stupid." "So that is what this is all about. You being embarrassed."

Mary stepped out of the car and yelled, "I don't really give a damn about my being embarrassed. But as I sat there it dawned on me that you don't trust me and there's a good chance that you might not even know me forreal."

By the time she had finished saying those words, Eli was at the driver's side door right in front of her. He placed a hand on her cheek and he wiped away the tears that were there, then he asked: "How can you stand here and honestly say that I don't know you Mary? I've known you ever since I got here to Kentucky. And I grew to know you better during our many late night conversing over the phone and whether I fell in love with you then or during the years we were together at middle school, I don't know. "But I do know that our hearts and our love was sealed on the night we spent together searching one another's souls!"

She then went into his arms, not based solely on the words that he spoke, but purely because of the truth that was contained within the words that he had spoken.

Through tears and sobs Mary told him, "Don't you ever doubt my belief in you."

"Come on, step back inside of the house with me for a few minutes," he said as he looked and saw his Granny Bee remove herself from the living room window.

When the both of them entered the front room, Mama Bee was nowhere to be seen. So Eli called for her after making Mary comfortable on the loveseat.

"Can I get you anything from the kitchen?" he asked.

"I have everything covered," Mama Bee announced as she re-entered the living room carrying a tray of cold cuts.

As she sat the tray down she told them to allow her to gather the rest of the things for the constructing of sandwiches and some beverages.

Mary's offer to help was declined by Mama Bee, who informed her that the things needed had already been prepared, but she would like to share a snack so they could discuss the direction Lynx would travel, despite the sudden pop-up of opposition.

When she returned to the living room again, Mary asked, "Ms. Bee was this sudden opposition anticipated by her?"

"Of course it was, as well as by other members. What did you think, that we would be allowed to guide black America into self-sufficiency and there would be no cleverly disguised flagitious move made by those who encourage and are willing to die to maintain negro ignorance?"

When she had left and then came back, she held in her hand a printout from her computer. She said, "This is an email I received earlier from a group of women who I have been in an ongoing correspondence with. "Their

396

desire is to form a Lynx chapter in Chicago, but they have already had people in political positions to threaten the stand that the new chapter would take. But this is what I would like to talk to the two of you about," Mama Bee continued as she spread Miracle Whip onto some bread.

"First of all, realize that we were not surprised by the recent criticism. As a matter of fact we expected it to have arrived much sooner. But it's understood that the reason why it has reared its ugly little head now is due to the sudden media attention which shows the oppressors that we're a threat to their continual employment." "So you knew that there would be some sort of forum put in place to attack what we are doing, but what about Eli's poem?" Mary asked.

"Obviously we didn't know that they would call for this particular panel, but of course we anticipated for there to be opposition, but only if we were successful in our mission to educate our children of their past and link that past to their present state.

"And although we had absolutely no idea that Eli's poem would be the catalyst or even spark their offensiveness, all we truly knew was that they would surely come if we were to succeed."

"It's obvious Granny Bee, judging by all of the research I've done, it shows and proves that whenever black folks make progress in standing on their own two feet, and then begin to walk without the aid of their crutches, then somebody grows paranoid.

"So even if America's scar did spark their displeasure, I don't regret that it did, because in order for us to truly grow as a whole nation, we all must be allowed to sit at the round table," Eli said with intensity.

"I have been accused of not knowing the essence of Lynx's plight, and although I do admit to not knowing in detail the all around efforts, I can now honestly say that actually it's no different than what we originally set out to do." "Beginning with our past history," Mary expressed her understanding.

"You're right sweetheart and again I apologize to you for falsely accusing you of anything," Eli said while moving closer to her on the loveseat.

Then he went on to say, "I was just a little upset, because I believed that you had taken without question the side of those who are opposing us."

"I'd never take anyone's side against you," Mary said as she kissed Eli on his lips.

"Okay, alright lovebirds, we're all on the same page. Now it's time we have the same focus," Mama Bee informed them both.

Then she went on to say, "I know that both Joann and Elaine are more than capable of handling their own on that panel, but I do wonder at the possibility of anything said in our defense being used against us."

After their hearing what Mama Bee had just said, it was apparent to both Mary and Eli that Mama Bee was more than just a little nervous.

When they had reassured her that Joann, and Elaine were more than capable, they then went on to discuss whether or not the new chapter in Chicago should be opened.

It was concluded that after the viewing of the panel, things would become much more clearer.

"Well, I'd definitely have to run it by the whole board. It was just that I value your opinions so very much." "We understand Granny Bee, and we appreciate the fact that you would even consider our advice," Eli said. Followed by, "I'm most appreciative and I thank you," Mary told her.

The three straightened up Mama Bee's living room all the while listening to Eli make mention of the fact that she would have to think you to be special and important to her to even allow you to eat anything in her living room these days.

Afterwards, they parted ways promising to call or come by tomorrow.

Mama Bee hugged and kissed on them and told them both how she planned to hold them both to their word.

It wouldn't be until Friday the twenty-seventh that Mama Bee would see Eli and Mary both together and at the same time again. And she was so thankful of it, because she had been nervous all that day she had forgotten exactly how many times she had phoned Elizabeth up in New York to basically ask her the same fifty questions again.

By the time Eli and Mary had arrived at Mama Bee's house, they were barely able to find a parking space.

When they made their way inside, they were greeted by many members of Lynx and even Larry, Darrick, and Reggie were there as well.

Eli embraced his cousin Reggie, because he had not seen him in a while. They asked about one another's well being and then promised to talk later.

400

Mama Bee wanted Mary, and Eli to meet Michelle Obama, from Chicago, Illinois. A woman who held a district seat and who was seriously adamant about forming a chapter of Lynx in her city.

After the greetings were complete, refreshments were offered and then the entire room was hushed into silence, because the news broadcast was just about to air.

Mama Bee's living room and dining room was packed with folks all concerned about the offensive that Lynx was obviously up against since there was a need to defend.

Wouldn't you know it, they saved the panel for the very last segment.

Anticipation was to the ceiling and it was so quiet you might have been able to hear what was being thought in each other's minds, but for the fact that no one concerned themselves with what was going on in thoughts, nor anywhere else besides what was going on right in front of them, on that television.

"Good morning and thank you for remaining with us throughout the broadcast.

"Now we come to our segment entitled, Lynx, Is This Wildcat Too Wild To Tame?

"I'll begin by introducing our audience and our viewers to the members of the panel.

"Thank you all for coming and being willing to voice your opinions and your concerns.

"I'll first introduce Dr. Ibe Green who is a psychologist from South Carolina. Then there's Pastor Jim Gravitt from Houston, Texas. We also have with us here this evening, GOP candidate, Isadora Dürer and superintendent, Thomas Bodiford, who's over Georgia's public schools for the southeastern district. Thank you for attending sir.

"We also welcome here with us this evening Mrs. Joann Lewis, one of the founding members of Lynx.
Accompanying here is Mrs. Elaine Jordan, and Elizabeth Lewis. Who are also founding members of Lynx as well. "Linking past experiences with present day situations in the hope of building better futures.

"We thank you all for being here, and now that everyone has been properly introduced I'll go ahead and set the forum," announced Ms. Soledad O'Brien. *"Obviously we are here to shine further light on the establishment known as Lynx, and here are some who*

oppose its establishment by voicing that it's not for the betterment of the people, but rather a platform to be used for its Anti-America Agenda. Is this correct"

"Absolutely, and it's evident that when this group obtained media coverage the very first thing they used it for was to exploit America's past history of slaveholding as you'll do well to see for yourselves when you hear the creative writing, "America's Scar," proclaimed the Pastor.

"Okay, why don't we have our producers pull up an excerpt of that poem that was read at Lynx's previous convention and has been traveling the internet as well as the world here of late."

'I now embark upon a scar that America has across its face. A scar so ugly that it's almost too hideous to look upon.

But we are forced to view it every day, a constant reminder of the wound so deeply entrenched, we wonder if it will ever heal.

It reminds us of the time the wound was first inflicted and of its residual pain still being slashed across the backs of the burden bearers till this very day.

I've called it a scar as well as a wound but the definition of them both is slavery.

"You see," continued Pastor Gravitt, "this does not better anybody, but it does reopen old wounds and constitutes the pain that boils over into rage. So, I stand firm, this group does not in any way promote refinement but rather takes us back to a dark time."

"I concur," spoke candidate Dürer, "and I further—"

"Excuse me," interrupted Elizabeth Lewis of Lynx. "If I may, I would like the opportunity to give a reply to the pastor's comments."

"By all means, please do."

"Not in defense of, but rather I reaffirm Lynx's stance. Beginning at the start we've made it our aim to show the youth and all those concerned, the importance of learning their past, associating it with the present, so that it provides a clearer path to their future. But it's obvious that the pastor, as well as others who may concur that it's not important for black America to know their past," Liz concluded.

"Important it may be," the pastor leaped in and onto his feet. "But if old wounds are re-opened, then how is it possible for anyone to heal?" "It's pastor, right?" Joann asked.

"That's correct," Pastor Gravitt answered as he regained his seat.

"Do you preach Jesus Christ crucified on the cross at Calvary?"

"Yes I do, but more often I tell of His resurrection. His return up on high is what we are to look toward. And just where are you going with all of this? We're not here to discuss the Lord Jesus, but rather your group that teaches America did bad things."

"So are you saying that our Lord and Savior being bruised for our iniquities is something that you'd rather not preach to your congregation?" Joann persisted.

"I don't believe it to be necessary to continuously upset the people by constantly reminding them of that abominable act."

"It wasn't just an act, it was an injustice performed against the Son of God, and if we should ever lose sight of what He did for us up on that cross, then the price He paid may cause us to become numb to sin."

405

WE SUFFER FOR A REASON

"On that note my producers are calling for a break, but first let me say I actually see where you've taken us Mrs. Lewis in your line of questioning. If your history is not remembered explained, and addressed, then all involved may become, well numb," Ms. O'Brien expounded.

"Exactly!" Joann touched and agreed.

"We shall continue momentarily. Please stay with us . . ."

"We're back. Thank you for staying with us where we are discussing a group's affect on the mindset of a country.

"Dr. Green, do you care to comment?"

"I most certainly would. I'll begin by stating that Jesus has absolutely nothing to do with the reason for our being here today. "The man died over two thousand years ago for Christ's sake. But the reason for our being here stems from this group of individuals promoting the past of a young America into the psyche of young blacks so that they may grow into rage. "As a doctor of psychology I'm here to tell you that it's not healthy and it only has the potential to catapult black America into a revolution of undocumented proportion."

"Would anyone like to respond?"

"Yes, I would," announced Mrs. Elaine Jordan. "I'll do so by asking a question. Is it correct that everybody on that side of the panel opposes the idea of young black Americans being taught their past and the importance thereof?

"I think it's safe to say that the four of you are able to agree on that. So my follow-up question is: Why is that? Why would you all go through all of the trouble to hinder the teaching of America's history to African Americans?

"I'll answer my own question and tell you all why. It's because equipped with such knowledge, they will no longer neglect the ignorance in fighting gangs against gangs. They'll no longer murder each other senselessly in the communities that their great, great Grandparents died to provide them with.

"Instilled with the necessary knowledge, young black Americans will see their destinys more clearer. Clear enough to see that they have always strived for greatness since the beginning of their existence."

"You speak enormous words for people who don't even desire to show up to school half of the time," interjected superintendent Bodiford. "In my overseeing of them there at our Georgia pubic schools, the numbers speak

407

for themselves. And I need not mention the dropout rate, nor the illiteracy stats.

"It just makes it plain to see that your group should not be concerned with teaching them about the ills of slavery, but more concerned about getting them to show up for school so they can learn to read, and write!"

"Mr. Bodiford it is extremely apparent to me that the state of Georgia may be in need of a more competent superintendent, according to your numbers and stats," Elizabeth said.

Then she went on to state, "You have said out of your own mouth that Georgia's public school has problems, yet you've failed to turn the tide. Now I sit here wondering just why that is. But for now I'll keep my opinion to myself and I'll only ask the question: Exactly who was it who employed you to such a position and was their aim really to provide adequate schooling, or simply push children through and out uneducated and unable to aim for a true chance?"

"I beg your pardon. I'm quite capable of performing the task given to me. I've simply pointed out their lack of desire to be taught," Mr. Bodiford professed in obvious discomfort.

"Well, it's a known fact that you yourself must love what you do and who you do it for in order to motivate others into enthusiasm for it. "But that's neither here, nor there," Liz continued. "Your own words have shown where your heart is when it comes to the 'blacks' in America. So, all that we wish to know, well all that I would like to know sir, are you of any relation to the Bodifords of Marietta Georgia?" Liz questioned.

"Why yes, yes I am. I'm not ashamed to admit," Bodiford stated proudly.

"You should be," Elizabeth concluded. "You should be.

"I just have this to say. It's obvious that Lynx has no problem with allowing individuals to speak out against America from their platform, so I'll ask, who will they allow next to speak out, Farrakhan?" "It's also obvious that America is being accused of being a fascist regime," proclaimed Ms. Dürer.

"Are you admitting to having a problem with the minister?"

"Oh no, not at all. I'm only pointing out—" "Would you have a problem with him if he went on record as saying political positions here in the United States should only be reserved for those of American descent?"

"I was born here in America," Ms. Dürer almost yelled.

"But are you American, or German?" asked Joann.

"I, I don't see what the question has to do with your Anti-American agenda. You people are always seeking some sort of retri—"

"I beg your pardon;" you people"! Ms. Germany, I would doubt very seriously if you will be receiving a single vote from us people ever again," Joann stated.

"I didn't mean it like, I wasn't trying to—" Ms. Dürer turned to Ms. O'Brien and attempted to clarify.

"We will be right back after some words from our sponsors

Back at Mama Bee's residence the excitement was overwhelming. Everybody ecstatic by the women of Lynx ability to hold their own on the panel. "They sure do make me proud that they didn't allow themselves to be suckered into a one-sided debate," Mama Bee exclaimed.

"I'm proud of them too. All of them for maintaining the course that you all set for Lynx," Eli said.

"We are all very proud of them," Mary added. "The overall commitment of Lynx is something that me and my friends would definitely like to be a part of and establish in Chicago," Mrs. Obama voiced.

"Hold on, it's back on, someone announced.

"Welcome back to our news cast where we have panel members of the group known as Lynx. They proclaim their mission is to teach and educate black America, young and old alike the importance of their black history here in America so that they may be better equipped to handle the struggles up ahead.

"Now we will allow Dr. Green to give in conclusion his perspective concerning this movement."

"Thank you Ms. Soledad. First of all if it is a movement it will surely come to naught, like all of those before. "I for one can only pray that it does, because this Lynx has not taken into consideration the mindset that it would cause its children to develop.

"By educating them of a past belonging to their ancestors, this has the tendency of causing them to become frustrated with their present state of condition and just may propel them into lashing out, or even rebelling against their own country for its treatment of their race. And then we will have a country full of these recalcitrants running loose, releasing their pinned up angers.

411

"We will not allow it, and as American citizens who enjoy their safety, we all must speak out."

"You've just heard the unquestionable truth being given to you by a highly accredited psychologist," Ms. Bürer began, then went on to say, "Why should we allow this group to exist any further. It should be dismantled and never allowed to cause unrest or future harm to this great nation of ours."

"Well, I guess that puts it in a certain way," Ms. Soledad O'Brien said sarcastically. Then she asked, *"Would anyone like to respond?"*

It was Liz who responded with, "There's actually no response to words such as those. But what I would like to say into the camera is hi Elisha and Eli. I love you both dearly. Hello Mary. I love you as well, and the last thing I would like to say is, Mama Bee, you were right. Critics will surely crawl out from under rocks and most of them shouldn't even be given a response. For during the course of the debate an onlooker may not be able to discern which is the fool."

"Thank you Bernice Lewis for your words of wisdom and for your insight, and your knowledge that has motivated us to form our coalesce, Lynx."

CHAPTER 27

It wasn't a good whole week that had went by before the media went into a frenzy. And everyone was being pulled in every which direction.

Mary, and Elizabeth traveled to Chicago to speak with Mrs. Obama and six of her friends about the opening up of the Chi-town chapter of Lynx. It had been unanimously voted in by the whole entire board.

Upon their return from Chicago, Elizabeth and Mary were informed of their need to return immediately back to Chicago.

"Why, what did we do wrong?" Mary questioned. "It's not for any wrongdoing," Elaine explained to them both while having a huge smile spread across her face. "We've been invited to appear on the Oprah Winfrey show!"

"What?" Elizabeth asked. "I don't believe it."

"Believe it," Mama Bee said. "I talked to her myself this morning and she's also requested for Eli to be present as well."

"WOW!" was all that Mary was able to say.

"Tomorrow morning after you two are well rested, we will all meet up downtown for a scheduled luncheon where we'll discuss the accomplishments of your trip and then we will be departing for our appearance on the Oprah show," Elaine explained.

"Mama, we are really on our way to reaching out to the entire globe, aren't we?" Mary asked.

"It really does seem that way, and if it's the Lord's will, there'll be a chapter in every city in the United States," Elaine said matter of factly.

"And eventually there will be Lynx chapters established in other parts of the world as well since we always aim for the stars," Elizabeth added.

That mission had begun. Oprah showed Lynx in a most favorable light.

Her and Mama Bee spoke on camera and off in great length. They both shared not having a father to give their daughterly love to and they confided in one another what they were not willing to share with others.

At their departure they, Mama Bee and Oprah, exchanged cell and home phone numbers, promising to keep in touch.

For video of the show order your copy of: "Mama Bee Wipes Away Oprah's Overdue Tears."

On the plane ride home as Eli sat in the seat next to Mama Bee she said, "See how your calling has been made more evident? You just showed the world that you are a skilled writer with something to offer others. A message in every bottle, that will truly guide others."

Eli answered, "Precious child of God was inspired by you Granny Bee."

And then they both slept the remainder of the flight home from Chicago—the Windy City.

CHAPTER 28

Eli obviously was destined for controversy to accompany him and his new found fame. Actually, he didn't consider himself as being famous at all.

There were several publishing companies that had contacted him, wanting to publish his work. But as mentioned before, there was controversy.

Groups of them to tell the honest to God truth about it. And they wanted to voice their protest to anyone who would give an ear. The object of their outrage was a poem Eli had on his website's archive entitled "Racist" and it reads as follows:

The hate that a white man illustrates towards a black man in this American twenty first century is cause for pause. Let us look into the mind of a human being who has such contempt, disdain, and pure hatred in its heart. A racist who's own core is being depleted from within unbeknownst to the racist. It's like a harbored sin that dries and rots the bones and causes the deterioration of the soul. Most of them are confessed alcoholic women beaters with a lust for abusing children.

WE SUFFER FOR A REASON

Compared to the wild animal, there's not much difference between the two.   Both are predators searching for prey.   With an appetite for destruction, seeking to destroy that which is weaker, or unable to defend themselves.

But, whenever placed on an equal playing field, the cowardice is displayed.

If we are to truly view the thinking of a racist, we may have to travel back in time and look at the roots of a poisonous tree.

The roots that go deep down into the soil of America, absorbing asp as a needed nutrient.

The vicious venom has been shamelessly spat into the face of the black race that it enslaved, freed, and now hunts down to lock in cages.

This obviously witnessed by their children. Children growing into adults willingly adapting to the hatred, never once considering the need to love, nor even to like those they have been trained to despise. Not just growing, growing into positions of power and control.

The same hooded clowns filling positions in government, police precincts all around America.   And in every penal system from courthouses to the jail houses.

WE SUFFER FOR A REASON

Especially so in their Jim Crow south. Cobb County Georgia Correctional Facility has twelve hour shifts of individuals you would recognize to be diehard Klan members, no longer hiding the fact that they hate the color black. Even more so when it covers the face of a man.

So, searching and seeking serves the purpose of sighting that these racists choose to hate other human beings for as many reasons as one could come up with.

But look with me deep into their eyes and you'll discover as I have the true deep seeded reason why their hatred runs so deep that it boils their blood and causes them to lash out at times for no apparent reason.

But there is a reason. And I conclude that flesh shall always contend with spirit!!!

The attention and the controversy was the last things on Eli's mind after having decided to stay in Louisville and attend the university with Mary and his cousins. His thoughts were only of his new transition into the college life.

And he had known early on that he could not leave his mother here alone. Although she had Granny Bee and forty seven members of Lynx who was hands on educating, tutoring and mentoring over a hundred and fifty participants by her side.

He still knew how much his mother needed him, and the real evidence of it showed in her eyes.

These are the thoughts which consumed him here of late.

And although Elizabeth probably would never say it, she still missed James and his untimely passing still pains her as if the automobile accident had just happened recently.

He knew this much, because it still pained him.

He often has had remembrances of the day. But he never talks about it with anybody, believing himself to have discovered a way in which to deal with it. That's by writing his heart onto paper, but never letting it go any further.

These writings will never be seen by anyone, even if the entire world desired to look into them, he knew he would refuse them access. This was his only way of dealing with his father's absence and he assumed that his mother had found her own way of dealing with it on a day to day basis as well. One in which he really didn't wish to intrude into.

What Eli believed he could do, he did.

He remained in Kentucky and attended school at the University of Louisville, so he'd be near to his mother for her inner comfort and ease.

"Hello Mom. Hello, oh I couldn't hear you at first. I thought we had a bad connection. Listen, are you busy? No, I was just wondering if you'd like to go out for dinner tonight? Good, then I'll make reservations and you just be sure to be ready by eight. I'm not telling you where, it'll be a surprise.

"Okay, don't work too hard. I love you Mom." Eli hung up the phone and he then instantly became filled with delight, just knowing he had just filled his mother's heart with the kind of joy that wraps itself around intrigue.

That night at the extremely nice, exclusive restaurant in the heart of downtown Louisville, Liz was shocked and surprised and she couldn't seem to be able to stop from smiling.

As they sat at their table, she took hold of her son's hand and she said, "Thank you son. This is truly a beautiful restaurant, and a wonderful surprise."

"Your presence adds to the overall beauty and Mama you don't have to thank me for attempting to show you how much I love and appreciate you."

"Well, do you mind telling the reason of my being here tonight, and not Mary?"

"I just told you that I simply wanted to express my love, and my appreciation."

"Eli, come on boy I know my child and there's something else to it. Now tell your mother what's really going on, or let it eat at you from within."

"Mama, why do you have to put it like that?"

"Because there's only one way to put the truth. Now come on and tell me what's on your mind son."

"Mama, let's enjoy our meal and one another's company and then we'll deal with my thoughts."

"Sounds fair enough," Elizabeth said.

Halfway through their meal, a bottle of some very expensive wine was sent to their table. The waiter informed Elizabeth that it had been sent to her by the table of gentlemen who sat near to the rear, just to their right.

When Liz looked in that direction, one of the men lifted his hand and gave her a smile, making her so aware that it was he who had sent the wine in order to show his approval of natural beauty.

"Please tell the gentleman thank you, but no thank you. We're just fine with the wine we've ordered." When the waiter reached and took a hold of the bottle, Eli took a hold of it as well and told him, "It'll be fine for you to leave it, and please be so kind as to bring us two fresh wine glasses, please sir," Eli instructed as he gave the waiter a folded ten dollar bill.

"Eli, why did you do that?" Liz wanted to know. "Because they are overworked, and underpaid. Most of them live off of their tips, yet and still people are serviced well, but tip less."

"I am not talking about the waiter and you know it Eli. I'm talking about accepting this bottle of wine, knowing what it signifies."

"And what would that be Mama?"

"Don't you dare play dumb with me boy. By accepting this wine, gives that guy the okay to approach."

"Tell me, what would be the problem with approaching?"

"Approaching leads to questions, and they lead to answering."

422

"Well, I sho hope you have some prepared."

"Have some what prepared?" Liz asked.

"Some answers," Eli answered.

"Answers?" Elizabeth questioned.

"Yes Ma'am, some answers to some questions, because he's approaching."

As soon as she turned her head in order to see she was greeted with, "Excuse my intrusion, as well as my assumption, if I have assumed incorrectly. But my guess is that here sits a mother out celebrating with her son, maybe even congratulating him for being a good college student. "My name is Todd, Mark Todd of Todd Communications. And while having dinner conversation with a few associates I couldn't help but to notice."

"Notice?" Elizabeth asked.

"Yes, I noticed a glow about you that let me know you've been spending time in your prayer closet with the Father."

The analogy caught Liz totally by surprise and she was speechless. The only thing she was able to bring to her mind to say was, "Well Mr. Todd. My name is Elizabeth. Thank you for the wine. Oh, and you assumed correctly, this is my son Eli."

"Hey Eli, you be sure to protect and cherish the precious gifts provided you by God," Mr. Todd said as he shook Eli's hand, never taking his eyes off of Elizabeth. He then removed a business card and placed it on the table, right in front of Elizabeth and told her, "Use this if the need to comes over you."

She said nothing. They said nothing as Mr. Todd turned and traveled back to the table from whence he'd come.

"Mama, are you okay?" Eli asked.

"Yes, of course. What do you mean?" she wanted to know.

"I thought you were showing the side affects of being wrong."

"About?" Liz asked.

"After the approach, then comes the questions quote, unquote."

"You do know better than to mock someone, especially if that someone is your mother, don't you?"

"Yes Ma'am, like I know the difference between mocking and joking."

Then there was silence until the meal had been consumed.

"Wasn't this entire evening supposed to be about the thoughts you wanted to share?" Liz asked.

"Some thoughts and concerns are eased just by spending a little time with the object of my affection," Eli said because he noticed Mr. Todd's business card had vanished, and more than likely had been transmitted into his mother's purse, by his mother.

"Mama, I would like to express this thought to you though."

"Express on," Liz told him.

"Okay, Christmas is only a couple of months away and I thought it would be a good idea if me, you, Elisha, Ella, and hopefully my great grandmother Glenda could all spend Christmas together down in Georgia.

"What do you think Mama? We haven't been there since I was a sophomore in high school. That was over two years ago, and we didn't spend a moment that we was there with Glenda."

"I know that we didn't, and we should have sought her out, but instead I called myself being considerate of Mama's feelings," Liz said, then added. "It's still not clear exactly where the two of them stand towards one another."

"Mama, wouldn't we be the blame if we neglected to do all that we were able to do to put our own family intact?" "Yeah, I truly believe we would be at fault. If not in the eyes of others, definitely in our own eyes."

"So, it'll be okay if I called and told Elisha of our plans to celebrate Christmas there?" Eli asked.

"It would be more than okay. Only don't mention your great Grandmother. I will need the opportunity to speak with Grandma and Mama just to provide myself a general idea."

"I already know that me carrying around this great news during this semester of school will probably cause me to be too anxious to concentrate."

To that his mother told him, "You know the word," and together they both said, "To be anxious for nothing but in all things make your requests known to God."

They then shared a laugh, and inadvertently Elizabeth glanced over to the table where Mr. Todd once sat, but only to discover him to be there no more.

CHAPTER 29

Eli found college life to be easy enough. The studying was made much much easier by internet downloading and all of the rest was a breeze due to his excessive ability to retain the knowledge learned.

What Eli found to be difficult was how to make adequate time to spend with his Mary.

Days were speeding by, turning into weeks that made the calendar read November the eighteenth. Less than six days before Thanksgiving and a little over a month until Christmas.

For Eli, first things were first. He had to call his Grandmother and make sure it was okay for him to invite Mary to Thanksgiving dinner. He knew she wouldn't mind it one bit, but he'd ask nonetheless.
The second thing he had scheduled to do was to upgrade his webpage by putting links onto his home page that would access his latest creation. A poem that would bless many and shine light on those who have been living in darkness.

Eli had realized beyond a shadow of a doubt that he absolutely positively loved to write. He loved to take in the finished product of his thoughts, emotions, heart, and his soul.   He knew he would one day conquer writing as musical greats had conquered their instruments.

CHAPTER 30

Eli and Mary entered Mama Bee's dining room and they both just stood there, because everyone's attention was locked in on them, and they both was trying to figure out why.

"What is it? Why are you all looking like I have a warrant out for my arrest?"

"Hi little brother," Elisha says as she walks in from the kitchen where she had been hiding.

"Oh my God," Eli says as he went over and embraced his sister. Releasing her he asks, "When did you get into town and why didn't you tell me you was coming?" "Then it wouldn't have been a surprise, would it?" she asked.

"No, I guess it wouldn't have been." Hugging her some more he says, "A wonderful surprise it is!"

When Elisha, and Mary had greeted one another they all sat down at the table to listen to Mama Bee tell them all about her good news.

"Listen," she said. "I have something to share with all of you. Me and Charles plan to be married come spring!" "Charles?" Reggie asked with a perplexed expression. Jokingly, because everyone knew Mama Bee referred to Poppa Charlie by his government name, Charles.

"Yes, Charles," Mama Bee replied. Then added, "Is there a problem Reginald E?"

"Congratulations," Liz said. "Congratulations to you and Poppa Charlie."

This was followed by many more offerings of congrats and a few hugs and kisses.

"I would also like to announce that Mary and Bridal Workz will be fashioning most of, if not all of the wedding planning, if she agrees to do it." "Ms. Bee, I mean Mama Bee, I would be more than happy to do whatever is needed of me that would cause your wedding day to be most beautiful."

"Thank you sweetheart. From the moment I knew I would say yes, I had you in mind, because you have worked so hard putting together, and overseeing the young women's established Bridal Workz shop." "Ms. Bee, you don't know how happy you've made me today by allowing me and my girls to be a part of your happiness," Mary exclaimed.

"Liz, don't you have something to tell to Mary?" Mama Bee asked.

"Mary, Lynx has allotted Bridal Workz the funds to open up a beautiful boutique downtown and obviously everyone would like for you to ready the place and prepare it to be opened to the public."

"No, you're joking," Mary said in astonishment and disbelief. with both hands over her mouth she managed to get out, "Mama Bee I won't disappoint you, or Lynx, I swear! Two boutiques, we're really growing. I can't wait to share this great news with the girls.

"Happy Thanksgiving," Cookie said as he came into the dining room followed by Lee-Lee who was carrying a beautiful little girl on her hip.

Everyone, the entire room was overcome with excitement and joy!

Debra rushed to Lee-Lee's side and took her little sister Faith into her own arms. She baby talked to her and kissed her all over her face to the point it caused Faith to wipe off her face with her hand and asked, "Why you talk like a baby?"

"Because you're my baby sister," Debra said.

"I'm no baby. I turn these many the last time I had my birthday," Faith said holding up four fingers, proudly showing her age.

Cookie was over there being smothered in Mama Bee's arms.

They brought her granddaughter over to her and upon taking her and placing her onto her lap, Mama Bee began saying, "Hi Faith, how are you?"

"I'm fine, and you? My name is Monique!" "Your name is Faith, but you like to be called by your middle name Monique," Lee-Lee said from the other end of the table.

"I like to be called my middle name, Monique," she told her Grandmother.

"Well, I'm your Granny Bee and I like to be called to supper on time."

"You my Granny and this is my Granny's house."

After informing Lee-Lee of their wedding plans, Mama Bee asked her daughter if she could depend on her to be in her wedding.

"Oh Mama, I'll be there, along with your ring bearer and your flower girl," referring to Cookie, and Monique

432

of course. Once Ray, and Joann arrived the families joy ,and happiness was absolute.

It was still left up in the air as to who would give the bride away; Reggie or Pretty Ray. All else would be left in the capable hands of Ms. Mary Jordan.

"Mama, Lynx keep throwing money around everywhere. How about you all purchase a rising basketball star a car?" Darrick asked.

"Why would we do that for someone who's academics are showing average grades and some courses being barely passed?"

"It appears that you're barely maintaining basketball eligibility," Liz exclaimed.

"Aunt Liz, so you're just going to put all of my business out there like that? Cool, you don't have to buy me nothing. There's other ways of getting a whip though," Darrick made them aware.

"And just what are you saying Darrick? Cause I know damn well you're not going to just sit here at this table and insinuate that you'll do something dumb and stupid, just so you can ride around looking dumb, and stupid," Mama Bee asked him.

"After seeing for yourself the end result of many who have willingly taken the pathway of ignorance. They show the dead end road so often taken daily on the news," Larry made mention. "Naw, we don't have to worry about Darrick, the boy is crazy, but he ain't stupid. He knows taking gifts could and definitely would end his career, and the next level, the pro's. Forget about it!" "Don't nobody want on their pro team somebody who has shown their stupidity by accepting gifts," Larry summarized.

"What if it's the pro team that's providing the gifts then?" Darrick asked.

"Then they're showing you proof positive that they don't give a darn about you, nor about your future," Elisha told him.

"Haven't we all learned from growing up here and being taught by these women who sincerely love us that those people who encourage wrong doing are the very demons that we've been instructed to fight against and resist," said Eli.

"How can anyone who claims to love you, or care for you turn around in the next breath and encourage you to do what is obviously wrong?" Eli further questioned.

"There's no sense in you feeling sad and having your heart downcast. You know right from wrong. You're just being convicted by the spirit of God, but that's a beautiful thing to have happen to you, especially before entering into sin," Darrick's Aunt Liz told him as her hope for him remained.

Darrick apparently came to his senses and said that he wouldn't let any franchise own him, or his decisions with a gift.

That's when Mama Bee said, "Everything that you all need has already been provided for you all, if only you would do right, and ask."

"What do I have to do?" Darrick asked.

"Get your grades up, nut," Reggie told him. "And think about something other than just basketball," he went on to say.

"Yeah, what if basketball ends due to an injury. Don't you want to have a career you can fall back on?" Elisha asked.

"Like Mama Bee said, do right and then ask. Who can say no to a child who makes his Mama proud?" Larry asked.

"I know, I know. Get a job Darrick," Cookie imputed.

Everybody agreed, and Thanksgiving dinner concluded in happiness and joy, instead of a sour note. Then came the deserts. The truth was, who really had the room in their stomachs for any of them delicious looking deserts that was placed before them.

But the moment allowed them to continue in wonderful conversations in which Poppa Charlie spoke. "I want to thank each and everyone of you guys for accepting me into this beautiful family. I'm honored to be a part of the lives of people such as yourselves. Compassionate God fearing and caring of others. Especially people who are less fortunate. I'm able to see how a part of Bernice's heart is flowing through all of your hearts.

"And my heart has been blessed two times over. First, by receiving the love of my Bumble Bee, and secondly by having the love of her family. I love you all, I put that on everything."

"You are a blessing to us as well," Liz said. "You have completed Mama's heart and we can't begin to express how much that means to us."

"Plus you know you have to treat her like the Queen that she is before we have to get on that ass," Darrick blurted. "Boy, how are you going to sit here and talk to us about doing good and turn right around and let that

436

forwardness come out of your mouth?" Mama Bee asked.

"Mama, I'm only joking. We all know that Poppa Charlie is good people."

"Poppa Charlie, I hope to be able to get to know you better," Lee-Lee said.

"That will be my pleasure, and really mandatory so your mother can have more of her some Cookie. And then there's this precious, adorable little thing," Poppa Charlie said to Lee-Lee as he picked Monique from her lap.

"I'm not little. I'm these many, see!"

"I know you're not little, you're four," Poppa Charlie assured her.

"I want to let you guys know that me, and the kids have moved back into the house over across Broadway", LeeLee mentioned as she made eye contact with her Mother.

That's what's up, definitely a better environment, someone made mention.

"Hey family you know Twill fell ill and I think we should take a moment to pray for my friend", Mama Bee told them.

When they had all stood and locked fingers, Eli took the liberty of placing their supplication into the presence of God Almighty, who's always willing to hear from His children.

When their prayers were ended, Mama Bee told her daughter Lee-Lee how much she loved it that she had moved back into a place where she could be reached and the children could be seen more easily.

She didn't feel the need nor had she the desire to ask of Rufus' whereabouts, or what caused their separation this time. She was just content to have her daughter right there, right now.

"Elisha, Me and Mama have something we would like to tell to you, and I'll let Mama do the telling."

" What is it Mama? Tell me."

"Me and your brother want to come and spend Christmas with you and Mama this year."

"Forreal Mama? Oh my gosh, that would be so wonderful. Nana is going to be so happy."

"You and Eli are all she ever talks about.

We just hope that all of us will be able to spend this Christmas together, including our great Grandmother Glenda," Eli added.

"I don't know how successful pulling that off will be, because I've tried to bring the two of them together on more than one occasion," Elisha said with a touch of sadness.

"It has been too long for them two," Mama Bee made mention.

"Even though we will miss you all not being around here this Christmas, at least we'll know where you will be, and why," Larry said in sort of a sadder sadness because it was bad enough that he had lost all contact with his Karen Mckenzie. Her mother had moved them to Tennessee somewhere.

As the deserts were eventually consumed and the conversations thinned, one by one they began to depart, but not before the telling of how they planned to call and/or come by in the following week.

At the door, Mama Bee gave out hugs, and kisses as Poppa Charlie gave firm handshakes and several hugs of his own until all were gone, save Lee-Lee and her two, Cookie and Faith who were sound asleep in the boy's old bedroom.

Lee-Lee told the both of them that her and the kids would be staying the night if they didn't mind it. They assured her that they didn't and Poppa Charlie took his que to leave the two women alone so that they could talk.

"I'm a go back and check on the children before turning in myself," he told them.

Mama Bee told him okay as they exchanged pecks on their cheeks.

Lee-Lee and her mother took seats in the living room where they both expressed their hearts.

Mama Bee was overjoyed to have her daughter and her grandchildren home for Thanksgiving. It had been a while since she last saw her Cookie, and even longer since she had seen Faith Monique. But down inside there dwelled in Mama Bee some anxiety, because she knew her joy would not last long.

Lee-Lee would again take her children and go, leaving Mama Bee with an empty void, but these thoughts, and feelings she knew she had to suppress.

Before the two said their goodnights Lee-Lee told her mother again that her, and the kids would be no further away than right across town and she would be able to visit whenever she liked.

WE SUFFER FOR A REASON

CHAPTER 31

Before leaving for Georgia, Elizabeth received from Mama Bee a few gifts for her and all the others who would be with her in Georgia.

Eli, and Liz gave Mama Bee, and Poppa Charlie their gifts and the gifts that they had purchased for others they had placed under Mama Bee's Christmas tree.

Before leaving out of the door, Mama Bee held her grandson in her arms once again and then afterwards she embraced her daughter-in-law Elizabeth, who over the years had become as her very own daughter; sort of like Ruth and Naomi.

"I want you to take this with you," Mama Bee said as she handed Liz a single slip of paper.

She didn't have to ask what it was when she looked at it and seen her Grandmother Glenda's name. She simply folded it and placed it inside of her purse, feeling a little saddened by the fact that she had not seen her Grandmother in along while.

They arrived at Ella's house in as little as seven hours, thanks to Eli's hasty, but safe driving.

"I'm wondering why we haven't made the journey much more often, seven hours isn't that bad." Eli made mention.

"I can't even begin to give a explanation that would be a reasonable one," Liz told him.

Before they even entered the house, Elisha was out the door asking if they needed any help with the luggage, and packages that they were gathering from the car.

"How are you going to help anybody with anything without having any shoes on?" Liz asked.

"I have on shoes," Elisha replied.

"Those are fluffy white rabbits," Eli reminded her.

"Girl get your behind back in this house before you catch cold," Ella told Elisha standing behind her in the doorway.

"Hi Grandmother," Eli said as he entered the house.

"I prefer that you call me Nana as Elisha does. As you both did when you were little and here with me. Now give your Nana a hug, cause she misses you so much!" When Liz had come into the house, tears began to flow from Ella's eyes and as she held her daughter she said,

"Liz, Liz, Liz, I have missed you so much and you hardly call the way you used to."

"I know Mama, it's just that I have been so busy with my responsibilities at Lynx."

"I have to say that I am so very proud of you and Elisha. The way you have provided a refuge for so many young women."

"Where's Ms. Pam?" Elizabeth asked after she had gotten somewhat settled.

"She's away attending to the needs of a elder of the church who needs her assistance far more than I do. "Would you just look at my grandbaby," Ella began. "Elisha has shown me on that computer some of your writings that have sparked so much fussing over."

"Controversy has become my middle name," Eli said as he took in his familiar surroundings. He loved this house; the safety, the comfortability, and even the smells, like there was something always cooking in the oven.

He began to travel from room to room recalling the very places he had played and even a couple of the places where he had been spanked. The floors still creaked in the hallway between the first bedroom and the bathtroom.

444

The next morning, Christmas Eve, they all were awakened to the smells of the huge breakfast that Elizabeth had prepared for them.

Afterwards, Liz and Elisha left, saying that they had some last minute Christmas shopping to do, which they intended on doing, but only after seeing the results of this important phone call that they were making. As Elisha drove, Elizabeth punched in her Grandmother's phone number, who answered on about the seventh ring.

"Hello. Yes Ma'am this is Elizabeth, Ella's daughter. Okay, me and my daughter Elisha are calling to let you know that we are only seconds away from your house. Oh yes Ma'am she's right here. Okay, just a second."

"Here Elisha, Grandma wants to talk to you."

"Hi Granny, I'm doing okay. Yes Ma'am. Yeah, my Mom. I don't know, does she seem nervous?" Elisha asked as she looked over at her Mother.

"Yes Granny, I'm sure she does. I'm going to hang up now Granny, because we're about to pull up to your house in just another second okay, bye."

"You're sure I do what?" Liz asked her daughter.

"Do what?" Elisha answered with a question.

445

"You just told my Grandmother 'I'm sure she does,' obviously referring to me."

"Oh, it was nothing. She was just wondering if you remember what she looks like."

As they got out of the car Glenda greeted them at the door, where she welcomed Elisha's embrace. Then she invited them both inside of the house.

"Hello Grandma Glenda. I know it has been awhile, almost three years, but I'll never forget my Grandma." Glenda ignored her words and she turned to her great granddaughter Elisha and said, "Baby do you mind going into my kitchen and washing those few dishes that I left in there?"

"No Granny, I don't mind at all," Elisha told her.

"Do you need my help?" Liz asked her.

"You wait right here. I don't allow too many people in my house, especially not in my kitchen," Glenda explained to Liz a little sternly.

Elisha returned to the front and said to her Granny, "Granny there are no dishes in there to be washed."

"There's not, oh I must have taken care of 'em before I took my nap."

Elisha was almost certain that there was something totally different with her great Grandmother. She just couldn't place a finger on what it was.

"Granny, do you remember my brother Eli?"

"Eli, yes I know Eli very well, but them white folks come by and they did Eli something terrible."

"No Grandma, we're asking you about my son Eli, not your Grandfather."

"Oh yes, that's right. Where is the child? Is he playing around back there in my kitchen?"

"No Ma'am, he's waiting on us back at Nana's house," Elisha said.

"That's right Grandma, he's at your daughter Ella's house," Liz tells her.

"My daughter; my daughter you must be mistaken!"

"Yes Ma'am, your daughter's name is Ella and I'm Ella's daughter Elizabeth."

"What is she talking about child?" Glenda asked, as she turned toward Elisha with such a look of fear in her eyes that it frightened her.

"There's nothing to be afraid of Granny, she's just trying to help you to remember. We both are," Elisha assured her.

Elisha and Elizabeth both sat there for well over an hour comforting and calming Glenda. Talking to her about her family and about some of the things they knew about Glenda's past, their family's past.

After they had a small lunch, Elisha asked her Granny, "You remember the last time I was over here about a month and a half ago and I told you that my mother Elizabeth right here; Her and my brother Eli were in Kentucky at my Granny Bee's house?"

"Yes, they are at Bernice 's house. How is Bumble Bee doing? You know that's what they called her when she was little, 'Bumble Bee.' And she didn't like it one bit. We would all tease her all the time. Run everybody before the Bumble Bee stings you."

"So, you do remember Bernice ?" Liz asks.

"Of course I do. Why would you think otherwise? She just hasn't called me in a good long while."

"We had thought that you had forgotten Bernice because earlier you weren't able to remember your own daughter Ella." "Ella? I know Ella very well. She's my only daughter. And she has a lot of heartache, and pent

448

up anger that she's carrying around with her. And she just can't seem to find a way to let it go. I wish she would let the pain go so it wouldn't wear on her so."

"Well Grandma Glenda, that's part of the reason why I came to Georgia for Christmas. To see if it would be possible for all of us to spend this Christmas together."

"Christmas?"

"Yes Ma'am, Christmas. It's tomorrow, today is Christmas Eve," Elisha informed her.

"Dear Lord I've been so busy here lately I just done forgot all about the Lord's birthday. Dear Lord, help me!"

"We want you to spend this Christmas with your family, over at your daughter Ella's house."

"I don't know, Ella is very stubborn. She might not want me at her house."

"Let us worry about that and when we call you later on this evening and tell you to start getting ready, you'll know we are on our way to get you, so you can spend Christmas with us."

"I'll be sure to do just that. Does that mean you are about to leave?" Glenda asked.

"Yes Ma'am, we're gong to shop for a few items and then we're going right to Ella's and talk to her about all of us spending this Christmas together."

"You can try to talk to Ella, but I doubt she'll let you get a word in inch wide. She's just stubborn that way. But you just remember to tell Ella that finding it in her heart to forgive wouldn't be so hard to do if she would remember how Rose forgave her and tried to take her secret to the grave with her. You be sure to tell Ella, because she sho is stubborn and headstrong too."

Elizabeth and Elisha cut their shopping short, because they both wanted nothing more than to have their conversation with Ella.

On their ride back to Ella's house, Elisha asked, "Mama what do you think Granny was talking about when she said, 'Rose forgave Nana and she even carried her secret to her grave?' "

"I haven't a clue, but we both know the one who knows exactly what she was speaking of."

They pulled into Ella's drive and they both took a deep breath and exhaled hard before traveling the few steps to the front door. Once inside they heard the laughter that was coming from the kitchen area.

Ella and Eli were engaged in conversation when Liz and Elisha entered the room.

"I see you two finally made it back. I was just telling Nana that I'll never ever attempt to figure out why it takes you two so long to shop and that includes grocery shopping as well," Eli emphasized.

"We weren't just gift shopping we stopped by Grandma Glenda's," Elizabeth announced while searching her mother's face for a reaction. She discovered that there was none. So she went on to say, "So we took the liberty of inviting her here to celebrate Christmas with her family."

"You had no right to invite anyone to my house without having my permission," Ella exploded.

"Mama, all of my life you did all you could possibly do to keep my Grandmother out of my life without ever giving me even a hint as to why. As if my feelings didn't matter to you one bit," Liz cried.

"Your feelings, your feelings! I was protecting your feelings from a woman who didn't give a damn about dismantling, tearing apart the feelings of others," Ella retorted. "I don't want to hear about your feelings where she is concerned, and I most definitely don't want to hear anymore talk about her coming to my house."

"Nana, listen for one second, will you? Granny is ill. She's not herself totally. She's not even the same as she was just a little over a month ago," Elisha said.

"What do you expect? The woman is almost a hundred years old. Add that with all of the evil she has done," Ella voiced.

"You two went over to Granny Glenda's and you didn't bother mentioning it to me at all, why?Eli asked in such a tone.

"Yes, yes we did go over to her house in hopes of bringing us all together for the holidays," Liz explained.

"I'll just have to go see her myself," Eli began. "It's been close to three years, and now I learn that she's not well!"

"I was under the impression that my family came here to visit with me, so that we may spend Christmas together. Not run all over the place visiting people who enjoy causing others pain, and grief," Ella said attempting to discourage Eli from leaving.

"She just wants to come over and spend the holidays with her family," Elisha said.

"What? She said that?" Ella asked, then added, "No, I won't have that woman in my house."

452

"That woman is your own mother," Eli told his Nana.

"Oh, I see how it is. The three of you are ganging up on me. So you're doing me like Bee did, taking her side."

"Mama, this has absolutely nothing to do with anyone taking anybody's side. What happened between you two, happened between you. So, you both will have to solve it yourselves."

"It can't be solved. It's far too late for anything to be solved, or salvaged. She made her bed and now she has to lay in it," Ella said in a fiery manner.

"All those years you've been going to church and reading the bible faithfully, but yet and still you haven't learned anything about forgiveness. But your mother knows her daughter well enough, because she said you would be stubborn. So stubborn in fact that you would have to be reminded that you yourself have been forgiven.

"Not only did your Aunt Rose forgive you, she also wanted to took the secret to her grave," Elizabeth had to say to her mother in such a way.

This caught Ella off guard and by surprise, to the point she could no longer stand. So she had to sit in the chair and as she did so she mumbled, "My mother knew, all these many years and she has known."

Ella remained there in the chair unresponsive for well over three or four minutes. When she finally arose, she went to her stove and began to prepare tea. She placed four cups on a tray as her daughter and grandchildren sat there and observed. After the preparation was complete, she invited them to join her for tea in the kitchen.

She led, they followed and they all sat in her historically styled kitchen and proceeded to sip their tea.

"I suppose it is about time I told someone about a past that may cause my soul to burn slowly in hell," Ella began.

"I won't try and blame it on them times nor will I blame it on the situation. But back in those days the white folks had a lot of influence over the black folks, especially the young and foolish.

"A lot of us couldn't discern whether or not if slavery was over or just a lie told us'.

I was thirteen and he was well over twenty-five. A white man who came by and bought all of my Daddy's cotton every harvest. He began by giving me the sweet

454

taffy, but one day well before the harvest, he came by and I knew he was drunk 'cause I smelled it on him strong.

"He grabbed me in his arms and after saying how he would make me out of a proper lady, he just began kissing me on my mouth. I fought him off 'cause I had never kissed anyone before, but something must have shown that I didn't mind it much, because that harvest time that later rolled around he took me out into the woods and I drank with him some, then afterwards we laid together.

"And despite the pain I allowed him to do whatever he wanted to do to me that night and several nights that followed. My Aunt Rose had taken notice first that I hadn't had my cycle so she kept an eye on me for awhile I imagine, long enough that she knew for sure. One day she had cornered me off, and all she asked was, 'Who's child is it?'

"Being that I believed she knew already I told my Aunt Rose the truth, everything,

She slapped my face so hard it took my breath away. She had to calm me and help me to catch my breathe again. I was hurt and scared, but I continued seeing him because he told me he would carry me and the baby away and take good care of us, long before anyone else discovered my condition.

'Because I had told him that my mother would notice soon if he didn't keep true to his word. That was the night I discovered that he was already married with children. When I cried, he slapped, and punched me asking if I really believed he would even consider leaving his family behind for a dumb stupid nigger.

Then he left me there to wallow in my own misery and self pity.

"I did the only thing I thought I should do. I took a metal rod used for the animals there in the barn and I fixed it. I bled horribly, but eventually I made it into the house and if it hadn't been for my Aunt Rose I wouldn't have made it through to the next day, I had lost so much blood.

"She convinced my mother and father to let her take me to her place, assuring them that it would do a world of good if I spent some time with her daughter Bernice.

"My health returned to me and soon after it did, me and Aunt Rose would begin to start having the most awful arguments, fusses, and fights. During those times I said things to my Aunt Rose that hurt her real bad, after all she had done for me, but she was always a forgiving soul.

"It wouldn't surprise me if all three of you looked at me differently. You could be no harsher than God Himself."

"Nana, we're not going to judge you. We'll always love you and care for you," Elisha said.

"Mama, you mean the world to us. Even in our absence our love has always and will always remain."

"And what do you say grandson?" Ella asked, because Eli had yet to voice an opinion.

"How can I, or anyone condemn when Jesus has died to free and to declare righteous in His sight," Eli said. Then added, "Nana, I can only pray you accept what Jesus has done for you by first asking God for forgiveness in Jesus' name.

"Your having faith in His Word will clear your conscience. Just don't neglect to show your trust in His love for you and remain a person of forgiveness towards others."

Eli allowed those words to marinate in his Grandmother's spirit and obviously they had taken root because Ella stood to her feet and stepped to her daughter Elizabeth and said, "Will you please go and get my Mother and bring her here to me?"

"Yes Ma'am, I most definitely will," Liz assured her Mother as Elisha and Eli hugged one another and then they embraced their Nana and Liz did likewise.

There they all stood while emotional tears washed over them, cleansing, and removing the stains of hindrance and stubbornness.

Elizabeth and Elisha hurriedly made their exit in excitement. Both of them riding on a cloud of anticipation while Eli remained with Ella explaining to her how he became versed in scripture.

Eli was more than happy to inform his Nana of his world religion course that was causing him to cross reference its teachings with the Word of God. And he didn't neglect to let it be known of God endowing him with a discerning spirit as well.

Ella hugged her grandson tightly again and then thanked him for helping to open her eyes. Then in speed Eli didn't know his Grandmother possessed, she moved, instructing him at the same time to assist her in the straightening up of her house in preparation for the arrival of her Mother.

Upon Elizabeth and Elisha's return with Grandma

Glenda, they found Ella's house to be Pinesol fresh and Eli sitting there in a state of exhaustion. Nonetheless he got to his feet and attempted to relieve Grandma Glenda of the oversized bag she toted.

"This here belongs to me," she said and refused to release it to him.

"Grandma, this is your great grandson Eli," Liz told Glenda.

"I know exactly who he is. I ain't blind. I can see the family in his face."

"Hello Grandma, how are you?" Eli asked. "I'm doing just as well as could be expected," she told him, then she said, "Ella, Ella what are you doing standing way over there? Come on over here and get these things."

When Ella came forward she was obviously at a loss for words, so she just stood there looking at her Mother as her Mother reached down into the tote bag she carried and brought up two sealed envelopes. Handing them to Ella she said, "Here, take these, I won't be around for much longer."

"No, mother don't say that. Come and have a seat here so we can talk," Ella said.

As they all sat there in Ella's living room their tensions were evident, but eventually their conversations inclined toward Lynx.

"Granny, do you remember me calling you on the telephone and telling you to turn your television to the channel so you could see our group on the Oprah Winfrey show?" Elisha asked.

"Yes indeed. I like Oprah a whole lot. She just don't realize that she is loved, and adored no matter what size she is."

"Yes Ma'am, I'm sure she knows that, but did you turn to see us on her show?" Elisha pressed.

"I couldn't. I mean, I looked, so I imaged I didn't have the right time," Glenda told them.

"Grandma, the reason why I asked is because we think there's a problem with you remembering things. Do you think that you sometimes forget things that you try hard to remember?"

"I can't say for certain. Sometimes when things slip my mind I believe that I may not have thought of it before then. I don't know. I guess sometimes trying to remember everything that has to be done over there in that big ole house all alone. I guess I just can't keep up with it all anymore."

460

"Mama, you'll have to let me make you an appointment with my doctor, so he can run a few tests," Ella told her Mother.

"Nonsense, it's not that serious. I have already closed off all of my house that I no longer have any use for, so I don't have to worry about it. Besides," Glenda went on to say, "I'm well able to recall and to recollect well enough to know that somebody here owes me an apology and I have the good mind to sit right here until I get it!"

"You are absolutely right. I do owe you an apology and so much more," Ella began. "Mother for all of the hurt, and heartache I've caused you, I truly apologize and I ask you to please forgive me, your daughter."

"Those words you just used were very nice ones," Glenda didn't hesitate to say. "And your apology is accepted, mostly because I'm unable to remember why you owed it."

"Grandma Glenda, you mean to tell me that you can't even remember what you and Mama were into it about?" Liz asked.

"I haven't the slightest idea. I do know that many a times I had liked to have called her and asked, but I couldn't locate her telephone number. And you realize she's far too stubborn to phone my house."

"Mother, we'll not even worry ourselves about it any longer," Ella told her. Then said, "Let's rather put our focus on getting you better."

"Getting me better? There's nothing wrong with me. Can't you tell I got all of my senses," Glenda stated.

"We can all see that you do, but we just want you to be looked at by a doctor," Eli explained to his great Grandmother.

"Have me looked at for what reason?" she wanted to know.

"We fear you may be in an early stage of Alzheimer's and it may be manageable if detected early," Eli exclaimed.

"Alzheimer's? You must be mistaken,"
Glenda told them. Then she turned to Elisha and asked, "Is this why you brought me all this way baby?"

"No Granny, of course not. We brought you to your daughter's house because it's been so long since you've seen each other. And because we all love you and were concerned about you," Elisha assured her, easing Glenda's fears a little bit.

"What do you have to say about all of this?" Glenda asked Elizabeth, since she had moved in closer and began rubbing Glenda's hand.

"Grandma, obviously your memory isn't what it used to be, so we are going to get a professional's opinion, because we only want what's best for you," Liz said before kissing her Grandmother's hand.

Their care for Glenda, which was expressed through their conversation, traveled well through dinner.

Night fell fast and their hearts were filled with the love that only comes from family affection. Glenda was comforted and Ella's peace was beginning to climb. After wrapping and placing Christmas gifts up under the tree, she just stood there and absorbed it all. Then Ella promised her daughter that she would never neglect to express her love for her Mother ever again. "I've been such a big ole stubborn fool."

"Mama, I know you'll be there for her and give Grandma complete and total care. I can see it in your eyes," Liz told her. "You be sure to get some rest," she concluded after kissing her Mother's forehead.

"I'll be turning in in just a moment," Ella informed her.

"Well I'm—"

"Excuse me," Glenda interrupted. "Lizzy" she began. "I was wondering if you would sleep in here with me, just for the night. Them furnishings are just so unfamiliar to me."

"Sure I will Grandma. I'd be more than happy to."

"Mama, you don't want to sleep in my room with me? The bed is more than big enough for the two of us.:

"I'll be just fine as long as I have Lizzy with me. I remember when she was wearing the two ponytails and those huge eyeglasses."
"Grandma, how do you remember— Never mind it. Just let me get you back into bed. Come on Grandma."

"Goodnight Ella."

"Goodnight mother."

"Merry Christmas, Merry Christmas!!" Eli yelled throughout the house. "Merry Christmas." Apparently he had become filled with joy, excitement, and Holiday spirit.

Elisha was the first to meet him out in the hallway, but her face wasn't one of holiday cheer.

"Boy, what's the matter with you?" she asked. "Eli, we're not little kids anymore."

"I know we're not. Like I also know we may never get this opportunity ever again."

"What opportunity?" Elisha asked as Ella and Elizabeth now joined them in the hall.

"This is our family, our family. All of us in this house right now. We have never spent a Christmas together. We have always been without Grandma Glenda," Eli voiced.

Upon hearing her name she entered the hallway wrapped in her robe and asked, "What is the matter with that boy, and why can't I find my pills nowhere?"

"Grandma we'll help you find your pills, but first I would like for everyone to realize that we were brought together on this very day for a reason," Eli said.

He then walked over and wrapped his arms around his Grandma Glenda and said, "Here is one of the reasons right here."

"You are right, we shouldn't take this blessing for granted," Elizabeth pointed out. "And we won't," she added.

"Let's find Mama her medication and then fix her a delicious breakfast," Ella stated.

"I put everything she told me she needed in the little blue bag and placed it inside of the tote bag that she was carrying," Elisha told them.

"I got it. I know exactly where it's at," Liz said as she went into the guest room.

Their breakfast was exquisite except for the fact that Glenda was obviously unfamiliar with her surroundings. She constantly spread her hands across the tablecloth, rubbing it and then she would tell everyone that she didn't remember buying it.

"Where did this come from?" she asked. They all explained to her that she was no longer at her own home, but instead she was at her daughter Ella's house. This caused her to become anxious, as well as concerned about her house being unattended to.

It took awhile to calm Grandma Glenda, but they finally did and it was actually a joy to see the way she allowed her daughter to soothe her by brushing her hair.

It was a beautiful thing to witness, but what truly captivated everyone's attention was when Glenda reverted back to a time long long ago. Calling her daughter Mama.

Momma, she began, "You brush my hair everyday momma, making it grow really long.

"When you get finished can I stay in here with you Momma, please Momma can I? Because the last time I went out to the field to listen to granddaddy tell about God, them white people came by and started fighting with everybody who was listening to granddaddy's story about God.

"Master Woodward, cause he don't like to be called anything other than Master, he was leading the pack. He snatched that ole book and yelled, 'Can't no nigger read no words. Cause if he could he would see right there where it say, 'Slaves be obedient to those who are your masters according to the flesh, with fear and trembling, in sincerity of heart, as to Christ.'

"Then he took to beating granddaddy with his whip and told him as he beat him that, 'You are to serve me unto your death. I am your Christ here on earth.'

Momma, the only reason why I run away is because I was so afraid he would

*turn his whip on me next Momma. That's
the only reason why I run off and leave
granddaddy Momma, 'cause I was afraid.
I'm still scared Momma, please don't make
me go out there no more Momma, Momma!"*

"Sh, shush, now. You don't have to go back out there
no more," Ella quieted her mother as tears traveled
down her cheeks.

She wrapped her arms around her from behind and
placed her cheek to her mother's haed and continued to
soothe and console her.

"It's okay, it's alright. You're in here with me now.
And I'm not going to let that mean ole Woodward, or
anybody else do anything to you ever again," Ella said
assuringly.

And she continued to express soothing words that
caused her mother Glenda to ask for a nap.

It was apparent that they all were shaken up by what
they had just witnessed.

Elisha was taking it really hard. When Ella and Liz
returned to the living room from laying Glenda down,
Elisha said, "Granny is getting worse suddenly. What
can we do?" she asked.

No one answered her, because it was apparent that no one had an answer.

Instead of there being longevity to their cheer and merriment, the room had become engulfed by gloom.

Eli was only able to stare at the wall as he remained there on the couch. His Grandmother Ella sat beside him and wrapped a arm around his shoulder.

Elizabeth sat on the other side of him and Elisha had stood, having both her arms wrapped around herself.

It wasn't but a brief moment later that Eli was able to draw strength from somewhere within. He knew that it was his obligation, and his responsibility to show himself strong, even though he felt weak, so that his family may be strengthened.

Eli said, "Listen, if we allow ourselves to be cast all the way down by this that has inflicted our family, then this Christmas and every one that follows will be labeled and remembered as a day of gloom and despair. "I for one am not going to allow that to happen to my family. Instead I wish that we would rather focus on the fact that after so many years we finally have Grandma Glenda with us in our lives, so that we may love her and care for her until her heart is content."

They heard and felt his words with their hearts, but yet and still they cried awhile longer and hugged one another a little stronger.

Then they dried their eyes and spoke out against despair, and sadness, confessing to walk in the joy of the Lord, not just for their sakes, but for Grandma Glenda's sake most of all.

Elizabeth checked the clock and decided that it was time to begin preparing the Christmas meal.

Eli, while looking in on his great Grandmother Glenda and seeing that she was sound asleep, put the blanket back over her that had fallen off and onto the floor. Standing there looking at the face of his great Grandmother, he recalled the stories told to him by his Granny Bee. How his great Grandmother had been named after a child who had been snatched from its Mother and killed by some evil wicked white man. Now his mind questioned the world, 'How can someone possess so much evil and hatred toward another human being just because their skin is a different color?' As he was turning to leave the room his great Grandmother whispered, "Child you be sure to let him know I love him, and I only run away cause I was so afraid."

"Okay Grandma," Eli returned the whisper, not wanting to wake her fully. "Get yourself some more rest and I'll wake you in a little while," he said in a whisper as he was easing back out of the room.

"Baby, be sure to tell him. You be sure to tell Eli!" As he came out of the room he was met right there in the hallway by his Mother Elizabeth who asked, "Is she still sleeping?"

"Yes Ma'am, she is, but for a moment there she was just mumbling some words in her sleep. She's fine though. She'll be okay, I'm sure of it. Come on, let's let her rest."

"There's someone on the phone who wants to talk with you."

"Who?" asked Eli as he followed his mother into the kitchen.

"Just get the telephone and you'll see," was the only telling that Liz was willing to do.

"Hello?" Eli asked when he had received the telephone from Elisha. "Hey Granny Bee, Merry Christmas! How are you?
Forreal, put her on the phone. Hey yourself. Hi Auntie, Merry Christmas to you too! Listen, kiss Monique for

me and tell Cookie I said we will play with that x-box together when I get back. "Huh, I don't know exactly, but tell my Granny Bee that we'll be certain to give her a call whenever we do head out. Okay, I love you all too!!!

"Everyone there seems to be happy and enjoying their Christmas. So it makes me happy to know that my entire family has had a Merry Christmas," Eli said as he placed the phone on its hook.

"Of course we have, as long as we are all here together strengthening each other, and keep in mind that faith in His word shields, protects, and comforts us all," Liz proclaimed as she wrapped her arms around her son, and her daughter.

The rest of their evening was spent exchanging gifts with one another. But most importantly they showered Grandma Glenda with Christmas gifts and increased their own joy by seeing the joy that she herself experienced.

When the holiday had passed, instead of Elizabeth and Eli immediately returning back to Louisville, they stayed awhile longer in order to assist Ella in taking Glenda to a doctor's appointment. And that they all did. Ella's doctor confirmed that Glenda was in the early stages of Alzheimer's and he made them all aware that her condition would worsen and eventually she will no longer be able to remember her own name.

"How can that be?" Ella questioned. "Just the other day she reminisced on her past in such vivid detail." "That very well could have occurred, but again I assure you, prepare yourselves for the worst," the doctor informed them. Then added, "What I will do is schedule her another appointment where I will further view MRI photos, but I am very sorry to say that they'll only confirm what the first images have already portrayed." After saying such, he patted Ella's hand showing himself to be a man of some sympathy, but a no nonsense professional nonetheless.

During their lunch after the doctor's visit Glenda insisted on being taken to her home. Her adamant demands were met with the assurance that they would be taking her to her own home directly.

Upon entering her house Glenda looked about as if she was searching for something or someone. With a look of despair all over her deep dark chocolate complexioned face, she sat at her kitchen table and said, "He must have gotten out when we opened the front door. He's always running out every chance he gets and there's no telling when he may return."

"Who Grandma? Who are you talking about?" Liz asked.

"My cat, my cat little Raphie. You've allowed him to get out!"

"Granny, you don't have a cat anymore. You told me so yourself awhile ago," Elisha tried to explain to Glenda, but she insisted that she did indeed have a little Raphie. So much so in fact that Ella was becoming unable to take it anymore.

She told the others to help her gather some of her Mother's personal things. Then she told her Mother that she was taking her back to her home so that she may stay with her until she got better.

But Glenda would have no part of it. She asserted with firmness that she had to remain at her own house in case little Raphie came home.

But thanks be given to Eli for his swift thinking. He was quick to say, "Grandma while you've been away at your daughter's house little Raphie may be looking for you there."

"Do you think that maybe he's there?" she asked as she stood to her feet and gave evidence that she was ready to go.

On the way to the car Eli told his Grandmother, "You absolutely have to purchase Grandma Glenda a cat, and soon."

A couple of days later Eli and Elisha agreed to forsake the New Year revelry and instead give some more comfort to their aging great Grandmother's transition, which was made a little bit easier after abstracting the color of little Raphie from her.

But the day came, January the third two thousand and nine, Elisha and Eli had to return to school, which wasn't a major thing for Elisha because she attended Spelman right there in the City. But Eli had to return to the University of Louisville, and Liz had to return to her responsibilities at Lynx.

Their departure was a heart wrenching one, and their tears flowed steadily. Even Eli shed a reluctant tear, or two as he observed his great Grandmother's blank stare. As Elizabeth hugged her Grandma Glenda, her Grandmother asked, "Who's going to sleep in the bed with me, if you're going away?"

After kissing her Grandmother gently, she told her, "Sweetheart you have little Raphie to sleep with you now and he don't like anyone else sleeping with you."

"Little Raphie don't like anybody period! The rascal even scratched me last night," Grandma Glenda said, then added, "I don't know exactly where that little Raphie has been, but he may need to be taken back there."

CHAPTER 32

Back in school and into the flow of things Eli found a little comfort and satisfaction, although he could not stop thinking about his great Grandmother's condition, despite the fact that Elisha would constantly assure him that she is being well taken care of.

He attempted to allow his writings to consume himself in his spare time, so he posted a couple of his creative writings onto the webpage. But for today he was only to come up with a line to the one that he desired to write the most. For some reason he was just unable to get past: "As our loved ones grow older and their memories they remember no more, let us not forget that which they've given unto us. The shaping of our character, the stability of our core." Eli was at a loss for words. His creative ability had fled, so he decided to give it a rest and give Mary a call. He was only able to reach her voice mail, which meant her, and her Mother must still be in their meeting. So there would be no use in going down the street to Granny Bee's house, because she's at the same meeting.

He decided to return a few phone calls. After activating his own voice mail he addressed the first one.

"Hello, yes this is Eli Lewis, and I'm returning your phone call. You say your name is Dr. Bach. Doctor, how may I help you, but first let me ask, 'You are a doctor of what exactly?' "

The doctor informed Eli that he was a doctor of literature and that he was very interested in discussing with him his writing techniques as well as a possible publishing venture.

Upon hearing such, Eli recalled speaking with someone who had phoned him previously on Dr. Bach's behalf with the same intention to discuss what he had posted on his webpage.

Eli respectfully declined, concluding that what he was providing on the web was causing enough controversy without him being published and then causing that much more troubles for Lynx.

But this guy Dr. Bach was persistent to say the least. This would be his second phone call to Eli after Eli's decision to allow the first one to go to voice mail. He attempted to tell the good doctor again that he wasn't interested. But the doctor broke in and said, "Mr. Lewis I shall be in your City come the beginning of the next month, where I will put forth my last effort to reach out to you."

"Have it your way Doc, but I'm convinced that less sometimes is better," Eli said simply before ending their call.

For some reason this winter wasn't as cold as winter's before, here in Louisville, Kentucky, Eli thought to himself as he made his way to his car.

He had decided that his best course of action would be to turn in a near due paper and hopefully receive insight on whether there was need for any corrections from his professor.

Once on the campus observing the intense enthusiasm that was laced with vibrant energies, Eli was soon filled with the capacity that he could hold the world by the tail and pull it in any which direction if its desire was not to be led in the right direction.

He witnessed other collegiates leisurely moving about, enjoying the decent weather in the latter days of February. But they too had that look of empowerment sculpted across their faces, as they made their way to their destinations.

When he made it inside of the hall, the buzz was electric there as well. This he knew was due in part to the majority having completed and turned in their paper and now experiencing the relief that it brings.

His professor was nowhere to be found so Eli had no choice but to hand his paper over to the instructor's aide, which he reluctantly did.

Afterwards he drove over to the gymnasium in search of his cousin Darrick. Inside, the entire Louisville Cardinal basketball team was practicing and being pushed to their limits by one Mr. Patino.

One who Eli was delighted to know had his cousin under his wing, because Mr. Patino treated all of his boys like sons and the ones that never knew a father figure, he filled that void.

Eli was content for the moment to just sit in the stands, watching a few drills and texting a few texts.

His cousin Darrick startled him as he stomped up the bleachers to where Eli sat.

"What's poppin cuz?" Darrick asked upon his approach.

"Nothing much," Eli replied, obviously a little startled.

"Check game," Darrick began. "Do you want to run with us over to the cheerleader's dorm after we get cleaned up?"

"Naw, I'm not gonna mess with it. I just come by to holla at you, because you've been so elusive here lately."

"Time is of the utmost importance, because after this, it's the league, so I devote ninety percent here and the other ten there."

"Ten percent where?" Eli asked.

"Over there at the girls dormitory."

"Man, you're trippin. What did you do, forget about your back up plan?"

"Naw, I haven't forgot, which is the only reason why I agreed to a male tutor."

"Listen cousin, I just wanted to drop in on you, maybe even question why you don't come by Granny's as often as you used to."

"You know how it is here on campus, plus now we're preparing for March madness. So, I'm just doing me, but I do call and I go by when I can."

"All I'm saying to you is, it's so easy to overlook who's sweat and tears got us here."

"I feel you cuz. Listen, I'm out though. You see over there by the double doors, it looks like the leader of the cheers is impatiently awaiting on me."

"Alright fam-o, you do you, but don't let your focus go to autopilot or you'll find yourself sitting on the

Wizard's bench," Eli told Darrick as they both made their way down to the floor where one of the finest women Eli had ever seen on campus stood.

He thought to himself how easy it is for any man to become distracted and sidetracked.

After the introductions and the invite, he declined again, then Eli was on his way to locate his welcomed distraction, 'Mary.'

His plan was diverted because he now saw his professor heading toward the campus chapel, so Eli ensued.

"Excuse me professor, may I have a word with you for just a second?"

"In order to do so you'll have to make it quick, because I have a situation that requires my immediate attention."

Inside the chapel Eli asked, "It concerns the paper I turned in today. I was wondering if maybe we could go over it before it's graded, because its grade will dictate my overall grade average." "Lewis, correct?" the professor asked.

"Yes sir, Eli Lewis. We spoke last semester in great length."

"I recall, but it's this situation that prevents me at the present. But I will encourage you to get with me next week and we'll go over the topic then."

"That would be great professor Woodhull. I really appreciate you making the time."

"Always a pleasure. Now if you'll excuse me I must go to the altar and plead my case."

"Your case, why would you—" Eli began. "My wife, and daughter were both involved in an automobile accident last night and before my heading back to the hospital I thought I'd make my supplication known."

"Sir, you mean to tell me that despite your troubles you still took the time to hear my request?" Eli asked. "You don't have to answer that professor, but please is okay for me to join you as you pray."

Eli's request was granted and fifteen minutes later the two of them traveled to the hospital together.

Eli's heart was twisted and torn as he looked upon the small child that lay there with various tubes running to her small body. "Lord have mercy," he mumbled as he looked at Professor Woodhull's tears stream down his face.

He placed a arm around the professor's shoulder and told him that God works through the hands of others so touch and agree that the Lord enables the doctors to perform with divine wisdom and enlightened skills.

After meeting Mrs. Woodhull, who suffered several broken bones, but was promised a fully recovery, Eli left the professor and his wife alone and made his way back to where their child lay.

As soon as he entered Clara's room the machines attached to her went berserk. He rushed to her side and knowing nothing else to do he dropped to his knees and placed a hand atop her small hand. There he pleaded with the Lord God Almighty on Clara's behalf. It wasn't but a second or two before nurses and doctors rushed in insisting he remove himself from the room. which Eli didn't hesitate to do.

Right outside of the door he ran directly into Professor Woodhull, wearing a confused look. He immediately began to ask what had happened. "What's going on?" Before Eli could explain, the doctor came out and told the professor that there was no need for alarm. Apparently the danger had passed.

"What the monitors had detected Clara has overcome!" Before leaving them, the medical doctor said, "I will need to order more tests to be run, but judging from my observation there'll be no need for a second surgery as previously believed necessary."

The professor expressed heartfelt thanks and then made an immediate departure so that he may inform his wife of the great news.

Eli thanked God on their behalf, then made his way to the waiting area to return an unanswered call from Mary.

He asked her to pick him up and assured her that he was perfectly fine and that he would advise her of the details upon her arrival.

The waiting area is where the professor found him. He told Eli that a weight of guilt had been lifted off of his wife and they all would be just fine. Then he offered to return Eli to the campus.

"No thank you Professor Woodhull, it won't be necessary sir. My girlfriend will be here shortly. You just remain here and watch over your lovely family."

"I'll do exactly that young man, and again I thank you sincerely for your prayers and your concern."

"That's appreciated, but not necessary, as long as we remain mindful to thank the Lord who always hears our prayers.

Just as soon as Professor Woodhull had walked off and before Eli could enter into thought, the same doctor from a moment ago approached him again.

"Son," he began, "I realize that you are apparently a friend of the Woodhull's and that's just fine, but I just need to ask you once again, what exactly took place in the young Miss Woodhull's room while you were present?"

"I don't know what to tell you other than the machines that Clara is hooked up to began to buzz and beep, then you all rushed in immediately thereafter."

"Yeah, yes I understand all of that, but prior to your arrival we were waiting for the child to stabilize so that we would be able to go in and perform a much needed operation.   But now, none of that seems to be necessary," the doctor informed Eli.

"I'm happy to hear that surgery won't be necessary and I'm certain that your decision to wait was the wisest choice, which is obvious when viewing the end result."

"Eli, hey what's happened? Why are you here in the hospital?" Mary asked as she came closer to where Eli and the doctor stood.

When Eli turned, he embraced Mary in order to calm her. Then he told her, "I'm okay, my professor's wife and daughter were injured in an automobile accident, but they both are fine now, right doc?"

"Absolutely, they are both doing well now, and again it was a pleasure," the doctor said as he extended a hand to Eli.

Before going to retrieve his car, Eli invited Mary to join him for dinner realizing how hungry he'd become. She accepted and they drove to a very nice restaurant just a few blocks away.

After ordering from the menu their conversation continued in the events that had transpired, and then Eli went silent suddenly for awhile. Too long actually, because Mary had to ask him what it was that was bothering him.

She reminded Eli that they held nothing from the other and whatever it was they would sort it out together.

"I don't think it could be sorted out so easily," Eli finally spoke.

Then he went on to say, "Basically, the whole matter is something I must work out for myself. But the problem is, I don't have a clue as to where to begin. Mary," he said, "I'll never be able to lead others if I'm lost myself."

She immediately and compassionately assured Eli, "You're not lost, maybe feeling a bit uncertain about which direction to go in next, but you are not lost, the way you help and assist, even come to the center whenever you can and give yourself to the kids, Eli you're anything but lost. Have you thought that maybe it's just that you haven't given total thought into exactly how you are going to focus your energies, and talents?"

"What are you saying?" he asked.

"I'm saying we have Lynx, which is a vehicle for us to use in order to apply our gifts. You need something whereby you are able to apply yours."

Over the rest of their meal and even while engaging in other conversation, Eli let what Mary had told him concerning applying his gift to take root.

CHAPTER 33

Eli seemed to be in a trance as he sat and listened intently to his world religion professor expound on the times of the inquisition executed by the papacy.

As he attempted to wrap his mind around, how could the church who made their claim of being followers of Jesus Christ, the humble servant who willingly gave His life as a ransom for the redemption of the whole world. How could this same Catholic church burn at the stake and torture, torment, and murder all of those lovers of Christ?

When Eli was just about to write down the historical facts that he wanted to further research, the door to the class hall flew open and there stood his Grandmother, Granny Bee.

"Excuse my intrusion instructor," she yelled, receiving the professor's attention as well as everyone else's who was in the hall.

"Granny!" Eli said as he stood.

"Yes, it is I, and I have a bone to pick with you young man! This here gentleman, Dr. Bach," who had just then entered the room and stood right beside her, "he has traveled all the way here from New York, just to talk to you about your writings and you won't even return his phone calls. Eli Lewis, you know we didn't raise you to behave in such a manner."

"Granny, I'm in the middle of a class," Eli exclaimed with a face expressing embarrassment.

Mama Bee turned to the instructor standing behind the podium and said, "Again, excuse the intrusion Professor Monroe, this won't take but a few seconds. You see this good man, Dr. Bach has come all the way from New York."

Before she could say another word Professor Monroe said, "By all means, be my guest."

Being given permission, Dr. Bach took flight. Swiftly he removed from his briefcase a silver flat screen device and placed it up on the podium, from where he began to speak. "I do believe it to be necessary that Eli receives from his peers their opinion and feedback as to the quality of his work. It's titled, 'The Battle," and reads as follows:

I'm in a constant state of fear, often mixed
with pain, and always laced with the
knowledge of the losing battle that I'm

engaged in. I think I only label it a battle because everyone around me are always saying to me, keep fighting. And I do! I fight daily, because I don't want to die!

This is what causes my fear, I fear the unknown. Not knowing what lies on the other side of life. So, yes I fear death! It terrifies me so. And not just for my own sake, but for the sakes of my loved ones and my friends as well. I see their fear, it's expressed in their eyes. They are in so much turmoil due to my condition—my condition,

I'm a patient of breast cancer.

Dr. Bach choked on the words, and began to weep before continuing.

It has taken a hold of me, and I sense my life leaking from me day by day," he managed to say but nothing more.

So Eli stood and his voice slowly filled the study;

I imagine my daughter senses it as well, because as strong as she tries to be I hear her weeping when my eyes are closed in rest. How I wish to God I could comfort her. To be able to take away my family's fear and pain would be an answered prayer. I'm so tired from the chemo. I'll conclude my message after I've awakened.

Taking advantage of Eli's pause Dr. Bach resumed, as he viewed his little device—

I dreamt a dream that was so vivid and real that it has to be placed right here. I was told by a voice that He would comfort my daughter as well as my entire family and they would be delivered of their pain in time and the removal of their fear would come as they witnessed my fearlessness. This is when I began to ball with tears, because I instantly believed I would never awake, ever again, but that I was already dead not ever being able to say my goodbyes.

Wet hot tears streaming down my face caused my eyes to open, but not before being made aware of my eternal destiny by Him who had spoken to me.

So in these last days I've gathered my family around me, assuring them that fear is false and freedom of pain is gain, The End.

"My wife," Dr. Bach began, "she discovered this poem over the internet and she went from being a terrified defeated woman to a strengthened woman having peace. She gathered all of us around her hospital bed and she encouraged us all. She even left that strength behind with our daughter Rachel.

"Eli, I've come to hopefully assist you in publishing your work, but most importantly I simply wish to thank you in person. Thank you son for providing an entire family with some comfort."

As Dr. Bach and Eli stood there clutching one another's hand, the study hall erupted into applause, with Mama Bee leading and clapping the loudest.

Class for the day ended on that note. As students left, they gave Eli approving head nods and pats on the back and almost all of his classmates viewed him differently.

Mama Bee apologized to Professor Monroe once more, then she made her way back over to her grandson and Dr. Bach where she instructed the two of them to join her at her house for brunch.

During brunch, Eli voiced his fears that his writings could very well affect the way people looked at Lynx and how he didn't want to cause any more unnecessary pot shots to be taken at his Grandmother, nor at her organization.

Mama Bee eased his concerns and put his mind at a serenity because she assured her grandson that their stability was stronger than ever and presently heading into further propriety.

So he thought and contemplated, contemplated and thought.

"I don't know. I mean, sure I've compiled enough to be converted into a book form, but who will edit it, who will publish, who will—"

"Son, if you will only utilize a little trust and allow me and my publishing company to do all of the necessary paperwork with your overview and final approval, we'll put together a book for readers of poems all over the world," Dr. Bach said in total and complete sincerity.

"What about my writings that I consider sheds light on the oppression of a people who possess a different complexion?"

"Are you referring to the one's that now have the watchdog groups watching you?"

"Those and others like those," Eli replied.

"All that I'm able to say to that is, an artist wouldn't be considered an artist if he, or she wasn't allowed to express themselves through art as they saw fit," Dr. Bach informed Eli.

"With that being your view I guess I'm ninety percent decided, but I know I'll need just a little more time. At least the time to go over everything with myself. Just to know that I'm sure."

"That sounds reasonable, especially considering how I've forced myself on you in the way that I have. So how about I phone you two weeks from today, or if you have something for me, you give me a call at that time," said the doctor.

"It seems like a good enough plan," Eli stated as the two stood to their feet and shook hands. "I'm definitely looking forward to working with you. You have convinced me to see the error of my ways," Eli said.

"Mrs. Lewis, it has been my pleasure, and I have enjoyed your company as well as your hospitality. I shall never forget how you've taught me how to bust up into a college!"

"Well, that's how we turn up around here," Mama Bee replied, knowing it'd probably go over the good doctor's head. But, give him something new to ponder on his flight.

When he had departed, Mama Bee asked her grandson was he going to give his best efforts at perfecting things that would bless others, as his poem, "The Battle" had obviously blessed the Bach family.

"Granny, my intentions are to do that exactly," Eli told her in all honesty.

"Imagine it though would you, being published, having written work that could potentially reach millions of people the world over?" Eli asked.

"Oh, I've imagined exactly that for you Eli. I know the Lord has called you and I hope you realize His purpose soon. I want to see His plan for you with my own two eyes."

"Granny, it's possible that your expectations for me are way too high."

"I don't believe that they are, and to prove it I ask a favor of you."

"A favor! Granny, what are you asking?"

"I'm asking my grandson to recite me something from inside of you, that's there but probably unbeknownst to even you."

Eli thought for a second, knowing exactly what his Grandmother was asking of him. She wanted him to free-style a poem. Come off the top of his head with something original!

He sighed deeply and turned his head and looked out through his Grandmother's living room window.

"As I reflect on all the many times we've argued and fought, the root to the cause stands out so vividly.

"I've been more than a fool, but now I'm not ashamed to admit it.

"By focusing on the minute character flaws that you sometimes emanate, those rare occasions that are but twenty percent of your being. I have allowed to blind me to the eighty percent that you daily offer of yourself.

"This question I ask myself, how could I have ever overlooked your true worth and the essence of the eighty percent that you willingly give.

"And it's not so much that I was unaware of your many attributes, it's that I've been oblivious of them due to my viewing of the twenty percent. And know that when I mention twenty percent, I had suppressed the fact that no one is one hundred percent. No, not one!

WE SUFFER FOR A REASON

"I now point out that here lately I've been overlooking all of the many wonderful characteristics that you possess.

"The very character traits that caused my heart to chase after your heart, but isn't it just like a member of the human race to desire and pursue the opposite sex and once obtained take for granted and then neglect. I now stand guilty of that!

"Forgive me, but not based on these words being spoken, view a repentative heart by actions taken. No longer will I concern myself with small matters that will cause me to turn a blind eye to all that you give, all that you take, and all that you are.

"A true soulmate is only appreciated when it's recognized and first realized that no one is perfect. I'm just thankful for the chance to share life with imperfection that has brought me to completion. "With the ability of a understanding spirit we've grown together realizing that twenty percent will always be, but will never be able to take away from the eighty percent which has established us in love, as well as propelled us toward a future filled with promise, the first one being; I promise to never ever again overlook all of that eighty percent that you've continued to give ever since our journey began."

"Grandson, not only was that beautiful and filled with insight, it also proves my point that God has blessed you to be a blessing to others."

"I appreciate your vote of confidence, even though I doubt it if those particular words will ever be put onto paper."

"You have to be kidding me, why not?"

"Because, they were inspired by Mary. How I sometimes overlook all that she truly is, so when I thought about that, I was able to speak as my heart compelled me to."

"So, put it on paper and add it to the rest to be published, so that it may open the eyes of others who are not appreciating who they have."

"Granny Bee, you actually interpreted its true intent. I'm impressed. You never cease to amaze me, or embarrass me," Eli said as he stood and leaned over to kiss his grandmother's forehead.

"Embarrassed, you want to see what embarrassed looks like? Be at Louisville's Saturday game and see me cheer for Darrick in my blue Kentucky jersey!"

"Granny, you can't be serious," Eli asked as they both laughed.

She, for her reasons and him because he knew Darrick had an embarrassing moment ahead .

CHAPTER 34

Mama Bee's house was filled to capacity as well as her porch and entire yard, front, and back. The scene is what you would call jam-packed, elbow to elbow, standing room only!

Well, what would you expect on the first Saturday of May in Louisville, Kentucky. It's the day of the Kentucky Derby known to some as the Run For The Roses. For the City of Louisville, state of Kentucky and surrounding areas it might as well be declared a national holiday. So the day has been perceived from its founding. Today it's being enjoyed by all who would partake of what the City has to offer. And the inhabitants of Mama Bee's residence were feeding off of the City's vibe, and their appetite for food was appeased by the many slabs of bar-b-q ribs that Poppa Charlie brought off of the grill.

The house occupants were in their most festive mood, having the joy and happiness that's contributed to a carefree state.

These folks did not concern themselves with any horses that were to run at Churchill Downs, despite them all being aware of the favorite.

Naw, this was a world all their own, and they were far too busy running around giving and receiving soulfulness, and love, that would last longer than a two and a half minute horse race.

When the excitement had overflowed out of Mama Bee's front yard and onto the street, more neighbors came and cars pulled over in order to become connected to that electrifying vibe.

And it was continuously flowinging well into the early hours of the following morning. This would certainly be a Derby day to be remembered.

CHAPTER 35

Before the school break the campus yard was filled to the limit, practically standing shoulder to shoulder. The students and some of the faculty stood listening to the members of "Voices" voice their opinions.

They spoke about utilizing the spring break to gain a clearer vision of what their contribution to society will be. And a greater sense of what legacy will they be leaving behind was the theme expressed. Acknowledging that everyone will be remembered for something.

Eli and Mary listened intently to Larry speak to the crowd some common sense.

Larry, aware of his cousin Eli's attendance, gave him a head nod and continued expressing to the entire campus their need to recognize that it is they who possess the ability to shape the immediate future. And having common goals, that which is fashioned and formed would be for the betterment of all. Equality, and justice being experienced all across the board.

Again Eli was able to feel the vigorous vibe vibrating throughout the crowd as if anticipation was climbing to a height of climax.

Larry passed the mic to Sherry who Eli recognized as being the cousin introduced to him by Larry at the Lynx convention.

After introducing herself as one Sherry Johnson, a graduate with a CPA in Accounting, she went on to speak of the potential financial woes that could and probably would consume all those who accumulate student loan debt and who lacked a sound financial plan.

She encouraged her fellow graduate students to search with her for means upon which to establish financial institutions that would not only benefit her sisters and brothers, but would also safeguard them against any financial disasters that the future economy may suffer, especially student loans.

Next to obtain the attention of the spectators was the highly anticipated Muslim brother; Brother Tito, who wasted no time in making everyone aware of a situation we all face.

"America has been afraid for too long to address the race problem, so racism is continuing to be acted out openly in the courtrooms of America. I'll take the blame for saying, 'Racism is the white people's brainchild."

He went on quoting facts, and stats that supported the bias measures exercised in America's courtrooms.

"The laws established by white majority legislature that imprison African Americans to life sentences and in many instances blacks, are sentenced to life in prison without the possibility of parole."

Brother Tito went further in his expoundence of the facts and the truths pertaining to America's unjust justice system.

"Brothers, and sisters, Christians and Jews, if their purpose was not to practice modern day slavery by means of incarceration, where they work the inmates on work details without pay, then laws or finances would be used to educate and then employ instead of using ten times the needed finances to build more prisons. "When you wake up, you'll look up and see there is a prison being built right by you. And if you continue voting these jokers into office, then those prisons will be built by you!"

After saying such, Brother Tito handed the microphone over to a fellow rally member who was quick to say,

"That was way deep."

Those who had felt the message spoken and realized the need to address the problem head on, let it be known as they clapped and stomped to a beat not unlike those illustrated by an African war cry!

Eli and Mary met up with Larry, and his cousin Sherry after the rally. They all expressed the uncertainty of America's future. But no one neglected the obvious fact that "pressure busts pipes."

If America continues to abuse and further oppresses her black citizens, those same citizens would eventually see no other way to remove the knee from their neck but by extreme force., if ever they should realize real freedom is worth dying for!

At the on campus eatery the four of them discussed this issue and several others until they decided to part ways. Before doing so, Eli felt it necessary to pull his cousin Larry off to the side.

"Cuz, we both know the truths that were spoken out there today, but my concern is how far you're willing to involve yourself."

"What are you trying to say?" Larry asked.

"I'm saying, voicing your beliefs so openly could bring on enemies that you're not even aware exist." "I know exactly who the enemies are, and so do you. See cuz, this was the purpose of the rally. To open the eyes of those who are walking around with their eyes wide shut."

"I'm simply telling you that whenever you are viewed as a serious threat, then you are silenced by the powers that be."

"That's fear talking, and although probably true, it's part of it and I'm prepared to deal with it in the hopes of leaving an example to that one who should come after me. Just to impart that knowledge would make it a willing sacrifice."

"It appears that your mind is all made up. And I'm not going to stand here and attempt to change it. Just be careful cousin, and give me a call if ever you should need the E!"

"I'll definitely do just that," Larry replied as the two embraced and then dapped it out.

As the four departed, they said their goodbyes.

CHAPTER 36

This was a most beautiful June the eighteenth. The sun was out and ablaze, shining brightly, and magnificently. But it wasn't a unbearable heat like June's of the past. Which was just fine by Mama Bee as she sat at the open window to Pretty Ray's upper guest room, where she looked out onto the back lawn prepared and arranged for her and Poppa Charlie's wedding.

She was obviously nervous and overjoyed at the same time, to be getting married today and to have all of her girls with her.

Lee-Lee, Elizabeth, Debra and Elisha, Joann, Elaine, Mary, Bunch, and even Faith, her little flower girl.

In her one and only attempt at expressing doubt, she was reminded of her love for Poppa Charlie! But it was Debra who refreshed her Grandmother's memory in this way'

"Mama, you are trippin. You're the one who told Poppa Charlie that if he didn't put a ring on it you would make him regret being born."

"I did, didn't I!"

"Yes you did," Liz confirmed.

"Granny Bee, we have a wedding to do here so please let me finish putting your makeup on," Elisha said as she brushed her face.

"I don't know Bee," Ms. Bunch began, "the way Charlie be looking at me, he might just be marrying you just so he can get close to me."

All heads turned toward Ms. Bunch and all gave her, The Look!

"Mama, you sure do make a beautiful bride," Lee-Lee told her Mother.

"You're pretty like a picture," Faith Monique added.

"Okay, lets do this," Mama Bee said as she stood to view herself in the huge floor mirror, then asked, "My butt don't look too big in this dress, does it?"

There was a pause, no one wanted to answer the question. So she asked the only one she knew she could get an honest answer from.

"Debra, does it?" she asked, still looking at it in the mirror.

"Mama, your butt looks big in any dress. You got a big butt, a big butt," Debra sung.

They all laughed, which caused Mama Bee to laugh as well. But then came the tears, tears of joy was expressed by the entire room to the point that Monique was made to ask, "Mama, why are everyone crying?"

"We are all just so happy for your Granny, because she's so happy!"

"Granny?"

"Yes sweetie."

"I'm happy too," Faith Monique announced.

"I know baby, thank you for being happy for me. We are all happy now. And thank you Mary for putting together such a beautiful arrangement."

"I enjoyed every minute of it, because I was doing it all for you."

"Come on out of there Mama," Reggie hollered from the other side of the door.

Lee-Lee cracked the door and said, "We're coming out now, go and tell everybody to be ready."

"We've been ready. We're just waiting on the bride and the rest of you women!"

"Here we come boy, now go on!"

Mama Bee and Poppa Charlie was united in holy matrimony.

When the pastor said, "You may kiss your bride," Poppa Charlie was all too eager to kiss his bridge and palm her butt with both of his hands.

"What are you doing crazy man?" Mama Bee asked.

"I'm taking into possession what rightfully and now legally belongs to me!"

"Man, you're throwed off," was all she could say.

"Crazy about my baby," he said and kissed his bride again.

She tossed her bouquet behind her and it was captured by the one and only Mary Jordan, thanks in large part to the other women stepping to the side and allowing her to do exactly that, catch the bouquet as well as the feeling.

"Don't be giving me that ole look," Bunch told Charlie.

"What look, looking all like somebody owe you a tow fee. Now gone some where's you pecuary pug puppy face looking," Poppa Charlie jonsed at Bunch.

"Don't treat my friend like that," Mama Bee warned him.

"Alright Bee I apologize, but you seen her start it." "It don't matter, you know better Charles. Let's just go say our goodbyes and take off on our honeymoon, where if we're lucky we just might make it out of our room long enough to see the beach."

Pretty Ray, along with all the other guests congratulated and gave their well wishes to the newlyweds.

Ray had rented a pearl white late model Rolls Royce and Mama Bee and Poppa Charlie rode off in the backseat of it as they waved goodbye to their family and friends.

What a truly beautiful June the eighteenth. One that has just been impressed upon the hearts and the minds of many who was in attendance.

Eli was elated and as he held Mary who held her bouquet, he whispered softly into her ear, "Your day will be as beautiful and even more so, because it'll belong to you, to us, forever!"

While Elisha and her mother walked the lawn, they talked about how things were going down in Georgia.

Particularly Elizabeth was concerned about her Grandmother's failing condition, but she was assured that her Mother was taking very good care of Grandma Glenda.

"Elisha, I just feel that I could be doing more. Like if I was there with you I could be helping with everything that needs to be done."

"There's really not much any of us can do, but sit back and simply be as supportive as possible as Granny's condition worsens, and Mama it's getting worser by the minute."

"Then that settles it. I'm going back when you go," Liz informed her daughter.

"If that's the case, you'd better start packing soon, because my flight leaves in about four hours."

"That will give me enough time to organize my affairs and say my goodbyes."

Elizabeth informed Eli, and Mary of her plans to travel to Georgia. She told them that she wanted to stay for a week, maybe two just to spend some time with Glenda and Ella.

Eli thought it to be a good idea and he asked Mary would she like to go to the A with him as he showed support for his family.

She was quick to say, she would love to. They all said their goodbyes and then went their separate ways in order to ready themselves for the trip.

WE SUFFER FOR A REASON

Several hours later their plane touched down in Atlanta, where Elisha's car awaited.

When they had entered Ella's house, Liz took notice of the somber look that defined her Mother's face. They hugged and then they cried. Words were not needed to express the emotions that were felt.

"Where is she?" Liz asked as she headed for the guest bedroom.

"And who may this be that my grandson has traveling so close to his side?" Ella asked.

"Hello Nana," Eli said as he hugged and kissed his Grandmother.

"This is my girlfriend Mary, the one who I was telling you about during the holidays."

"Hello, it's nice to finally meet you," Mary said. "It's nice to finally meet you Ms. Ella, I've heard so much about you, it's truly a pleasure."

"It's nice to meet you finally as well. Why don't you all come on in and have a seat while I get you all something to drink. Are you good and hungry?" Ella asked as she headed toward the kitchen.

"Nana, why don't you let me get Mary and Eli some sodas and you can sit down with them," Elisha told her as she followed her into the kitchen.

"I'm okay," Mary said to Elisha who was already halfway into the kitchen.

"I'll let her know that we both are fine on the drinks, while I'm looking in on my Granny."
"You'll be fine for a second?" Eli asked Mary.
"Of course I'll be perfectly fine," she said.

"Oh, okay here's Nana. I was just going in to look in on Grandma Glenda."

"Eli, if you don't mind, sit here with your Nana awhile and let your mother spend just a little time alone with mother," Ella said. "She sometimes cries out for Liz in the middle of the night, so I think it would be good for them to talk awhile alone."

"Oh, that's just fine by me Nana."

"Grandma, hi sweetheart. It's me, Liz. I've come to see you!"

"Lizzy, that's you. Oh my God that is you. Did you come to spend the night with me baby?"

"Yes Ma'am, if you want me to I most certainly will."

"Grandma, why do you have this huge quilt all over you, aren't you hot?"

"My legs get so cold I have to have something to keep warm, but if you don't want to sleep under it we'll take if off."

"No Ma'am, if your legs are cold we will just leave it on. But I was wondering if you wanted to get up for a little while so you could talk to Eli and meet his girlfriend, Mary?"

"Eli has a girlfriend?" Glenda asked, having a puzzled look on her face as she raised herself up in the bed.

"Yes Ma'am, do you remember us telling you about their relationship the last time we was here?"

"It's his girlfriend, do he love her?"

"Yes Ma'am, I truly believe that they are very much in love with one another."

"Dear Lord, have mercy. If my Grandmother was to find out about it, it would just break her heart so."

"No, no Grandma, I'm telling you about Eli. My son, Eli. Come with me into the living room so you'll be able to see for yourself."

"Grandma, you look wonderful," Eli said as he stood to give his great Grandmother a hug and a kiss.

"Eli, Eli baby I thought you was never going to make it back. Now promise me you'll be careful the next time, cause they'll be looking all over for you!"

"Who will Grandma?" Eli asked in confusion.

"Don't you mind that at all," Ella advised. "She sometimes carries on that way."

"I'm not carrying on about just nothing, I'm telling you, you have to be careful, and that's just the truth. You can't go hiding underneath them floorboards, because they know all about that."

"Okay Grandma, I promise you that I won't do that."

"Mama now come on over here a little closer and meet Eli's girlfriend, Mary."

"It's so very nice to meet you. I've heard so much about you already," Mary was saying as she made eye contact with Glenda.

But Grandma Glena just remained there unresponsive, but staring. Until all of a sudden she started to scream and rant. "No Eli, no! Don't trust her. Don't you dare trust her. Don't trust that girl," Glenda screamed. Then she sobbed, "Daddy, why come you didn't listen to me?" It took Liz a moment to calm her down, while Eli tended to Mary, explaining to her that his great

Grandmother's condition was in a terrible state. And that she shouldn't take anything that was just said about her to heart.

Despite the explanation, Mary made an effort to assure Eli that she would never betray him. She took Eli's face into both of her hands, and looking him in his eyes Mary said, "Eli you know that you can always trust me, don't you?" she asked.

The following day an emergency appointment was secured for Glenda, and they all accompanied her to the doctor's office.

After her examination and following Ella's one on one with the doctor, she told everyone that what the doctor had just informed her of was the obvious. Glenda's condition would more than likely be all down hill from here.

As Elizabeth sat there holding and caressing her Grandma's hand, she kissed her forehead, giving her gentle reassurance.

To her surprise, Glenda looked her in her eyes holding them captive long enough to say, "I'll finally be able to go and see my Momma and Daddy. And I know my Granddaddy and Granny are waiting for me. I'm so happy Lizzy."

Eli had the opportunity to take Mary to shop at the underground, but under such circumstances it was a brief and unenjoyable trip to the mall.

A few days later it was time for them to say their goodbyes, or better put, their farewells, but even they were expressed with heartache. But the worse moment of all was experienced when Glenda cried because her Lizzy couldn't sleep with her anymore.

Elisha hurried them away in hopes of lessening the pain that she saw overwhelm her Mother's eyes.

Back in Kentucky, Eli made sure to keep an eye on his Mother, because he too saw how his Mother was so affected by her Grandmother's decline. It was certain that everyone was deeply moved by Glenda's mental state, but Elizabeth had fallen toward a depressed area. One in which Eli had vowed to monitor closely!

It couldn't have been three weeks that had elapsed before Eli had received the telephone call from his Mother telling him how much she needed him to come home as soon as he possibly could. And it was the tone of her voice, or better put, the lack thereof that caused Eli alarm.

"What is it Eli?" Mary asked watching him jump to his feet and get dressed in neck break speed. "Eli, please

519

don't leave me here without telling me what's going on."

"Mary, I'll talk to you later. Right now I don't even know what's going on myself."

"Who was that that was on the phone? It was your Mom, wasn't it?"

"Yeah, that's who it was, and apparently something is wrong."

"Well, wait for just a minute. I'm coming with you."

"No, you just stay here Mary and wait for me to call you."

"Eli, why won't you let me be there for you? You've changed ever since we got back from Georgia."

"Mary, please stop it, and just stay here until I'm able to get back at you, okay?"

"Okay Eli, if that's what makes you comfortable."

"I don't know about being comfortable, but I believe it would be better," Eli said as he leaned down and kissed her on her lips.

When Eli made it to his Mother's house, he was a little shocked to see his Aunt Lee-Lee and his Granny Bee both there with his Mother.

As soon as he reached the kitchen's threshold, his Mother leapt into his arms and started to cry aloud.

"What's the matter Mama? What's wrong?" he asked, while holding her tight, but looking at his Aunt and Grandmother for an answer.

His Mother continued to cry and he was unable to console her, so he decided to allow her to cry out her tears.

It was Mama Bee who stood and wrapped her arms around the both of them, and it was Mama Bee who said, "We lost Glenda this morning Eli. She passed while she slept."

The emotional impact caused Eli to cry, and the pain went deep and it hurt hard. The tears continued their flow for a long while. Then after the late morning traversed into the afternoon, Mama Bee rallied her troops and told them both that their need for strength was most important in order to make it through.

But at the time all Liz could muster was the ability to say, "It's so sad, because we just now got her back. And we've never had the chance to be a family to her for as long as I would've hoped."

And instead of holding Ella's former selfishness against her, Elizabeth had made her mind up to overcome vengeance with unconditional love. She found cause to thank God for impressing her spirit with the guidance she needed.

Later that evening Ella called and asked Liz when was she coming to Atlanta.

"Mama, we booked a flight for tomorrow morning, so let Elisha know there's no need to pick us up at the airport, because
Eli's going to rent a care."

He must be intending on bringing that girl to my Mother's funeral."

"Mama, she wishes to be there for him while he's grieving, but why do you ask?"

"Because my Mother didn't like her, so she shouldn't be at her funeral."

"Don't you think you're being a little dramatic considering Grandma's condition before she left us?"
"I don't want her here, because I desire that my Mother rests in peace."

"Are you concerned about Grandma's peace, or your own?" Elizabeth asked as she was losing control of unconditional love.

'What is that suppose to mean Elizabeth?" Ella asked. "Nothing Mama, nothing at all. Listen, I'll talk to you when I arrive, alright," Liz said before hanging up the telephone.

CHAPTER 37

Glenda's wake was pleasant. Her family and church members filled the funeral home. The flowers was a beautiful arrangement and as Elizabeth gave the eulogy she cried uncontrollably.

Eli spoke of death and life, but also he spoke about what one generation leaves behind should be used for the benefit of others.

"Let us search our hearts, because there we will discover the spirit that connects us all."

It wasn't until the actual funeral where Mama Bee could no longer hold in the pain she felt for the loss of her Great Aunt. She cried as Glenda's body was lowered into the ground.

When she had thrown a single flower atop of the casket, she insisted on being taken back to Ella's house.

Oftentimes death brings a family together in such a way, due to shared pain causing all to reflect on what they'll never have the chance of doing or saying ever again. But how many times must the process be repeated before it's realized that only in the reciprocating love of Christ is the sting of death removed here on earth and throughout all of eternity.

The following day Mama Bee, Eli, Mary and Lee-Lee returned to Louisville, Kentucky, leaving Liz behind to provide comfort to Ella and Elisha. Also to sort through Glenda's personal and legal affairs.

While doing so it was discovered that Glenda's entire estate had been willed to her Lizzy, more than twenty years ago, but nonetheless still legally binding.

Elizabeth both overwhelmed and shocked, concluded that it was her obligation and her duty to move into and straighten up her Grandma's house. This responsibility she immediately assumed.

For over a week she worked relentlessly to turn the house she had inherited back into a nice residence. So diligent she was in her pursuit that Elisha became concerned, prompted by Eli's inquiring of his mother's absence she decided to drop in on her.

When Elisha had come to her Granny's house she found it buzzing with workers going in and out, which included having a landscape service tending to its exterior.

She entered the house to find her Mother standing in the midst of a newly furnished dwelling. They both sat at the glass table in the freshly painted kitchen where Liz assured her daughter that she had not lost her mind, but in fact had found her center.

A pivotal point from where she could utilize the resources of Lynx to aide single Mother's across the country.

"Although my first contribution goes to a young woman who's yet to have any children, but she's so deserving that words may not ever be able to express how much so," Liz said as she handed Elisha the keys to the house.

"Mama, are you serious, this is my house? I can't believe it," Elisha exclaimed effusively.

"I want you to believe it due to the fact that you are my inspiration. And I will never forget to remember all that you mean to me."

The two women hugged and they cried in the middle of that little white kitchen for what seemed like at least an hour.

Their embrace was interrupted by, "Excuse me do you mind if I was to invite myself into this affection?"

"Eli!" both women screamed with excitement as they extended their open arms for him to enter.

"When did you get here?" his Mother asked.

"I just arrived a short while ago and I came directly here from the airport."

"I'm so glad that you did son."

"I am too," Elisha said still embracing them both.

"I've noticed the house has been refurbished. And it looks real good!"

"It belongs to your sister now. I just gave it all to her. Under one condition, that I had forgotten to mention," Liz said having a look on her face.

"What's the condition?" Eli and Elisha asked in unison.

"I'm glad that the both of you asked, because the task requires the two of you."

"Which is?" Elisha especially wanted to know.

"I need for my two children to go up into the attic and bring me down Grandma Glenda's belongings so I can sort through them."

"Oh Mama, of course we will. It'll be no problem seeing how you've done all that you have," Elisha said as she began to lead Eli by the hand.

"Come on little brother. I'll need you to pull the stair chain."

Up in the attic it was a complete mess. Old furniture from a time long gone that made one wonder how, how long have these things been up here. And how did anybody ever get them up here. Dust covered everything; the chairs and stools, the table, and the dresser drawers.

Elisha opened an old storage chest only to discover yet even more old belongings. As she moved items inside around, she came upon her own image being reflected by a girandole. She lifted the old candleholder and wondered how old it really was.

Then another object from within the chest caught her attention. It was an antique box only so big, and when she lifted it she noticed it had its key sticking out of its lock. Elisha discovered it contained photographs of people from a time in a distant past. The paper was yellowing and very outdated, but this fact only intrigued her more.

She placed the box onto her lap after closing the chest, upon which she sat. Elisha stared at a picture of her great Grandmother Glenda being held by a man who appeared to be much younger than she.

She searched through other pictures and witnessed her great Grandmother go back in time and transform into an overwhelmingly beautiful dark-skinned woman. Having hazel eyes, long dark hair, and nice long legs, Elisha noticed.

Elisha then looked at a larger photograph. Possibly the biggest of the stack, and judging by the paper it was developed on, it was definitely the oldest of the bunch.

As she looked and searched the photo, her mind became locked onto the scene she saw before her.

"What is it?" Eli asked as he pulled up an old rickety stool to where she sat.

Elisha obviously enthralled by what she held in her hands, finally spoke. "It's pictures taken a long long time ago," she told him.

"Forreal, let me have a look?" Eli asked as he took a hold of the photograph Elisha held in her hands. "Hold on Eli, I'm not finished looking at it." But by then it was too late. Eli had wrenched it away from his sister's grip.

Now he sat looking at this old photograph dating back to only the Lord knows when. He wasn't able to immediately identify any of the occupants of the picture as he looked over it with a deep intensity. But what he was able to ascertain was the obvious fact that this picture had been taken of people in bondage.

Eli looked over the back row consisting of four men in clothing that seemed to have been stitched of rags. Their faces somber, but yet at the same time he was able to recognize the pride that was eminent, but somehow was able to reach the surface of their black leathery faces.

The three women who sat on the steps of the old rundown shack showed a sense of pride and self-respect as well, but their countenance was stern which showed resilience.

529

And then there was the two little girls who both appeared to be wanting the very same spot in between the legs of the woman who sat center. The two children looked out from the photograph with eyes that showed their depth. And it was those eyes that caused Eli to become mesmerized in an almost trance like state.

He stared into those eyes as if he was searching into a pair that were alive.

"Eli, Eli I wasn't finished looking at that one yet," his sister Elisha insisted.

At his being jolted back to the right now, Eli turned the photograph over so to be able to view its back in search of any names of the occupants. As he struggled to make out the date that was there, he moved on and came upon a name that he had heard told to him in stories by his Granny Bee.

"Give it back to me Eli. You're acting like a child right now," Elisha said in such a tone as she grabbed a hold of the picture's edge.

Eli had resisted without being fully aware of doing so, because he only wanted to look upon the faces again before releasing the picture to anyone. In his reluctance, he reared back and away from her grasp only to cause the old rickety stool to give way. He went down so hard that the force and his weight caused the floor to cave in beneath him.

Elisha's screaming was only drowned out by the explosive crashing sound that Eli's body made as it smashed through the glass kitchen table on the first floor below.

"Oh my God!" Liz screamed as the instant realization grabbed a hold of her. She ran to her son's body laying there bloodied and motionless. "Eli, Eli!" Elizabeth screamed and yelled her son's name, but received no response.

Elisha had reached her mother's side, hollering and screaming his name as well. She then scrambled back to her feet and snatched the phone from the wall and frantically dialed nine, one, one.

WE SUFFER FOR A REASON

CHAPTER 38

Wake up, Wake up, Eli faintly heard words being spoken, but he did not understand nor did he know from where they'd come. Everything was black, total darkness without there being any propensity for light, so his mind returned to nothingness.

"Get him up and into my bed," the woman instructed the two men who were standing over Eli's cut and bruised body.

They immediately obeyed the woman's command and took him into the old shack and gently laid him into her bed.

She gathered a pail of cold water and some rags to tend to the cuts that covered his face.

"If'n theys find this'n here there'd be trouble brought on us all," Leroy told his Mother in obvious fear. "Be that as it may, he's here now and we ain't about to just let him stay out in the woods to die, or to be torn apart by them vicious dogs they got out there roaming the land. For now he seems to be alive and living. For how long, we'll have to wait and see what God decides."

"Now don't go carrying on about there being a God up in the heavens Mama, because if there was such a thing as One we wouldn't be enslaved by people who hate the color of our skin so that oftentimes they put the whip to us for no reason at all," Leon voiced.

"There is a God high up in the heavens, just like your Daddy tells us there is."

"Well, why won't He come down and right this wrong that's going on right here before His eyes?"

"Now you just hush up your foolish talk, right this minute, and I mean it. It's talk like that that causes His anger to boil over and spill out on us in a most terrible way."

"If thats the case, it's impossible for us to anger Him any further than what we already have then. Just look around. Or you need not look any further than your own bedroom where that boy lies terribly beaten and cut all to pieces by those who God allows to do so to us all."

"I won't hear no more of it. Everything you say is altogether against what your Father teaches from that there bible."

"That there bible Mama, that there book of words. The very same book that he had to have gotten from them.

534

The book that tells you just how right and proper it is to obey our master and pick his cotton until our fingers bleed. 'And anytime he feels the desire to, he should come out to his barn and beat us with his whip until our backs blister and split open and our clothes soak up with our own blood."

"We are gonna have to let God have His own way until He sees fit to bring about change."

"His own way? It's easy enough to see that them white cracks are the ones who are having their own way, and if God is allowing it to be so, then He's in partnership with them," Leon said with a fierceness that caused him to tremble. And one that made his own mother recede just a little, but not due to fear, but more so to surprise, having never heard her oldest boy say such words against the God who her husband teaches them all of. She was relieved to see their front door open and her husband enter in.

"I'm so glad you're back. A child has been found by the boys beaten to almost an inch of his very life! He's in the most terrible shape," Bernice exclaimed.

"Where is this child," Eli asked as he stepped closer to his wife.

"He's in the bedroom. I've done all I could do. The rest is up to the Lord."

"There it goes again," Leon voiced.

"I've told you that there will not be any more of that talk of nonsense in here Leon."

Eli went into the bedroom and looked over the young man that lie there. He had no way of discerning the young man's exact age, but to him he looked to be in the latter part of his teenage years. He definitely looked to be very bad off. But Eli had to smile to himself as he now focused his attention on his wife's doctoring. She had bandaged the boy well. Always the one to care for anybody who's in need of her care.

"I just had to bring him inside and tend to his wounds. I couldn't leave him out there in the dark to die, now could I?" Bernice asked.

"Of course not Bernice , you did the right thing. We just have to be careful not to let Tom the overseer discover him here. Now, does anyone know where this child came from, or who he belongs to?"

"He was just lying there as we made our way back from the barn after chasing down them darn turkeys," Leroy said.

"Well, he had to come from somewhere. He didn't just fall from the sky, now did he?" asked Eli.

"Wherever he has run away from, he's bound to bring us nothing but trouble. We will be accused of hiding a runaway," Leon pleaded. "Daddy you've always taught us to avoid these troubles and to never let 'em land on our doorstep where it'll bring danger to the women of our house."

"This here is a little different. This here concerns our duty to care for strangers. The Lord will bless our house with goodness for doing so."

"I know you'd bring the Lord God Almighty into this, the same Lord that sat back and watched that treacherous Tom beat Leroy into a retard," Leon said in a malevolent manner.

"The good Lord has his reasons for everybody's steps of suffering. That means our plight in this world is no different. There will come a time when those who have stayed trusting in God will be instructed by Holy angels on what to do."

"Holy angels, will you just listen at yourself daddy? You sound like your mind has been removed from the cotton field and has made its way to some magical land where no whips exist," Leon told his father.

"That boy over there with half the sense knocked out of him is your son," Leon added.

"I dare you mouth me in such a way in my own home boy. Now you just do well to remove yourself from my house and go to your own dwelling," Eli exploded.

"I will do just that exactly, but remember my warning. There will be trouble when them bloodhounds come sniffing around after that there runaway."

"Be that as it may, I'll not turn that child aside and allow worse harm to befall him," Bernice said to her son's back as he left out through their front door.

After shutting the door, she turned to Leroy and asked, "Leroy think carefully, have you ever seen that boy laying in there ever before?"

"No momma, that's all I've ever seen of him ever before. Is he not from around here?"

"Well baby, that's what me and your father are trying to find out," Bernice said.

It took several days of Bernice 's constant care in order to bring the injured boy to a state of consciousness.

As she was tending to the bandage around his head, he asked, "Where am I? What's happened to me?"

"I can't rightly say what's happened to you, but I can assure you you're in good and able hands. Now, do you care to tell where you've run from as well as who's after you?"

"Who's after me?" Eli questioned. "I don't know. All I know is—" he paused, and tried unsuccessfully to search his mind for some answers. The attempt caused his head to throb, so he closed his eyes and laid back.

There came a pounding on the door of the shack that made the door fly open and almost made it come off its hinges. In stomps, Terrible Tom, the overseer, hollering,

"Eli, Eli where have you gone off to boy, and who have you got ill at this place?"

"I'm here," Eli strained to say in the weakest voice, only to be shushed to silence by Bernice as she nervously made her way out of the bedroom and into the presence of Tom Woodward.

"Where's that damned Eli of yours? Has he fallen ill all of a sudden. I've received word there's been inquiry made concerning infectious ointment of some sort. Tell him to get out here now and explain it all."

Then he began to yell past Bernice , "I can't have none of yous falling ill around here. We have bails of cotton to be picked. Whether your fingers or your backs bleed makes no matter to me! Did you hear what I say Eli?"

"Yes sir," Eli replied as he walked in and up behind the overseer, causing him to jump and expose his fright.

Tom turned fast and faced Eli, screaming, "What's the meaning of you sneaking up on a man? I have a good mind to knock some sense into yous."

"I, I mean you no harm sir. I only just now hear the yelling and I come in to see the cause for it." "I'll tell you the cause, you've been seeking some medicines from the main house cause it was overheard and related to me. But you're standing here not looking a damn bit ill, nor does she."

"I had asked sir if'n it be possible to have something for the bare feet that have become sore and bleeding sir. That's all sir." Eli bent the truth.

"I come personally to tell you that there will be no nothing of any kind. Only more bleeding if this crop doesn't get picked on time to be taken to market. Am I making myself clear enough for you boy?" Terrible Tom asked as he made his way back out of the little old shack, stomping and shouldering Eli as he went.

"Surely I thought he had received word of the boy when he come in here hollering about somebody being here ill," Bernice said as she made her way closer to Eli.

"Now don't you worry yourself so Bernice ," Eli comforted his wife as he pondered on who could have leaked word to the overseer.

"The boy had come to, but only for a brief moment. Not near long enough for me to learn anything about him," Bernice told Eli as they entered their room and looked over the boy.

"Not even his name, or where he come from?" Eli asked.

"Not yet I haven't. You just go and tend to the field so we don't have 'em coming back around here snooping. I'll do my best to get this'n into good enough health," Bernice told Eli as she ushered him out of the room and to their front door.

He stopped there and turned to face her, then he simply said, "I thank God for sending me you, and Bernice one of these days we will be married in one of them churches."

She pecked him on the cheek and told him, "You are always concerning yourself with my little ole feelings."

541

After closing the door and turning to tend to her business, she came face to face with her patient who looked her in her eyes and said, "I'm Eli!"

"Dear Lord," she said. "Let me get you back into bed. Surely they done knocked the sense out of you."

"Where am I and how did I get here?" he asked. When she had gotten him back in the bed she said, "You must be suffering a fever, causing you to speak things that ain't so."

"Where am I, who are you?" Eli interrupted.

"Well, you're here at me, and my husband's home, and you've been in pretty rough shape until here of late. I thought you was getting better, but I'm unable to tell for sure."

"What happened to me? All I can remember is me, and my sister sitting at the house looking at pictures, then I just blanked out."

"You have a sister? I figured as much, because while you were trying to come around you would ask for Mary and say other names that I couldn't make out." "I remember my sister's name. It's Elisha, and Mary is my girlfriend. Where am I, so I can go and find my family?"

"Your family, who is your family and where have you come from? Ever since you have been in my care you have been unable to tell me much of anything. Are you able to remember where you are from?"

"Yes, of course. I'm from Georgia. I was born in Georgia, but we moved away with our Mother after our Father died, he explained as he was slowly recovering some of his memories."

"Are you trying to tell me that you, your sister, and your Mother were all sold off after your Daddy died?"

"No, we weren't sold off. We moved away and drove up to Louisville, Kentucky."

"Drove, Louisville. Child have you done gone crazy? What are you speaking of?"

After an hour or so of back and forth talk between Bernice, and her patient, she had come to the conclusion that the boy had been given a terrible hit to the head.

"It's time I start preparing the meal. After you've eaten maybe you be given some more senses."

"I feel just fine. I'm only having trouble understanding where I'm at, and how I got here."

"I have told you already, you are here at me and my husband's home. At least it's what we've come to refer

543

to it as. A home, given to us to rear children in and raise into able working bodies.

Being that our Leon is in charge of making sure all the other workers make it out to the fields, the master saw it fit to give to us our own little shack."

"Did you say, the master, and the fields? What are you telling me exactly?" Eli asked.

"Sh, hold your tongue down. You done went and woke the baby."

Before another word was able to escape Eli's mouth, Bernice left the room to tend to the cries of her baby daughter, Jessie.

"Now, now there. That's a good girl," Bernice said to soothe the baby as she picked little Jessie up from the makeshift baby's bed.

Once she had her all quieted down, the quiet didn't last long due to Eli's stomping in to where she was, asking loudly, "How'd I get to this place?"

"Why so loud child, you done gone and got this little one all riled up again. Now sit here and hold her while I go over to the wood stove and prepare her something to eat."

As she handed her daughter to Eli she told him, "Meet lady Jessie. She's as feisty as a wild cat, but once she gets a little something inside of her belly she's much easier to deal with."

"Her name is Jessie?" Eli asked.

"Yes it is. I like to call her lady Jessie. And now that you know our names, do you mind sharing with me your name child?"

"My name is Eli, I'm Eli Lewis."

"Child, they must have hit you upside of your head awfully hard in order for you to think your name is my husband's name."

"No, my name is Eli. I was named after my relative who's name was Eli."

"Well, that could very well be, and I have no right to doubt your telling of the truth. So, if you're able to remember so much about your family, their naming and such, how about you telling me where they are, and where you come from. And just as important, how did you end up out there in them woods only half alive?" Bernice asked as she gathered up lady Jessie and placed her on her own lap.

"Your husband's name is Eli?"

545

"That's right, apparently it's the same as yours," she answered with a slight chuckle.

"And your name is Bernice ?"

"You're right once again. Not only that, but we haven't had any trouble remembering our names," she told him as she gave him a look that could only be saying, 'But one of us sitting here may not be able to confess the same.'

Eli ignored the knowing look and went on to say, "This may sound crazy, because it definitely feels crazy, but my Grandmother's name is Bernice . It's obvious to me that I've somehow woken up in a different place and in a different time. But all I can remember is being in Georgia with my Mother and my sister, and something happened to me and I don't know exactly what to make of it, because what I'm thinking can't possibly be real."

Bernice said, "I guess that depends entirely on what it is that you're thinking. I can tell you rightly so that this here Georgia is real. The birthplace of Satan himself."

Eli stood and went for the door so he could take a look at the outside. He was frightened into a frozen position at Bernice 's abrupt shout,
"NO! If you let yourself be seen by anyone, the sooner you'll be returned to your owner."

"My owner? Nobody owns me," Eli said but he heeded her warning and peered through the makeshift curtain that covered the window instead of opening the door. What he saw stunned him into an awful realization. From that window he could see a cotton field that went on for as far as his eyes could see. And just off to the left in the distance, he was able to see what he knew to be one of his worse fears growing up digesting his Granny Bee's stories.

There sat the Big House, a huge plantation house along with all of the fixings. There was even a couple of horses, and buggies sitting to

the side of the place.

CHAPTER 39

Inside of the Big House a few men had gathered to listen to James Bodiford as he spoke about their plight for a better, greater, and richer Georgia.

In attendance was his brother-in-law Henry, his wife, Nancy's brother, Tom Woodward, the overseer, George Hill the sheriff of their newly formed town of Marietta, the Reverend Tom Parish who's son Tim was known to hang with the Bodifords on more days than not. Also in attendance was Billy Floyd who bought and sold slaves with such finesse at times and at other times he used his power and brutality to attain negro human beings. The latter method had earned him the name, Bill the Bull.

There was also present a couple of men who had hopes to become involved in this lucrative business of purchasing souls to be worked until the soul was no more.

And let us not forget to mention, Ms. Emma, the only woman ever allowed into this exclusive mens only gathering. And her right of passage was mainly due to her marriage to the unchallenged and obvious next Governor, Nathan B. Forrest. That and the fact that her family has traded negroes ever since she could remember.

"Gentlemen, if you all would listen to some real reasoning," Emma began. "I'll share with you all how it's been done around here for the longest of time. "Ever since I can remember the purchasing of these niggers and our benefit there from has given us all the power we need to map out this states infrastructure.

"My Daddy has always said, 'The blood of niggers fertilizes our crops to abundance.' "And we all know that these abundant crops is what grows our wealth."

"This we all know to be true," Bodiford interposed. "Well, I vote yes to allowing Mr. Richard and his brother Walter Kay here to purchase the three hundred acres of land that's adjacent to their property, as they are now included in our circle.

They should also be allowed the use of Bill the Bull," ?Bodiford concluded.

Emma's reasoning did bring about an agreement, as she knew it would. With her possessing the wealth, power, and influence that she wielded, this to be compounded with her marriage to Nathan Forrest, no one but Bodiford himself could possibly oppose her sway.

But even he was reluctant to show any objection to a cause that would extend his own power, and control.

"Emma, Emma," James Bodiford interjected once more. "We are all in agreement to the Kay's purchase, and I give them unlimited access to Bill's talents. So you see there's no need to convince us of something that we already see so clearly.

"Henry here will see to all of the necessary paperwork. And gentlemen, you both will be well on your way to enjoying the fruits of your labor. Or should I say, 'The fruits of your salves labors.' "

Then Bodiford laughed his devilish laugh which caused the others to join in the laughter.

CHAPTER 40

"This can't possibly be forreal, but it is real Lord God, how can this be happening to me? How can this be happening at all?" Eli asked himself as he backed away from the window.

"Child, are you well?" Bernice asked as she looked at the distraught face of the young Eli.

"Why don't you have yourself a seat right here before you fall over now?"

"I'll be okay. I just need a few minutes in order to gather my thoughts. This is unbelievable," Eli exclaimed as he took a seat on the floor right in front of where Bernice sat.

She finished feeding lady Jessie and then placed her back in the makeshift cradle.

"Get up from the floor child and let me warm you a bowl of my soup. That will fill your stomach and loosen your tongue some."

A short while later Bernice and her guest were both finishing up their bowls of bean soup, which contained such spices that Eli's mouth had never experienced before.

"The soup was delicious and you are an excellent cook. I really appreciate all of your help," Eli told her.

"You don't have to speak of it, because I would've done the same for anybody found outside lying half alive, and half dead. But in order for us to really be of some help to you, you'll have to tell more than just what you've been telling."

"What I've been telling, what I've been telling is the truth. My name is Eli. I'm not from here, but somehow I've been brought here. The last I remember is being with my Mother, and my sister at my great Grandmother Glenda's house."

Bernice gave Eli a look that was in between astonishment, and shock before asking, "Your great who?"

"My great Grandmother Glenda," he said again, and went on to say, "If this dream I'm living is as real as it seems, then there was once a baby Glenda in your life before she was snatched away and killed."

"Boy, what do you know about it? What right do you have to come in here and—"

"No listen" Eli interrupted. "I haven't come to upset you. Honestly, I don't know why nor how I've come,

552

but if you'll listen I will share with you all that I do know."

An hour later after Eli had shared with Bernice many of the things shared with him by his Granny Bee, it left Bernice confused, but not totally unbelieving. For now she just sat there and searched Eli's eyes as if she was seeking some sort of revelation. That or at least a family resemblance.

She must have found something to be familiar, because she took Eli's face into the two of her hands and she continued to look until the tears began to roll down both of her dark and lovely cheeks.

"My God child, I've carried the sight of my own child's death around with me for such a long time now, allowing it to tear my soul apart, piece by piece a day at a time. And at times the pain has caused me to ask the Lord for my own death.

"Now, well now I believe He has a greater purpose for us, even at the cost of my own soul."

Entering into the shack came Eli, followed by both of his boys, Leon and Leroy. Bernice stood to her feet and announced to them all, "This here boy is our own kin! Don't ask me how, cause I don't rightly know the exact how of it. I just know that he is."

"But Bernice , how can this be?" Eli asked, needing just a minor amount of evidence.

"I just told you, I don't know the exact how of it."

"Momma, this boy was found by us out in the woods, knocking on deaths door. And none of us had ever seen a hair of him before then. So he being of any kin is a little far fetched, wouldn't you say?" Leon asked, enjoying his logic.

Bernice ignored her son's question and she led her husband toward their room. Right there at their door Bernice told him, "Eli, I know what I say is right. Now you just take notice of it, cause I ain't never told you no wrong."

"I know, I know Bernice . That's why I'm telling you now that I intend to do whatever you feel to be for the better. Now tell me, what would you have me to do?"

"I don't know Eli, I honestly don't know what to do. We just have to take good care of him and make certain he stays safe."

"If I'm not mistaken, that's what you've been doing. And looking at the way he's up and about, you've done as good of a job as any. But I do know what you're telling me and seeing how they got the Big House spilling over with folks, there may be dangerous times up ahead."

"What are you telling me?" Bernice asked him.

But it was their son Leon who answered. "It's looking like them white folks are getting themselves together in order to search for something missing, lost, or runaway!"

"We can't rightly say that that's their gathering reason, but there's something in the air and it just don't feel right," Eli, the elder told them.

Blaam! Boom! Right then their door came crashing in and in came Tom the overseer accompanied by Walter and Richard Kay, but it was Bill the Bull who rushed on in and took Eli by the arm and neck forcing him face first to the floor.

"Eli, I'm very disappointed in you boy. You've been harboring this new fellow here and obviously you have forgotten about the consequences," the overseer Terrible Tom voiced.

"We had no idea this boy here was a runaway. All I know'd is that he was injured awfully bad and in need of some help," Leon spoke up.

"So you are admitting to having knowledge of his existence?"

Before Leon was able to respond to the obvious, he had been snatched up by Tom. And while Tom held Leon by his throat, he looked him intently in the eyes and said, "You shall bare the burden and save your Daddy the suffering!"

At the mention of the word suffering, Bernice burst into tears for her son's sake, then she wailed aloud, "No!"

Her cries fell on deaf ears and so Eli, the younger and Leon were dragged outside and away.

"Leon boy, do you care to tell me from where this runner has run?" Tom asked. "If you refuse to give the truth, your time on the Post will be longer spent and much more painful, that I promise you!"

At the mere mention of the post, Leon's face showed a terrifying fright as his entire body tensed, for he knew from experience that the Post was where slaves were tied and beaten with lashes that not even Satan himself could mete out more brutally.

The remembrance of that night several summers past, engulfed him in a fear that now gripped his soul!

Before he actually realized it, he was bound facing the Post, having his shirt ripped apart exposing his bare back.   Standing in front of him was Terrible Tom clutching his whip and revealing a look of anticipation.

"I'll ask you this one last time boy. Now you'll do well to tell the whole truth nigger, you hear' Where did this here other nigger come from?"

"I don't know sir. As I say to you before we just come across him there laying in the field, bleeding something awful. I swear it's the truth. I swear to you it is!"

"You know you should have immediately come and let us know that there was this new nigger here on Master Bodiford's property. For all you know he could have been a great danger to you all, like the last runaways killing everything in their path and causing the deaths of many of your own kind. But instead you rather hide the truth and take the risk. So let this be a lesson to you," Tom said uncoiling his whip and walking around to his exposed bare back. The moon light revealing scars for beatings past.

The first lash ripped Leon's skin open and struck him with excruciating pain. He yelled out, but after so many repeated lashes, his yelling stopped as well as his consciousness.

It was as if Terrible Tom enjoyed the sight of blood leaking, because as it ran down Leon and onto the ground, Tom continued to beat him with his whip all the while instructing the Kay's on how they are to properly break the nigger's will. "Only then will they serve passively," he explained.

After the whipping had finally ended, they left Leon there for dead, and they then turned their attention to their runaway slave.

"Listen here boy, you have only one chance of telling the honest to God truth so help you. Now tell us plainly, where have you run away from, you disgusting bastard?"

"Sir, I've run away from nowhere. I was born free and I—"

Before Eli could complete the sentence, Tom had taken flight on him with his whip.

Eli screamed out and attempted to make a break for it, but he was instantly subdued.

Tom yelled, "Oh yeah, you're one of them there halfway smart niggers. Maybe yous a house nigger, and you done run away from your good master who has taken such good care of yous. But look at the way you show your gratitude."

"This 'n here has a lot of rabbit in him. I can tell," said Bodiford as he approached the others.

"Before beating this one to death Tom, why don't you chain him in the pit until he comes to submission. By then he'd make a real good gift to the Kays here, as a semblance of our forward progress."

"That's mighty kind of you Bodiford and we would accept the token and not to mention all else you're willing to share in the fine art of breaking the will and self-pride of the high niggers."

"So you see it as well, in this one here?" Bodiford asked.

"Yes, I must say that I do. This one here shows a certain pride and knowing that just shouldn't be shown, nor expressed in the eyes of any nigger."

"I agree totally," replied Bodiford. Then he commanded Tom to carry the runaway away to the pit.

By the time night had fallen, Bernice was apprehensive. She had no idea, absolutely no way of knowing rather or not if her son Leon was still alive, or dead. With pleading eyes she looked into her husband's face, desperately wanting him to go out and see about his son, but at the same time fearful of what would happen if he was caught out at night.

Believing herself to know the truth about the younger Eli's origin, she now feared for the child as if he was her very own.

Her very own; what the child had said, is it possible? Could it be?

By now she had convinced herself to believe, I mean, how else could he possibly know the things that he did.

It wasn't possible, unless—

"Eli, we have to do something. There has to be something we can do to see about their well being."

Before Eli had the chance to respond to her, he removed himself from the window and opened the door and allowed Marsha, the girl from the Big House to enter in. The little colored girl Marsha, came through the door, passing Eli and went right to where Bernice stood.

"Ma'am, I come to tell you that your boy Leon is about half dead and still tied to the Post. I did want to go myself and untie him, but I feared I might be found out. So, I just come straight to here as soon as I was given the chance to."

"We certainly appreciate your concerns. Tell us please of the other they took as well."

"You do mean the runaway, don't you Ma'am?" Asked she.

"They say he's run from somewhere, but if there's no place to run from, then how could you be a runaway?" Bernice questioned.

"I don't rightly know the answer. All I do know is when I overheard their talking, they say he belongs to them now and they aim to give him away as a gift to the ones who are taking up land up here on the other side of cotton fields." "Where's he now?" Bernice asked with the tremble of fear to her voice.

"Well Ma'am, they've chained him down deep in the pit!"

"Oh my God, Eli did you hear? They've put the child down in their pit. He will never survive there. He'll be dead before long."

"So, you really don't know where he come from, nor who he belongs to?" Marsha asked. "They believe he has traveled a good distance to get to here. He maybe even became lost and y'all stumbled up on him, since that's all they were able to beat out of your Leon. But

561

they knows he's been here a good while, and you've nursed him back to health.

"They know as much due to the medicines you've been asking from the big house. So, they take away his nice shoes and his clothing and put him in the slave rags and then chained him in the pit."

"As we say to you before, we haven't any idea where he come from, even if all you say be true," Eli attempted to make Marsha understand.

"Well, I've only come to let you both know what's going on up there at the Big House, hoping I could be of some help to y'all."

"We really do thank you and we appreciate all of your concerns," Bernice tells her.

"I dos whatever I can when I'm able to sneak away," Marsha says then adds, "It be wise of you to go after your Leon and bring him down from off of the Post, cause you know how they'd just as well leave him there until the other half of his life leaks right on out of him." Bernice , Eli, and Leroy left shortly after Marsha had left.

Eli tried to dissuade Bernice , but she simply refused to listen to a word of it. So, with lady Jessie wrapped and secured, they all traveled to the Post where they saw with their own eyes the torture that had been administered to their own flesh and blood.

Bernice handed the baby to Leroy and she went to her son, still tied to the Post unconscious and as Marsha had exclaimed, half dead. She took the rag and bottle of water and used it in an effort to wipe the disservice from Leon's face.

Once untied and awakened, she forced him to drink from the bottled water. They finally managed to get him back to their dwelling, where Bernice went to work at her nursing skills, mingled with motherly love, occasionally taking a hold of the string made Red Cross she wore around her neck, praying while she dressed his wounds.

Her prayers were increasing as well as her concern for her son's survival. It did appear that they had beaten the life all the way out of him.

She remembered witnessing with her own eyes this form of brutality being poured upon her people for so many years, even the murders of her own brothers.

And the Lord only knows how they brought about the demise of her very own father. The details were never discovered. As she thought back to that time over forty years since, she remembers her father's pridefulness and his resiliency.

Even bound and beaten, he made certain his family knew their inner strengths. The well he had taught them to draw from during the hardest of times.

She recalled the way he had looked into her eyes. It was as if her and her father had communicated soul to soul before those white men took him away. Now, as she looked into the vacant eyes of her oldest son, she was just thankful to see that they still held life in them.

When she had done all that she could possibly do for now, she went out into the front room and joined Eli and Leroy.

"Glad to see that the baby lay sound asleep," she whispered to her husband and son. We must do whatever we can to rescue that boy from that hellish pit. There's no way we are just going to sit by and do nothing."

"Momma, I want to help. I can help, can I help you momma?" Leroy asked.

"Of course you can Leroy, but first we have to keep our voices down so we don't wake the baby. Then Eli you must gather some help from the field tomorrow. Just a couple of them that you know to be willing to do me this favor."

"I don't know Bernice , by morning word of this been done spread all over. Surely the fear be deep."

"Maybe so, maybe so, but we just have to do all that we can Eli, cause that boy Eli, he belongs to us too." "Huh, what exactly are you saying Bernice ?" "I'm saying that boy has told me things that lets me know for sure. Oh Eli, we must free him from that awful pit so you can hear him for yourself, then you will know just like I do. That's the only way you're going to believe the truth."

Before sun up the next morning, Eli and Leroy was gathered up for cotton picking.

Leon was thoroughly looked over to make certain that he wasn't able to make it out to the field.

After Tom declared him to be unfit, he said, "Serves him right. This is what always results when you niggers sneak around your master's back."

Once out in the fields Eli cleared rolls and filled bags of cotton. This being his forty-forth year picking cotton, day in and day out, his hands had calloused and become numb to the thorn pricks, but nonetheless at times like this when his nervousness caused him to tremble, the thorns would somehow hit Eli in places he didn't have any defense for.

Making his way over a few rolls he was able to commune with Thomas, who he had been friends with for some number of years.

"I heard what's done happened to your boy, and I be really sorry for you, and your Bernice ," Thomas said.

"Thank you, I appreciate your kind words, but Thomas we got another problem that needs some dealing with."
"Say on," Thomas encouraged.
"There's this boy they have put down in the pit that I have to—"

Thomas stopped Eli mid-sentence and said, "There was a youngin in the pit, but in my passing they done brung him up."

"Where did they take him to Thomas?" Eli asked with intense eyes.

"Can't say that I know for sure. All I seen is what I saw, and like I said, it was in passing."

Several days went by and although Bernice was worried a great deal abut the younger Eli, her worries didn't make his whereabouts any clearer.

"Momma, momma here comes my Auntie," Leroy said aloud as he went to open the door wide.

In walked a wide woman, but her gait showed her confidence, or you could say, you could see her pride in her stride.

"Hi Auntie. You been gone too long," Leroy told her.

"I know honey, I know, but they got me doing everything under the sun up there at that house."

"How'd you get away from up there?" Bernice asked as she wrapped her arms around her Mother's sister.

"I told 'em I must be going to listen to Eli tell about the Lord God in heaven, which is my Christian duty. They seemed to have no problem with that since they be on their way to church this morning to hear about the same

God."

"Eli done gone down by the opening. I just stayed and tend to Leon. He insisted that Leroy stay here with me just in case I needed him."

"I must go in and take a look see at that Leon and see with my own eyes how bad they did to him."

"You know I don't mind it at all. He's always been just as much yours as he's been mines."

They both stood over where Leon lay, until he finally opened his eyes.

Bernice went over and made him drink from the bowl of broth and then sip some water.

He sat up in bed and was able to utter, "Hi Aunt Tee!"

"How are you feeling baby? I come by to check on you and to bring you these things here."

She began bringing things she had wrapped in a kerchief out from her breast. Foods and medicines that she had gathered from the Big House.

It hadn't been but ten days since Leon was tied to the Post. And although he was showing his self to be strong and recovering rapidly, the fact remained that he was nothing more than a child trapped in a man's body.

At nineteen, the child looked to be in his early thirties.

When Bernice and Aunt Tee were back in the front room, Bernice sat her down and asked, "Aunt Tee, what did Bodiford do with the boy he had put down in the pit?"

"The runaway who done caused you these troubles?" Aunt Tee asked.

"You have to tell me where they've taken him, if you know," Bernice pleaded.

Aunt Tee looked at her niece acutely for a short moment. Seeing her sister's features in her face she perceived her concern for this boy, and how could she refuse her Bee Bee anything, including information. "Child settle yourself and I'll tell you all that I know, which ain't much, not much at all.

"There was two men who came by the Big House a few days ago, around the time I was clearing master Bodiford's table.

"Joseph had showed the two in, knowing that they was the same men from days ago. The ones who had recently purchased that land down over on the other side of here. Well, they come in asking if the runaway was still living or was he dead.

"When they was told how alive he was they asked to take him away and master, he give 'em the right to."

CHAPTER 41

Eli was brought out of the Kay's barn and placed in the dirt at the feet of the two brothers. The eldest brother, Richard, put his boot to Eli's neck and began to speak,

"Listen closely boy. My brother, Walter here, believed it to be just as well if we had left you in that well to die, being that you were on your way to death anyhow. But me, I'm see something altogether different in you. Being that you speak differently than the rest of them, like if you've been educated somehow.

"Maybe that's the reason why the look in your eye is different. But I know you'll work out just fine here once we knock that there look of pride and resilience out of your eye, or knock your eye out, whichever one comes out first." The younger Kay said, as he moved around his brother, rather quickly, and kicked Eli in his face.

With a foot still on Eli's neck, Richard says, "You're here to guide some sense in the rest of them. That's the only reason why you're here. And your only reason for being allowed to live. So, as soon as you neglect to do your duty then your reason for living ends.

"Do you understand my brother plain enough nigger?" Walter yelled as he made his way over to do more harm to Eli's swollen face.

Now here it is two months after Eli's arrival to the Kay's plantation, and he was feeling physically fit and mentally sound. He had already conditioned his self to believe his only course of action would be, no action. It was paramount that he first learn the lay of the land and at the same time, plan. Plan his escape and search daily for a way to return through the apparent portal from whence he come.

Today, him, Richard and Walter stood in front of the place awaiting the arrival of what was slowly approaching—the two wagons full of black negro cargo most recently purchased by the Kay's.

As Bill the Bull jumped down from the first cart, he made way to the back and unlatched the latch. Using the handle of his whip he knocked his cargo into a line formation before the Kay's. And likewise was the brutality administered to the second wagon's cargo.

"As promised Mr. Richard. Mr. Walter this the best able body niggers that the square had to offer. I've brought to you strong hands and broad shoulders.

Healthy females with child baring hips like they all have.

"Your farm will soon have plenty of them little black bastards running around here. All you needs to do is train 'em up to obey, and you'll both be running the half of the State that James Bodiford don't possess," Bill proclaimed and then he broke out into a loud cackle. Richard and Walter walked up and down the two rolls of butt naked negro slaves looking at them all from head to toe.

Walter, paying extra close attention to perfectly perched breasts belonging to the young negro women who stood obviously terrified of him, but even more fearful of their uncertain futures.

"Tamer," Richard called, but since he received no reply from Eli, he reached over and knocked the I don't know what out of him.

When Eli was able to gather himself and stand to his feet, he hurried over to master Richard's side and began to say, "Sorry sir, so very—"

But Richard told him, "If need be I'll implant your name in your brain with my fist, but do know that I take no pleasure in it."

Eli knew that to be a damn lie, but he simply bowed, lowering his head in a cowardly submissive manner of defeat. Seeing how his acquiescence makes them believe that they have broken the negro and have finally proven to him his own inferiority.

Richard snatched one of the younger women from the rows and then grabbed her hard by her face. Obviously enjoying the fear he saw in her eyes, he threw her to the ground over by where Eli stood.

"Tamer, she will be your mate. You are to breed with her and produce the second crop of this farm," Richard said with a look of possessing a secret only he knew.

Eli helped the girl who he thought couldn't have been no more than nineteen to her feet, but she snatched away from his grasp looking at him with about the same amount of fear as she showed to have for the white men.

When Eli attempted to tell her that he would not hurt her, she screamed, "T-ke Too-Too, Too Tomadure." At least this is what Eli heard and he hadn't a clue as to its meaning.

When Walter slapped the girl's face so hard she fell into Eli's arms, Eli turned his body so that he was now positioned between her and Walter.

WE SUFFER FOR A REASON

Walter recognized it for what it was. He knew it was the nigger's showing of protection, so Walter commenced to beating the hell out of Eli. So much in fact that Richard had to finally pull his brother off of Eli.

Afterwards he instructed Bill and his crew to escort the cargo of slaves into the barn where they had stocks and fetters prepared to chain them to. And it was there that they all stood cuffed in the stocks for hours.

Eventually, Eli was allowed to go and attempt communications with the new arrivals.

"Where do you think you are off to boy?" asked Inman, the dog handler who's pleasure it was to let the dogs loose on a nigger whether they were running or not.

"I've been told to go and see about the people who are inside the barn."

"Them aren't no damn people. Them there are animals like yourself. And you can see about them all you want, but they aren't able of knowing a damn thing you say, you dumb ignorant bastards that you are."

Eli bowed his head and carried on his journey to the barn, knowing himself that there are apparent language barriers, but he knew that this didn't necessarily mean that communications are impossible.

574

Once inside the barn he went over to the same girl who he had received a beating for trying to protect. When he reached for her face, she immediately turned, not wanting his touch, nor his concern, so Eli had gathered.

"I just want to see if there's any swelling or if there's anything I can do to help you."

"Neffi Aah, nuh Ell jar ra ta," is what Eli heard being spoken to him by the man who was chained next to the girl. So he faced him and made an attempt to speak with him by repeating back to him what he had spoken.

Fifteen minutes and about a hundred hand gestures later, Eli had made out that this man's daughter Neffi was in desperate need of water and food, even more so than the rest since she was already with child.

The water was not a huge problem, but even he himself had trouble getting any food and whenever he did, it was always scraps.

After giving them all water he went back over to the girl and said, "Neffi jar ra-oul."

When she heard her name being spoken to her she provided Eli her full attention, but her countenance remained perplexed. So he repeated to her what he believed to mean 'more water for Neffi.'

575

She slightly nodded indicating that she did want more water.

Eli knew he couldn't spend too much more time in the barn because the Kays were forever suspicious of his doings, and they constantly kept him under scrutiny.

He left the barn after having promised that he would return. So, off he went perfecting the act that he had to perform. His mind constantly on the bigger picture, which was to convince the Kays that he had truly submitted mind, body and soul. For that was the only way that they would allow him enough room and free time to move about as he wished.

The following morning Eli was awakened into the new day by a kick of a boot belonging to Bill the Bull.

"On your feet boy, yous got much work to do," yelled Bill as he put his boot to Eli's backside.

"What'll you have me to do for you sur?" Eli asked in a sleepy voice, but with an attitude of passivity nonetheless.

"You just follow me boy and be quick about it," uttered the Bull in his piercing tone.

As Eli followed Bill, he could plainly see that dreadful whip in his hand, so he's instantly thankful that he wasn't awakened by the skin splitting braided leather.

A brief moment later they entered the barn where Eli discovers an extremely horrific scene. The brutality that had been dispensed on some of the men held captive in the barn was repulsive, to say the least.

He squinted his eyes in the dimness in search of Neffi, to make sure she hadn't suffered any harm.

Eli was made aware of his task. It was now his duty to accompany these souls labeled incorrigibles to the fields to pick cotton.

Since he has been here on the Kay's plantation, Eli has witnessed them acquire roughly eighty able bodied men, women, and children. All put to forced labor here in the fields. First sowing the seed and now reaping the harvest.

Selling cotton and negroes are the most lucrative businesses here in their Jim Crow south. And somehow, some way, Eli has been made to suffer this atrocity that his race has already had to endure. He's constantly telling himself that this cannot be his kismet. And Since he has traveled back in time, there must be a way for him to travel back into the future. But until then he's focused on escaping to the North. For he has learned from his Granny Bee's history lessons, there his chances of survival increases. There he may live long enough to figure out what must be done in order for him to revert—

Snap! The crack of the whip shocks Eli back into the present relm.

Not being the recipient causes him to immediately seek out and then recognize who was. Bill the Bull had just unleashed a ferocious flogging unto one from the barn, while his right hand man Trump held his rifle on the other incorrigibles.

"I'll be the one that knocks you down from your high horse, cause I've told you tramp you'll pick this cotton until your fingers bleed," yelled Bill.

Eli doesn't know why his mind told him to, but he took ahold of the Bulls' swinging arm and demanded that Neffi belonged to him, given to him by Richard Kay.

Having snatched away from Eli's grip, Bill left crossed Eli, knocking blood from his mouth, loosening a tooth, and sending him to the ground. While Eli lie there dazed, Bill the Bull resumed the lashing he was putting on Neffi.

When Eli had regained his composure, he flung himself atop of Neffi, and by doing so he was successful in protecting her from further torture, but he received one of the worse beatings he'd ever seen or even heard of.

And it was only discontinued by Richard's authority, when he approached the scene riding upon his mare and commanded the Bull to cease.

"But sir this is an uppity nigger, doing as he wishes and having sayings of a smart nature that should never be allowed to come from the likes of a nigger," Bill pleaded to Richard Kay.

"Nonetheless, he's my property and I intend to get out of him my purpose," Richard exclaimed.

Eli was then ordered to be taken to the back of the Big House to receive necessary medical attention. After being treated with an ointment of some unfamiliar kind, Eli was placed in the barn by Trump.

He immediately sought out Neffi so that he may treat her with the ointment he had cuffed while they thought him to be unconscious.

Fortunately, Trump, having discharged Eli, he didn't chain him up. He only kicked the unresponsive Eli and then off he went chirping, as was common for Trump to do.

It had grown dark while Eli laid there on the back porch of the Big House and now it was pitch black inside of the barn. He could only see the sclera's of his co-captives eyes and their bright pearly white teeth whenever they opened their mouths to speak in their native tongue.

He located Neffi and thankfully she was lying in the area where the moonlight shined through the slits of the boards that made the barn.

Eli found her eyes and searched them for a brief moment, then he showed her the ointment; although knowing she wouldn't have a clue as to its pain soothing ability. But she soon would. He took the initiative and began administering the ointment to the lacerations on her arms, before he gently applied the remainder to her back.

She said not a word, not because she was too tough to, but rather half the life had been beaten from her. Add that with malnutrition and you'd question where would the strength come from to speak out her pain.

In those few hours that followed, Eli had learned a great deal about his co-captives, although he was no polyglot.

The big guy whom he had noticed make an attempt to break loose and destroy whomever, offended Neffi or even looked at her for too long was her father, Ră-zī-elle or as he had been corrected by the others; King Ră-zīelle. And all of their concerns was for Ra-elle, the King's son, who had been taken from the barn the night before and had not been returned.

While listening intently to and learning the basic of their dialect, he was able to ascertain that they were one tribe of people taken from Africa, brought directly to Georgia, then purchased by the Kays.

As silence consumed the barn, Eli pondered, and he then grew strength along with the excitement of what he was about to do.

He made his way over to the far corner of the barn. Once there he commenced to dig, using his bare hands. But it didn't take him long to realize that this method wouldn't work. It was at that exact moment his memory allowed him to recall the broken piece of a shovel that lay to the left as you enter the barn.

The retrieve took awhile due to the darkness, but Eli was successful and it aided his motivation. Twenty minutes later he had achieved a hole that was deep enough, but it had taken an additional five minutes or so to convince the others why it wasn't feasible to free them from their bonds.

Even in her weakened state Neffi still managed to utter; jăr-ră. As he repeated to them several times, "water," he then made his way through the aperture he had created. Once outside in the black and still night, fear made its attempt to overtake him. But Eli knew his mission and he was determined despite fears efforts.

So he surreptitiously moved about in the quiet of the night, all the way to the wood structure, that was his purpose. To his misfortune, its door had a padlock attached. This would not deter Eli; it only meant he must improvise. As he made his way to the rear of the structure he was met by a pair of eyes that revealed confusion and curiosity.

As Eli began to ease backwards, the mouth belonging to those eyes began to bark. He froze in place and remained frozen until the barking subsided. It was only then that he made his way back to the barn. Not in failure, but to snatch up the broken piece of shovel. Having obtained it he made his way back to the wood structure that had the smoke rising from its roof.

Now Eli knew not to venture to the other side, due to the kennel of dogs being there, and on high alert.

He dug and made his hole large enough to enter in through. Once inside he almost fainted from the aroma alone.

It had been so long since his stomach had ingested even the smell of some real foods. And here he was in a smokehouse surrounded by more meats than a truck could haul off.

With his two hands he began tearing and ripping, and grasping and snatching and then filling his mouth to the full, but in the midst of his devouring he saw the faces of those who were beaten, broken, and literally starving to death.

Eli became impetuous as he searched for and found what he needed; a half of a burlap bag. And once again he began to rip and tear meat from everywhere.

As he made his exit he contemplated the most dangerous aspect of the mission; concealing his crime. But not only was he determined to succeed, Eli was resolute in surviving his ordeal. Crouching, he made a trail of small pieces of meat from the hole in the smokehouse all the way around to the North side. Once there, the dogs began to bark immediately. It was as if the ones in the first kennel alerted the others and together they made efforts to summon the entire plantation.

Eli knew then he mustn't hesitate, but move quickly. As he traversed the distance to the first kennel, the dogs barking had become deafening. Suppressing fear he eased to the gate that stood between him and four vicious beasts that wanted nothing in life but to tear, rip, and devour him as he had done unto the smoked meats. Eli gently unlatched the kennel's gate and to his surprise these vicious animals took a couple of steps backwards.

Apparently their concealed fear was being revealed. This gave him a little more courage to proceed. As Eli pushed the gate open he heard it—a voice that was in extremely close proximity, yelling ;

"What in the hell is going on out here?" Then he turned and saw it. A lantern being carried by him who approached.

Eli had no choice besides the worse one imaginable. So, cautiously he entered the dog's domain and slowly he offered delicious smoked ham to the curious inhabitants.

As the lanterns glow illuminated the kennel, Eli eased into the furthest doghouse in the fenced in area. At that instant he heard Inman's voice calling the animals by name, but they, being reluctant to heed his calling because Eli had the meats.

Two of the four initially being undecided, eventually obeyed Inman's command, but the remaining two, Eli had to provide hush hush money.

So by patting his pocket and then dispensing the goods, they were quietly eating out of Eli's hand.

After about a minute or so Inman departed, convinced that nothing was out of order. Eli cautiously made his way to the gate and continued on with his initial plan. So leaving the gate wide open he led the dogs to the aperture at the south side of the smokehouse.

He was the first to enter, because his mission wouldn't be a success without refilling his bag and snatching up a canister of water.

Eli was crawling back through the hole in the barn a few moments later and discovered almost everyone to be awake and awaiting his return. He went directly to Neffi and slowly poured water into her mouth. Then he gave her a whole smoked drumstick.

Likewise, he administered to them all, water and meats. Then more water until it was all consumed. And not a moment too soon either, for they all heard the ruckus that was building outside.

Men yelling, dogs barking in the distance. This caused Eli to move with a great amount of speed. Recalling from memory the entire layout of the barn, he first gathered every piece of evidence pertaining to their smoked meats, and buried them in the aperture along with the burlap bag. He used the piece of shovel to put human waste in the hole before covering it all up. Afterward he made sure no one was emitting any of the meat's aroma. Then he laid face down in a far corner just as Walter Kay and his men came busting through the door with Inman and a couple of dogs bringing up the rear.

They searched the barn, discovering that nothing seemed to be amiss. Yet Walter Kay was extremely vituperate as he delivered kicks to the slaves who he deemed to be in his way.

The light from the lanterns revealed nothing, but the animal's barking grew louder. This did not cause much alarm due to their knowledge of their dogs lust for black flesh.

One of the beasts that had been guided to where Eli lay wasn't barking at all. It was instead licking. Licking

Eli's exposed hand and arm. He had to shunt, which caused the animal to become sibilant.

Now he wondered if his malaise was palpable. Finally, Walter and his clan exited the barn, but despite their departure Eli became stertorous as he sat up placing his back up against the barn's wall. He sat there trying to gain some kind of composure. As his breathing steadied, Eli made his way over to the injured men.

Thankful that dawn was allowing its light to spill through the slits in between the barn's boarding, Eli took the opportunity to tend to bruises as best he could.

It wasn't twenty minutes later that Eli was sent for by Richard Kay himself.

Upon his arrival to the back porch of the Big House he was commanded to stand at attention until Richard made himself available.

having stood there for quite some time, Eli was now face to face with the eldest of the Kay brothers, who illustrated impetuosity as he reminded Tamer of his responsibility and duties.

"These properties of mine that are presently confined to that barn, are to be encouraged by you to do the work required of them. Do I make myself clear?" questioned

Richard and then he went on to say, "This will be the absolute last time that you are warned concerning this matter. Do you understand my manner of speaking?"

"Yes sur. I do sur, perfectly. It's just that their reluctance is derived from their concern for the whereabouts of one of their members," Eli explained.

Given no response from Richard, only an ardent stare as he reflected on this young nigger's articulation. Finally he replied, "What Walters pleasures entail are of little to no concern to me. You'll do well to relay to those individuals that they'll probably never encounter that missing fellow ever again."

That information gave Eli a numb feeling, because he knew how desperate the others were to receive the King's son back to them safely.

Eli was taken to the field where Neffi, her father, and one of the other women were located.

Seeing how the overseer put hands on them in order to get them to pick cotton and place it into the burlap bags, he intervened with caution, expressing to the overseer that he'd been given explicit orders to encourage this group to do the work without further malice.

As he was about to knock Eli upside his head for using words that he had not a single clue as to their meaning, his hand was stayed by Willie's words of agreement.

Willie, the Kays other dog handler was a rather large man, and he had just given the overseer a look that made him instantly comply with what he had agreed to be the truth. So much in fact that the look given by Willie caused Taylor to walk off to another area of the field to harass and brutalize other slaves.

Eli grabbed a bag and illustrated to them what was required of them in order to prevent further abuse. Yet they still refused, collectively, all having defiant, tenacious expressions etched across their faces.

Eli did the only thing he could think of to do at the time. He spoke a lie to King Rǎ-zī-elle.

"Rǎ-zī-elle, do it for Rǎ-elle's safe return."

Upon hearing his son's name he spoke words to Eli that Eli knew not the interpretation of. So Eli placed the bag in the King's hand and repeated "Rǎ-elle's safety." Rǎ-zī-elle looked at them all and simply nodded as he began to pick and place cotton into the burlap bag. Then they all began picking cotton as did Eli. Several hours later as they drew near to where Richard Kay sat atop his mare, Eli began to be a little too enthused in his cotton picking performance.

"Massuh Richard," he began. "These here will do all that you ask them to sur, if you'd just tell your men to stop beating on them. You purchased these individuals to make a profit. What would be the sense in killing them dead Massuh Richard?"

"Well Tamer, seeing how you have them doing what's their duty to do, there won't be no need for any killings," answered Richard before riding off.

Unbeknownst to Eli at the present moment, he had just encouraged his co-captives to choose slavery, whereas their prior mindset was that they'd rather receive death, as they believed death was a better choice opposed to slavery.

Back inside of the barn, King Rǎ-zī-elle asks Eli, "Where Rǎ-elle?"

Eli is surprised to hear this man speak English for the first time.

"You speak English?" Eli asked. "We learn little from white men I let come into village. White man betray, white man wa-kī."

"Wa-kī?" questioned Eli. "Oh, wicked white man wicked," he translated. "My son?" asked Rǎ-zī-elle.

"I believe your son is still alive, and safe. But I think they sold him off to some other plantation." Eli tried to perfect a lie.

There was a erie silence for over an hour then,

from out of Neffi's mouth comes, "Ba-foo." And they all broke out into laughter, even the King briefly. Everyone besides Eli. Not only because he didn't understand the meaning, but mainly because he knew it was aimed at him.

So, he approached her and asked for its meaning.

She repeated the word with emphasis, "Ba-foo." But it was Tac, the extremely large, extremely dark fellow, the King's nephew and soldier who demonstrated by performance.

Showing how Eli looked while out in the field dancing a jig for Massuh.

The butt of the joke, but at least it allowed him to learn that some words have the same meanings, regardless of its origin. For he was being called a buffoon. Eli didn't let the raillery get to him. Instead he used the opportunity to explain to his group the fine art of acting, and playing a role.

An entire month past, with Eli remaining in custody with those formerly labeled incorrigibles. He and the seven that form his group are doing the work of twenty men. But instead of receiving incentives or respect, they are driven harder by the taskmaster at Walter Kay's behest.

While in the field becoming more acquainted with the other field hands, Eli learns a great deal concerning the going on's of the entire plantation.

Walter Kay occasionally took a slave away. And he or she are never to be seen, nor heard of ever again. Eli summarizes and concludes that Walter is the sole person responsible for Rӑ-elle's disappearance. But he must discover for himself the details before the King and his tribe explode into full blown rebellion.

That night King Rӑ-zī-elle meets Eli's anticipation. Becoming irate as he shouts, "No more!" Using a more thorough English, being that Eli has been teaching them all.

Eli calms the King by pointing out the swelling of Neffi's belly and he assures them all that their departure would be soon in coming. For Eli himself had a longing and burning desire to find a way back to at least say his goodbyes to his Grandmother's great great Grandmother. Just feeling, and knowing in his soul that she is a progenitor of his. And possibly a key to his purpose for being here.

CHAPTER 42

"I've called this meeting so we could all be assured that we are all on the same accord," stressed James Bodiford. "Now the business at hand is pertaining to the land by the swamp that you Kay brother's would like to acquire. And as I've previously made known to you both, I gave that parcel of land to Henry here, and my sister Ruth as a wedding gift," he expounded.

"I'd be willing to part with the land indeed, but I'm curious to know your intent with such useless soil.

No disrespect James, but it's been of no use to us since receiving it," proclaimed Henry.

"None taken," Bodiford told him. And then went on to say, "I am still in possession of the deed and I too am curious as to why you are willing to pay three times its value. So, yes I'm curious to learn your interest."

"Well, I'll tell you my interest and intentions if that's what's necessary to close the deal." "Please, by all means," urged Bodiford.

"Well, I've obtained plenty of field hands and I'm now able to fill that swamp and make the land useful for cotton," Richard explained.

"Cotton," exploded Bodiford before catching himself.

"Well, I'd like to witness the likes of that," he continued.

"And you will if you'd be so kind as to present to me the deed," stated Richard.

"Lets see, four acres of land at a thousand dollars an acre. Well Richard you'll receive said deed just as soon as I receive from you four thousand U.S. dollars."

"In two days time you produce the deed and I'll be forthcoming with the proceeds," Richard expressed.

"That being taken care of, let us get on with more important matters," began Bodiford.

"Say on," voiced Walter speaking for the first time.

"We see your prosperity in these few short months that you've been permitted here amongst us. And don't get me wrong, we sincerely encourage your continual growth. It's just a matter of sharing in the political costs," proclaimed James Bodiford.

"How do you mean?" questioned Richard. "It's a matter of placing the correct funds into the appropriate hands in order to pave the way into a more prosperous tomorrow," said Bodiford in a circuitous way.

"Exactly who's hands are you referring, and how much are those hands requiring?" Richard Kay asked directly.

"Well, there's the matter of putting funds behind the right candidate in order to assure him to be the one who governs. And also, we'll have to provide money in order to maintain George's sheriffs' position. Although he's quite naturally a shoo-in. But why take any chances?" Bodiford put it all out there.

"The totality of these funds should come to around three thousand dollars, which ensures the necessary vote counter we'll need," James announced. He then went on to say, "You see Emma here, well her husband is running for re-election of governorship of this great state of Georgia and it's in all of our best interest that he wins that office, because it will guarantee us the luxury of maintaining another hundred years of free slave labor."

"Oh, you better believe we're not going to lose that Governor's mansion. You can bet your Granddaddy's will on it," Emma voiced in pure confidence.

Her being the only woman ever allowed into Bodiford's inner circle was not necessarily the greatest joy for Emma; the opportunity to obtain and wield her own power was. Her Grandfather's Father, Grandfather, and

Father had acquired properties from Georgia to the Carolinas and back. And with it, enough black souls to populate a large city.

Nonetheless, for all of her family's wealth and power, it provided little to no power, respect, or independence for the female species.

So, here Emma sat under the umbrella belonging to James Bodiford. She, being in search of her own slice of the American pie. Most recently she had become a major asset due to her husband's insured appointment into the Governorship.

"Now if James here says that you Kay brothers are allies then I'm all for it, but make no mistake about it, my husband is always going to do exactly what I advise him to do," she said in such a way.

After the gathering was concluded and no one remained, other than James, his only son Jimmy Bodiford, and Henry. James spoke more candidly.

"Jimmy I want you to go fetch the sheriff for me. It's time we put a closer eye on those Yankee Kay bastards. It's apparent they have an influx of revenue and it damn sure isn't coming from no damn cotton. Besides, I saw it in the younger ones eyes, they got something going on. And I aim to make certain that it doesn't affect us in a negative way."

"Henry there's no reason for you to look at me as if I didn't sale something that wasn't rightfully mines." "That being that, I will provide you, and Ruth with some more nigger labor. But I tell you for the last time Henry, you're going to have to find a way to keep them niggers from running off. You and Ruth are wasting my damn money, and at the same time making yourselves look like you're not capable of taming them niggers over there," voiced Bodiford in an amplified tone.

"To be honest with you James, I'll never be able to understand why they run away as good as Ruth treats them over at our place, but I guess they're like any other animal that you let off of its chain," Henry asserted. "But concerning that swamp, wasteland, I don't feel no certain way about it," he added. And mostly because he knew there was absolutely nothing he could possibly do about anything that James Bodiford did to him.

An hour or so later Jimmy Bodiford returned having Sheriff George Hill in tow.

After their greetings, James jumped right to it. "George, I'll share with you all what must be done immediately, because I'm not sure how much time we may have," Bodiford began. "this concerns those Kay brothers and

598

whoever else they may be allied with. In the beginning I believed they'd be a valued asset to our federation, but after today I have a much better understanding.

"It's evident to me that those fellows would never be content in working together for the whole. Their satisfaction would only arrive by their controlling of the whole. And I just can't allow that. Now, I'll allow them to purchase the swamp land because that'll be much needed cash for our cause, but I don't believe they'll live long enough to see any good come from it. But until then we need a close eye kept on them Yankee sons of bastards," expressed James Bodiford.

"I see," George spoke. He then went on to say, "I have a man, or two that I could employ for the task, but if you're talking about around the clock observation then we'll probably need to get some outside help."

"Too many eyes would probably make the surveillance too obvious. What we need is something a little more clandestine. And what I was thinking was we could supply the Kays with a couple of our own field niggers and one bright house nigger that would report back to us the inner goings on's over at that Kay plantation," spoke Bodiford with impiety.

"Just who do you have in mind?" asked George.

"What's that boy's name over there at your place Henry?" asked James.

"Who, Pete? James, Ruth would never part with that there Pete. She depends on that one for almost everything and I'd go further to say he'd be useless without her aiding him every step of the way," spoke Henry in a pleading manner.

But such words would not deter Bodiford.

"I'd say he'd make the ideal individual being a nigger and all, to do the job that we require of him," he said with finality.

"What is it exactly that you want me to do?" asked George.

"It's your responsibility to detain, capture, or abduct a couple of them house niggers belonging to the Kays, so they'd recognize their need for replacements," James pointed out.

"That high yellow nigger that comes into town on Thursdays belongs to them Kays. Me and Tim could easily snatch that one up this coming Thursday and have him to do with as we see fit," proclaimed Jimmy Bodiford.

"You'll do no such thing," his Father James voiced in a tone of high decibels. Then he added, "I've sent you off to be schooled for one purpose and one purpose only. And It's not to come home and be a punk thug. I'll tell you that much.

"You will occupy the seat of executive judge of Marietta, Georgia as soon as I erect that city in the very near future. Your future Jimmy."

"But Daddy, I want to do my part in securing my own future. And you deny me the right to do that at every turn," responded Jimmy.

"I do what I know to be best for you son, and you do well to take heed to it. End of discussion," he replied.

"Now Sunday night I want you all back here and we'll initiate the next step and see if we're able to place this entire situation back under my control," Bodiford announced before dismissing his inner circle.

WE SUFFER FOR A REASON

CHAPTER 43

Another two weeks had passed and Eli drew no closer to a means of fleeing to the North. Although he had been given a little more leisure, which meant that his plan was working somewhat, and the spare time given him was due in part to Richard Kay's belief that the child inside of Neffi was put there by Eli.

During those times of being out and about, he had gathered information from the yard boy who tended the gardens. He shared with Eli that a couple of more folks had gone missing, even a child of around twelve years of age.

It's been rumored that Walter Kay was killing these poor souls for no apparent reason. This belief was due to the fact that the abducted were never seen, nor heard of ever again.

This caused him to search for more evidence, because there was no telling who would be Walter's next victim. Maybe even someone else from the barn.

Real late in the still of the night Eli was prepping for another one of his missions. For two distinct reasons this mission was going to take place tonight. The first one being, he could no longer stand to take anymore of the King's rambunctiousness, and the second reason being, his stomach was on his back. They were all starving, despite their continued show of willingness to do their work and some. So off Eli went.

By stealth he'd made his way out to the smokehouse. But to his disbelief it had been reconstructed. Now it sat upon a platform. there would be no digging in through the bottom, but he didn't take this extreme risk for nothing. He used the front door and entered as though his wages awaited him inside. Once inside Eli helped himself to a nice chuck of beef and said aloud, "Heaven must be filled with smokehouses."

Having filled his bag and taking the extras in order to place blame on his voracious co-conspirators, the dogs. He re-entered into the black of the night. But before Eli began his trek around to the kennels, he heard something, or someone that was out there with him concealed by the darkness.

Then he heard it again. A whimper, or a moan. So he inched closer in the direction of the sounds. Crawling around the brush he was now able to see by the candescent of the lantern. A child in protest of Inman's assault. He now lay atop of this black little girl of no more than thirteen or fourteen. As Eli stood indecisive, he took a baby step toward where they lay, but that baby step made the sound of a firecracker, being that he stepped on a dried twig.

Inman sprang to his feet. After snatching the lantern, he then nervously asked, "Who's there? I know somebody's there."

Eli back pedaling, then crouching down made his way back to the smokehouse. The animals were barking now and Inman was in hot pursuit.

Eli continued his course in extreme fear now, because he knew he had to do the only thing he could do. So he dug in his pocket, unlatched the kennel's gate and provided delicious smoked meats to ravenous beats. Thankfully they did not bite the hand that fed them.

As they remained there devouring their portion, Eli made his way to the rear doghouse and entered in. From inside he heard Inman unlatch the gate. His fear escalated instantly.

"What is it boys? Where'd he go, come on, where'd he go?" he questioned.

They answered with barks and excitement that caused Inman to shine his light around. As he reached the back and was putting his head down to have a look, Eli charged him, knocking him backwards and onto his backside. Dazed and confused he knew not what to do having lost hold of his rifle in the clash.

Seeing where it landed, he and Eli went for it at the same time. And both of them reached it at the same time. Inman the barrel and Eli the stock.

The dogs were in a frenzy by now, not knowing which human to aid. They knew Inman the longest, but he had never come all the way into their doghouse with them bearing delicious meats.

"Now look here boy, you let go this here shotgun and I'll see to it that Bill the Bull leaves some skin on your back when he's done," Inman said exclamatorily.

After making further threats, assuring Eli that the whipping he'd receive would be remembered for the rest of his short life, Inman suddenly and without warning gave the shotgun a yank. He nor Eli being aware that

Eli's finger was there on the trigger. The blast shot the projectile and fire into Inman's chest cavity stopping his heart and his threats instantly.

Eli remained stationary and startled, not being able to move an inch as the dogs began to howl, bark and jump about.

The ruckus being caused by the dogs in the other kennel had an acute effect and the night was engulfed in noise that now exploded in Eli's ears louder than the shotgun's blast, due to its continuous audible that echoed.

As Eli regains his bearings, his mind begins to shift into overdrive. Thoughts upon thoughts that he has to sieve and then move into action according to its importance. He heaves Inman onto his left shoulder. Taking the meats in his right hand he makes his way back to the brush where he had first spotted Inman with the child.

Running back to the kennel to retrieve the rifle is when Eli's worse fears are realized. Looking towards the Big House he could plainly see the mob approaching. There was no way for him to make it back to where he had laid Inman. But, he had to, 'cause hiding the body was peremptory.

He ran as fast as he could around the other kennel, disregarding the dogs barking out their urgent summons. Eli circled around and came up behind the torch and lantern bearing mob.

The run to the brush where Inman lay causes Eli to become extremely stertorous, but he doesn't allow this to retard him of his goal.

After hiding the rifle just so, he heaves ole Inman once more and carried him to the woods.

Eli eventually makes his way back to the barn. Once inside, he refills the hole, then climbs up into the rafters where he stashes the sack of meats.

Having informed the others that there's trouble coming, he begins erasing the night's excursion from off of his person.

Hours went by without incident. Listening intently Eli could only make out the dogs barking, but it was in the distance. Finally the bolt of the barn's door was released and Walter did a walk through bearing a lantern, illuminating each and every individual's face. When he came upon Eli he paused for a brief moment before turning and exiting the barn.

Eli didn't know what to make of it all. Being too afraid to retrieve the smoked meats, he just lay there and whispered the details of his activities to his companions.

The next morning it was back to the drudgery that's demanding of one held in bondage by overbearing slave owners. The only thing that Eli and his group had to look forward to was the fact that they had a bag full of smoked meats awaiting them back at the barn.

WE SUFFER FOR A REASON

CHAPTER 44

It was a Sunday evening of a nebulous atmosphere, but it had no affect on those in attendance at Bodiford's gathering. Or did it? You wasn't really able to tell due to the moods of these men varied from day to day. And at other times they set their countenance according to their deception.

So for the sake of understanding, lets just say that everyone's face was covered with curiosity and anticipation, including Ms. Emma's.

After everybody was seated with drinks in hand, James began his colloquy. "I called this meeting for several reasons, and the first one being the land transfer to the Kays." He illustrated by producing the deed and having Henry to place it in the hand of Richard Kay.

In turn, Richard produced a stack of large bills totaling seven thousand dollars and placed them onto Bodiford's huge oak wood desk.

"You will let me know if there are any more funds needed for your electorate?" Richard asked as he returned to his seat.

"Indeed," replied Bodiford as he began his count.

Also in attendance was George, the sheriff, Tom Woodard, Jimmy Bodiford, and Walter Kay who possessed the only truly discernible facial expression. His was one that showed how much he'd rather be somewhere else.

Without a knock the parlor doors came open and through them came Nancy Bodiford having refreshments, and Ruth in tow.

"Gentlemen, Ms. Emma, I thought you all would enjoy some fresh beverages and sandwiches," Mrs. Bodiford said in a cheerful voice.

Having placed her tray of hot tea onto a table, Ruth went to her husband Henry's side.

"Thank you so very much dear," James said.

When no other words were spoken, Ruth and Nancy took their leave, with Nancy saying as she went, "If there's anything else."

"It's come to my attention that you lost a few of your slaves over there at your place," James began, and then he went on to say, "That's the reason why I employ the sheriff here so that him and his deputies can round up the runaways and return them promptly. I'd be more than willing to allow you the use of George's services.

In the meantime, I've decided to provide you with two of my niggers and Henry here has agreed to lend you his best house nigger. Now that's merely a showing of our belief that if we work together we'll prosper together."

"I don't think it'll be necessary that you give us any of your workers. We'll manage," spoke Walter in such a way.

In turn Bodiford looked intently into the eyes of Richard and voiced, "I insist, due mainly because, what would it say of our friendship if you was to turn down such a sincere gesture?"

"Walter let us accept these gentlemen's act of kindness and in turn we'll seek an opportunity to return such kindness," Richard stressed.

"That won't be necessary, as I've already explained. Our being of one accord is what's necessary to reap a future of prosperity," said Bodiford.

"Now let us move on to more pressing business. This election takes place in less than forty five days and all appears to be going according to our expectations. But what's of the most importance is what transpires after the Governor and other officials have taken office. "There will be a council created that will guarantee our control over these parts for the next hundred years or so.

There will be a greater influx of free labor to continue the building of our great state of Georgia. Those buildings and structures will cost us little to no out of pocket costs. But the one thing that guarantees our success is our transparency as we take these huge steps into the future," said Bodiford.

And he went on to say, "Richard, Walter and you as well Emma, I know that you all have a great deal of these negro laborers and it's in all of our interest to provide one another with access to these most able bodied workers as you see plainly how it's to your own benefit.

"In conclusion, I add, the three promised to you will be forthcoming this very night."

"James you almost convince me to invest in a slave ship," Emma voiced half jokingly.

"All that you've spoken appears plausible and me, and my brother Walter here are in alliance, and intend to do whatever's necessary to strengthen your confederation," Richard conveyed.

"Well, it's a democracy and we are the only people that will matter in its equality," James was so proud in saying.

"As always James Bodiford, it has been a pleasure," Richard spoke as he stood to shake James Bodiford's hand.

"You're leaving so soon? I believe Nancy and Ruth are back there conjuring up more refreshments for us to enjoy."

"I hate to disappoint, but I have an early morning tomorrow. Actually, I must travel and meet associates of mines and I wish to be on my way by first light." "Well, I'll not hold you any longer. You travel safely and be assured that I shall tend to your best interest in this matter that we're engaged in together," spoke Bodiford as the Kays departed.

Outside in the cool, crisp night, Walter asked, "Brother, why do you entertain the likes of such narrow minded individuals such as a Bodiford?"

"It's like a game of chess. You must first engage in play before determining if you have a worthy opponent. Besides, what better way to learn the true intentions of a man than to listen to his lies," confabulated he with his younger sibling.

Bodiford was deep in thought as Emma asked him if he needed her for anything other. He ignored the question, because he simply did not hear her ask it. He was in another place where he alone traveled to see matters and people for who they truly are.

"Dad?" said Jimmy as he walked over to his father's desk. Then he continued, "I've noticed a look in that Walter Kay's eyes that's most disturbing. I mean he's not a guy I'd wish to come into contact with alone on a dark night."

"Yeah, well if all goes as planned the Kays won't be around for too many more dark nights, nor bright days," Bodiford spoke his thoughts.

"But this here is the matter at hand. Henry, you go round up that house boy of yours. You'll do good to do it while Ruth is here and explain it to her later," said James leaving no room for debate.

The bruises, sore bodies, and swollen, bleeding fingers are almost forgotten this night, because this night Eli and his companions are feasting on all kinds of smoked meats.

Some of the turkey pieces actually reminds Eli of some cold cuts from Krogers. But the memory causes him to ache in his heart for his family back home, and for his Mary. Oh, how he miss her so.

After contemplation, Eli says, "Listen, winter is almost upon us and we don't want to be trying to make it to the North in nobody's cold weather. So it's best we gather whatever we can and then make our escape. But I must go to my relatives place first."

Four days later, on a very, very dark Sunday night, Eli, the King, and one of the women, Thes-nō-ă ventured out into that darkness.

The King had assured Eli that, although a woman Thes-nō-ă was beyond capable. This Eli couldn't deny, for he had witnessed her resilience on more than one occasion.

On their mile and a half trek, Eli explained to them how he believes they'll be able to receive much needed supplies from the Bodiford plantation. This would offset suspicions of their escape from the Kays.

Not wanting to just rush in head first, they kneeled down at the tree line of the woods approximately a hundred feet from the Bodifords. Circling around to the east side they made their way through the thick brush and came to the rear of Eli's and Bernice 's shack. Eli asked Rǎ-zī-elle and Thes-nō-ǎ to remain at the tree line while he goes to the shack.

The King orders Thes-nō-ǎ to stay back as a lookout, and he insisted on accompanying Eli.

Making it around to the front was easy enough. Now came the task of waking his relatives in the dead of night without causing them extreme fright.

It had been nine months since he'd seen them last. So, to be truthful, he didn't know how he'd be received.

Tapping on the door in the still of the night made explosive sounds that he was unable to muffle. The door came open and there in the doorway stood Eli, the senior.

Eli, and Rǎ-zī-elle was allowed into the house where Bernice stood confused, until the candles' glow allowed her to see the boy's face, and then tears began to stream down her lovely face. Bernice embraced the boy while saying, "My prayers have been answered, you're safe." After their embrace, Eli introduced them to Ră-zī-elle. After which he exited the tiny shack so that he may stand guard on the outside.

A few moments later their catching up was interrupted by the whimpering of lady Jessie, the daughter they'd had in their old age. When Bernice returned from gathering up lady Jessie, the child reached for Eli and he warmingly took her into his arms, where she began to gently rub his face with her tiny fingers.

Eli gave his relatives a anecdote of what had befallen him and he went on to express his desire to make it to the north with his African tribe.

"Tell him Eli," Bernice urged her husband.

"But is it possible Bernice ?" Eli asked.

"Sure it is, and he's right. It's far safer for him than staying around in these parts."

Upon her urging, Eli the elder began to relay to Eli a anecdote of his own.

"There's a white woman by the name of Ruth. She's the sister of Master Bodiford. She's a great help in getting runaway negroes and even some of her own slaves up to that north. She has a hideaway out in them woods, where she stores them until she can get 'em on their way. I'll have to speak to one of her slaves by the name of Pete in order to get you to Miss Ruth.

"But I'll do it 'cause it'll make my Bernice more at ease about you," Eli added.

"Eli!" They all heard the shout from right outside the door. But before anyone had time to react, "Blaam!"

The door literally came off of its hinges and landed onto the floor right in front of them. Young Eli stood to run, but there was nowhere for him to run to.

Tom had his men to take ahold of Eli as he himself moved over to Bernice and went to snatch up lady Jessie. Bernice moved just quick enough, but terrible Tom was persistent. Grabbing the arm of the child he and she tugged, but she not wanting to be the one to bring harm to her child, released her grip.

Tom raised the child to eye level and spoke to her parents, "You both know what I'm capable of, yet you still insist on defying me."

"This is no fault of theirs Master Tom. I's the one to come here and they was just telling me that they would have to tell you and Master Bodiford 'cause it's their duty to do so sur. That's all, I's swear to it," Eli expressed earnestly.

"Is that the whole truth Eli? If'n you swears to it then I'm going to believe the words of a God fearing man," Tom says as he places lady Jessie back into her mother's awaiting arms.

"It's just like he says Master Tom. We don't need no more trouble around here," Eli Sr. expresses.

"Boys take at one on outside and I'll teach him a lesson he'll never forget," exclaimed Terrible Tom.

Outside in the midst of the darkness, Eli was able to see that three of Tom's men had Rǎ-zī-elle pinned to the ground with both hands tied behind his back.

Now Eli's sorrow began to be made manifest even more so than his immediate future, because he had caused Rǎ-zī-elle this extreme misfortune.

"On your knees you black bastard," shouted Tom as he kicked Eli in the back of his knees. "You two have earned yourselves a trip to my post," he said with maleficence.

Thes-nō-ǎ had made her way close enough to see and hear what was happening to her King. As she lay there in the grass concealed by the black of the night. But there was nothing she could do.

Just then a lone horse rider approached and dismounted alongside of Tom. Once there he asked, "Tom, what do we have here, more runaways?"

"Yeah Jimmy, that's exactly what we have here and I'm about to whip that rabbit out of the both of them." "Don't you think we ought to learn just who they belong to first?" questioned Jimmy Bodiford.

"I really don't give a damn who they belong to, because I've caught them trespassing on this here land," voiced Tom in such a tone.

"You caught them on this land, my land you say?"

"Your Daddy's land. Now let me tend to what your Daddy pays me good money to tend to."

"Well Daddy obviously has never paid you for being a thinker," said Jimmy as he moved over to the huge black man tied and laying face down on the ground. Then he took a step or two further, making his way to where Eli was still kneeling.

"Where you run off from boy?" he asked as he stood Eli to his feet.

Eli had already thought his answer through before the question was even posed, due to the fact that being honest could spare them at least one beating. So he willingly answered. "We run off from the Kays plantation sir."

"The Kays, that's the only names you seem to hear around here is those Yankee bastards," voices Jimmy using a great deal of his father's terminology. "But I have an idea," he stated.

"Tom, put these men in chains and don't you lay not one finger on either of them," stressed Jimmy as he mounted his animal.

After doing as he was ordered to do, Tom went to the Big House just to see if by chance James might be awake. And Jimmy continued on to his clandestine destination.

Having followed in the shadows, Thes-nō-ă witnessed the location of Eli and her King's confinement. Once the coast was cleared she made it to them, but was unable to free them from their bonds. She was ordered by her King to return to Neffi and the others before her absence was discovered.

Upon her return she did two things that was considered sagacious. She unlatched the bolt to the barn's door and she then refilled their escape hole. And she had not a moment to spare either, 'cause just as she was about to explain to Neffi and the others the fate of Eli, and the King, the barn's door came open and in walked Richard, Walter, and Jimmy Bodiford.

To the Kay's surprise Jimmy's information was accurate—two of their slaves had escaped, or was let free judging from the latch being undone from the outside.

"As I've already expressed to you both I have those two runaways over at our place. And I'm guessing by now my father has been apprised of the situation. But that will not hinder you from reclaiming what's rightfully yours," Jimmy was saying.

And then he went on to express to the Kays that if and when his Dad's reign comes to its end he would make an ideal partna for their prosperity, and longevity.

"Well young Bodiford you've certainly made a good gesture tonight, but how can we be assured that you will not prove to be the same scoundrel in sheep's clothing as your father?" Richard Kay asked frankly.

"I wouldn't be here tonight if I had ill intentions. Now any further conversations will be for another night if

623

you want to reclaim your niggers before they're sold off
to

Alabama this very night."

"Walter you tend to this matter and upon their return
don't be too brutal, before discovering who helped them
flee," instructed Richard.

Just as dawn approached Walter returned to the
plantation with his two escapees in tow. He sent for
Richard who came with haste. Then he launched his
inquisition.

"I'll ask you this only once fellow, who helped you with
the barn's latch?" Walter began.

By this time Eli had ample time to formulate a tall tale.
But he couldn't have prepared for this question, so he
simply spoke the truth.

"No one sir."

"Then explain to me how you was able to exit through a
unlatched door?" he asked.

"That's the thing Mr. Walter sir, the door was unlatched
and me, and Răzī-elle went out in search of a sorrel,
that's similar to the iboga, the one that's proned to grow
in a wooded area. The leaves of this particular African

herb is needed in childbearing to assure no birth defects in the child."

"Is that a fact?" questioned Walter.

"It is indeed Mr. Walter. Me and Rǎ-zī-elle wasn't running away from here sir. I'd never run off and leave my unborn child, having never seen its face sur. It's just that these are African people who have traditions and rituals Mr. Walter," Eli explained earnestly as though his life depended on its receptiveness.

And in a sense it did, because had it not been for Richard's presence, Walter would have beaten, and tortured them both until nightfall.

The only reason for his sending for his brother in the first place was due to Richard's fury if he hadn't.

"You'll receive no reprieve from me. You ran off for whatever reason and I must show that such behavior is not, and shall not ever be tolerated here," voiced Richard sternly. Afterwards he added, "I'm very disappointed in you Tamer. I had hopes that your intelligence would set you apart from the others."

"I'm so sorry to disappoint you master Richard. I just want me a healthy child like everyone else." Eli continued to be a fabulist.

"Be that as it may, you'll suffer the consequences for your actions. Here it was that these incorrigibles were doing so well under your guidance." Richard further stressed his disappointment.

"Walter you have these two chained to the tree. When I've changed clothing I'll administer just punishment," instructed he before departing.

CHAPTER 46

"James I got him out back. Now what you'll have me to do with him?" asked Henry.

"Well, bring him on in here," Bodiford advised.

They brought Pete into Bodiford's study and put him in a chair Bodiford had arranged for the purpose.

"You listen intently boy," began Bodiford as he bore into Pete's eyes from behind his huge oak wood desk. "You're being sent to the Kays plantation temporarily. Once there you are to use your ears more than your mouth. You listen for their talk about us Bodifords and their plans here in Georgia. Do you understand everything I've just explained to you boy?" questioned Bodiford in his overbearing way.

"Yes sur master Bodiford. I's believe that I do," replied Pete.

"You believe that you do, or do you, you ignorant nigger?" James exploded.

"Well sur you tells me to go listen and if'n I's hear any talk about you or any talk about Georgia, but you never tell me what am to do if'n I do hear," Pete explained.

"You're right. I haven't and you're not as ignorant as I first believed you to be. You just may be the right boy for this task. Now pay close attention. Whenever you see anybody from here over there you get the information to them, if possible. Otherwise we'll find a way to extract you, meaning we'll get you back here periodically," explained Bodiford.

"I's do all that you ask me to do sur," he assured.

That same morning James Bodiford wanted to know in detail the occurrences that transpired last night. And the question was directly imposed upon Jimmy.

"As I'm sure you've already been informed Daddy, two of the Kays' slaves were caught on our land by Tom here. So, I took it upon myself to return them to the Kays as yet another form of our showing a good faith gesture. That way, they may feel a little more at ease in divulging at least some of their plans to us," explained Jimmy.

"Well, I'm unable to see where any harm could come from it. Just remember next time you allow me to make the final decision.

"But being that I can't figure out why them kays would pay me three times the value for some wasteland, I'm appreciative 'cause it aids in my purchase of the twenty two thousand acres that will become Marietta, Georgia," he announced with glee.

"James do you really believe that the Klan is going to sell you land that has their huge nigger tree on it?
They've been hanging them niggers from that tree since before we all were born," Henry reluctantly stated.

"They'll sell and be assured that they'll be able to continue in the use of their nigger tree as will I," James replied.

"Now Tom, here's an errand that only you can accomplish. While we're all attending Emma's Governors' shin-dig you go over to Texas and deliver to Bob his requested funds for the gunmen you'll be bringing back with you."
"Say less boss, I'll make it happen at your command," expressed Terrible Tom.

"Daddy what's your intentions with these additional guns?" questioned Jimmy.

"You'll see all in due time dear boy. Until then just know that we're making the appropriate moves to assure your place in the future. A future that seats you in the executive judges' chair over all of Marietta."

After beating Rǎ-zī-elle to within an inch of his life, Richard commenced to whip Eli unmercifully, while at the same time telling him that,

"This hurts me as much as it does you Tamer." When he had finished, he ordered the girl from the house to tend to their wounds.

That deed being done, Richard and Duvalle, his business partna and understudy from east Texas, were off on a journey of more pressing matters. Several days later they reached their destination of Lexington, Kentucky. There they met with Richards' financial backers from New York City.

"Gentlemen, it's always a pleasure," Richard greeted Ernie Fletcher, and Jim Devoe. Both extremely wealthy businessmen from the east coast.

"Richard, the pleasure is all ours. Every time you send a chest filled with U.S. currency to the north, we're able to provide the necessary financial backing for our political ambitions," spoke Ernie.

"Now to the purpose of our gathering together here this evening," voiced Devoe.

"I've encountered an obstacle, but one I'll soon surmount, rest assured. And I can also assure you both that our businesses are intact. The final stages of our next venture is underway. We'll send you a healthy profit in as little as a year. That's my word," Richard expressed.

"Your word has always been sufficient for us, And our partners back east will be advised of your commitment toward continuous profit," Fletcher conveyed.

"Now, concerning this matter of an obstacle," questioned Devoe.

"Yeah, it's a fellow by the name of James Bodiford who believes he's entitled to autarchy, but I'm in the process of setting a trap that will fit him perfectly."

"Is our method of removal required?" asked Fletcher.

"No, not at all," Richard answered.

"What say you Duvalle?" Devoe wanted to know.

"It's like Richard has said. The trap will fit this Bodiford just fine," Duvalle confirmed.

"Gentlemen, please accept this quarter's profit from my hands and a guarantee that I'll personally place Georgia into your capable hands, as well," exclaimed Richard Kay.

631

WE SUFFER FOR A REASON

On their way back from Lexington, Richard expresses to his partna the importance of the soil in the swamp area. "Duvalle that land is so valuable to our future growth and success that I would have given that old fool ten times its market value.

"But be clear we must use our negro resources to cultivate it just right and we'll reap over a hundred thousand dollars annually."

"I am aware of our future tobacco crops, but my present concern is as our associates from the North which is this James Bodiford."

"Our next stop should ease your concerns somewhat dear Duvalle."

They arrived in Rome, Georgia in three days time. It's there that Richard shows Duvalle the hotel/brothel, and finally the huge ranch.

"The ranch was purchased for you and your men. The hotel is managed by Sloan, so be sure to get to know him at your earliest convenience. And allow your men to meet the womens' acquaintance and I'll send you definite instructions in as little as two weeks from today. At which time you'll be receiving a few of your friends from Texas as well."

"Sounds great, you have a safe return home and I'll just enjoy the fruits of your labor until I receive your word," said Duvalle.

As Richard Kay's carriage pulled up to the front of his huge plantation mansion, he was greeted by his staff, a few gunmen, and his brother Walter.

"Brother, how was your trip?" Walter asked.

"It was a successful one, successful indeed," replied Richard.

CHAPTER 48

Neffi had given birth to a healthy baby boy two weeks ago, but upon the child's arrival, his Grandfather was unable to hold him due to the beating he had received from Richard Kay.

A beating that left him and Eli devitalized, and what made it that much more poignant was the recrudesce that it caused.

In their third week of recovery, King Rǎ-zī-elle musters up the strength to hold his grandson high above his head and uttered words of a sacred language.

Eli witnessed the tear that rolled down Rǎ-zī-elle's face and is saddened to his core because he knows the depth of his pain.

While he's been laying there recovering from his own torment, Eli has had to draw strength from a unknown source. He's assured that either he has to escape this nightmare or die trying.

The bolt from the barn's latch is removed, the door is opened, and in walks Walter accompanied by Bill the Bull and another rifle totter.

"On your feet," Bill screams. "What about this one, and her newborn?" Bill turns to Walter and asks.

"Bring her, leave the child," instructed Walter.

While they disregard Neffi's cries of protest, they march them out in the cold and down by the swamp. A half a mile journey barefoot, and carrying axes and saws, shovels and pick axes. Once there they're made to cut down trees, remove dead brush and shovel out a road. For nine hours straight, no rest, no water, and no warmth.

WE SUFFER FOR A REASON

On the fourth day, upon their return from the swamp they were met at the back of the Big House by one who introduced himself as Pete. He distributes hot soup to them all before they are led back into the barn.

As always Neffi goes directly to her child and unwraps him to make sure he's still alive. After inserting a nipple into his mouth she's satisfied and relieved. "How much more of this will we be able to suffer?" asked Rǎ-zī-elle.

Eli did not have an answer and he felt as though he was dying right then. But he mustered up the ability to speak, "Where are we to run to in this weather?" "We don't run, we fight, we kill, we destroy!" shouted the King a little too loudly.

"We're chained. They have numbers, and they have weapons," Eli pointed out.

"We take their weapons as we destroy them one by one." "Yī kiz cha da!" exclaimed Tar Ka, speaking for the first time that Eli had ever heard, which causes him to ask,
"What did he just say?"

"He say, We fight, dai-dī," answers Neffi.

WE SUFFER FOR A REASON

CHAPTER 49

Everybody who was anybody was in attendance for the Governor's inauguration. Afterwards at the Governor's mansion the guests kept pouring in. Emma had gone above and beyond the call of duty in arranging, decorating, and making it a very festive, elaborate affair. She employed entertainers as well as a live orchestra.

And while the festivities were in full affect, a very clandestine gathering was taking place in a secluded area of the Governor's mansion. In attendance at this secret gathering were men of a secret society.

A sitting U.S. senator, Earl Duke, the brother of David Duke, Paul Chambers, a wealthy land owner who also owned more land in the Carolina's than he did in Georgia. James Royal Goss, a native of Alabama but one of the richest slave traders in Georgia, and Mississippi. And there was James Bodiford, the self imposed head of this society. But don't let us forget Mr. E. Hoover who is their mastermind and grand strategist. It was he who plotted and executed the demise of those who once held the positions of power that they now possess.

"I call tonight's meeting to order, and let the minutes reflect that this isn't a regular meeting, but one that was formulated for a particular purpose," stressed James Bodiford from the podium.

"Now allow me to introduce to you all, Mr. Richard Kay from New York City, New York.

As Richard Kay was being led into the room, the men in attendance began their applause. As the clapping subsided, Bodiford continued in his oration.

"Gentlemen, it has come to my attention that Mr. Kay is not only clever, honorable, wealthy, and judicious, but he's also German, but we won't hold that against him. Today our desire is to welcome him into our fold as a brother. As a person who's able to visualize as we do the direction that this great nation is intended by God to travel in.

"We are a society of men who's constitution shall never fail nor be altered. For it has been written in red hot blood that we shall subjugate those provided to us by God himself. They shall always and forever until the end of time remain the burden bearers. It is our responsibility to keep the nigger in bondage for his own good. Being less than a man and even less than a human he needs us to show him his rightful plight in life. "It is our pledge to our country to grow our strength and power so that its foundation shall never falter from these truths, so let it be innate in our offspring throughout our generations. And let inferiority be instilled in the nigger."

At Bodiford's conclusion of the summarization of their constitution, E. Hoover took to the podium. "Mr. Kay do you swear to your death that what our intent is shall be your intent and this constitution will be upheld by you until your death, knowing that any regression by you may cause your death?"

"I swear," voiced Richard Kay.

CHAPTER 50

The new year had come and gone and Eli and his bunch were still no closer to the North, not even closer to the North of Georgia.

It was around mid-February that Eli's mind and courage was made up, so he picked his collar lock and began to make an opening in the side of the barn. Once he was able to squeeze his head out, he wedged his body through. Now he was crouched low to the cold earth, inching forward.

There wasn't another soul out on such an extremely cold night such as this, or so he thought until he heard the sounds of one whimpering. He made his way to the far east side toward the direction of the sound. The closer he got to the Big House, the more audible the cry. He was now able to make out the figures heading toward the side of the Big House. So he became as a frozen statue. Now despite the night making it caliginous, Eli was able to make out Walter Kay strong arming a reluctant slave.

This was a black man of age, Eli was able to ascertain as he moved in closer. Walter had just forcefully took this man down into the cellar of the Big House.

Eli was more than petrified, but his curiosity drove him down the steps of the cellar, and to the cellar's door. But it was no ordinary wooden cellar door. No, this was some sort of heavy metal, or iron door. he placed a ear up against the door, but is unable to hear a sound. So he concludes that the door is soundproof. With no windows or even a ventilation flow, he's unable to obtain a view of the inside nor what's exactly going on.

Eli takes up an obscure position in hopes of learning what it is that Walter Kay be doing with the slaves that causes them to go missing. Having planted himself in one spot for so long, Eli was about frozen to death. He didn't know how much longer he could endure the freezing cold. The thought of going to the barn to thaw out and then return entered his mind, but left just as fast.

Then he saw it, a flicker of light. The cellar's door had briefly come ajar. Oh, there he is, Walter Kay ascending the cellar stairs, but without the slave that he had entered in with.

This got Eli's blood circulating again. He waited out Walter, then made his way back down the cellar stairs. Eli pushed up against the heavy door, but to no avail. It was locked up tight. He spoke through the keyhole, but received no response. At the present moment Eli had no choice but to return to the barn. He was so cold that he was losing a few of his motor skills. His fingers were so numb that he knew they may be borderline frost bitten.

When he had made it back to the opening in the side of the barn, Eli believed his bodily fluids had frozen inside their vasculars. After squeezing back into the barn, he fell to the ground and there he laid until Neffi, realizing the problem, came over and laid her body atop of his.

It's May the twenty-fourth and Bodiford has been anxious for over a week now. Being in a state of not knowing is what's killing him.

His initial plan was to first convince Richard Kay of his acceptance into their council, then when he let his guard all the way down, smite him and his brother Walter with one astounding blow.

But Richard has been proving himself of tremendous value to the other council members. He has even allowed them all to choose from the best of his cargo vessel of pristine negroes and little nigglets.

"Tom, I can see through that Yankee bastard's cunning. He may have the others fooled, but I'd be damn if I allow that son of a vermin to pull a wool over my eyes," Bodiford stressed.

"Here he is Dad," interrupted Jimmy as he ushered Pete through the door and into the parlor. Once seated, Jimmy began, "Now, tell my father exactly what you told me and don't you leave out a single word boy."

"James, explain to me this instant why you've taken what's rightfully mines?" Ruth asked as she came

643

barging in unannounced. "You've taken Pete away and this is the first glimpse I've had of him in several months," she continued.

"It was of my understanding that your husband Henry, explained to you the importance of the task I have this fellow Pete performing," Bodiford voiced.

"Henry has been saying some incoherent mumble jumble that has only driven me to further frustration. And whenever I mentioned coming directly to the horse to hear from your mouth, he has forbidded with his begging and pleading. Now you tell me plainly, when do I get Pete's safe return, so he can do the work over at my house that I've learned him to do?" she asked.

"Ruth, you're all worked up over nothing. You can see for yourself that the boy has had no harm come to him. There he sits right there," James stated the obvious. "Now if you'll leave us be he'll be able to complete his work for me."

"What work?" she questioned.

"Listen, it's best that you didn't learn of the particulars. Just know that this boy's safe return is imminent."

"Well, is it possible that I borrow him for just a few hours? Things over there remain in shambles. No one else is capable of tending to them horses, nor the bundling like Pete does. Just allow him to instruct the others on doing it like he does."

James knew his sister's persistence better than anyone. He also knew they'd go back and forth until he relented. And they both knew that he'd relent eventually. It's been that way since they were little. She becoming like a surrogate after their mother died when they were young. So, he almost never told her no.

"Allow us to conduct this matter in your absence and once our discussions are concluded then I will consider your request," expressed James.

Having left and the doors being shut, Bodiford began his interrogation of Pete.

"Let's have it Pete. Apparently you have something to share. Speak slowly and don't you dare leave anything out."

"Well massuh, it's just like I's telling yung massuh Jimmy. Them Kays have plenty to say about ole massuh Bodiford, but nothing so bad. They only say yous use their money wisely and doing business with you has proven to be profitest."
"Profitable?"

"Yeah, that's it, profites profit-abow. They also say when they don't think I's bees listening that in the month after this one, they meet wit da devil that sits on the seat in Rome."

"You mean to tell me in all of them months you've been over there at the Kays' plantation, that's all the news you're able to bring back to me?" James Bodiford asked becoming angered.

"Well massuh James, they don't allow me into them areas where they gather, and they don't right leave them doors open either. They don't trust me like they really need me around there massuh, no. And that's the way it's been all my time there."

"But you do say that they gather together for meetings over there? How often would you say that they have these meetings?"

"Well massuh, let's see, umm I's seen at least three since I's been there. One around the brand new year, another the time of that awful cold."

"February?"

"And this last one just a few days ago. You know a day after weez come over here, and hear Reverend Eli preach to us."

WE SUFFER FOR A REASON

James Bodiford sat back in his huge chair and began his contemplation.

CHAPTER 52

Over at the Kay's plantation everybody was bustling about. It was the beginning of June and the summer brought with it nonstop work for Eli and his tribe. Most days they were driven fifteen hours straight with only occasional water breaks provided to them. And everyday upon their return they'd receive food scrap, and a little water from the hands of Pete.

Everyone on the Kay's plantation knew that the slaves held captive inside the barn did the work of thirty men. Although they were only four men and three women, one of whom always had an infant strapped to her back, they plowed longer straighter furrows, they sowed more seed, chopped more trees, and hauled off more earth than thought possible by so few. Eli's logic was finally understood, accepted, and implemented.

"Pardon me master Richard. I beg of you one brief moment sur?" Eli bowed and asked on this particular evening as they were returning from the swamp area.

"I shall never pardon you, but you do have my permission to speak," instructed Richard.

"Well sur it's just that you have no proper irrigation for your garden and that's why this heat is destroying most of your vegetables, and the heat will do equal damage if not more so to your tobacco crop."

When Richard heard mention of damage being done to his tobacco crop he was at Eli's mercy. "What do you suggest for me to do Tamer?"

"Master Richard it would be a pleasure for us to run you an appropriate drip irrigation system for the garden and then for the tobacco, first thing in the morning sur."

"Will you? Lets say you begin now with your irrigation system and if I approve, you and yours will receive an incentive."

"Master Richard we'd love to sir, but it's just that we've been at it since before the sun came up until now sir."

"If you would like to witness another sun come up then I'd suggest you begin the assignment just given to you before this sun sets completely."

"Yes sur Master Richard. Right away sur, just allow us the picks, hoes and shovels sur and we get right to it."

Every single person in Eli's group was beyond angry with him. He even thought that the baby Fat Daddy was mad at him too. And it was him who had nicknamed the little fellow. Nevertheless, they toiled into the wee hours of the night, but had completed their mission. Now they all lay in the heaps of dirt exhausted.

When awakened by Richard Kay, they all stood to their feet. All being chained together by a long length of chain they looked at him extremely wearisome, and exhausted.

It wasn't until morning that Eli demonstrated how the water would run through each and every roll and all excess water would make its return and then repeat the process.

Richard Kay was most impressed. Before his departure he voiced, "Upon my return you all shall be escorted to the swamp where you will perform the same irrigation system, but for now remove this dirt, then await your double portion and biscuits like you've never tasted before."

Eli didn't allow himself to become disappointed. It wasn't like he was expecting Richard Kay to grant them all a furlough.

It was around the fourteenth of that same month that Eli presented Richard Kay with his invention, or we could say his re-invention, which was an apparatus that extracts the oil from the cotton seed. After explaining to

Richard the many uses of such oil, he began to realize the income this would bring.

And at that very moment Richard began to view his Tamer in a brand new light.

Eli noticed the difference in Richard's eyes so he shared with Richard Kay a detailed explanation of the cotton gin. As Eli continued in his providing Richard with the specifications, he knew his inveigle would be successful.

It wasn't long before Eli was proven correct. Richard Kay provided Eli with the necessary material needed for his re-invention of the cotton gin. But most importantly he was provided with permission to have his fetters and iron collar removed. Now all he had to suffer with was the leg irons.

But he would manage as he labored to construct the equipment, using meager tools and his ability to envisage from books he'd read a long, long time ago.

Eli also had to complete this project in the midst of friends who were not remotely friendly toward him at the time. They viewed him as a traitor, one who was too eager to do for the white man, and then only gain favor for himself. He dealt with the ex-communication, for he alone could also envisage what lie ahead in their near future.

The next morning on the twenty-fifth of June while out in the fields, Eli continued his ongoing communications with the other workers having learned that they were as anxious as he was to be rid of the Kay plantation forever. But he had to be extremely careful, for he had learned that all negroes are not negroes of unity nor for a common cause.

So, he spread his intention through third and fourth parties.

CHAPTER 53

Absolutely and positively in the afternoon on the twenty fifth day of June, Bodiford was addressing two gentlemen from Texas in the comfort of his parlor.

"Gentlemen I'm extremely thankful that you were able to answer my call. Now I've been assured by a mutual friend of ours that you are capable of handling this situation with extreme discreetness. That knowledge alone has caused me to provide you both with a twenty percent increase upon completion of the job."

"Well, that's most generous of you Mr. Bodiford and I assure you that all that you've heard of us is most accurate," spoke Jack Wells with a slow Texas accent.

"And what say you?" James asked Wells accomplice.

"I concur," came a reply in a deep Texas drawl from Sam, the eldest of them Wheeler boys from east Texas.

"Would you two like to have a drink as we await the arrival of George?" asked Bodiford.

"I believe a couple of shots of your whiskey is exactly what me and Sam needs," answered Wells.

Having consumed over half a bottle of very expensive Kentucky bourbon the two from Texas were feeling themselves. It didn't loosen Sam Wheeler's tongue any, but Wells shared in detail their journey to there from Texas, the greatest state in this God blessed Union!" Finally, George arrived and was introduced to the two Texans. He immediately voiced his belief that he and his right hand man Edwards, were more than able to complete the task they had begun.

"These men here are professionals George, and I see no reason why you shouldn't welcome the expertise of such men," Bodiford pointed out.

"It's that my luck has never been any good when dealing with outsiders," replied the sheriff.

"Don't be like that friend. We're on the same side, we're employed by the same generous soul," said Jack as he stood to greet the sheriff.

George reluctantly took the hand of Jack Wells but shook it firmly.

They were then introduced to Edwards, and after the introductions were complete the four were given their marching orders by Bodiford.

CHAPTER 54

Eli enjoyed sharing the extra portions he received with Fat Daddy. He had fallen in love with the child as did they all. They often expressed how his generation would witness the end of bondage.

Eli taught him English as Neffi taught him their native tongue. Eli appreciated her knowledge of the importance of the next generation not being allowed to forget.

WE SUFFER FOR A REASON

That night on the twenty-eighth of June Eli handed the child over to Thes-nō-ă and began to whisper, "We are leaving this place in six days from now. It will be on the night of their Independence Day. We're going to rise up and declare ours. "Listen very carefully because we all have a part to play. While they are in a drunken state we shall relieve them of their weapons, and then we are going to locate our passage to the North."

Eli had never seen so much glee in the eyes of his companions who had become his family, his tribe. But in the back of his mind ringing like an alarm, was that one thought, that one possibility; what if they failed? What if he failed them? There's absolutely no telling how many lives would be lost.

But his other thought that slightly outweighed that one was, look at how many of his race who are dying daily. They just hung Worm for reaching out to catch Emily as she stumbled out of the carriage.

Eli concluded that the futurity was uncertain but a man places his own fate into his own hands and he is willing to sacrifice his life for the betterment of his family. For this reason we suffer. The other choice is slavery for centuries.

He continued to lay out to them their roles that they were to execute and he explained to them the roles being done by the slaves on the other side. He detailed to them how he would use the very same oil that he had been allowed to abstract from the cotton seed to burn this place down to the ground.

Tac, your job is to hook the horse up to the wagon full of tobacco and anything else we find that will burn. After setting it and the wagon ablaze we send it off into the cotton field.

It will be a good enough diversion for us to commandeer this plantation, tie everyone up and make our departure out into the unknown.

CHAPTER 55

On their journey to North Georgia the town of Rome, the four riders had little to no communication between each other.

It was like four horses being ridden by monks. Around the second day of their journey the sheriff asked the two Texans if they'd be so kind as to take the lead at least until sunset. This he suggested due to his uneasiness of having them at his back.

"Why are you so hostile toward them?" Edwards asked at one point.

"Outsiders Edwards. I don't trust them," he replied. It was dusk when the four arrived at the hotel, slash saloon, slash brothel. They were all dead tired. Too tired to even consider to enjoy the amenities offered by the establishment.

"Where do you fellows come from?" questioned Sloan the barkeeper, slash hotel manager.

"We're just passing through," offered George evading the manager's question.

"Well, if you fellows are seeking lodging we have rooms available right above you."

"we'll be in need of two rooms, four beds if you're able to accommodate us," inquired Jack Wells.

"Certainly, alls you need to do is pay up front and little Rosie here will see you to your rooms.

The pairs are shown to their rooms by little Rosie Carter who politely informs them that if they should require food or liquor she would be more than happy to obtain their request.

George, being all business and focused on that alone, refused as did Edwards. It was Jack Wells who obliged her by requesting a bottle of the saloon's finest. Inside their room George was now able to converse with Edwards more freely. So he asked,

"What's your take on the quiet one?"

"I can't rightly say George, can't get him to let go of his tongue. So it's hard to get a read on him."

"Yeah, I agree and that Wells fellow he won't shut up long enough to swallow, so the both of them has me curious. So I don't trust them."

"George you don't trust nobody, never have for as long as I've known you, you've been like that."

"Yeah Ted and most of the time I've been dead on. Go ahead and get you some shut eye old friend. We got us a big day tomorrow. We gots to locate da devil. Also known as Du-valle. That old nigger Pete gave his best understanding of, Taylor Duvalle as best he could I guess."

It seemed like as soon as George placed his head onto the pillow it was morning. But he didn't allow that fact to make him keep his head there. He was up and in his boots in seconds. As he woke Edwards up he informed him that he was going to get a jump start on the others and hopefully question the barkeeper before the others even woke up. When George had made it downstairs, there sat Jack at a table eating, and drinking coffee.

"Come on over George. I'll order you a cup of coffee. They have some very good coffee here George."

As George took a seat, he looked around in search of the other Texan Sam, but he was nowhere to be seen. maybe he was a late riser and jack was the early bird of the two. But George had this uneasy feeling so he asked,

"Where's your friend; Sam is it?"

"Oh, he's around. I believe he's been smitten by one of the ladies of the night," Wells offered.

Moments later Edwards joined them at the table asking, "What's on the menu?"

Having ordered up eggs, toast and coffee they now discussed who would be the one to acquire the knowledge of Duvalle's whereabouts from the hotel manager.

"No need to worry yourself about it George. We've already learned from this guy Sloan that Duvalle has a huge ranch just right outside of town," Wells explained.

"Is that so? Cause I've been in these parts a couple times prior to this one and I wasn't able to learn from anybody that a Taylor Duvalle even existed," stressed George.

"Well, maybe you're not a very likeable guy. You have to admit, you're not the most sociable fellow in the world," Wells expressed.

"That being neither here nor there," said George as he gulped down his coffee. He then added, "If you possess the location of this guy's ranch let us be enroute and performing the duties for which we've been paid."

"Exactly what duties are those George?" Jack asked as he looked intently into the sheriff's eyes.

"Listen you damn cow herder, I didn't come here to play your games with you. We've both been hired to talk to this guy Duvalle and if you're backing—"

"Talk George. Is that what you come to do, talk to Mr. Duvalle? 'Cause me and Sam have come all the way from Texas to eradicate Taylor Duvalle like weeds, like unwanted dandelions."

"Then that's my assignment as well, and I just prefer to be getting to it instead of sitting around here doing nothing."

"You're not sitting around doing nothing George. You're eating, you're talking, and you're waiting."

"Waiting for what?" George almost shouted.

"Waiting for confirmation on the information given to us by Mr. Sloan here. And if it's false information then I can deal with the manager accordingly," voiced Wells in a most calmn fashion.

At this point the sheriff was too enraged to say anything, believing it would be better to just shoot Jack Wells in his chest right where he sat. He believed that Bodiford would somehow understand his actions to be justified.

"Let us be on our way," instructed Wells as he stood to his feet. "I've taken the liberty of having your horses brought around," he added as they followed him outdoors and into the morning.

While mounting their animals, Sam pulled alongside of Jack and delivered to him a slight head nod.

"Let us follow Sam," jack informed the others as he put his heels into his horse's sides.

Every mile out of town that they traveled the sheriff experienced a little more queasiness. He wanted to voice his concerns to his partner Ted, but he thought better of it.

663

As they approached the entrance to the ranch they were met by a lone ranch hand who asked, "Would you mind stating your business here fellows?"

"Not at all kind sir. we are here to make the acquaintance of one Mr. Taylor Duvalle," replied Jack. As the man opened the gate. Allowing them to enter he voiced, "He's expecting you."

I don't know if anybody else caught it, but it did not fly over George's head. He whispered to Edwards, "He's expecting us?"

When they had reached the extra large porch area they were met by two men bearing rifles. These men escorted the four inside the house and into a very large room containing a few couches, several chairs, a desk larger than Bodiford's, which had been made of a recherché quality, and a fireplace that was large enough to turn a horse around in.

A tall, slender gentleman of around the age of forty seven, slightly greying at his temples, entered the parlor. "Gentlemen, welcome. How was your trip?"

Being in such an extremely uncomfortable situation, George began to work his mind harder, but the malaise that he was experiencing made it impossible for him to formulate any plan of action.

"By now I'm sure you all are aware that I'm Duvalle, Taylor Duvalle. The one whom you've been inquiring of. Please be seated gentlemen and together we will be able to learn of your intentions."

"Our intentions are simple enough," began George after being provided with something to stand on. "We were sent here by our employer to understand your involvement with one Richard Kay. You see, he's in business with our employer and he's concerned about whether Richards' dealings with you conflicts with what they're engaged in."

"George, is it? George I thought we were all being cordial, so why not disclose the name of your employer as a show of our being of one accord?" asked Mr. Duvalle.

"Sir, we are employed by a prominent businessman, a slave trader named James Bodiford of Marietta, Georgia."

"I see. Would you gentlemen care for a drink? I have an extensive selection of the finest liquors," offered Duvalle.

"No sir, drinks are not necessary. We just soon be getting back to Mr. Bodiford with whatever information you'd be willing to provide," expressed George as he stood.

"Information, yes I do have a bit of information for your employer," quoted Mr. Duvalle.

Suddenly, all of George's feelings of queasiness and bad luck, and gut feelings all added up to his knowing when Jimmy Bodiford walked into the room and made eye contact with him.

George yelled, "You traitorous, turpitude," as he went for his gun. But it was Jack Well's prestidigitation that prevailed, as he drew his gun in what seemed to be a blur, leaving a hole the size of an acorn in the center of George's forehead.

"I've been called worse. As a matter of fact, I'll be called a patricide not too many days from now," voiced Jimmy Bodiford as he stood over the former sheriff's corpse.

"What say you Mr. Ted Edwards? Would you be interested in new employment? We could use a good man close to the situation down there in your area?" Duvalle asked.

"Sure, what choice do I have. I have to feed my little ones," he answered a little shaken, but not stupid.

"Gentlemen it is Richard's desire to engage James Bodiford's might swiftly, and thoroughly. So you'll be joined by valiant gunmen from Kentucky and Texas a couple of days from now," explained Duvalle.

CHAPTER 56

It being the bright and beautiful morning of July the 4th, everybody on the Kay's plantation was in an upbeat, festive mood. The Kays having promised every slave their own watermelon, but only if the celebration goes off without a hitch. And be one that will be talked about for years to come.

Eli would personally guarantee massuh Kay satisfaction concerning the latter.

I believe it was when Richard Kay recited to Eli how perfect everything had to be due to Governor Nathan Bedford Forrest being in attendance that evening that caused Eli's reply. "Yes sur, we'll make certain that it be a night spoken of for many years to come sur."

Since Eli had done such an exceptionally well job irrigating the tobacco fields as well as his few inventions that had made Richard Kay the topic of discussion in a few circles. Eli was allowed to work on arranging the Kays Independence Day party as well as oversee the labors of others who had been put to the task of obtaining the same festive goal.

The small victory gave Eli access to the whole entire plantation on the most important day ever. The day of their revolt. As he made his way about, he shared vital strategic information with everyone who held key roles to play.

It was unfortunate for them that he could not locate Pete anywhere. For it was Pete's responsibility to unlock the door that would allow them access to the Kay's cache of weapons.

He was grateful to discover how many of the others who had ambitions of making it to the town's armory and relieve them of their stronghold. This let him know that he should not overly concern himself with each and every individual's wellbeing.

As he traversed over to the barn, he was able to give the flint for igniting the fire to his people, who were still being chained in the barn. But thankfully since they'd been worked harder than any, they were liberated of the neck irons. Those awful tools of bondage that rubbed and cut and sawed into the neck of a human being.

When Eli had made it back around to the front of the Kays' mansion, he observed how perfectly he and his group had manicured the landscape leading all the way up to the large stairway. This being irrigated by the same water supply as the garden.

Speaking of which, he went and retrieved the bag of vegetables they'd need for their departure. The word departure sounded so well when he said it to himself. Then Eli began to wonder just how he would ever be able to depart from this entire nightmare or could he.

"God this cannot be my kismet. I've trusted in you my entire life." having spoken to God, Eli realized that it was his first time being intimate with the Big Guy in a long, long while.

"So you think your inventions affords you this idleness?" snapped Walter as he walked up on Eli and stared him down. Actually, Walter Kay was sizing him up, because so much toil had caused Eli to put on mass, a lot of mass. "No sur, master Walter. I's just on my way to having plenty room cleared away so as to make room for the buggies arriving."

"You can cut the shenanigans boy. I'm well aware of your being the smartest nigger I've ever come across, and I believe it's the reason why I've yet to become successful in my endeavors," expressed Walter freely.

"Oh no sur, there's no shenanigans. I's just don't want master to be displeased with me sur."

"In a little while you'll only be concerned with whether I'm pleased or not, 'cause I swear by my own name that I'm going to have a talk with my brother pertaining to my good uses for you. Now you do well to carry out your duties to my satisfaction," voiced Walter in such a manner, causing Eli a great deal of concern.

Eli made straightway to the vegetables and a small cutting utensil that he had hidden in the dirt and slid the items into the barn through the removable piece of board.

The overseer made his presence felt by coming out and slashing the backs of a few slaves for no apparent reason other than the fact that he could.

On its way up the road taward the house was exactly what Eli had been waiting to see. The wagon which contained the alcoholic beverages that these party goers would be consuming until their thoughts grew further and further away from beating the backs of blacks.

All Eli needed to do was make sure he was able to procure at least three to four bottles of the highly flammable substance.

Looking out into the distance he was able to make out the first wave of guests that would be attending the Independence Day party of the decade.

He advised a young lady to run and inform Mr. Kay that his guests were arriving rapidly. "go child, hurry!" he said.

CHAPTER 57

Bodiford had converted his parlor into his war room, having turned down the Kays invitation. Claiming to have succumbed to a sudden illness, he now issued orders that were to be executed without delay.

"You eight men are to lay in this area south of the Kay's property in seclusion. There you'll await the signal that will come from the second wave of our strike. It will be led by Tom here. Tom, you and your six men will go onto the property right after the first strike.

"The first strike will be executed by two separate squads. One led by Dale here, and seven of the Texans. The second squad led by Eddie and the other seven Texans. "Dale, you and Eddie White listen up carefully. Your two groups are the most important aspect of our assault. You must creep up on them using extreme caution, because everybody there won't be boozed up and disconcerted due to too much Independence Day partying. You both will simultaneously breach the properly from the east and west side, but only after making certain that the Governor has left the plantation. Dale, you'll signal to Tom, but only after engaging the Kays men at the perimeter. "Gentlemen we've covered all the bases, so let tonight be a victory that eliminates the opposition and redresses this situation and allow power to remain totally and completely at my capacity. Let us not forget nor neglect to understand our main objective, which is to completely and absolutely annihilate Richard and Walter Kay.

"Let us rid our great state of Georgia of the likes of these nigger loving Yankee bastards forever. And by doing so we'll send a clear message to the rest of them yellow belly bastards up there in their rotten apple," he concluded as he sent them all off to prepare for tonight's attack.

After everyone had left out, in walks Jimmy Bodiford carrying with him a huge smile that went well with his huge ego.

"Daddy, it appears that when this night is over you'll have succeeded in your quest for absolute power and control. You'll also have everything you need to complete the construction of this here Marietta, Georgia."

James Bodiford looked up at his son, knowing him to usually be insouciant, now wondered why the sudden interest in his declaration of war on his enemies.

"Dear boy, it is not my quest for power, but rather my desire to ensure that my family, my descendants, my offspring maintains a prominent position of authority. I've prayed that you'd become a proponent of that goal. But here of late you've fought me at every turn. I continue to overlook the fact that you are a naïf, being your mother's son. Now, if you'll excuse me, I have some last minute preparations to make before tonight's conquest transpires."

"My being naive is completely mendacious Father, to prove to you so, I've taken the liberty to call to arms four men of my own to guarantee your safety here in the comforts of your abode," spoke Jimmy as he exited his Father's parlor, securing the doors behind him.

CHAPTER 58

Night had fallen over the Kay's estate and with it a gloom that possessed its own palpitation.

Eli and the others had long been put away. This being a common procedure, mainly due to the slave owners inability to see his negro against the blackness of the night. Unless of course he has him chained from neck to ankle, to ensure the negro's inability to flee his bondage, or attacked his person.

Inside the barn all were awake and being given last minute instructions by Eli. The moment of truth had

674

arrived. The only thing awaited was a knock that was to come from a loose captive from the other side. "Tac, you will have no trouble hitting this flint and igniting the wagon full of cotton and tobacco. After sending it into the field, hurry back and go with me into the house to get their weapons. Răzī-elle, you and Thes-nō-ă must go over to the other side and help free as many brethren as possible before meeting me and Tac back here. Together we'll fight our way to the swamp. Neffi, you Ra-kar, and Iz-lă take Fat Daddy and go ahead of us, but safely to the edge of the swamp and wait for us there.

"Knock, knock." It was time. Everything that had been gathered for this night was retrieved. Eli made his way through the new and improved aperture first, having his blade at the ready. He was followed by Tac who went with him to the door. Being unaware of the guards' whereabouts, they unlatched the barn's door and freed the others. Everyone immediately separated in order to initiate their role. Only Neffi and her two companions were instructed to remain in the shadows with her son until the diversion was implemented.

The horses being full of fear, took off through the cotton field with the wagon attached engulfed in flames. They zigged and they zagged, setting the cotton ablaze in

675

their wake. This illuminated the night on the front side of the plantation.

The sudden and unexpected blaze caused a tremendous stir. Bodiford's men believed beyond any doubt that this was their awaited signal.

The men on the east side having a line of vision all the way across the face of the mansion, moved in with calculated speed.

Eddie had witnessed the field of cotton go up in flames as well. He being to the west, directly in front of the road leading to the estate. He, and his men had to circle around the flames and grow closer to the mansion by way of the south side. There they encountered Tom's group of men who immediately sent out one of their own to signal the others with a waving of a lantern. The Kay's men were first discombobulated and in a frenzy as they fumbled about awaiting instructions on what to do. Walter stood there on the porch shouting incoherently.

It was Richard who after walking the full length of the veranda, announced that there was nothing to be done, but to allow it to burn itself out.

Those men of the Kay's estate who were just on their way to the burning field due to their inebriety were met by Tom's and Dale's men who slaughtered them effortlessly.

One gunshot rang out, causing all hell to break loose. Eli and Tac were inside the mansion, Tac urging the negroes to tear a path to freedom, but none would take heed, especially those of a quadrone lineage. Eli was rummaging through an upstairs bedroom in search of some weapons, preferably a pistol, but he only came across a wad of bills which for some unknown reason he shoved down into his pocket.

Hearing the gunshot, Eli raced back down the stairs to Tac's location and encountered his puzzled facial expression. Not being able to locate the cache of weapons that Pete informed them of, the two made their exit to the outside. There they witnessed more gunfire as whites and blacks battled for their lives. The negro in his rage was willing to die for that in which he fought for. He fought for his freedom. A freedom denied most since birth, but all was equipped with a soul that gave assurance of their God given right to live free or die trying.

He sent Tac to the rear of the barn with instructions to wait for him there. Eli himself made his way around to the other side of the house in search of Rǎ-zī-elle and

Thes-nō-ă, for it was time for them to make their escape to the swamp area. As he turned to peer through the sea of dark faces, Eli was struck in the head with the butt of a shotgun. The last thing he remembered was darkness.

As Bodiford's men fought vigorously with Kay's men, they both were being assaulted by the raging negroes. So, for the purpose and intent of self preservation, they combined their forces. In doing so, they quashed the situation by slaughtering dozens upon dozens of negro combatants.

With no more shedding of each others blood, Richard Kay was able to announce, "For each man who brings back to me a runaway nigger of mines, will receive a twenty dollar note. For each man who delivers to my doorstep a dead nigger, will receive a fifty dollar note."

CHAPTER 59

The doors to James Bodiford's parlor flew open, startling him slightly. When he noticed that it was only Jimmy, he relaxed himself and asked, "Is there any news of the total destruction of them damn Yankees?"

"No news has arrived pertaining to the Kays as of yet, but much more important news has just arrived hot off the press."

"Well, let me have it," demanded James.

"Indeed," voiced Jimmy as he drew his weapon.

"I might of known," spoke James Bodiford as he sat down into his huge leather chair behind his desk.

"Nobody is capable of seeing everything, except God. Who by the way you believe yourself to be.

So, Jimmy my son, you're standing there telling me that you're going to kill your own father?"

"Who better to put an end to the tyranny?"

"That's how you view your old man, as a tyrant?"

"You wear the hat well."

"What about your dear Mother? What will she do without me around?"

"She'll manage."

"I see your mind is all the way made up and there's absolutely nothing I can do to dissuade you of your decision."

"No Father, my partnership with the Kays is elaborate enough to keep my decision as it is."

"All your life I've done nothing but pave the way for you a successful future. By the sweat of my brow I've done things with your position in life in mind. And this is how my only son honors my efforts."

"Spare me your pathetic speech of a better tomorrow for me," voiced Jimmy as he raised his weapon.

"I wish I could spare you son, but your actions have exhausted my ability too," he said as he squeezed the trigger of his concealed pistol that was attached to the underside of his huge oak wood desk.

The slug hit Jimmy's abdomen with such force that it knocked him off of his feet. He released his hold of the pistol as his body hit the hardwood floor. James remained in his chair peering over his desk at his dying son. With a tear running down his face he stood to his feet as Nancy and her colored maid eased into the parlor cautiously.

When Nancy Bodiford saw her son lying there dying on the floor writhing in pain, she turned to Aunt T who stood in the doorway and asked, "Can't you do anything?" Then Nancy looked up at her husband and screamed, "Why?"

James walked out of his parlor in search of those men who Jimmy claimed to be his.

The entire Bodiford plantation was in an intensified state of uneasiness.

Just as James made it to the front of the house, Tom came in with his explanation. After Bodiford advised Tom of Jimmy's demise, they both stood there speechless for a spell.

It was Tom who broke the moment by voicing, "James I have to get out here and get a handle on these niggers of yours. Surely by now they've caught wind of what's taken place at the Kays. It'll only cause them to grow their own crazy ideas."

Having splashed water into Eli's face, it caused him to come back from his place of unconsciousness. Eli immediately realized the fact that he was strapped wrists and ankles to some sort of metal table.

"Yes, you are exactly what's needed to put me many levels above all others who's ever attempted this kind of dianetics," informed Walter.

"What, are you crazy? You're killing folks with your stupidity," voiced Eli.

"I'll not be deterred by your rantings boy. Yours is the brain that I've been in search of, one that already possesses a certain level of intelligence above the norm."

"Your experiments will never work, not now, not ever, and only a lunatic would continue to try and expect a different result."

For said comment Eli received a diabolical blow to his midriff that knocked all the wind out of him.

"I dare you insult my abilities and skills. I've accomplished grand and remarkable feats, but it's too abstruse for you and your kind."

"Oh I comprehend extremely well. That's why I know you've never had a patient to walk away from any of your so-called feats. You and all of your primitiveness."

This caused Walter to pause. He then turned with scalpel in hand toward Eli and looked him in his eyes very intently. "You know something that you're not telling me! You'll be more than willing to share it all with me before you lose your ability to speak completely."

Just then there was a loud banging at the cellar door. Walter walked over, slid the flap and demanded to know who had the gall to interrupt him during his time in the cellar.

"Mr. Kay it's Jones. Sir, Mr. Richard needs you urgently."

"Go away and leave me be for your own good," suggested Walter as he slid the flap back into its closed position.

"Bang, Bang, Bang," came the sound of impatience from the other side of the door. This time Walter Kay didn't take the time to speak through a flap. He unbolted the cellar door and yanked the heavy door wide open so he could address this imbecile who dared to interrupt him in his work.

Now he stood face-to-face with Tac, a very angry, very large African who had a issue he needed to get off of his chest.

Tac took hold of Walter and pushed him all the way back into the cellar's caliginous. He then turned him so, and wrapped his massive arm around his neck and squeezed until sleep fell upon Walter.

Then he freed Eli.

Before their departure they strapped Walter to the table, fixed the large table so it would jam the door. Then the two made their way to the swamp where the others awaited.

When they were all together again, Eli wasted no time explaining the grave danger that they were in. "We are not safe here at all. They are going to be tracking us and if they catch us, they are going to kill us all," he said with a recognizable fear etched across his face.

"Let them come. I am ready for them now," spoke the King brandishing a well made spear, and a short blade in the other hand.

"We can't fight them all. They have guns. We must run for now," urged Eli.

And just then they all heard the noise at the same time. Dogs barking and some even seemed closer than others. When they peered around the brush that concealed them, they were able to see the torches and lanterns in the distance, yet steadily approaching.

"Lets move," voiced Eli in amore contained tone.

"Which way?" asked Tac.

"Lets move this way," he said as he began to lead. "Wait, allow Thes-nō-ă to lead our way. She has great vision for dark," uttered Ră-zī-elle.

And off into the dark they went, traveling at a steady pace. The King carrying his grandson Fat Daddy in one of his arms as if he was carrying one of his weapons.

Having run nonstop for roughly forty minutes, it was time to take a pause and that mostly due to Eli wanting to know if they were travelling in the right direction.

Eli asked them to remain where they were while he went into a bend to make sure they were headed toward the wooded area at the outskirts of the Bodiford plantation.

But what he encountered was a portion of the swamp that appeared to break off into a shallow lake. He signaled the others and they all traversed the lake in a group. Once on the other side, Eli believed it to be a good opportunity to rest awhile. But as soon as the suggestion left his mouth he heard it, they all heard it. The barking of animals in extreme close proximity.

By remaining in complete silence, and placing a hand over the child's mouth they thought the beasts would not come near. But the illumination of the moon showed them otherwise. These predacious animals began snarling as they inched closer, occasionally barking and at the same time half circling their prey.

Eli attempted to keep the others behind him at his back as they all circled in complete opposite to the animals.

They could hear the dog handlers calling out to the animals.

"Where are you boy, whatcha got for me?" Eli knew he had no time, so he made his move. He eased toward the voracious beasts so that they may be able to have a better look at his actions.

He then began to pat his right front pocket. When the animals were completely focused, Eli dug into his pocket and brought out a vegetable that he had been eating on. He told the dogs to go get some smoked meat as he chunked it across the shallow lake that they had just crossed.

Off they went without hesitation, and off Eli and his tribe went in the opposite direction without hesitation.

The dog handlers made it to that exact same spot several seconds later to discover the dogs hot on the trail of something, so they went after, yelling and screaming, "Tear him to pieces boys, but don't kill him." Having run nonstop for over an hour, Eli and the others eventually made it to a wooded area where their bodies demanded rest. Eli explained to them how it would be daylight soon so fifteen minutes of rest and then they'd move deeper into the woods.

Two and a half hours later a new day began to dawn. The tribe was deep into the secluded woods. It was day, but from their position the only way you could tell it was day was by the little rays of sunlight that beamed down from above.

"It won't be safe for us to move until nightfall," expressed Eli as Neffi and the other women passed out vegetables to the men.

"Why do we go to this shack once more? We was captured there, remember?" questioned King Ră-zī-elle.

"Yes, I remember, but we can't make it to the North without their help. We must get the information from my family."

CHAPTER 61

James Bodiford's rampage lasted all through the night with evidence of more to come. He beat, kicked, punched, and whipped unsuspecting negroes as he traveled the length of his plantation. It was liquor and pure exhaustion that put an end to his madness.

Afterwards, everyone awoke to a new day filled with the same fears. The trepidation was palpable.

Terrible Tom was up at the crack of dawn cracking his whip, ordering slaves to do things that didn't even need doing. It was chaos due to uncertainty at the Bodiford plantation.

They assumed that the Kays wouldn't strike back, but they weren't for sure. So, on one end they were on high alert and at the other end they were punishing those closest to them.

Nancy left for Ruth's that morning with the dead body of her boy. She said no goodbyes. She simply dressed herself in all black, packed a few things and summoned a carriage and driver.

Henry tried to calm James by making efforts to receive from him an idea of what his next move might be.

As evening approached, two of Kays men did also. They had been sent to Bodiford to discuss damages that the Kays had suffered, damages that they were there to make sure he was totally liable for.

Bodiford listened, but did not admit, nor agree to anything.

Several hours later, as nightfall arrived so did Mr. Dukes, he being accompanied by two of his fellow riders. The three made their way to Bodiford's vestibule, where Mr. Dukes removed the vesture that he wore over his vest.

He asked James' whereabouts and then made straightway for him. When the two were seated and the doors closed, their communications were furtive, but the overall message imposed on Bodiford was one of a compulsory nature.

Bodiford made straightway to the slum area of his property, where he housed some of his slaves. He and his men took up a man, a woman, and their eleven year old daughter. They dragged them out yelling and screaming to the awaiting wagon.

WE SUFFER FOR A REASON

With the night came Eli's opportunity to venture out and into the unknown. It had been decided that he and the King would travel a mile or so through the forest in hopes of reaching the place where it meets the Bodiford plantation. Having never traveled this way before Eli was uncertain.

The two traveled for over an hour. It seemed as if the woods had no ending. For as far as his eyes could see there was more forest to traverse. At one point it seemed as if Eli and King Ră-zī-elle turned westward. They both decided that one more hour in the direction that they were headed in and if nothing was discovered, they would head back to the others. At least they would know when they moved in a group it wouldn't be in this same direction. Through the trees and thick brush the King and Eli could see the light that shone brighter and brighter the closer they drew nearer. Having made their way to the edge, they came upon a clearing. But that's not all they came upon. In that clearing stood a very tall wooden cross. A cross having a perpetual burning. It appeared as if it generated its own gasohol. It lit up the entire clearing, exposing the fact that there also stood approximately fifty white hooded individuals who were paying extremely close attention to that which was taking place right in front of them.

Right in front of them was a platform raised about ten feet off the ground. Standing on the platform was Nathan Dukes, Richard Kay, James Bodiford, and a black father, mother, and daughter having their hands tied behind their backs.

"Again I make known to my highly esteemed league of brothers that last night there was a great deal of bloodshed by niggers who thought they were capable of executing a revolt. But they quickly discovered that the white man is capable of executing their demise when we join together. Last night taught us to always remain united and forever keep them animals devided and we shall always conquer them keeping them under our feet.

"Now every man present here tonight in the beginning had quite a bit of a fright, believing that them niggers was making way to your homes to slaughter, disembowel, rape, and murder your wives and your daughters. And they would have done exactly that, because it was their purpose and intentions. They having such a lustful desire for the white woman and her flesh.

But thanks be to the unity and the expeditiousness of our brothers Richard, and Bodiford standing here, they were able to squash those lecherous, lascivious nigger rodents and save you all the trouble of having to bury your loved ones.

"The sole purpose of our gathering tonight is to acknowledge the fact that we've lost a few of our own and their deaths are to be honored here tonight by us all. James Bodiford has been generous enough to provide us with these three pieces of property and he willingly extends their souls to Richard Kay so that he understands they both experienced the same loss. But now standing here as brothers, all is forgiven and the pursuit of prosperity is restored tonight as these niggers hang from our sacred tree until they are dead. Richard Kay will be welcomed whole heartedly into our brotherhood and when he has recited our creed while having his right hand atop the head of the male standing up here, he will then be a brother for the rest of his natural life and welcomed home by brothers who have gone before us into the afterlife."

After the reciting of their creed, Eli and King Rǎ-zī-elle witnessed a thing truly horrific. The execution, the blatant murder of that eleven year old little girl will forever be etched into the brains of both of them.

Ră-zī-elle drew back, not wanting to see no more of this child's life escape from her body. He had witnessed with his own eyes many beatings. He'd witnessed them brutally beat his own daughter. He'd been beaten. But this was the first time he had ever seen them murder such a small child.

It hit the King profoundly and as he and Eli traversed the distance to make it back to the others, it was as if some of his vigor had been depleted. When he made back to the others he took a hold of his grandchild and held him throughout the rest of the night.

The following night it was Eli accompanied by Tac who traveled in a totally different direction. It took them slightly under two hours to get there, but they eventually reached a familiar area. From their concealed location at the edge of the woods, Eli could make out the small wood structure that his relatives referred to as their home.

They inched toward the property and then to the rear of the shack. This is when the King's words reverberated throughout Eli's mind. 'Isn't that the same place we were captured at?'

He refused to allow himself to become tremulous, so he took a deep breath and gave the back of the shack two hard knocks. But not too hard.

Moments after, they heard the front door creak open. Eli and Tac continued to move furtively as they made their way to the shack's entrance. Once there, they were questioned by Eli the senior, "Who's out here?"

"It's me, Eli," he answered as he allowed the moonlight to reveal his face.

"Oh dear boy. Yous come on in here for you be seen."

Once inside the door, they were met right there by Bernice . She having lady Jessie on her hip. Apparently Eli's visit had awakened the house.

"I'm so glad to see you still alive child. We have heard many bad things that's taken place over there at the Kays plantation. But I's show glad to see yous safe," spoke Bernice as she sat the child down and took Eli into her arms.

They spoke of all that had taken place since the last time he had seen her face.

A couple of hours later she served them all her own special vichyssoise. It was cold and delicious; they all agreed. Eli supplied lady Jessie with plenty of attention as he osculated her all over her pretty face and little hands.

The elder Eli had supplied them with all the information necessary to contact Ruth so she could provide them safe passage to the North.

Having heard of the others who awaited them out in the woods, Eli and Bernice 's hearts went out to them, especially to the small child out there being made to suffer.

"What's it mean?" Bernice asked Tac, referring to the words Vlies elle ză, that he was teaching to lady Jessie.

"It means, village of zi-elle in my native tongue."

"It's beautiful," Bernice replied.

Everyone heard the noise at the exact same time.
Somebody had just stepped up on their makeshift porch. While everyone remained frozen in place there came three light taps on the front door. Eli and Bernice made ready the concealed hole in their floor and urged Tac and Eli to hide there. Tac was down in there in seconds; him and all of his brawn. He being approximately six feet four inches, weighing at least two hundred and ninety five pounds, there may have been just enough room for Eli's 6 foot one, hundred and ninety-five

pound frame, but his great Grandma Glenda's voice now sounded in his head,'don't go down there they know about the hiding place', So while

standing there being indecisive as to what he should do, the shack's door came open and in walks the young girl from the Big House who usually assists Aunt T.

"Marsha, what you doing coming so late honey?" questioned Bernice .

"Ma'am I was told by Aunt T to comes down here and gives you word of hers having to go to young Bodiford's funderal first thing in the morning so she's needed you to come up to the Big House bright 'en early so yous can prepare the foods."

"Mary?" Eli asked as he was drawn closer by the appearance of this girl.

"Is it possible, is it really you Mary?" he asked again.

"No sir, it's I, Marsha," she replied.

Eli stepped even closer until he was only inches from the girl's face. And what he now saw was that this girl was a spitting image of his Mary, back home.

Whether from fright or otherwise, Marsha hurried off after having told Bernice that she'd tell Aunt T how she gave the message.

When she had departed, Tac came back to the surface questioning if it was time for them to go. Eli assured him that they would be leaving soon; for he was searching for a way to regain his bearings.

After a spell, Eli began to ask Eli the elder, exactly what must be done in order to get ahold of this white woman Ms. Ruth.

Eli senior explained it in detail and then he gave Eli the younger, directions to Ms. Ruth's residence as well as a secret place in the woods. Then decided it would probably be best if he lead the way. Eli having stressed that it was paramount that him and his group make it to that secret location before morning arrived completely.

That very night Eli escorted Eli to where his tribe awaited him and Tac. After introductions, Eli escorted Eli and his companions to a secret location in the woods, where they came upon a trap door in the floor of the woods. Eli gave the trap door a couple of taps before lifting the door and going down alone. When he resurfaced he had with him a runaway slave and what appeared to be some kind of book in his hands.

"I left my bible here last time 'cause I had to run off 'cause of all the footsteps we heard going through these woods searching for yous I suppose. This here good book had been put in my hands by my Granddaddy a long, long time ago," Eli expressed. He then introduced Eli to Mr.Hillman a.k.a. Rev. the runaway.

"How long before Ms. Ruth will come here?" "Can't rightly say son. These are very dangerous times. But no later than Sunday's service, I'll get word to one of her slavers and she'll catch wind of it," he explained. When Eli and his group made it down under the earth, the three rooms down there was lamentable. One, the smallest of the three was used entirely as a place for waste. And for Eli the smell was unbearable.

Eli explained to them all how unhealthy it was to allow those conditions to remain. So he, Ră-zĭ-elle and Tac decided to venture out and into the unknown in search of anything they could use to remedy the conditions.

The first thing Eli did when they made it to the surface was to locate a piece of a tree branch to prop the door open with and allow fresh air to enter in.

After doing so, he stood with the others, having not a clue as to what to do next. Then it hit him. "Didn't Eli say that Ms. Ruth's place was over that way?" He asked no one particularly.

Less than twenty minutes later they came upon a huge house. Not quite a plantation, but considerably large.

The three remained together as they searched around for anything that may be of use, especially some food. Awhile later everyone having hands full of various items made it to the fence where they had come over and as they were about to hurtle it a voice from the darkness spoke. "You's three hold it rights there."

As they turned and the owner of the voice drew closer, recognition was deduced.

"Pete? Is that you Pete?"

"It's me Eli.

Son, you just about caused ole Pete to put a beaten on to you with this here hands of mines," explained Pete.

Eli then sat his items down and took the old man into his arms.

"This here is Ră-zī-elle and Tac with me."

"What's the meaning of yous out here in the dark of the night stealing from the missus?" questioned Pete. "Having run off from the Kays, we've been informed of a Miss Ruth who may be able to help us to the North. We've been in the woods down inside of the hideaway waiting. Everyone is in need of food, water, and a few other items in case we have to be down in there awhile waiting for this Miss Ruth."

"Keeps your voice down now. Don't speak her name so loud. Yous never know who be in the shadows a listening. Now, wait there on the other side of that there fence till I's return," instructed Pete.

The wait was done in fear, but it wasn't a long wait at all. Pete returned in less than three minutes, bearing in each of his hands a bag. He handed them both over the fence to Eli and told him that he would see to it that the missus be made aware of everything. "And let Reverend Hillman know that his family made it."

"You know about the secret place Pete?" asked Eli.

"I do, now get going. These are the worst of times."

Once they was back down inside of the hideaway, Eli immediately furnished the place with light from the lantern's candescence.

After he delivered the message to Jenkins he then went to work in the other room with the shovel and bucket. After several trips to the surface to dump and bury human waste, the place slowly became bearable.

Four days later Eli the elder came to the secret place. Once down below, while gripping his bible tightly, he told them of the gathering together that they had and how he preached to them all how Jesus died to set them all free.

This causes Eli to reflect back on how powerful the word of God truly is, and it also causes him to remember a particular story told to him by his Granny Bee.

So, he asks Eli if he could see his bible. After being allowed to, Eli brings his elder and the bible over toward the glow of the lantern.

Eli caresses the book, feeling the wear of the leather and appreciating its feel. He opened the book delicately having noticed the browning of the pages. His fingers led him to Jeremiah, chapter twenty-nine, and so he read aloud verse eleven. "For I know the thoughts that I think toward you, says the Lord, thoughts of peace and not of evil, to give you a future and a hope."

"My son, you can read them there words?" asked Eli. "Yes sir and I'm going to teach you how to do the same."

That very night Eli the senior's lessons began. And for seven nights afterward Eli returned bearing water, some foods that Bernice had prepared, and his leather bound bible.

WE SUFFER FOR A REASON

Eli learned to read and he learned how to receive Jesus as his Lord and Savior. Everyone else followed suit and they all became Christians that night.

Eli was looking intently in the margin of the bible trying to make out the words that were inscribed there. To him it appeared to read, rever, or maybe reverend something or other. Then he continued to read aloud from the margin; meditate on the promise of God. Psalm 91:14-16.

It was so old and worn he didn't know if he had read it correctly. He basically was filling in the blanks.

Having handed the bible back over to Eli the elder, they embraced. Eli accompanied his elder to the surface and before saying their goodbyes Eli told him, "I want to share with you that your little girl lady Jessie is going to name her second daughter Glenda. I just thought it to be a good idea to share it with you."

Eli shed a tear and embraced his descendant. His crying caused his body to shake, as he continued his hold on the lad.

Despite the occasional trips to the surface for some fresh air, they were all still feeling more than a little confined. Eli the elder hadn't come to the secret place in three days and Eli had become worried and somewhat anxious. Because he had a feeling that the elder Eli may have been seen leaving, or returning from the woods.

On this particular night Eli and King Ră-zī-elle went up to the surface. They both was shocked into petrification and it being equally reciprocated upon those they encountered.

"No, no, calm yourself missus. These are the ones I's already tells you of. These 'n here was held at the Kay plantation as was I," explained Pete, as Miss Ruth attempted to quiet her stertorous.

"Ma'am I'm Eli and this here is Ră-zī-elle and we have five others and a small child," Eli began, but was cut off by her question.

"What of Hillman and the other two?"

"They're still below. We've all been waiting on you to see if passage to the North is possible. That's the purpose of our being out here. The ship leaves tomorrow at eleven o'clock, but passage has only been secured for the three I had paid the captain for."

"Are you hungry? We've brought some food," she said. "Yes ma'am, we are, but may I ask how can we obtain permission aboard this ship?" "It's impossible with this captain, because he'll not bend. You see he hates your skin color, but loves money or anything else of good value more."

"Is there any way for you to talk to him and see if—"
"There's no way. It's too late. It's impossible for me to make it down to the docks and then . . . no, it's just impossible and extremely too dangerous for us all. But there is another ship that travels. Lets see, in seven days that could transport you all to the next destination, but for all of you the cost will be very high and I've just about depleted all of my funds and a large portion of my jewelry. I do desire to help you all though, especially the
little one. Well, all of you, but I'm simply unable to at the moment."

That which had become a nuisance to Eli, balled up, and poking his thigh, he now dug for and retrieved.

Eli handed the wad of cash over to Miss Ruth and asked, "Would this help?"
Viewing it up close she made out the denominations and had to ask, "How did you get all of this money?"

"Oh that, that's just back pay," he said in humor.

She questioned no further, but rather assured him that it would be more than enough, before departing having Pete at her side.

Eli, and King Ră-zī-elle returned to the others elated and they could detect the excitement in their voices as they shared the news with them.

He explained to Hillman, Gilbert, and Joe P. that they would be leaving tomorrow night according to Miss Ruth.

The next night came and went as well did Gilbert, Joe P. and Jenkins.

The next week dragged on and as their water supply dwindled they became restless. It was the middle of the day when Eli couldn't take it any longer. He had to go to the surface. If he didn't stretch, breathe, and walk about in the outdoors he'd die. And as he reached up to open the trap door he heard it.

There were dogs and people up on the surface in very, very close proximity. So close in fact that he couldn't move. Eli became frozen in fear, and not just in fear for his own life, but also for the lives of those whom he now loved. He could very distinctly hear Fat Daddy down there with the others and wondered if those on the surface could hear them as well.

Eli let go of the handle and eased his way back down the stairs to the others. Having placed a finger over his lips and at the same time pointing at Fat Daddy, he waved

Tac over to himself and asked Ta-Kar to give him the shovel.

Tac and Eli secured the trap door with the shovel and both held on incase someone tried to open the mysterious lone door out in the center of the forest. They held on having their arms stretched out and their weight pulling on the shovel for what seemed like thirty minutes. Eli could no longer hear the dogs or anything else, so he felt safe enough to take a peep.

The danger had passed for now, but they all knew for certain that they couldn't survive there for much longer. That same night Eli had awaken from a dream, nightmare, or something. He wasn't sure because he could only remember fragments. As he pondered, he now recalled seeing Eli the elder's leather bound bible. For the next few days Eli's dream danced around in his subconscious. There was something scratching the surface of his conscious, but couldn't break through.

That night he, Neffi, and Fat Daddy went up to the floor of the forest. And as always they both had to hold on to Fat Daddy who she had recently given a Christian name of Lamondre.

This kid always wanted to tear it down, despite the darkness. He too had been cooped up for too long.

Eli and Neffi enjoyed one another's company. She, forever bringing to memory the few times he had sacrificed his own body for her safety. He looking into her eyes in the moonlit night was easy enough. What was hard was finding the words to express how in another lifetime she would be his princess, even as facts suggested that he was living in another lifetime. So complicated and confusing to him. She kissed his lips so very gently and said, "You are more than a prince to me, and my son."

Seconds after they went back down beneath the forest, they all was caused to pause in fright, because someone had just hit the trap door three times. But not using the three light taps, pause and then two taps.

Eli believing it not to be danger, went back up the steps and removed the shovel. When the door opened he was staring into the eyes belonging to Pete.

"Hurry, hurry. Everyone weez must go now?" urged Pete.

He then escorted them all to the trail that led to where Miss Ruth awaited behind the rein of a horse driven wagon. When everyone was loaded into the wagon, Ms. Ruth explained to her passengers the rules and procedures if encountered by anyone while they traveled to the vessel.

"What is da matter Eli?" Neffi asked as she was able to see the look on his face much clearer now.

"Neffi, it's these images and thoughts that keep popping into my mind," he attempted to explain.

"Images?" she asked.

The bible verse, the message in Eli's bible. It wasn't reverend, it was revert!

"Stop!" Eli shouted to Pete who was now driving the wagon.

As Pete brought the wagon to a standstill, Eli explained to Neffi and the others that he had to go back.

"I must decipher the message contained in the bible. I'm so sorry. I can't go with you," he expressed while making his way to where King Ră-zī-elle sat. "This is to be used when you get you and your family to the North," he said as he placed in the King's hand some folded bills.

Eli kissed the top of Lamondre's head and whispered, "Go to school." Staring into Neffi's eyes once more as tears streamed down her beautiful face, he was at a loss for adequate words. So Eli kissed her lips. A osculate that expressed a bond shared.

Once on the ground he told Pete to get a move on it, and to travel safely. He thanked Miss Ruth and assured her that God has a special place in His heart for her.

Eli then retraced their path and made his way back to the trail leading to the secret place. From there he had no trouble making it to the shack.

But things wasn't going so smoothly for the others for they were being detained by two drunkards looking for trouble.

"Hold this here wagon still boy," ordered one of the two as he took hold of the horse's rein. "Tell us why you got with you this here white woman so late into the night?" questioned the other.

Pete, being too terrified to answer, just sat there staring. "Boy is yous hard of hearing? I's plainly asked you a question."

"This man belong to me, and we have to pick up some supplies from the docks, so you best let us be on our way before you make trouble for yourselves," she threatened. "Ma'am, with all due respect, it'd be wise for you to shut your filthy nigger loving cake hole," he said with a chuckle afterwards. "We seeing with our own eyes how you and this darky been groping one another out here in the black of night, ain't that so Clive?"

"I couldn't believe it until I taken a closer look. And sure enough they's kissing and carrying on like two animals in heat."

"What? This is all nonsense being fabricated by you two drunkards," stressed Miss Ruth in anger.

"You can call it what you want to Ma'am, but it all boils down to who will be believed," he said as he attempted to slide his hand beneath Miss Ruth's dress.

He didn't get the chance to touch her flesh because Pete leaped from the wagon and onto that fellow like a wildcat. Half shocked, his buddy, the one referred to as Clive went to snatch Pete off of his friend and by the time he made it over to Pete, King Rǎ-zī-elle and Tac had made their way to the both of them.

Seconds later the two were severely injured and broken in places, then placed onto the side of the road in some thicket.

Having made their way to the ship that they was to board, Miss Ruth secured their passage. Before departing, she began to encourage Pete to travel to the

North 'cause she had made it possible for him to do so. "No, missus, my place is right here beside you. Don't you knows as much by now?" he asked while gazing into her steel grey eyes.

"I believe I do," she replied with a fluttering heart.

Eli went into his relative's shack and hugged Bernice so tight and long causing her tears to wash away her fears. When he scooped lady Jessie up into his arms, she just giggled, then she rubbed his face with her little fingers as was her thing to do.

Having sat her down he moved to where Eli the elder stood and embraced him so. When they released their grip, Eli asked, "Where's your bible? May I see it?"

When he returned, Eli began to explain. "There's a very important message on the inside of that bible. I believe the message is the key for me to return to my family and yours," Eli shared with them as the senior placed the book into his hands.

"Well, you know Eli is always saying that them words are for all of us so we'd be close to God forever," Bernice had to say.

"That's true as well, but if you'll look right here you can barely make out the word revert, which means to go back to a former place. Then there's this bible passage,

713

Psalm 91:14-16. this is a promise from God who cannot and will not lie. So I have to do my part and allow God to do His.

"Do my part—" Eli pondered the thought as the door came crashing in. Terrible Tom busted in and before anyone could make a move he was all over Eli the younger.

Terrible Tom was followed in by a couple more of Bodiford's men, who was followed in by James Bodiford himself. He having the house girl Marsh at his side. "You see, I's tell yous the truth all along massuh. I says I's sees him come up out them woods over yonder," said Marsha as she pointed an accusing finger at Eli.

"Eli, Bernice I'm very, very disappointed in you both and mark my words, I'll deal with you both personally," threatened Bodiford.

He then turned to Eli the younger and grabbed him by his collar as Tom held him and voiced, "You've caused nothing but trouble since you arrived here. And you're definitely the cause of the uprising over at the Kays. Believe me you, you'll pay dearly for your revolt, and insurgence.

"I don't have no problem receiving whatever's coming to me, but why harm Eli, or Bernice seeing how they've been so loyal to you all these years doing all you've ever asked of them. Even raising you up as a boy?" he asked as he returned Bodiford's intense stare.

"What I desire to do with my property is of no concern to you boy," shouted James as he put Eli to sleep with a short right hook.

Having done that, he instructed one of his men to go fetch Richard Kay and inform him that he had captured the ringleader who ignited the massacre.

Eli was awakened from unconsciousness by the splash of water thrown on his face. Now he was looking eye to eye with Walter Kay, who held a devilish grin as he held eye contact with Eli.

They tied Eli to the post and Walter beat him as Richard, Bodiford and the others looked on. Walter was like a savage as his whip tore into Eli's flesh.

It was Richard who halted his brother's maleficence as he voiced, "We can't kill him Walter. It would deny us his true purpose."

"Yes, of course, but I was hoping that after he healed up some I could use him to complete my research brother," Walter communicated.

"His is a greater cause Walter, and you'll just have to trust me on this. For doing so I promise to provide you with whatever necessary funds needed for your experiments," Richard assured his brother.

That night, unable to walk. Eli was dragged and thrown into the back of a wagon. The wagon took him to what Richard called his final destination.

When they arrived, everything was arranged and apparently the entire town of Marietta was in attendance, as one could see by the illuminationb given by the burning of the cross. James Bodiford, Richard Kay, Nathan Forrest, Earl Dukes and a few other members of their council were up on the platform as Richard took position to give an oration, which began,

"Brotherhood, it gives me great pleasure and I'm honored to be allowed to come before you this night bearing a great gift for you all. The leader of a sect that attempted to destroy what I have built, as well as what I have promised to make available to you all. Our security in being able to live our lives without fear of danger from a pack of illiterate, ungrateful, ignorant niggers. Now we must all remember to embed in the minds of our offspring that we are the superior race and they shall forever be the inferior. We cannot and we shall not ever allow them to obtain any kind of awareness of being men of the human race. Not even an inclination. We must suppress any and all acts of unity or love expressed by them We can't allow the fathers to become fathers to their young. Separate them immediately by any means necessary. We can't allow the Mothers to raise daughters into soulmates and supporters of the negro man. No, they must be molded and fashioned into what our forefathers brought them here to be, whores and breeders of ignorant nigglets. It is our duty to instill into them our purpose which is nihilism.

"Of course we'll face a very small amount of resistance, but to counter, we must entrap, enslave, and when deemed necessary murder the unarmed bastards as they attempt to flee.

"We are forever of one accord. To execute our right to make our niggers the burden bearer throughout their existence.

WE SUFFER FOR A REASON

"Brothers and sister, I, Richard Kay execute my right to destroy the soul of this here nigger who is rightfully my property."

They placed the noose about the neck of Eli as he sat atop a horse being held steady by another.

Richard Kay continued, "I make my pledge to pit one nigger against the other, causing their distrust, and hatred for one another, young against old, dark against the lighter skin, eventually even they will begin to believe that black lives will never matter. And in due course he'll grow to love me more than his brother.

"This method will forever keep the nigger in check, and in his place. Seeing they are too ignorant to recognize our methods and overcome their hatred with love, and unity for him who looks exactly like he does. "Our method will remain intact for the next thousand years. I declare this to be our way of life as well as our right by destroying the soul of this here insurgent nigger, we shall forever be masters." Concluded he as he gave the signal that caused Eli to be hung from their sacred tree in the center of downtown Marietta, Georgia. Eli's legs jerked and then twitched as his soul escaped his body.

WE SUFFER FOR A REASON

WE SUFFER FOR A REASON
CHAPTER 63

In the hospital room the television was up rather loud as the viewers watched the aftermath of yet another group of officers being acquitted of killing another unarmed black man in the streets of America.

Black Lives Matter, Black Lives Matter!! was the chant as the television was being turned down.

"Oh my God you all, look! Eli's eyes are open, he's smiling," yelled Mary.

"Didn't I tell you that he would pull through having my DNA all in him," Mama Bee exclaimed!

About the Author

I am most appreciative to be provided the platform to glorify and thank God Almighty for the breath of life and for His Christ. I was born in Louisville Kentucky. I have two adult children that I absolutely love and adore. Brandie Larrisha Tillman, and Terrell Johnson, a.k.a. Legacy. But I haven't always been there for them. Not even during times when they needed me most. I shall forever regret wrong choices made while growing to become a man. So, the remainder of my life will be lived proving to them and to my grandchildren that my love for them is unwavering and eternal. The remaining chapters of my life will consist of investing my time and love into my family. Totally committed to doing my part to assist in it's necessary healing and growth. My main and most sincere prayer is that God will take the hurt and pain out of my sister Faith Monique's heart. Please God. Only a Mother who has lost a child could even begin to understand that kind of pain and agony. So, I'm compelled to dedicate this book to my nephew, DeAnthony Taylor, a.k.a. Dooda, Rest In Paradise nephew. Shout out to my city, Louisville! Birth place of the greatest boxer ever, Muhammad Ali. When you combine your gift with your dream then all things become possible. I dreamed of writing this book and God gifted me to complete it so that I can now proclaim; that I can do all things through Christ Jesus who strengthens me.. Sincerely, Larry Williams the author.

Back Cover Summary